THE **GYROSCOPE** OF **GUILT**

George Wilgus III

 FriesenPress

Suite 300 - 990 Fort St
Victoria, BC, V8V 3K2
Canada

www.friesenpress.com

ISBN
978-1-4602-8938-9 (Hardcover)
978-1-4602-8939-6 (Paperback)
978-1-4602-8940-2 (eBook)

1. FICTION, MYSTERY & DETECTIVEERY

Distributed to the trade by The Ingram Book Company

DEDICATION

For Barbara, Jen, Jake, and to the memory
of my father, mother, and brother

He who writes the facts determines what is justice. What history recounts as justice may be just an illusion or far worse, pure evil. Peel away the facts, and uncover the truth.

PROLOGUE

January 1945
Germany

It was time. All was lost. The Führer's Ardennes offensive had failed. No chance existed now for a favorable peace. There would be no classical empire like Greece. Berlin would not be Caesar's Rome. Linz would not become Europe's cultural capital. The rapine Russians were nearing the Oder. Art meant nothing to those barbarians.

His plan had to be implemented now. The statuettes, grave stellae, amphorae, kraters, lekythoi, and busts were ready for shipment to Buenos Aires. So were the paintings. Argentina would be his safe haven until his eventual journey to the States. The Allies would uncover only some of the salt mines, tunnels, and caves where the Führer's minions hid Europe's confiscated masterpieces and sculptures. Only he alone would be able to divulge the rest. Surely, the Allies would trade his life and safe passage to America for that knowledge. All he had to do was wait. The curators, restorers, and historians would plead his case. So, of course, would the mendacious and avaricious dealers. The clamor would be immense. Greed trumped everything else.

He was young, German, and single. He was educated in the arts. Archaeology and art were his upbringing and passion. The crude and porcine Reichsmarschall Goering had trusted his expertise, as Carinhall's walls were a testament to his skill and acumen. Little did he know what lay ahead.

Late December 1999
McCormick Hall Art Building Princeton University
Princeton, New Jersey

It was a study befitting a classical scholar. The walnut bookcases enveloped the room and were weighted with tomes on Hellenistic architecture and sculpture. Intermingled were texts on Greek and Roman painting and pottery.

The elderly man moved the most current journals and periodicals from his cherry desk. At eighty-five and with a weakened heart, he knew his days were numbered. Yet there still was so much to pursue. As professor emeritus, he would come and go as he pleased. Occasionally, he would give a guest lecture or precept. His wife had passed twelve years earlier. Only his research provided a salve for his sadness, which was heightened during the Christmas holiday.

Having completed his review of Professor Bellington's proposed lecture outline for the spring seminar, Art 518: Greek Sculptures and Roman Copies, he grabbed his coat and attaché. He heard a clap of thunder in the distance so he reached for his favorite umbrella. Black and embossed with an orange crest containing a Latin inscription, the umbrella also identified his graduating class of 1936. His eyes brightened as he looked at the Latin inscription, Dei sub numine viget, meaning, "under the name of God it flourishes." A slight smile crossed his wizened face. No, undergraduates, the university motto didn't declare that God went to Princeton, he thought.

Locking the front door, he immediately realized that the evening's chill was accompanied by a driving rain that augmented the surrounding darkness. The art museum's walkway was deserted. Students wouldn't return from break for another week. As he turned left on to McCosh Walk, he anticipated that even with the umbrella, he would be drenched upon arrival at his Dickinson Street residence. During the fall, he would traverse under a canopy pathway of trees. Now, the swaying limbs were barren.

As he approached the intersecting steps that led off to the right toward Whig-Clio, he saw the outline of the two crouching tigers on opposing sides of the stairway's apex. With ears back and teeth bared, the bronzed figures looked ready to leap.

As he turned forward, he felt fingers on his collar. An icy sensation suffused his neck. His heart sped and fluttered. Darkness engulfed him before his face hit the pavement.

The assailant stepped over the splayed body and ascended the stairway between the Vermont-marbled Whig and Clio Halls. He casually glided past West College and then the ivy-covered Stockton-sandstone Nassau Hall, once the home of the Continental Congress. Only the denuded white ashes, sycamores, and elms observed his presence as he exited Fitz Randolph Gate, crossed Nassau Street, and disappeared down Witherspoon. Now he believed the secret was safe forever.

January 2000
Pan Hellenic Monthly

Dr. Alexander Clarendon, professor emeritus of classical studies at Princeton University, died on December 29, 1999. Princeton's Department of Art and Archaeology was nearly sixty years old when World War II commenced. The department was considered one of America's finest. Professor Clarendon was a "Monuments, Fine Arts and Archives Officer" during the war and utilized his expertise in Greek and Roman antiquities in uncovering and protecting art works looted by the Nazis.

He returned to his alma mater in 1960 and taught in the Classics and Arts and Archaeology departments, while continuing to assist the world's art curators in retrieving confiscated European art. Over the years, he received many awards and commendations, including the Gold Medal of the Archaeological Institute of America. His knowledge, kindness, and wonderful sense of humor will be sorely missed.

PART ONE

1.

February 2015
Hopewell Township, New Jersey

He was enveloped in darkness on this moonless night. The air was still. He had been waiting much longer than expected. His black neoprene suit provided much-needed warmth. Finally, from the rear corner of the house, he saw a beam of light illuminate the trees on the curved driveway. Shortly thereafter, he heard the garage door open. Within five minutes, the faint illumination that seeped through the living room curtains was extinguished. Now his waiting would be in earnest.

Two hours later, he removed the glass cutter from his knapsack and silently commenced his work. Once completed, the suction cup removed the oval piece. Through his infrared goggles, he located the latch and quietly unlocked it. He stepped out of his moccasins and onto the carpet. His stockinged feet masked his footfalls.

He saw her arise from the couch and move forward. From behind her, his gloved left hand forcefully applied the cloth to her face. She violently grabbed at his left hand and screamed, "Richard! Help me!"

As he was struggling with her, a dazed figure emerged from the adjacent bedroom. With his right hand, the intruder fired twice. The man fell backward. The woman went limp. He released his grasp. Unconscious, she fell forward. He quickly bent over the fallen man and placed the gun close to his forehead. The third round solved the problem forever.

2.

Mercer County Civil Courts Building
Trenton, New Jersey

"Ladies and gentlemen, we enter this world drooling and incontinent. If we live long enough, we exit the same way. My client, Jerry Howard, is thirty-three years old. Normally, he would have a life expectancy of another forty-five years. Now, he breathes through a tube. His legs and arms spasm uncontrollably. A catheter removes his urine. He communicates by blinking. He didn't sign up for this fate when he trusted the presurgical confidence of Dr. David Lewis. This horror all could have been avoided had Dr. Lewis used the care and skill that any reasonable neurosurgeon would have used when performing this particular surgery, an operation that neurosurgeons perform routinely in operating rooms throughout this country. Unfortunately, you can't change Jerry's life, but as Judge Fleming will instruct you shortly, you can award Jerry that sum of money that reasonably will compensate him for all his past, present, and future pain and suffering.

"Based upon the testimony of our economist and our life-plan expert, you also have reasonable projections as to past, present, and future costs Jerry will incur for medical expenses and home healthcare. Three years ago, Jerry was an up-and-coming architect in this community. At thirty, he was lauded for his revolutionary design work in commercial construction. He was earning $150,000 a year and, no doubt, had many successful years before him. The defense would have you believe that some other tragedy could have occurred to him, or that his dynamic architectural style would have fallen out of favor. The defense has no proof of that. Such a 'smoke and mirrors' defense defies common sense. Don't you think Jerry, based on his schooling and creativity, would have adapted to any changes in architectural taste? Do you really believe that someone as young, bright, and vibrant as Jerry wouldn't have altered his style if the situation arose? The defense wants you to forget those witnesses who already have painted an independent picture of Jerry. Unfortunately, Jerry can't speak to you so you could hear his words, measure his sincerity, and judge his truthfulness. Believe me, we wish he could have shown you through a rigorous cross-examination all those traits.

"In closing, all we ask is that you be fair and reasonable. On behalf of Jerry, I wish to thank you for your kind attention and patience."

As Johnnie Fitzhugh watched Jerry's attorney walk slowly toward the counsel table, he wondered how it all had come to this. Repeatedly, he had beseeched the insurance carrier to "pony up." The claims manager's response was that familiar refrain, "But, Johnnie, you never lose." Despite urging from Judge Fleming and his own repetitive admonitions, Sam Tagliardi refused to open the proverbial wallet. Well, Johnnie's intuition told him where this was heading, and the front page headline wouldn't be pretty.

As a successful trial lawyer, Johnnie knew it was the defeats, not the victories, that an accomplished trial lawyer remembered. And this trial had all the trappings of a nightmare. Fellow members of the defense insurance bar would offer their condolences, but he knew they were gloating at the very distinct possibility that they now could steal the carrier from his firm. The carrier always expected victory. Any defeat was the lawyer's fault, for, of course, the carrier's judgment was bulletproof.

The adage that the "law is a jealous mistress" was so true. Johnnie preferred to refer to the law as an unctuous whore, because, he thought, she tempted you to neglect your family, friends, and church. She seduced you into believing in unsurpassed powers of persuasion and clairvoyant thinking — a hubris that, at best, fostered a manic depressive state of extreme peaks of self-importance and deep valleys of utter worthlessness. As cases and years went by, Johnnie questioned whether the money and so-called fame really were worth it. He tried to find balance in his life, but it was a constant battle. At forty and unmarried, his only release was his unabated love for, and participation in, sports. Still referred to as "speedy" due to his years at Princeton as a flanker and sprinter, Johnnie believed that his body was his temple and that if that temple cracked, he was done with the law. Dreams of an NFL career were destroyed after two knee surgeries and a severely fractured jaw. Through his father's urging, he obtained his JD and joined "Pops" at Fitzhugh and Fitzhugh.

Johnnie expected that after this verdict Fitzhugh and son might take a huge financial hit.

Startled from his intermittent daydreaming during Judge Fleming's charge to the jury, Johnnie heard the familiar words, "Counsel, before I send the jury to deliberate, would you both check all the evidential exhibits to see that they dovetail with the court clerk's exhibit list?"

Having satisfied themselves that all the exhibit boards, diagrams, and photographs were marked properly, both attorneys returned to the counsel table. The judge then requested that the sheriff's officer take the six-person jury to the deliberation room, located off the hallway to the rear of the judge's bench.

"Counsel, please provide my court clerk with your cellphone numbers before you leave the courtroom. It's now 12:45 p.m. My clerk is taking lunch orders for the jury. They likely won't get past looking at the exhibits before their lunch arrives. I would suggest, however, that you not stray far from the courthouse in case they have any questions. Okay. Court's in recess".

As Johnnie turned toward his client, Ed Cranston, the judge's law clerk, quickly approached.

"Mr. Fitzhugh, your office called. It's urgent that you call your dad's secretary. Also, the judge wants to see you for a moment before you leave for lunch."

"Ed, tell His Honor I'll be in immediately after I make the call. Thanks."

Johnnie then turned to his anxious client.

"Well, Doctor, it's now out of our hands. It looks like I'll be tied up for a while. You may as well go across the street to the luncheonette. I'll join you as soon as I can. Keep your cellphone on."

"What's your read on the jury?"

"I've tried lots of trials in eleven years, and like I told you earlier, it's always a crapshoot. Throughout this trial, I have glanced surreptitiously at the jurors as critical responses were coming from the witness box. Frankly, I can't read this jury. To stay successful in this business, you can't lose many cases. It's the ones you lose that stick in your craw and awaken you with night sweats."

Dr. Lewis curtly replied "Well, this damn jury better get it right. I didn't do anything wrong. That bastard attorney never should have taken this case. No offense to you, Johnnie, but lawyers are like ticks. If you walk long enough in the woods, one will latch on to you."

As his client opened the swinging door separating the counsel tables from the empty spectator benches, Johnnie turned away to mask his irritation. The "good" doctor had been a thorn in his side from the moment of their initial conference. It took months of coaching and cajoling to bury his client's haughty demeanor. Now that the testimony had concluded, the normal persona returned. As his dad counseled him, "Son, you don't have to like or respect your client. Just stay calm and take the money. If you don't, you won't last long in this profession."

3.

Johnnie hurriedly left the courtroom and found an alcove from where he called his father's secretary, Eleanor Dodson. Eleanor, long-widowed, had been with the firm for twenty-five years. It was her life-blood and security blanket. Loyal to a fault, she fielded calls graciously like a minister, but when conversing with opposing lawyers, she didn't suffer fools gladly. Even the local judiciary knew rank didn't equate with privilege in her hazel-blue eyes. Silver-tongued and silver-haired, she presented a formidable presence on her five-foot-two-inch willowy frame. As the office's factotum, she wore many hats: confessor, confidant, interpreter, placater, ally, and friend. She was always there when trouble brewed or sorrow arose.

Everything and everyone went through Eleanor. The attorneys were in or were available only when she said so, at least until the advent of that dreaded cellphone. Even then, she circumvented that obstacle by purchasing separate "court" cellphones for father and son Fitzhugh. Only the "court" cellphone numbers were given to the judiciary and clients. That way, the attorneys could leave them off and conduct their normal lives on their personal phones, which she would call only if a real urgency arose.

"Eleanor, it's me. What's the crisis?"

"Johnnie, you have to call Burnside immediately, and I mean immediately. Something's up. He sounded very rattled, far out of character for the 'ice man.'"

"Maybe our cocky trial adjustor is providing him a more realistic portrayal of this trial that he presents as rosy to me on a daily basis. No. That can't be. After all, our adjustor friend just pontificates. He's never engaged in the actual battle. I'll call Burnside post haste. When does Dad get back today from his Rhine River Cruise?"

"It's tomorrow night, not today."

"Oh, well, I guess time doesn't fly that fast when you're having the fun I've experienced the last three weeks. Talk to you later."

Glen Burnside was a tougher-than-nails seventy-five-year-old former Vietnam decorated marine lieutenant who rose through the ranks to become president and CEO of Supreme Insurance Company.

Located in a sylvan setting in semirural Hopewell Township, the carrier was known for the ardent defense of its insured. Its shibboleth was "Money for the defense, but none, or very little, for the injured and wronged." Burnside would not often consider deviating from that philosophy. The fact that he personally placed an urgent call startled Johnnie. Typically, an insurance adjuster would report the day's trial events to his litigation supervisor. For three weeks, the trial had ebbed and flowed. From what Johnnie observed, not much was flowing in his favor.

Fortunately, Judge Fleming was a seasoned jurist. Having been a former trial attorney, he vividly understood the courtroom stressors. Calm, courteous, and fair, he allowed the attorneys to try their case at a reasonable pace. While his evidential rulings were precise, Judge Fleming didn't provide them in a brisk, supercilious fashion. He heard any objections at sidebar and allowed frequent breaks so that the jury's attention wouldn't wander. He covered for the inevitable witness delays so neither attorney would be penalized by the jury. All in all, Judge Fleming was a trial lawyer's dream. It was no coincidence that he routinely was assigned the most complex cases.

With anticipation and curiosity, Johnnie returned the CEO's call.

"Mr. Burnside, I'm glad you called. The jury's out. I wanted to..."

"Right now, I don't give a damn about the trial. Melanie's been arrested for her husband's murder. She's in the lockup at Hopewell Township. Her one obligatory call was, fortunately, to me. She sounded hysterical. Between her sobbing and hyperventilating, I heard her mumble that she didn't do it. Frankly, her husband's death isn't the greatest loss, but that's for another day.

I called Police Chief Lawton. They have cordoned off the house and called the prosecutor's office. A search warrant is being issued for the home. Forensics are still at the scene and will be there apparently for some time. Melanie's maid arrived for cleaning, discovered the body, and called 911. The chief wouldn't say anything further other than Melanie needed a good lawyer. And, Johnnie, that's you."

Johnnie cringed internally. While he had spent three years in the Mercer County Prosecutor's Office trying every type of case, including murder, that was eight years ago. Since then, he had honed his skills in personal injury law. While the evidence rules were the same, the nuances and the cast of characters were completely different. Left unsaid was the amount of resources at his disposal. On the civil practice side, as a defense attorney, he had the vast reserves and monetary resources of insurance companies, corporations, and municipalities on which to rely. The tables were turned, however, on the criminal side. The prosecutor, with his herd of investigators, detectives, and experts, easily had the upper hand.

The prosecutor could find, threaten, and influence witnesses. He could interview, hire, and then discard experts and retain others. Although a prosecutor's budget wasn't unlimited, it far exceeded what could be expected from an accused, who, more often than not, was rightfully charged and lacked the intelligence, education, and poise to withstand a blistering cross-examination.

Burnside noted the lack of a quick response and quickly assumed the offensive.

"Johnnie, let me make this perfectly clear. It will be you! From what I remember, you were a very skilled prosecutor. What? You lost only one case, and that involved a rival gang shooting, where the jury probably concluded that more members should have killed each other."

Johnnie politely but quickly replied, "But, Mr. Burnside, this is your daughter. I haven't tried a criminal case in eight years, and I never crossed over to the other side. You need the best criminal defense lawyer. I can think of three immediately. They practice here, obviously know the prosecutors well, and are above reproach."

Burnside emotionally replied, "Johnnie, I already spoke to former Prosecutor Sapienza, your old boss. He gave me a rundown on the criminal defense bar and its pros and cons. I mentioned you.. He replied, 'dynamic, thorough, tremendous courtroom presence and awareness.' All these attributes apply to civil or criminal, Johnnie. Melanie needs you. I need you."

Johnnie wished this conversation could have been face to face. He was certain that he could dissuade Burnside in person. Body gestures and postures could convince Burnside that he wasn't the right fit for the onslaught that was to follow. Also, with his crowded civil trial schedule, how would he devote the interminable hours that would be required to defend an accused murderer? What if he lost, which was most likely? Wouldn't Burnside be vindictive enough to pull all the carrier's medical malpractice files from the office? While Supreme Insurance wasn't the firm's only client, it paid the best hourly rate and yearly sent a considerable number of files. Most importantly, each file required a tremendous amount of research and leg work, which translated into a very considerable legal bill. It seemed this was a no-win situation for him and the firm. He had to conjure up a plausible excuse.

"Mr. Burnside, you have been so good to Dad, me, and the firm. Frankly, I fondly regard you and Supreme as a member of the Fitzhugh family. One of the things that is ingrained in a lawyer at an early age is that you never represent a family member. As much as you would love to, nothing good can ever come of it. While it is a very difficult decision to make out of your love and attachment to the family member, such closeness only clouds your thinking and decision making when representing a family member. Judgments often are made rashly and emotionally due to your mutual closeness, leading to consequences and outcomes often unfavorable, if not downright disastrous. I'm afraid that nothing good can come if I represent Melanie. While I would defend her to the best of my ability and leave no stone unturned to prove her innocence, there will be times during the process that critical decisions will have to be made. Those determinations have to be reached dispassionately, devoid of any relationships, emotions, and outside pressures. Due to our closeness, that can't be done. I wish it were otherwise."

Without hesitation, Burnside emphatically replied, "Johnnie, if I recall, an experienced counselor advises his client never to say 'never' on cross-examination when responding to past behavior or conduct. Maybe, Johnnie, you haven't strayed from not representing family members, but this isn't a 'never' situation. We are not family. I'm a businessman, and you're essentially my employee, albeit an excellent one. Lest you forget, I hold the purse strings. How many millions have I paid Fitzhugh and Fitzhugh over the years? Remember, I can pull the files as quickly as I can dole them out. It's your call, Johnnie. Defend or see the spigot run dry."

Intuitively, Johnnie realized his options had dissipated quickly. Now, there really was no choice. All he could hope for was that as events unfolded, Burnside would realize his mistake and seek other counsel. Until then, he would placate, assuage, and investigate. He carefully chose his words as he replied.

"Do you have any questions about the possible pitfalls that would occur through my representation of Melanie?"

"None. You have made your concerns crystal clear. I will provide all the resources and money you need to ensure the best possible defense. I will spare nothing on experts. Find and hire the best. Your undevoted attention to my daughter's plight is all I ask. Now go immediately to the county lockup and see her. Any questions?"

Differentially, Johnnie responded, "I've got a problem. The jury's out. The judge said not to stray too far because the jury might have questions."

"Sam told me we offered twenty-five grand. Melanie's more important than this case. I need you out of that courtroom now! Settle the damn case within the policy limits, even over Dr. Lewis' objection!"

Burnside knew his company's parsimonious reputation. He prided himself on being known as a prick. A lawsuit against a Supreme Insurance insured meant a full-blown trial with all its concomitant expenses. The plaintiff's bar was forewarned. Thus, experienced practitioners didn't file cases with little value or questionable liability. Of course, the novice attorney might initiate a suit, but typically the court would toss it at the summary judgment stage. If not, then the jury would toss it. Having eaten the time, the deposition costs, and the expert fees, the forlorn lawyer quickly learned his lesson.

Burnside knew, in this instance, an exception would be made, and the experienced practitioners would understand the reason. His adjustors would spread the word that the company's philosophy hadn't changed, and the plaintiff's bar shouldn't assume that the Burnside family would experience future calamities.

As Johnnie entered the judge's inner sanctum, His Honor put down the newspaper and looked up and over his tortoise-shell half glasses. Before the judge could vent his spleen, Johnnie rushed in, "Sorry, Judge, I've been on the phone trying to convince the powers that be we should make a more palatable offer. With your help, we can settle this case, provided the carrier doesn't have to pay its entire policy."

Johnnie and Judge Fleming discussed reasonable parameters and then summoned the plaintiff's attorney, Silverman, and the matter was settled.

By the time Johnnie exited the chambers, Dr. Lewis had reentered the courtroom. Now came the hard part.

"How much longer do you expect the jury to be out?" queried Lewis.

"Doctor, the carrier has agreed to settle with the plaintiff," Johnnie replied gravely.

Lewis angrily retorted, "What do you mean settle? I didn't give you, the adjuster, or the carrier that permission. I told all of you not a penny was to be paid. I didn't do a damn thing wrong, and that son-of-a-bitch Silverman knows it."

Calmly, Johnnie answered, "Doctor, I don't control the carrier's funds. It gives me my marching orders, and I must follow them. I was engaged by the carrier, not by you. The carrier offered you the right to have your own lawyer at your own expense. You decided not to do so. I have defended you to the best of my ability. I have reported each day's trial events to the carrier. Additionally, the carrier's adjuster sat through the case from opening to closing. I don't know what the adjuster told the carrier. I just recited all the entered testimony. I know the carrier clearly was concerned a verdict against you would exceed your policy limits. Any overage would have subjected you to personal responsibility for the excess. Under our law, the carrier had an obligation to offer your policy limits if required to reach a settlement. Otherwise, it would be responsible for the excess. The judge was able to resolve this matter without the carrier having to pay those policy limits. Plaintiff's counsel has agreed that he will not tell the press the settlement amount. He will mention only the amount received from the other defendants.

"We also are not putting the sum on the record, so it will not be public knowledge. If you want to know the settlement amount, you can call the carrier. I will be asking Mr. Silverman to forward the settlement release directly to the carrier, which then will issue a draft made payable to the plaintiff and his counsel. The carrier will forward the draft directly to Silverman. Both counsel will sign a stipulation of dismissal, and I will file it with the court and forward you a copy. The stipulation doesn't mention the settlement figure. I know you're upset, but your personal assets have been protected. The judge will be putting the settlement now on the record. The jury will not be told the settlement amount. In fact, both Mr. Silverman and I will be leaving the courtroom before the jury learns of the settlement."

"Well, I want the jury to render its verdict," yelled Lewis.

Johnnie placed his hand softly on Lewis' shoulder, looked at the doctor's graying beard, and stated, "That would be the worst thing you could ask for. If the jury ruled against you, the verdict and its sum would be in the morning newspapers for all to see. Nothing good can come from that. This carrier thought it was in its and your best interests to resolve this matter. It believes the sympathy factor is enormous. The other defendants paid their policy limits. Even the hospital, which was blameless, paid its limits, because of Mr. Howard's condition. Furthermore, neither Mr. Howard nor Mr. Silverman wants to hear the verdict. They and the carrier have agreed. The judge will not take such a verdict, no matter when it is reached. Of course, if you want to call the carrier and inform it that you will relieve it of any financial responsibility, I guess the carrier could enter a separate agreement without your name on it and then pay Mr. Silverman the agreed sum. That settlement, however, will not protect you. Any award entered against you will be your responsibility, not the carrier's. By now, you should assume that Silverman, under those circumstances, would attach your assets until any award was satisfied. I don't think that is a viable alternative for you, but it's your decision."

Lewis's shoulders slumped. "No, I guess it isn't." Then he glared at Johnnie and coldly stated, "You and your carrier have ruined my career. I can just imagine how high my next malpractice premium will skyrocket. And then what? Who will want me as their neurosurgeon? Would you engage a surgeon whose patient came out of the operating room a quad?"

Johnnie started to reply, but Lewis cut him off with the wave of a hand, announcing "No, you fucking wouldn't! You, that fucker over there," he said pointing to Silverman, "and Supreme haven't heard the last from me!"

Lewis then turned and stormed out of the courtroom. Silverman shook his head and surprisingly muttered to Johnnie, "If you want to work for the good guys, call me. My clients might be maimed, and even stupid, but they appreciate me. You look like you could use a little lovin'."

With that, Judge Fleming entered the courtroom, and counsel put the agreement on the record. Johnnie then grabbed his trial briefcase and slowly rolled it out of the courtroom. He contemplated how much worse matters could get in the next several hours.

PART TWO

4.

Exiting the courthouse, Johnnie walked to the State parking lot across from the aluminum-and-glass exterior of the angular Richard S. Hughes Justice Complex that housed the Supreme Court, Appellate Division, Attorney General's Office, and other agencies. Leaving the parking lot, he observed a group of middle schoolers exiting from the adjacent brick façade of the William Trent House, the oldest remaining building in Trenton. William Trent, for whom the city was named, erected the building in 1719. During the summer of 1798, a yellow-fever epidemic inundated Philadelphia, then the nation's capital. The Trent House served as a temporary location for federal agencies until November, when workers returned to Philadelphia.

Johnnie turned south on Market Street and entered Route 29 that paralleled the Delaware River as it flowed past the city. In the late nineteenth and early twentieth centuries, Trenton was a prominent manufacturing site for ceramics, rubber, and wire rope, produced by companies such as Roebling, Maddock, and Scammel. Populated then by Hungarians, Italians, and Jews, the city thrived. In the last several decades, however, the city had fallen on hard times, leading to a mass exodus to surrounding Jersey municipalities in Ewing, Lawrence, Hamilton, Hopewell, and Pennington, as well as Pennsylvania suburbs in Morrisville, Yardley, Newtown, and the Makefields. As the emigration continued, urban blight took ugly root, and crime increased. The Crips and Bloods arrived. The drug trade flourished, despite the best efforts of those left behind. Now the city basically was a nine-to-five locale populated by state employees, who, during their lunch hour, could be observed in droves walking or jogging across Trenton's bridges to adjacent Pennsylvania.

En route, Johnnie passed through Washington Crossing. On a bitterly cold sleet- and snow-driven night, George Washington and his army of 2,400 men arrived at Johnson's Ferry after crossing the ice-floed Delaware from Washington Crossing, Pennsylvania, in Durham boats — large open boats used to transport pig iron along the Delaware. The Continental Army then marched south to Trenton and attacked 1,500 unsuspecting Hessian soldiers garrisoned in a barracks constructed in 1758 during the French and Indian War. The battle, often referred to as the "Turning Point of the Revolution," was followed by the Second Battle of Trenton on January 2, 1777, and the Battle of Princeton the following day. Johnnie fondly recalled that Christmas day surprise when, at age ten, his parents took him to the annual Christmas crossing and reenactment. His eyes had widened in amazement as he observed the authentically clad Washington and his troops struggle to cross the rapidly moving river.

Within moments, Johnnie arrived at his destination. The Mercer County Corrections Center, located in Hopewell Township, is a short-term jail facility for approximately 900 inmates with minimum, medium, and maximum security classifications. The population includes those convicted and sentenced as well as those who are awaiting trial. Inmates sentenced for more than a year are housed there while awaiting transfer to one of the state prison facilities. Those sentenced to less than a year serve their time at the Corrections Center.

Upon entering the jail, inmates are booked. Property is inventoried, medical information obtained, prints and mug shots taken.

Pulling into the parking lot, Johnnie hoped that all of that already had transpired for Melanie. He still had that gnawing sensation that his representation would not end well. He recalled a noted attorney once advised him, "Every case is filled with choices to be made. As a lawyer, you believe you make that choice, but often the choice makes you." What choices lurked for him?

5.

Clad in a loose-fitting orange jumpsuit, Dr. Melanie Stafford shuffled into the visitors' room. Johnnie immediately noticed the bandage on her forehead and the smaller one on the bridge of her delicately modeled nose. Her black curly hair appeared unwashed and disheveled. Her deep-set moss-hued green eyes were bloodshot. Her lids appeared swollen and bruised. Her high cheek-boned, elongated face was ashen. Her thin lips quivered and intermittently revealed her porcelain white teeth. She slowly bent forward and sat on the plastic chair. Raising her head, she mumbled, "They killed him. They finally did it. Richard waited too long. I pleaded with him to go to the authorities or the FDA, but he insisted that he wanted the evidence to be air tight. I don't know how." She then broke down and sobbed uncontrollably. A female attendant approached with tissues. She took a wad of tissues, wiped her face, and bit her lip.

"Dr. Stafford, your father hired me to defend you."

She stared directly into Johnnie's eyes and quizzically replied, "Why? I didn't kill Richard. I loved him. We were so much in love. I knew from the moment we met that we would be together. How could the cops believe I killed him? For what reason? My God, I've got all the money I need. I'm an anesthesiologist with a thriving practice. He has a…" Then she broke down again. Johnnie looked away. Regaining her composure, she added, "I mean, he had a wonderful job at Wellington Pharmaceuticals until he uncovered irregularities in their trials testing."

Johnnie cut her off and interjected, "Dr. Stafford, we can talk about that later. My immediate objective is to get you out of here. Tomorrow, you will have a bail hearing. The prosecutor will argue for no bail or very high bail due to your assumed assets and your possible flight risk. Whether you committed the crime or not, the issue here is bail. I will be there for you. Did the police question you?"

"Yes, they did. I told them the truth from what I could remember."

Worried, Johnnie asked, "Did they have you write a statement?"

"No, my head hurt. I told them I couldn't write well, because my vision seemed blurry, and I felt somewhat off balance, but my head wasn't spinning. I just felt off mentally. The officer then asked if I would give a recorded statement. I assumed that he wanted to know whether I got a look at the intruder or intruders. I assumed there must have been more than one, although I never felt more than one. I just felt an arm like a vise around my chest and a hand with some cloth with a distinctive smell being pressed tightly down on my face. I tried to struggle free. I kicked backward. I seem to remember falling forward. The next thing I recall is being groggy, hearing Inez scream, looking over, seeing Richard on the floor, blood all around, and a gun next to me. Later, I saw what appeared to be the cloth on the floor. I guess they just left it. I remember pulling at it. I tried to rip it away from my face, but he was too strong. I remember his fingers being very thick. My right foot may have hit his right shin."

Johnnie interrupted, "Did you give a recorded statement?"

With sudden emotion and emphasis, Melanie answered, "Yes. Even though I wasn't feeling well, I wanted to help the police get the intruders. I knew from seeing crime shows on TV that the sooner the police get the details, the faster they can catch the killers. I knew my head pain might be interfering with my recall, but they killed my husband. I wanted the bastards caught and executed!"

Johnnie noted the sudden fire in her eyes and the flaring of her nostrils. From a subdued broken woman suddenly emerged a fiery persona. He could picture her thrashing backward at her assailant, resisting with all her force before succumbing to the anesthetic.

Taking a yellow legal pad from his briefcase, Johnnie inquired, "Did the police have you sign the transcribed statement?"

"Yes."

"Did you read it before you signed it?

"No! I had a splitting headache and still didn't feel right mentally. The medics had taken me to the hospital where I was examined. As you can see, I had lacerations on my forehead and nose. I must have received them when I fell to the floor. I forgot to tell you. When I awoke, I saw an overturned table and lamp on the floor. I must have hit them when I lost consciousness. I needed stitches to my forehead but not to my nose."

Johnnie noticed that his client's composure again had changed. Her responses sounded like that of a clinician or physician describing a medical diagnosis. Her voice seemed impersonal and detached. It was as if Johnnie was conversing with a completely different person. He noted that even though her eyes were bloodshot, the greenness was mesmerizing. He had heard that some women had green eyes but never had encountered it. Even in her present state, Melanie's eyes were alluring. They seemed to draw Johnnie inward, like a diver being drawn to a Caribbean blue hole.

Johnnie realized that Melanie was staring at him. He recovered his thoughts and reflexively picked up his legal pad from the table, made some random notes, and prodded, "Who is your maid?"

"Inez. She comes once a week. That was her day. Both my husband and I leave early for work. Due to my surgical schedule, I often leave at four or five o'clock in the morning. My husband leaves around six thirty. Inez has a key. She often arrives early. That allows her to clean our house yet still have time to do someone else's. Today, I actually had the day off. Richard had flown back from a conference in Hawaii with a layover in Dallas. He was supposed to be home by 11:00 p.m. When he didn't arrive, I decided to wait for him on the living room couch. Our bedroom is adjacent to our living room. We have a ranch home. At some point, he arrived home and awakened me from a deep sleep. He kissed me on the forehead. Knowing he was home safe, I immediately fell back to sleep. At some point, I awakened to go to the bathroom. As I arose from the couch, I felt some cool air coming from the drapes behind the couch. I swore I had checked the sliding glass door earlier that evening. I went to check it. Suddenly, I was grabbed from behind. I screamed in the darkness, and you already know the rest."

"What's Inez's last name?"

"Garcia."

"What's her address and phone number?" After Melanie provided the information, Johnnie addressed his client, "Have you talked to any of the inmates?"

"No. Should I?"

Johnnie replied quickly and forcefully, "Under no circumstances are you to tell anyone anything about what happened. You should not mention that you've been arrested for murder or what your occupation is. Under no circumstances are you to have any conversations with any of them, no matter how friendly they may be. You are surrounded by people rightfully charged who will do anything to cut a more favorable deal with the prosecutor's office. They will lie, tell half-truths, and create fictional accounts in an effort to curry favor with the prosecutor. You are their ticket to a reduced charge or even to freedom. Nothing, and I mean nothing, should be said to anyone other than hello in response to any greeting. If someone intimidates or threatens you, scream your lungs out.

If you hadn't been arrested, were you scheduled to work at the hospital tomorrow?"

With a faint wan smile, Melanie replied, "You mean hospitals. I cover all the area hospitals as the leading anesthesiologist for all major surgeries. By that, I mean lengthy surgeries, such as cardiac, neurosurgical, and, if needed, sudden major traumas. I have a full schedule from tomorrow through Friday. I don't know who will be covering for me tomorrow. When I called my father, I told him to reach out to the hospital administrators. By now, I would assume they know of my arrest."

"Dr. Stafford, I need to know the names and numbers for those administrators. I would hope that one or more would appear at the bail hearing. I need them to show how critical it is for you to be released on bail."

Melanie provided Johnnie with the requested details and added, "From what you've implied, it appears that we will be seeing a lot of each other for a while. You should call me Melanie. I want my lifeline to feel connected to me. My father advised me that he was engaging you. When my father says what he wants, he always gets it. He said you were the best and that I'd be free and cleared. Not to put any pressure on you, but both he and I expect it. I'm innocent and have no intention of rotting my brains out in some prison cell!"

Taken aback by her forcefulness, Johnnie started to rise, and answered, "I'll do my best. It's your show tomorrow. Look bewildered, but act the intelligent and graceful woman that you are."

Melanie raised her chin and offered, "I'm here, but I'm already there".

With that, she arose from her chair, turned her back on him, and walked away without a shuffling gait. Johnnie tried to hide his perplexed look as he exited the facility. His client seemed to have a chameleonlike personality. Having not defended an accused murderer before, he really hadn't formed any preconceived opinion of his client. As a prosecutor, he had encountered and cross-examined numerous young men accused of murder. Almost all were street-smart yet basically uneducated. Cross-examining them was like shooting fish in a barrel. Their alibi witnesses were even worse. Times, dates, and places never coincided, thereby leading to fairly quick guilty verdicts.

What his present client lacked in street-smarts she made up for in striking features and superior intellect. She should prove to be a formidable adversary for any cross-examining prosecutor. A prosecutor could not bait and control her, but that begged the question: Could Johnnie harness her moods, mannerisms, and responses? If the evidence was as she depicted, was the prosecutor looking at this as murder or manslaughter? Obviously not as self-defense, or no charge would have been lodged so quickly. There was no question that Melanie was a Burnside. Beneath that sometimes demure demeanor appeared to be a granite backbone. At trial, that spine had to be concealed. A grief-stricken widow, a victimized wife, and a caring, mild mannered, well-spoken educated woman had to appear. Controlling Melanie Stafford would be no easy task. Her life and his job security depended on it.

6.

Approaching the cell area, Melanie heard the constant chattering. It reminded her of crickets on a hot summer night, except this staccato was punctuated with profanities, slang, and venom. She felt like a cornered animal. She was surrounded by crack whores, black and white. For the most part, the teenagers were emaciated. Their vacant stares portrayed a haunting portrait. The older inmates, in their twenties, thirties, and forties, supplied the chatter. Sometimes boisterous, often scatological, the din was nerve-racking. No one could be trusted or befriended. Melanie braced herself for a tumultuous night, bereft of sleep. Tomorrow was the first step in what she feared was an arduous and terrifying journey. Her lawyer had to get her released from this hellhole. She never envisioned actually getting charged with Richard's murder. The sliding door glass had been broken to free the lock. She had lacerations on her forehead and nose. A table and lamp had been overturned. Inez had discovered her semiconscious on the floor with a scented rag near her body. How could the police conclude that she drugged herself, knocked herself out, and still killed Richard? She knew Inez was loyal to a fault and would provide the details to corroborate the scene. What were the police thinking?

Her lawyer seemed perceptive, though young. Her father had assured her that he was brilliant, and that, in the courtroom, ice streamed through his veins. He definitely was handsome. Close to six feet and rock hard solid, he projected a powerful presence that, coupled with his ruggedly handsome good looks, would hold the attention of any juror, especially a female one. As a physician, she had come to detest attorneys. Most she encountered had a quiet arrogance. Others blatantly projected a hubris that was downright nauseating. The worst, in her eyes, were those that preyed on her profession, filing baseless suits and grandstanding before the cameras and the press. Although her profession contained some unsavory characters, most were upstanding and felt an attachment and caring for their patients. With the constant long hours, sudden family interruptions, and inevitable undercompensated insurance reimbursements, no sane individual would enter the medical profession without a deeply rooted passion for the practice. Presently, she was out of her element, but she had steeled herself for this scenario. Fitzhugh knew her fate was in his hands. How it played out was in hers. Tomorrow would be the opening act.

7.

Leaving the Corrections Center, Johnnie phoned Burnside and instructed him to call the named hospital administrators, request their assistance, and tell them to expect to hear from Johnnie in the evening. He briefly summarized his meeting with Melanie and indicated that he would arrive at Burnside's Princeton home sometime after six o'clock. That done, he called his office and asked for his assistant Erika Svenson. Within a minute, she exclaimed "I hear we've got a doozy."

As best he could, Johnnie laughed and retorted, "I'm glad you used we, because you're tag-teaming this problem. What do you know?"

Erika hurriedly rejoined, "It's all over the local news. She murdered her husband. Three shots: head, chest, and lower abdomen. Was she aiming for the groin? Sounds like a cheating husband and a spurned spouse to me. Count yourself lucky that none of your old short-lasting flames have had that predilection."

Johnnie laughed again and uttered, "Erika, I need you to find out who is hearing the bail requests tomorrow. Contact that judge's secretary, and ask that she advise you the time of the video hearings. Tell the secretary that we will be requesting bail for Melanie. Then call my cell and leave the info. I will need you to be present at the hearing. Wear your finest. Just make sure you haven't worn the same garb before that judge. Being I haven't been in a criminal court in years, it's doubtful unless the judge was rotated recently from the civil side. If you hear anything from the gossip or police hotline, let me know ASAP. Thanks, talk to you later."

Johnnie's thoughts momentarily drifted toward Erika. She was his special courtroom asset. Usually present through the jury selection process, she routinely sat at counsel table when an adversary's expert was on direct examination. Her striking appearance created a welcome distraction to the expert's critical testimony. Well prepped as to the expert's report and deposition testimony, she had a knack for knowing when to utilize her distraction qualities. A lithe blonde with long, shapely legs, saucerlike hazel eyes, and pouty lips, her presence would stop anyone midsentence. As Johnnie's trial assistant, she attended bar association functions and hobnobbed with the local attorneys and, more importantly, the judiciary.

With a degree in Criminal Justice from the College of New Jersey and a private detective's license, Erika possessed the requisite investigative skills. Of Swedish heritage, she had attended college on a tennis scholarship and had played on the professional circuit for several years. After not cracking the top one hundred, she concluded that the international grind no longer had its allure. A chance meeting with Johnnie at a tennis-sponsored charity function led to her present employment. Most assumed that their relationship was more than professional. Colleagues were bewildered that marriage wasn't on the horizon. Johnnie and Erika did little to dispel their assumed linkage. It provided Erika with her needed cover. She was ardently gay but treasured her privacy. She still maintained a secret relationship with one of the circuit's top-ranking females. Erika, however, was not without feelings for Johnnie. She understood his moods, assuaged his frustrations, and even provided his sexual releases during periods of self-inflicted depression. Their emotional relationship at times could be intense. What was left unsaid was the lack of possible permanency. Johnnie was too needy to cement a relationship where Erika needed an alternative release. A hookup was one thing; an everlasting bond was another.

After traversing Route 29 south and Route 95 east, Johnnie entered Route 206 north and passed through charming Lawrenceville, home to one of the country's most elite and esteemed prep schools. With attendees from all over the world, the school's campus and facilities rivaled that of a small liberal arts college.

As he approached Princeton, Johnnie passed Drumthwacket, a Greek revival mansion, now the official residence of the state's governor. On land once owned by William Penn, Charles Smith Olden in 1835 commenced construction of "wooded hill," which eventually evolved into a mammoth edifice containing a large portico with six detailed Ionic columns. Gated and set back far from the roadway, the building projected an imposing presence.

Turning left on Elm and then right on Hodge, Johnnie entered Princeton's most prestigious neighborhood. Library Place, Hodge, and others were streets known for their stately mansions with winding or circular driveways. Cross-gabled and half-timbered Tudors with massive chimneys crowned with decorative pots and steeply pitched roofs competed with brick Georgians with their paneled front doors capped with elaborately adorned crowns supported by decorative pilasters. Here and there, a Colonial with its elliptical fanlight and small entry porch or a classically columned façade dotted the landscape. Almost all were situated on ample grounds. Maples, oaks, sycamores, and pines lined the lawns and curbings. On Hodge, the massive trees formed a canopy over the roadway, creating a sylvan effect.

Johnnie wound through the area and eventually reached Burnside's four-columned red-bricked residence. Burnside greeted him at the door and then led him past the impressive circular staircase and into a massive cherry-paneled study with floor-to-ceiling bookcases. The ceiling was high and coffered. Several Persian rugs graced the oak floor. Two leather tufted chairs fronted an intricately carved desk on which rested a miniature bust of Napoleon. Off to the side sat a Chesterfield sofa. Dark plantation-style shutters enclosed the study.

Burnside walked behind his desk and gestured for Johnnie to sit in the burgundy leather chair. Behind him, he heard heels slowly clicking on the oak floor. Before he could turn, he heard a softly spoken stammering voice.

"Mr. Fitzhugh, how is she?"

Johnnie arose from his chair and turned. A diminutive woman in a light-gray cashmere cardigan and black gabardine slacks approached. Her silver hair was in a classic French twist. Her somewhat frail appearance contrasted sharply with Burnside's tall muscular frame. Her perfectly coiffed hair seemed out of place with her obviously distraught face.

"Mrs. Burnside, I'm sorry to meet you under these circumstances. Your daughter is a strong woman. She's holding her own. As I told your husband, my immediate concern relates to tomorrow's bail hearing. I have to convince the court to provide a reasonable bail."

Burnside forcibly interjected, "Money isn't an object. Our home and Melanie's are mortgage-free. Each, by itself, should provide a sufficient guarantee. If not, we can post a cash bail, but that would require some asset moving."

"Mr. Burnside, as we discussed, I will need at least one of the hospital administrators to accompany you to the hearing. After we talk to Mrs. Garcia, we may also need her."

"I've already spoken to her. She is awaiting our call," Burnside replied.

"Mr. Fitzhugh, would you like something to drink?"

Realizing it would be too stressful for her to hear their discussion, Johnnie politely requested hot tea.

As his wife entered the corridor, Burnside quickly closed the door behind her.

"I don't know how she is going to bear up. She and Melanie have been so close. My daughter will confide in her. Knowing my mercurial temperament, I fear she has hidden some things from me, which brings me to my dead son-in-law. It's no secret I never approved of their marriage. His sarcastic and supercilious attitude never appealed to me. Melanie thought he was handsome and brilliant. I guess she thought him to be her intellectual soul mate. To me, he was an oafish bore. For my daughter's well-being, I bit my lip on many occasions. In her thirties, Melanie contracted ovarian cancer, which necessitated a hysterectomy. Melanie wanted to adopt, but the selfish prick refused. In retrospect, maybe that was a good thing. The world didn't need a Richard junior!

"One other thing, I think the bastard was cheating on her. I don't have any concrete proof, but it's a very good hunch. At one point, I thought of hiring a PI but decided against it. I feared that if my intuition proved correct, I would do something rash that would turn my daughter away from me. I couldn't bear that. I didn't want her forced to choose between him and me. As it is, I'm not so sure she would have forgiven him. Although Melanie is a very sweet and caring woman, she is also incredibly proud. As a teenager, I remember her ditching long-time friends over even insignificant slights. Other than her work, if Melanie is fanatical about anything, it is her bedrock belief in loyalty. She didn't lie to or deceive her friends. In the back of my mind, I've always considered what she would have done if she discovered he had been unfaithful to her. I guess now that's a moot point."

"Mr. Burnside, please keep those thoughts to yourself. Nothing would be more disastrous to your daughter's defense than that scenario. Television plotlines abound with that entanglement. From what I've observed, most prospective jurors watch CSI and 48 Hours. They're preconditioned to the predictable result. It would be very difficult to convince them otherwise."

Mrs. Burnside knocked on the door and reentered. "Would you like something to eat?"

"No, dear, Johnnie and I have to make some phone calls regarding the bail hearing. We'll be tied up for a bit. Try to get some rest. We both must be strong when Melanie comes home."

Mrs. Burnside slightly nodded and replied, "Mr. Fitzhugh, I'll be praying for you and Melanie. Glen is almost always right. We all will get through this with God's help. Both of us will do whatever you need. Thank you again."

Johnnie watched her steady herself, turn, and walk deliberately out of the study. As the door closed behind her, Burnside inquired, "What time is the bail hearing, and who's presiding?"

"My assistant, Erika Svenson, is checking on that now. She should be calling shortly. Let's call your daughter's maid in the interim."

Burnside picked up the phone and dialed the maid's number. "Mrs. Garcia, it's Glen Burnside again. I have Mr. Fitzhugh, Melanie's lawyer, on speaker. Please answer all his questions. Anything you can remember will help us. Okay?"

In somewhat broken but very clear and hurried English, Inez Garcia replied, "I do my best for Melanie. I tell you what I see. All I see. It was so terrible. I still shaking. I never forget. The blood on him, on Melanie. The gun on the floor. The blood on the floor. On Melanie's face, her hands, her blouse. My screaming, her screaming. Her lips all bloody. Her hands. Bloody chest. Pounding. Chest no move. I call 911. The sirens. The police everywhere. The ambulance. I still screaming. Melanie screaming, crying. It so terrible, so terrible. I still shaking, still shaking. My husband he try calm me down. I no can do. He say, get nerve pills. Where I go? I don't want to leave house! Who do this? They wonderful people to me. So nice. Never yell at me, even if I'm late. So wonderful. Why do this? I no understand. Why police take Melanie? She so good and nice. I pray for her. For his soul. What wrong with world? Violence everywhere. Mexico I understand. Drugs and more drugs. Here, I and family come. Now this. Oh God! Oh God! I no understand."

Johnnie interrupted, "Mrs. Garcia, my name is John Fitzhugh. You can call me Johnnie, okay?"

"Yes. Okay."

"I am Melanie's lawyer. I need to ask you some questions. Okay?"

"Yes, it okay."

"When I ask you a question, I want you to tell me everything you remember, even if you are afraid it could hurt Melanie. If I know everything you recall, nothing will hurt Melanie. Do you understand?"

"But what would hurt Melanie? I no want to hurt Melanie. She good person."

Burnside interceded, "Mrs. Garcia, in order to help Melanie as best we can, we must know everything you saw and heard. Even if you think something could hurt Melanie, you must tell us. Mr. Fitzhugh and I can make sure nothing will hurt Melanie, but we can only do that if we know everything you saw and heard. Will you tell us everything so we can help Melanie?"

"Yes, I tell everything. I no want to hurt Melanie. She my good friend. She help me and my family. I tell all to help Melanie. I do my best."

Johnnie stated, "Mrs. Garcia, I want you to tell me in order everything you saw and heard from the moment you opened the front door. I know this is frightening for you, but I need you to tell it to me slowly, so I and Mr. Burnside can write it down. Please try to tell me slowly. Okay?"

"Yes, I do my best. My husband is here next to me."

"Okay, but tell your husband that only you can tell the story, because he wasn't there. Okay?"

"Yes. I understand."

"Okay. Tell us what you saw and heard."

"I open front door with my key. I go inside. I see Mr. Stafford on back on floor just outside open bedroom door. Blood on forehead, shirt, and pants. Blood all over white rug. I scream. I then see Melanie to left. She on floor and trying to get up. She screams. I see gun on floor not far from her. I see white cloth near gun. I see table knocked over on floor. I see table lamp on floor. Glass from light on floor. Melanie has blood on forehead and on nose. Melanie run to Mr. Stafford. She screams again and says, 'Call 911!' She gets on Mr.

Stafford. She puts hand on his chest and pushes. She keeps pushing. She gets blood all over her hands. I call 911 on my cellphone. She puts face on Mr. Stafford. Her lips touch his. She blowing. More blood from him on her face. She keeps pressing hands. She then stops and falls on Mr. Stafford. She screams, 'No! No! No! They killed him!' I no understand what she means. She keeps saying 'They killed him.' Police and ambulance arrive. I think ambulance first. I not sure. First aid go to Mr. Stafford. They also push but for very short time. They stop. Melanie she still crying and yelling 'They did it!' Ambulance people go to Melanie. Put bandages on forehead and nose. Yes. They come first. I remember now police come next. They talk to Melanie. She still crying. She say, 'They killed him.' Melanie go with ambulance. Melanie have trouble walking. She look dizzy. They put her on stretcher and strap her. She still crying and screaming. Blood all over her clothes and hands and feet. Big policeman leave with Melanie and ambulance. Other policeman stay and talk to me. I tell him what I tell you. Soon other police come. They take photos and apply black dust all over room. I see them enter bedroom. They also go to sofa, chair, and lamp. They pick up gun and white cloth. I forgot. I see sliding door open. I feel breeze. Curtains moving. I hear policeman say door glass broken. They take pictures. Police go through rooms of house. Take pictures. I see them. Police take me to station and take statement from me. They ask me to sign typed statement. I ask them to read it to me first. Then I sign it. They drove me back to Melanie's house. Other police cars there. I see yellow tape in front of house. I get in my car and drive home. That's all I remember now. I am tired. I try nap but no sleep."

"Mrs. Garcia did the police give you a copy of your statement?" Johnnie asked.

"No."

"Did you tell the police what you just told us?"

"Yes. I think so."

Burnside then took over. "Mrs. Garcia, thank you for your help. If anyone else should ask for a statement, don't talk to them. Don't talk to the newspapers or to the TV people. You can't trust them. They will say you said things you didn't. If they try to put you on TV, they will change your words. They will say only part of what you said to them. They will make you look foolish. They will make it look like you are lying. They can't make you talk to them. No one. The police can't even talk to you unless you want to. If the police try to talk to you again, tell them they first must get Mr. Fitzhugh's permission. Do not talk to anyone else about what you saw unless Mr. Fitzhugh is with you. We don't want anyone to make you say something that is not true. Promise me that you won't tell anyone else what you saw. If the killers know you exist, they could come after you. Don't go on TV. They then will find you and your family."

Inez responded, "Oh, dear God, no!"

Johnnie reinforced Burnside's warning. "Mrs. Garcia, Mr. Burnside is right. Promise me that you will call me if anyone asks for a statement as to what you saw. Don't speak to them unless I am standing next to you. Promise?"

"Yes."

"You can reach me at either of these two numbers." Johnnie provided his office and cellphone numbers. He and Burnside thanked her for her help and concluded the conversation.

Burnside looked at Johnnie and spoke, "What do you think of her narration?"

"It definitely helps us. I just hope that is what she told the cops. I also hope they didn't edit her oral statement. If they did, you can bet the tape has already been destroyed, and only the typed, signed statement remains. We'll know if my discovery request fails to produce a copy of the recording."

Johnnie's cellphone vibrated. Pulling it from his jacket pocket, he saw it was Erika and answered it. "What did you find out?"

"Bail hearings are by video starting at nine thirty before Judge Warren. Judge Scholman, however, is hearing Melanie's at eleven thirty in his courtroom after he hears in person the bail reduction requests. Scholman's secretary suggested that we not broadcast the time. She's already made a similar request to the prosecutor. Apparently, they're trying to avoid a media circus. How much you wanna bet the prosecutor leaks it?"

"Erika, whatever you have planned for tomorrow morning, postpone it. You'll be with me at Scholman's. See you at the office at nine o'clock. Thanks."

"What do you know about Scholman?" Burnside inquired.

"Not a lot. Since he's been on the bench, he's sat criminal. Got promoted to Criminal Assignment Judge last year. Used to be with a large Newark firm where he specialized in corporate work. Firm had some multinational clients. Used to travel back and forth to Europe for the firm as well as for his father's export-import business. When the firm opened a Princeton office, he became its managing partner. Through the firm's lobbying efforts and political connections, he made the right inroads, worked hard for the governor's election, and got his judgeship. Had a lot of trial experience in corporate and equity matters and served on various state bar committees. Before he ascended to the bench, I briefly talked to him on occasion at Princeton Bar Association functions. He has a high opinion of himself but can be charming in public when he wants to be. His wife was a biochemist with a pharmaceutical company in Morris County. Never met her. She died several years ago in a car crash. He was not with her at the time. Apparently, had no criminal trial experience before he was elevated to the bench. My friends who practice criminal defense say he's very bright and a quick learner. He tightly controls his courtroom and embarrasses those attorneys who try to bend the rules of evidence or editorialize before the jury. From what they tell me, he dislikes the press. That's probably why he's handling Melanie's hearing separately."

"Do you expect him to be hard on our bail request?" asked Burnside.

"I really don't know, but it's critical that we have the hospital administrator present in case the judge wants him to confirm what I will be stating on the record. Now that we know Mrs. Garcia signed a written statement, I can allude to that document without needing her present. I don't expect the prosecutor to let me see it at this early stage, but it has to confirm to a degree what she told us. Even if it doesn't contain everything, there have to be some favorable parts, should the court want to peruse it.

"You should bring your property tax bill to court. That will show the value of your property. If you can get Melanie's, that also would be beneficial. It's a public document. Hopewell Township will provide it if asked.

"Plan to meet me at Judge Scholman's courtroom by eleven o'clock in the morning. If anyone asks why you are present, state only that you were told by your lawyer to meet him there. Obviously, don't mention that you're Melanie's father, and don't make any comments to anyone about your daughter. Do you have any questions?"

"What else can I do?" replied Burnside.

"At this point, nothing. I would suggest Mrs. Burnside not attend the hearing. I fear it will be too much for her to bear."

"You're very perceptive. I'll have our next-door neighbors sit with her. They're dear friends and will do their best to distract her."

Rising from his chair, Johnnie stated, "It's not just Melanie who will be tomorrow's attention getter. All eyes will also be on you. No matter what is said concerning Melanie, remain stoic. Let me handle any unpleasant ramifications. You must appear like the dignified professional you are. Portray your normal powerful presence. Wear a dark suit, white shirt, and power tie. I want the prosecutor to realize that he has met his match."

Burnside grasped Johnnie's hand and shoulder, saying, "They don't know what going to battle really means. Believe me: They're about ready to find out."

As Johnnie exited, he wondered whether Burnside understood that he, not Burnside, in reality, would be issuing the commands, shoring up the defense, and directing the line of attack. He also wondered why Judge Scholman was not handling Melanie's bail hearing by video from the Corrections Center. Was he doing this because Melanie wasn't the typical accused, or was he doing it at the prosecutor's request, even though Scholman's secretary had inferred that the judge wanted to minimize the publicity? Whatever the reason, Johnnie realized that logistically it eased his ability to have Burnside and the hospital administrator present and actually before Scholman. That would increase Melanie's odds at receiving a more reasonable bail.

8.

Trenton, New Jersey

Johnnie and Erika approached the four-story building housing Mercer County's criminal courts, located at the corner of South Warren and Market Streets. The stone and masonry exterior containing glass and metal panels contrasted sharply with the pillared classical façade of the old courthouse, located at the top of the hill at South Broad and Market. Johnnie's outwardly calm appearance masked the knots he felt tying his stomach. It had been several years since the criminal courts were his domain. Judges before whom he regularly had appeared had retired, been elevated to the appellate level, or rotated to the civil side. Although he knew some of the criminal judges through bar functions, he lacked the crucial intimate rapport that he had fostered with the criminal bench when frequenting their chambers as an assistant prosecutor. He no longer had the access to request favors, mutually exchange critical information, and delay trial dates and motions, as was the custom of prosecutors and public defenders who daily roamed the hallways of the criminal courts. Now, he was the outsider.

Burnside had promised all the necessary resources, but they still paled when weighted against the assets of the prosecutor's office. On the other hand, he really had no choice. Many of the insurance carriers the firm once represented had gone in-house, hiring young staff attorneys to handle the routine auto accident and slip and fall cases, which had been the bread and butter of the outside defense firms. Those cases were "easy lifting" and through their volume guaranteed a steady and very profitable income. While the unique cases still were "farmed" to outside counsel, those were not as frequent, and many defense hands sought the work through fishing trips, golf outings, lavish sporting events, and mini Caribbean vacations. Fitzhugh and Fitzhugh steered away from buying business. As more players entered the picture, the stakes grew higher. The ethical line didn't blur. It broke. Some would sleep without misgivings. Johnnie and his father refused to partake. The risks, in the end, were far greater than the reward. The firm was "old school." Honor, probity, and loyalty were its trademark.

Although the firm still had a stable of well-known and well-heeled clients, Burnside's company really controlled the spigot. Malpractice cases flowed often and paid reasonable hourly rates. The volume insured the firm's financial well-being. Burnside had reassured Johnnie that all he required was Johnnie's best efforts on behalf of Melanie. Not for a moment did he believe him. If he didn't represent Melanie, Burnside would pull his business. If Melanie was convicted, the result would be the same. Either a not-guilty verdict had to be returned, or some event had to intervene to warrant Johnnie's removal from the case without incurring Burnside's vindictive wrath. As he entered the court-house, presented his attorney identification card, and passed through the metal detector, Johnnie prayed that event would occur quickly.

Johnnie and Erika entered the elevator and approached Judge Scholman's courtroom. Standing outside were Burnside and a tall gray-haired man whom Burnside introduced as Robert Sutcliff. Burnside clearly was not his usual self. His voice was hesitant, and he seemed subdued. Johnnie probed Sutcliff as to the hospital's immediate need for Melanie's release. Sutcliff elaborated upon the importance of her release and reiterated that he would vouch for her sterling reputation and character before the court if requested. Burnside added that he had copies of the requested property tax evaluations, which would validate the bail values of his and Melanie's residences. The group then entered the courtroom.

Immediately, Johnnie noticed that someone had leaked the hearing to the press. At the rear of the courtroom sat reporters from The Trenton Times and The Trentonian. Standing next to the prosecutor's table was First Assistant Prosecutor Terry McGuire. Redheaded, cherub-faced, tall, and somewhat overweight, McGuire smiled toward Johnnie. McGuire had joined the office shortly before Johnnie left. During the intervening years, they occasionally would exchange courtroom war stories when they ran into each other at the local courtroom luncheonettes. Not much had changed over the years with McGuire. He still talked in a fast-clipped pace while glancing about with his hazel, darting eyes. Very self-conscious about his growing weight, he habitually wore dark suits to streamline his expanding frame. During the short time Johnnie mentored McGuire, he recognized his protégé's burning desire to succeed. Hidden behind that warm smile was a fierce determination to ascend the prosecutorial ladder.

McGuire had the look of a career prosecutor. While pleasant outside the courtroom, he was merciless within it. McGuire regarded defendants as a blight upon society. Most deserved severe punishment within the confines of law, so as to deter others living in the county. If the accused was indicted, he or she was guilty, not presumed guilty, and definitely not presumed innocent. Rumor had it that the prosecutor was next in line for a judicial appointment once a seat opened. There was no doubt in Johnnie's mind that McGuire, as first assistant, had his sights on the top job. He had paid his dues within his political party. The fact that Melanie had been arrested so quickly, despite apparent conflicting evidence, led to one conclusion: An indictment would be forthcoming quickly. McGuire's appearance at counsel presaged that result. Melanie was McGuire's path to ascension.

Johnnie told Burnside and Sutcliff to sit in the gallery's first row. He pushed open the gate and, with briefcase in hand, walked toward McGuire who had turned to say something to the court's bailiff. McGuire then rapidly turned and stated, "Do you feel like a fish out of water, Johnnie?"

"I'm bringing much needed light to the dark side, Terry. What's the rush to judgment?"

"Justice must be served, Johnnie. The high and mighty travel the same path here as the poor and downtrodden. Their fall, however, is a lot further. She should take a plea quickly, Johnnie. It looks like a triangle murder to me. Three shots. One in the lower abdomen. Can't believe she missed the poor bastard's penis. She was right on with the two other shots. Guess her anger strayed the bullet's path. Boss might accept first degree aggravated manslaughter, if she pleas pre-indictment. Tragedy in a way. She had it all — prestige, money, looks. Man, what a waste. Well, at least you'll get paid real well by her and her old man. On second thought, maybe we should play it out for a while. Get those fees up. Let her see she's getting her money's worth. Whatta you think?"

Under his breath, Johnnie replied, "Terry, word has it that the boss man might be elevated. You hankering for the post? Might want to look at all the evidence, or lack thereof, before swimming upstream. You know that dam could burst. Stellar careers can be broken as well as made. As young prosecutors weren't we warned? Evaluate, scrutinize, cross-check, and only then prosecute. Even the boss man should remember that dictum."

Johnnie and McGuire then heard the bailiff state, "All rise."

Judge Scholman entered quickly, mounted the bench, and firmly stated, "Please be seated." Turning to his right, he said to one of the sheriff's deputies, "Please bring in Dr. Stafford."

Clad in the corrections jumpsuit and handcuffed, Melanie entered and was escorted to the first row of jury seats. She remained standing until told to sit by the judge.

To Johnnie, her appearance looked the same. The bandages were still apparent. Her hair was askew. Her eyes were deep-set. Her shoulders slumped. She seemed weary and afraid. She looked pleadingly toward Johnnie and then spotted her father and Sutcliff. Embarrassed, she turned away quickly and looked downward.

"Good morning, Mr. McGuire. Good morning, Mr. Fitzhugh. I see you'll be representing Dr. Stafford."

"Yes, Your Honor, I will be," Johnnie uttered emphatically.

The judge then turned to Melanie and said, "Dr. Stafford, as a result of your arrest, this is a bail hearing. You need not and should not say anything to me about the facts of this case. The lawyers are here only to argue the issue of your bail. The prosecutor cannot ask you any questions about the shooting. We are not here to discuss your guilt or innocence, only the monetary amount of your bail. If you were to say anything about the incident, it could be used against you. Therefore, I strongly caution you that you should not say anything about the event that transpired. Do you understand me?"

Melanie softly responded, "Yes, Your Honor, I understand."

Johnnie was somewhat taken aback about how thoroughly Scholman had warned Melanie. When he prosecuted, the prisoners were led in and usually not provided with such detailed instructions. On the other hand, Melanie wasn't your routine unemployed and uneducated defendant. It was clear that Scholman was treating Melanie more as an equal than as an inmate.

The judge then addressed the prosecutor, "Mr. McGuire, What bail are you seeking?

"Your Honor, we don't believe the facts warrant that the defendant receive any bail. She is a highly educated woman who poses a tremendous flight risk. She has the means and wherewithal to flee the county. She has been arrested for the heinous cold-blooded murder of her husband. She was found at the scene. The murder weapon was present. She was covered with his blood. This is an open-and-shut case. The State fears that if bail is set, she will flee the country and live happily in some foreign jurisdiction, most likely one that won't honor our extradition process. Therefore, we request that Your Honor deny any bail."

Johnnie heard Melanie groan. He saw her weeping silently. A bailiff handed her some tissues.

"Mr. Fitzhugh, I'm sure you don't agree with Mr. McGuire's request."

"Your Honor, with all due respect to Mr. McGuire, it seems he already has tried and convicted my client even before any indictment has been returned. Even then, an indictment is not proof of guilt. It is just a vehicle by which a case is presented for trial by a jury of my client's peers. This case cries out for justice for my client. I don't know if the prosecutor's office has provided you with any police reports or witness statements. We obviously haven't received anything, yet we know from the one living witness present besides Dr. Stafford that evidence exists that refutes any charge of murder.

"Your Honor, the purpose of bail is to ensure the accused's appearance at trial. It is not meant to penalize the accused or to hinder her in the preparation of a valid and legitimate defense. Dr. Stafford has an unblemished reputation. She is this area's leading anesthesiologist. The county's hospitals rely upon her expertise for the most serious surgical procedures. Sitting in the gallery is Mr. Sutcliff. As a hospital administrator, he will attest to the necessity for her release to ensure that the most urgent surgical procedures are not impeded.

"Dr. Stafford has practiced in this area for many years. She resides in Hopewell Township and sits on various hospital boards. Also in the courtroom is her father. Mr. Burnside is president and CEO of Supreme Insurance Company. He also resides in the community. Dr. Stafford is anxious to prove her innocence. She has lost her husband, her partner of many years. We are not dealing with some hardened criminal. My client never had been arrested before this travesty. Mr. McGuire knows my client has sufficient assets to meet a reasonable bail. His request for no bail is meant, purely and simply, to punish her, to keep her in jail to hinder in the preparation of a legitimate defense. This is unseemly, Your Honor. Dr. Stafford will relinquish her passport if Mr. McGuire is so terrified that she may flee. Dr. Stafford already has suffered enough. She is entitled to a reasonable bail, Your Honor. On her behalf, I would request that Your Honor set that bail. Thank you."

Judge Scholman looked toward the hospital administrator. "Mr. Sutcliff, Mr. Fitzhugh stated your hospital's position correctly?"

"Yes, Your Honor. Not only is Dr. Stafford a wonderful and caring person, she is a critical part of our surgical unit. As you may surmise, we have numerous surgeries per week for which Dr. Stafford's oversight is indispensable. On such short notice, we don't have the luxury of engaging an anesthesiologist of her caliber from an adjoining county. Even if we had, that individual would serve only as a stopgap. There is no question that our surgical flow would be hampered severely as would our other local facilities'."

The judge slowly turned toward the prosecutor, inquiring, "Mr. McGuire, any reply?"

"Yes, Your Honor. Murder is the most serious crime. The killing of a spouse tears at society's social fabric. Left unpunished, it weakens marital bonds and the sanctity of the union. Without the requisite punishment, our mores become chaotic and unstable. This defendant is a highly intelligent and sophisticated woman. She was not raised on the streets. No psychologist will opine her act had its roots in an impoverished background, full of neglect, beatings, and lack of self-esteem. Quite the contrary, she comes from an environment of privilege. Her act was cold and calculating. If bail is granted, she will find a way to disappear. This killing depicts how resourceful she really is. For these reasons, bail should be denied."

Before Johnnie could respond, the judge replied, "Mr. McGuire. Divorce weakens marital bonds. Divorce also can cause an upheaval to children. Poverty also tears asunder familial bonds. Are you claiming that perpetrators of these acts also should be denied bail if accused of a crime other than murder?"

"No, Your Honor."

"Mr. McGuire, the law requires that I set a reasonable bond unless I believe the defendant will flee upon a moment's notice. I don't see that here, and you haven't provided ample justification to the contrary. To lessen your fears, I will require that Mr. Fitzhugh tender to this Court Dr. Stafford's passport as a pre-condition of her release. Bail is set at $1 million. That bail may be met by cash, bond, or property. Thank you, gentlemen. That is all."

Johnnie sighed a breath of relief. He nodded to Melanie and then turned around to speak to Burnside who leaned forward and mumbled that McGuire was a prick. McGuire grabbed his papers and walked toward Johnnie. Within earshot of Burnside, McGuire emphatically asserted, "Expect a quick indictment."

Johnnie commented, "I guess I don't get any discovery until then."

Looking toward Burnside, McGuire quipped, "You got that right," and walked out of the courtroom.

Johnnie nodded to Burnside and counseled, "He heard your description. That was his way of reply. Let's get Melanie out of here. We have lots of work to do."

9.

May 1974
Northern New Jersey

He had fled the Fatherland in 1944 and, at twenty-seven, had found a welcoming sanctuary in Buenos Aires. Some compatriots had preceded him. Many had waited too long. They were exterminated when the Russians entered Berlin and exacted their revenge.

His looted antiquities and paintings also had found safe haven in Argentina.

For fourteen years, he had kept a low profile, working by day as a commercial illustrator and by night as a portrait artist. Only a few trusted German expatriates knew his secret and were willing to assist him, provided they shared in the eventual profits.

With a new passport and identity, he entered the States in 1958 and obtained citizenship in 1960 upon his marriage to an American.

With the assistance of his wife's family, he founded an export company. By all accounts, he had become a success. Yet he still longed for Germany and for Munich in particular.

What had become of his beloved country? The barbarians still controlled the east, including a portion of Berlin. West Berlin had prospered. It was free and enlightened, a sharp contrast to its dilapidated and thought-controlled eastern neighbor. The communist wall was more than an impregnable barricade. It was a fortress barring access to free thought, speech, and movement.

For thirty years, his secret had been safe. The art world longed for the still-hidden antiquities and paintings. Some discoveries had occurred, but much, very much, remained unearthed.

Could he find a reliable and trusted conduit?

The hidden works should see the light of day. That, of course, would come at a price, yet, in the scheme of things, it was a just bargain. He would remain free and prosperous. In return, the art world would gaze again on the priceless treasures that had been enshrouded in darkness far too long.

A trip to Munich would be required. Could he uncover there someone who shared his passion and greed?

10.

February 2015
Trenton, New Jersey

While Burnside handled the bail processing, Johnnie and Erika exited the courthouse. Several reporters tried to pry a statement. Johnnie's sole comment was that his client was innocent and that he would try the case in the courtroom, not through the media. He left unspoken his belief that McGuire would not act similarly. If his hunch was correct, he would move swiftly to obtain a gag order from the court.

As they walked toward the parking lot, Johnnie considered his next course of action. Pre-indictment, McGuire wasn't obligated to release the police reports, forensic data, or witness statements, if any. During the interim, he had to probe Melanie. Had she killed her husband, or was she truly innocent? If he asked her, and she admitted her guilt, he would be faced with a real conundrum. Burnside's hubris never would allow his daughter to cop a plea to a reduced charge of manslaughter. He was certain Burnside would urge his daughter to employ a self-defense strategy.

From a trial standpoint, if Melanie confessed her guilt to him, he could not put her on the stand. He had an ethical obligation as an officer of the court not to be a party to perjury. He could be sanctioned or even disbarred if he knowingly allowed Melanie to perjure herself by testifying that she was innocent after revealing her guilt to him. For his own sake, however, he wanted to explore the issue of her guilt or innocence. He would not ask her directly. At the Corrections enter, she already had proclaimed her innocence. From a legal viewpoint, that was sufficient for his purposes. Yet he would delve further on his own. If the surrounding facts illuminated a contrary belief, he subtly would share those facts with Burnside. Perhaps, Burnside then would see the light and engage alternative counsel without harboring ill will toward him and the firm. This, of course, probably was a pipe dream, but he believed nothing should be foreclosed at this early stage. As with a trial, the ebb and flow of any investigative process warranted an open mind, razor sharp in adjusting to cross-currents and riptides.

"You're awfully quiet. What's bothering you?" asked Erika.

"Just figuring our next step. What did you think of the bail hearing?" he inquired.

"Johnnie, she might have looked withdrawn and frail at the bail hearing. Don't let that fool you. Rage overcomes frailty every time. You don't have to be strong to pull the trigger. My guess is the woman you saw at the bail hearing wasn't the same person immediately before her husband's demise. Like I said before, I still like the spurned spouse theory."

Erika's sudden pronouncement interrupted his musings. From McGuire's bail hearing comments, he knew that jealousy, humiliation, and rage would be the prosecution's bullet points. All McGuire needed was to connect the dots, find a paramour, and make the logical connection. Then the issue wouldn't be denial of the act but rather one of self-defense. That would be a game changer. Would there be any evidence of a paramour at the crime scene?

Johnnie suddenly stated, "I want to see the crime scene before we meet with Melanie."

Johnnie then called McGuire, ascertained that the investigators had left the crime scene, and asked permission to enter the premises.

Johnnie then called Burnside and requested that Melanie remain at Burnside's home for the evening. He informed Burnside that he did not want the crime scene contaminated before he and Erika inspected the scene and took the necessary photos and measurements. Without a key, the most he and Erika could accomplish would be to walk the grounds and possibly interview Melanie's neighbors. Surprisingly, Burnside didn't offer any resistance. Burnside acknowledged his own concern for his daughter's physical and emotional condition. Uncertain whether the authorities had possession of the house key, he told Johnnie that he would obtain the key from Inez Garcia if needed.

Johnnie and Erika meandered through Hopewell Township until they arrived at Melanie's road. Johnnie turned right and proceeded approximately three miles on the roadway before Erika spotted the Stafford mailbox. The area was densely wooded. Johnnie made a right turn on to a winding gravel driveway enveloped by elms, oaks, and spruces. After proceeding a couple of minutes on the curving path, they spotted a sprawling stone and cedar one-story contemporary home that blended into its surroundings. Johnnie had travelled through rustic areas of the township, but this location really was secluded.

Johnnie and Erika exited the car and approached the front door. On each side of the entrance was a coach lamp. The police had locked the door, but the lamps still were lit. As they circled the house, Johnnie observed that the elongated windows were several feet off the ground and were too narrow to allow easy access. Johnnie spotted the rear sliding glass door. His attention was drawn immediately to a broken area adjacent to the interior lock. The hole corroborated Melanie's comment that she was drawn to the sliding door because she felt air blowing toward her. Johnnie noted dusting powder on the exterior and interior portions of the glass door near the opening created by the intruder or intruders.

While the area in front of the house was gravel except for a flagstone walkway, natural vegetation covered the ground behind the home, except for the brick patio adjacent to the sliding door. There was no rear garden. Johnnie surmised that Melanie's profession probably left her little time to dabble in gardening. Johnnie estimated that distance from the rear tree line to the outer edge of the patio was only twenty feet. The natural vegetation would have hidden any footprints had the intruders approached from the rear forest. There had been no rain for several days. The ground was hard. Clearly, there were no homes behind the residence. All Johnnie saw was a vast expanse of densely populated trees.

They returned to the front. The garage doors were remote-controlled. He noticed dusting powder on sections of the garage doors and front door. No search warrant had been posted. He was certain McGuire would have obtained one. If his intuition was correct, the document would be found on the dining room table or kitchen counter. He would have to interrogate Melanie deeply regarding the seized items. It was imperative that she be candid with him regarding the confiscated items. Often, it was the little supposedly inconsequential items or comments that damned an accused. The skilled cross-examiner delved into the minutiae.

Most witnesses could produce a plausible narration for the big story line. Very few, however, were court-wise enough to comprehend that their credibility could be eviscerated by the smallest of details. The big lie always collapsed when probed with precise questions on relatively insignificant matters. The guilty entrapped themselves with illogical responses. Each succeeding question eroded their initial believability. Supposed sincerity and candor collapsed into disingenuousness and falsity.

For each seized item, Melanie had to reveal any negative fact that could lessen her credibility. The favorable facts took care of themselves. They couldn't be altered. The harmful evidence could often be explained away provided its appearance was not sudden at trial.

Johnnie assumed that the detectives would have seized computers, diaries, calendars, address books, and cell phones. They would contact the phone carriers and subpoena them for landline and cell phone bills covering a twelve-month period.

Through pretrial discovery, Johnnie would get to review the expropriated items, but that could be weeks away. McGuire had boasted that the indictment would be quick. A review of the taken evidence, however, could cause the prosecutor to delay the matter's presentation to the grand jury.

Typically, a prosecutor would want all loose ends shored before seeking an indictment. Post-indictment, the discovery rules mandated that proposed evidence be shared mutually within specific time periods. This was a high-profile case. McGuire would want to control the flow of the evidence. To do so, he would need to cement the critical parts of his case before proceeding to grand jury.

That body basically was a rubber stamp. McGuire would produce hearsay evidence through one of the investigating officers. There would be no cross-examination. The grand jury would be told Richard Stafford was shot three times and bled out at the scene. His wife was found on the floor with the pistol nearby. She had her husband's blood on her clothing. Typical domestic killing. A twenty- to thirty-minute presentation with skillful responses by the presenting officer to any inquisitive questions from the grand jurors. The indictment would be simple and quick.

If Melanie had anything she wanted hidden, Johnnie had to convince her to the contrary. The prosecutor had or would obtain any damning documents or information. It was best to confront the negative now. Surprises at trial were difficult to counter and overcome. At this stage, logical explanations might be possible and would be buttressed by corroborating testimony.

In a murder case, everything was in the details and the preparation. If Melanie revealed any reluctance in being candid, Johnnie would have to approach Burnside. The man's overpowering personality could be used against him. Burnside always had to be in control. Warned that his daughter's hesitancy could sabotage her defense, Burnside would cajole and, if necessary, overwhelm her. Burnside was a survivor. He had been tested repeatedly and had overcome all obstacles. Johnnie had no doubt that Burnside would surmount his daughter's intransigence.

With his cell phone, Johnnie took pictures of the house's exterior. He shot all sides of the house and took close-ups of the broken sliding glass door and of the fingerprint powder marks. He then took views from the patio to the rear woods. When he and Erika drove to the driveway's entrance, Johnnie stopped, exited his car and took a panoramic photo of the wooded expanse leading to the Stafford home. He assumed that the police had obtained similar views, but he had no intention of relying on their actions. He would do his investigation his way and in the manner his present adversary had schooled him. He would ascertain how thorough his opponent had been. Had the neighbors been canvassed? He would know shortly. The question remained whether they would cooperate with him.

Johnnie turned right from Melanie's driveway and travelled half a mile before he sighted the next mailbox, which was located on Melanie's side of the road. In a clearing sat a two-story black-shuttered white-sided Colonial, approximately one hundred feet from the roadway. Smoke was emanating from the red brick chimney. As Johnnie parked in the macadam driveway, the red-paneled front door opened. An elderly man wearing a green plaid flannel shirt and gabardine trousers viewed them warily. As they approached, the man gruffly inquired, "What do you want?"

"Good afternoon, sir. My name is Johnnie Fitzhugh and this is Erika Svensen. We're sorry to trouble you, but we represent Dr. Stafford, who was assaulted and whose husband was murdered."

"I've already talked to the cops. They were here last night. Scared the hell out of me when they pounded on the door. I had been watching a college basketball game and had dozed off. The wife passed away couple years back. Really miss her. It's pretty lonely out here. Only thing that really keeps me going is my grandkids. Daughter lives in North Jersey but visits often with the kids. It's all over the news about Melanie. I just don't understand it. She and Richard been good neighbors. Didn't see them that often due to their work schedules, but they were always there when Martha and I needed them. Melanie and Richard hosted the wake. I'll never forget that. I was all torn up.

Melanie, she took right over, did everything. I just don't understand why she would kill anyone. She is so good and caring."

"Sorry, I didn't get your name."

"It's Alan Lethridge."

"Mr. Lethridge, we don't believe Melanie murdered her husband. As her attorney, I am conducting an investigation and frankly want to know the truth. If Melanie killed her husband, I have to know. If she didn't, then I need all the evidence to convince the prosecutor or a jury of her innocence. That's my duty. Could we ask you some questions? By the way, here's my card."

"I don't know how I can help, but come on in. It's nice to have some company for a bit."

Johnnie and Erika followed Lethridge down the hallway and into a pine-paneled den. At the far wall was a fireplace. On its mantle were pictures of Martha and Alan as well as several photos of their daughter and grandchildren. Lethridge motioned them toward a threadbare tan couch.

"Can I get you some tea?"

"No, we're fine, thanks. Mr. Lethridge, did you hear any gunshots the late evening or early morning of the day on which Mr. Stafford was murdered?"

"As I told the cops, I didn't hear a thing. Even if I had, I wouldn't have thought anything of it. This is a wooded area. Hunters often hunt here. Gunfire is a common occurrence."

"Did you know whether the Staffords owned any guns?"

"Not that I know of."

"Ever been to their house other than for your wife's wake?"

"Several times over the years. Usually for summer cookouts. They were very hospitable."

"Ever see any arguments or tension between them?"

"Never."

"What did you think of Mr. Stafford?"

"He was quiet but pleasant. Now Melanie, she was a real extrovert. She would have been a great pediatrician or family doctor. She had a real nice way about her."

"When did you last see either or both of them before the murder?"

"Probably two weeks before. Melanie brought over some brownies she had made. She knows I'm a chocoholic, especially dark chocolate. They say it's good for the heart. At my age, everything helps."

"How did she seem then?"

"Perky as usual and those green eyes, they just draw you toward her."

Johnnie smiled, thinking the same thing.

"Did they have any close friends?"

"I really couldn't say. When we visited, it was just the four of us."

"Did you see them at any neighborhood parties?"

"Well, I couldn't really call this a neighborhood. As you probably saw, any homes on this road are pretty far apart. There's not much interaction. Other than Melanie, the closest neighbor is maybe three-quarters of a mile away."

"We noticed that the house just before Melanie's had a For Sale sign. Do you know who lived there?"

"Young couple moved in about two years ago, but the house went to foreclosure. They moved out maybe three months ago. Never knew them. Only reason I know that is Earl Jensen told me. He's a realtor. We both belong to Kiwanis. That's where I get the local gossip, for whatever it's worth."

"Did you see or hear anything unusual the day or night before the murder?"

"Nothing, as I told the cops."

"Do you remember what the police asked you?"

"Basically same as you. There were two who interviewed me. One was from the township. The other was a detective with the prosecutor's office. I got his card in my wallet. He told me to call if I learned anything about the murder."

Lethridge reached into his left rear pocket, extracted the card, and handed it to Johnnie who immediately recognized the name. Domenic Carlucci had been with the office when Johnnie started. Even then, he was a homicide detective. Dom would leave no stone unturned to solve a crime. He was an expert interrogator. He had an easy way about him. People naturally opened up. When he needed to, he could charm a malcontent. One moment he could be diffident and the next, assured. His investigation was unrelenting. If Melanie was hiding something, Dom would find it.

"Mr. Lethridge, did the officers ask you anything that we haven't?"

"They asked me what cars the Staffords drove. I told them Richard had a gray Acura SUV and Melanie, a red BMW convertible. They also asked whether I had seen any different car there often. I told them no. Obviously, people visited their house, but I didn't know whom and didn't pay any attention to the types of cars. I knew Melanie's because you couldn't miss her car. I knew Richard's because I would see it on the occasions Martha and I visited their house. When Melanie dropped off the brownies, she was driving it so I knew they still had it."

"Mr. Lethridge, can you think of anything else important or out of the ordinary that we should know?"

"No, not now. If anything occurs to me, I got your card. I'll call you."

Johnnie and Erika thanked Lethridge for his time and left. In the car, Erika checked the tape recorder that was in her purse. It recorded their conversation clearly. In the office, she would have it transcribed. Lethridge appeared forthright. If the officers had made notes to the contrary, the tape would be used to blunt their testimony.

Johnnie dropped off Erika at the office and left a message on Burnside's cell. He was concerned about the funeral preparations. The autopsy should have been completed by now. If not, it would be soon. He would call McGuire to determine when the body would be released. In the interim, he suggested to Burnside that the service be private. He didn't want gawking onlookers at the funeral, much less photographers or detectives spying on the grieving widow. Johnnie ended his message by telling Burnside that he would call early the following morning to obtain the key to Melanie's house. He and Erika wanted to inspect the interior crime scene before allowing Melanie and Burnside to enter. He then headed for the gym. He needed some time to clear his head and release his pent-up trepidation.

11.

Johnnie arose early, picked up Erika and her crime scene gear, and drove to Burnside's residence. It was evident Burnside hadn't slept well. The prior evening, mother and daughter had undergone a tearful reunion. Burnside related that he had been awakened several times by Melanie's pacing and sobbing. He had attempted to quell his daughter's agitation with little success. Around daybreak, Melanie's body gave way to exhaustion, and sleep finally overcame her.

Burnside agreed with Johnnie's suggestion that the funeral service and burial be private. Rather than viewing Richard and Melanie as both victims, Burnside regarded his deceased son-in-law an afterthought. His ill will was so apparent.

Johnnie gently cautioned him to veil his thoughts. Melanie couldn't be exposed to additional stress. She had to be clearheaded and steady. They needed to garner critical facts. Now was the time to commence a vigorous defense. There would be enough distraction and conflict for Melanie once she returned to work.

Friends and associates could view her differently. While most would be outwardly supportive, doubts as to innocence would remain. To some, civility and trust would be mutually exclusive. Smiles and greetings would mask inner thoughts of deception and guilt.

Melanie would have to wall herself from the whispers, awkward glances, and turned heads. She had to focus solely on the daunting task confronting her. Johnnie would plot the strategy, but Melanie needed to plant the seeds from which the truth would grow.

Once she was stable enough to view the crime scene, she would have to reenact those terror-filled moments for Johnnie and Erika. Every thought and movement had to be relived. Johnnie and Erika could scrutinize the scene. Only Melanie could provide the horror that had unfolded. She would need to supply the details from that chaotic tableau in sequential order no matter how squeamish that ordeal would be.

Burnside could not interrupt that process. He would be kept from the crime scene until after Melanie had narrated the intrusion and killing cogently, logically, and, if possible, dispassionately.

Before entering the Stafford home, Johnnie and Erika again walked the grounds. Nothing appeared changed from the prior day. Johnnie made a mental note for them to return that evening to photograph the house and surroundings in darkness. They also would need to take photos with the front light illuminated and drapes closed. Once Johnnie ascertained from Melanie which lights had been on earlier that evening, they would take exterior pictures to duplicate the setting that would have presented itself to the killer, or killers, lying in wait for Richard's arrival. The police may have obtained those photos. Johnnie would not rely upon their supposed thoroughness. Erika would take the night shots from all angles and under different lighting conditions.

McGuire would argue that there were no intruders. The killer lying in wait was Melanie.

To depict the area as remote, words were not sufficient. Erika's photos would reveal the home's isolation. The area's desolation would provide the ideal backdrop for Richard Stafford's execution.

While the burden of proof rested with McGuire, Johnnie knew, in this instance, that he had to prove Melanie's innocence. He had to plant reasonable doubt. The more evidence that could sow that indecision, the better. He would have to center the proverbial scales of justice in equipoise or tilt them ever so slightly in Melanie's favor.

The court would instruct the jury regarding the State's high burden of proof of "beyond a reasonable doubt." But reasonable doubt didn't mean you couldn't convict if you had some doubt. You only couldn't convict if the doubt was reasonable.

Although the average juror might be clueless regarding recondite medical terms and standards thrown about in a medical negligence trial, even the most uneducated had been bombarded by mindless and repetitive fictionalized crime dramas.

Spousal killings were a featured staple. The more the surviving spouse protested innocence, the more likely he or she was the perpetrator. On the other hand, viewers of such dramas were accustomed to the presence of highly sophisticated techniques that guaranteed, within sixty minutes, the resolution of the crime and the accurate arrest of the felon. Such narratives inferentially increased a prosecutor's burden. If similar techniques were not implemented or, far worse, produced equivocal results, reasonable explanations had to be forthcoming.

After Melanie's indictment, once he was granted access to the prosecutor's mandated discovery, Johnnie hoped that he would find those gaps that would cause her jurors to question the thoroughness and validity of the State's evidence. Even if the State survived his motions to dismiss at the end of its case, if the gaps were there, the chance of his success would increase. Then it was up to Melanie to sell herself and her story.

Johnnie could accentuate her account with the corroborative supporting details, together with logical inferences and deductions that would flow from the evidence. By evidence, he meant not all the exhibits introduced by the prosecutor but rather those exhibits, whether proffered by the prosecutor or by him, that created and augmented the doubt of Melanie's guilt.

Johnnie opened the front door and preceded Erika into the foyer. Approximately forty feet ahead was a massive living room with a cathedral ceiling and dark-stained crossbeams. After traversing several feet, he opened a door to his right and observed a spacious dining room with Brazilian cherry floors upon which rested a light-colored oriental rug and a double-pedestal table surrounded by eight Chippendale chairs. A cherry sideboard with an antique Staffordshire soup tureen and silver candlesticks adjoined one wall. On the opposing wall were several hunt prints. The room was undisturbed and devoid of print dusting. Nonetheless, Erika took the requisite photos. She would photograph each room in its entirety. What today might seem unimportant could become paramount during the trial.

Leaving the dining room, they entered the kitchen. Johnnie immediately noticed the search warrant on the black granite countertop. He would peruse it after they familiarized themselves with the home's layout. Beyond the kitchen were the laundry room and the interior door leading to the two-car garage. Fingerprint powder covered the area surrounding and including the door handle. They then retraced their steps, crossed the entranceway, and proceeded to examine and photograph in order the half bathroom, library, media room, and the two guest bedrooms with their separate bathrooms. Nothing seemed out of place in any of those areas. It was apparent that the Staffords favored a clean and orderly home.

The state of the living room presented a different picture. Blood stains and blood spatter were present on the wall-to-wall carpet. The table and lamp were still overturned and covered with forensic powder. Richard Stafford's body had been outlined on the rug before its removal. Portions of the floor-to-ceiling drapes were covered with powder. The police had used both latent and magnetic powders. They used white powder on dark surfaces and dark powder on light-colored objects. Additionally, they applied bio-chromatic powder on both the light and dark surfaces and fluorescent powder on wooden surfaces.

The outlined figure was several feet from the master bedroom. As they entered, they saw a king-size four-poster bed. The comforter and sheets on the near side were in disarray, as if someone had quickly exited the bed. The room had not been ransacked. The armoire and dresser, if opened by the police, now were closed. Johnnie and Erika opened each and found everything in order. They searched the walk-in closet and vanity. Nothing appeared out of place. It was patent that neither a robbery nor burglary had occurred. The two skylights were intact. Wood shutters covered the two unbroken narrow elongated windows. Richard's embroidered slippers were to his side of the bed. From their placement, it was clear that he had rushed from the room without them. There was no blood evidence in the bedroom. Richard had died where he fell, which was logical due to the bullet placement.

Johnnie wondered how Melanie would hold up when viewing the blood-stained carpet. Would she break down or stare blankly at the carnage's site? He and Erika needed her to relive the incident before her memory clouded. She would need to see the room as is, not in a pristine blood-free state.

Johnnie and Erika inspected the cut sliding glass door. A circular piece of glass had been removed adjacent to the exterior door handle.

What bothered Johnnie was that everything else was too neat. Melanie's version was that she had been asleep on the living room couch because Richard's flight had been delayed. He later returned, awakened her from a deep sleep, and kissed her on the forehead. Assured he was safe, she quickly fell back to sleep. At some point during the night, she arose to go to the bathroom. She felt a draft coming from the drapes and went to make certain she had closed the sliding glass door. She then was grabbed from behind by a silent assailant. Inferentially, the intruder, or intruders, already had entered the house silently and without disturbing anything. The table and lamp had to be in their proper place before she was attacked. Otherwise, she probably would have heard a noise or, at the very least, would have tripped over one, or both, as she headed toward the bathroom. For such silent entry, the area must have been survielled when unoccupied.

The prosecutor's adverse version would be that Melanie staged the murder. Why would she have had to check the sliding door? It was winter. Why would she even have thought it was open? A professional killer would have needed one shot to the head or, at most, another to the heart. The shot to the lower abdomen would have been unnecessary, unless it was meant for the groin, as Erika jocularly had surmised earlier when theorizing it was a spousal killing. Fingerprint evidence would bolster one side or the other. Johnnie caught himself. He was back in his prosecutorial mode. That life no longer existed. The circumstances had changed. Like it or not, he had been compelled to cross to the other side. Burnside had left no alternative, at least not yet. Melanie had clamored her innocence. He had assumed her cause and would fight for her freedom. The burden was McGuire's. Let him prove it.

Johnnie and Erika returned to the kitchen to inspect the search warrant.

As he had surmised, the warrant listed the usual items: two laptops, one desktop, a calendar, an address book, two cell phones, cell phone and landline bills from the preceding month, and Richard's briefcase and luggage.

Erika photographed the warrant before Johnnie removed it. Johnnie made a note to look at the crime scene photos to ascertain whether forensics had fingerprinted Richard Stafford before his body was removed from the scene. A thorough investigator would perform that task before allowing the body to be transported to the morgue for a pathological autopsy. Prints from both Staffords would be compared to those prints lifted at the crime scene. The absence of any foreign prints at the scene would make Johnnie's task more difficult but not impossible. Melanie's version aligned with a professional hit, and professionals used gloves. Gloves normally didn't leave prints. As long as the gun couldn't be traced back to Melanie or Richard, that argument still had merit. If Melanie's prints were discovered on the exterior surface of the glass cut-out, it would be destroyed. Johnnie could only hope that those prints didn't exist. Nothing could save her if they were present, because she had reiterated that she was attacked from behind before she was able to touch the sliding door. There was nothing Glen Burnside could say or do, regardless of his wealth, if his daughter's prints were on the outside circumference of the glass opening. She then would be doomed. Until he received the print results, there was nothing he could do but plow ahead.

Tomorrow was another day. "Pops" would be back. His insight and guidance would be welcomed and accepted. The old man often bragged that he had seen it all, and Johnnie didn't doubt it. In conferences with the local judiciary, he often was regaled with the zany cases and exploits in which his father had been intertwined. Unfortunately, Burnside had picked youth over experience in this instance. Johnnie still harbored the hope that Burnside would see the error and substitute senior for junior.

Johnnie asked Erika if they had overlooked anything. Erika smiled and stated that he had failed to comment on her change in lipstick. With that, she kissed him on the cheek, and he locked the front door. Tomorrow was just another day with all its uncertainty.

12.

"Well, look who's back," Johnnie said with a big smile as he entered his father's office the following morning. As usual, Jack Fitzhugh was the first one in, even before any of the secretaries. Spry, wiry, and animated as usual, he looked younger than his sixty-nine years. A couple of inches shorter than his son, he had the same blue eyes. His impish smile contrasted with his short-cropped silver hair. One look at the elder Fitzhugh, and anyone recognized his fun-loving nature. While some attorneys pontificated before juries and urged justice for their wronged clients, Jack Fitzhugh was a man of the people. His easygoing and friendly demeanor charmed his juries. He regarded them, though strangers, as friends. His summations were just chats friend to friend. Soft spoken, he kindly reasoned in a humble way, not urging his position but rather explaining in modulated tones the clear but obvious reason why his client's position was the correct one, while always reminding his jurors that they, not he, would use their God-given talents and common life experiences to render the proper and fair verdict.

"It appears your batteries are recharged. What did you see?"

"Well, I started out on the Rhine cruise. Saw Cologne, Koblenz, Rudeshein, Main, and Worms. Food was great. Then I visited Wurzburg and took side trips to Barahurz, Rothenberg, and Heidelberg. Loved Rothenberg — great medieval walled city. Then I went to Nurenberg and visited where the trials took place and ended up in Munich for three days."

"What's with Munich? How many times have you been there now — five or six?"

"Somewhere around that number. I love the city's history and its museums. Great galleries. You know that was the last European city your mom and I visited before she died. I guess it still holds a place in my heart for that reason alone. So what's happened since I've been gone? Anything interesting?"

Johnnie half-heartedly laughed and said, "I've got a problem." He then described Stafford's murder, Melanie's arrest, and Burnside's unyielding demand that he defend Melanie or see the firm lose Supreme's very profitable business.

"Dad, I explained to him the various pitfalls with our representation of Melanie, but he refused to budge."

"Son, I think we're stuck. He obviously wants you, not me. Frankly, for that I'm thankful. It's been decades since I've handled a criminal matter. I'd be out of my element. I also don't have the energy or the patience to deal with Burnside over any extended length of time. Fortunately, you inherited your mother's patience and calmness. I know your insides are probably churning, but you hide your fears well. At my age, I have trouble suppressing my inner thoughts and feelings, especially when dealing with combative people like Burnside.

"Look, you can only do your best. Don't let Burnside interfere, but keep him apprised of everything. Decisions will have to be made. All you can do is advise. Melanie will have to make the ultimate decision. If Burnside tries to interfere, then let father and daughter decide.

"If things get dicey, you can always put your advice on the record, so long as you convey to the court that you instructed Melanie that the ultimate decision was hers. All you can do is provide the best defense that is available. The evidence will speak for itself. Even a resistant Burnside will recognize the evidence for what it is.

"If the verdict or plea is unfavorable, we will have done our best. Candidly, we have no control over Burnside and never will. If he pulls his business due to a guilty verdict, so be it. We have survived and thrived so far, and we will continue to do so with or without Supreme Insurance."

"I've learned over the years that somehow everything works out. I'm here to support you in any way I can. If Burnside becomes a real problem, I'll intercede if you think it appropriate. Hell, even if we lost Supreme's business, I think I still have enough influence within the state bar to get you a judgeship, so don't worry about your future. One way or the other, it's still going to be bright."

Johnnie nodded to his father and stated, "Thanks for the encouragement. With you thousands of miles away, I felt a little like a shipwrecked sailor holding on to a broken mast. I didn't want this case, but I sure as hell wasn't going to allow the practice you built to be destroyed by some sanctimonious bastard who has a God complex. I made the decision to accede to his ultimatum.

"If Melanie is convicted, the verdict will be on his conscience, not mine. This firm will provide her with the best defense. We were not the players in this drama. Only the actors created the facts. We must deal with those facts, maybe even try to reshape those facts, but, in the end, we didn't create those facts. Burnside, Melanie, and the late Richard Stafford, in one way or another, created those facts. Thanks for your counsel, I needed it and probably will continue to need it through this ordeal."

"What's your next step?"

"As soon as Melanie has her emotions under control, I need her to revisit the scene and relive the horrors she experienced. She has to walk Erika and me through that evening in the minutest of detail. I don't anticipate McGuire will seek an indictment until all the forensics are in. Hopefully, there is no damning evidence contained in the items seized under the search warrant. Once that indictment is returned, I intend to file discovery motions immediately if McGuire tries to delay releasing discovery. Erika and I must explore Melanie's premise that Stafford's employer had him silenced. We have a lot to do but need that discovery to accelerate our investigation. Until then, I have to delve into the mind of Melanie Stafford. I have a feeling that she holds the key to everything. With a dead husband and no eyewitnesses, she's our only witness. From her, other evidence has to flow."

There was a gentle knock at the door before it opened slowly. In peeked Erika grinning radiantly. "How was the Germanizing?"

"I see you haven't lost your skill of vocabulating," laughed the elder Fitzhugh.

"It's how I differentiate myself from the crowd," retorted Erika.

"Dear, I think you stand out for a myriad of other reasons, in addition to being a superb investigator. From what Johnnie has recounted, those skills will be tested on the Stafford case."

"Well, we already have a difference of opinion. Your son thinks she may be innocent. My intuitive powers say she's guilty, but I'm duty-bound to keep an open mind. One way or the other, we eventually will be on the same page.

"Now Burnside is another story. I don't think his ego will ever accept the possibility that his daughter's guilty. We've been forced to defend her or lose a good part of our livelihood.

"I've told Johnnie that if we conclude that she's guilty and advise him of our conclusion, he'll probably pull his business even if we get her off. So we stay mum and plow ahead.

"If the evidence points unequivocally to her guilt, maybe she sees the light and pleads to a lesser degree over her father's objection. If she still clamors her innocence, we provide the most logical defense and hope for an acquittal or hung jury.

"Burnside told Johnnie that all he wanted was the best defense possible and that he would be satisfied regardless of the outcome. I don't believe it for a moment, and neither should you, Johnnie," Erika stole a quick glance at Johnnie and then continued. "If we lose this case, Supreme will pull its business the next day. Get as much money upfront, because we won't receive any voluntary payment with a guilty verdict. I can see it now. Burnside fires us and hires new counsel who immediately files a post-trial motion asserting inadequacy of trial counsel. Although that motion won't go anywhere on the trial level, the local papers will regurgitate the motion's content.

"Our lawyer friends will understand that the motion is bogus. The general public, however, will not. Make no mistake, we will suffer. I've told Johnnie that he has to find some conflict of interest that will cause the court to remove us from the case.

"Burnside won't relent voluntarily. He has his talons in us and realizes that we have no viable option but to maximize our efforts to defend his daughter. He wouldn't have that control over any other firm. Other firms would view him as just another wealthy client. If they lost the case, so what? They would still have the regular book of business from their established clients. We don't have that luxury. Sure, we have other clients, but even I know Burnside's business guarantees we never incur a lean year. He's got us where he wants us.

"I've told Johnnie that I'm going to investigate this case from two fronts: one, to find out the truth, and two, more importantly, to find some conflict that will remove us from being Melanie's trial counsel. We then could advise Burnside from the sidelines while being out of his crosshairs.

"I apologize, Mr. Fitzhugh, for being so blunt, but you've been away. We all know your son is an excellent trial lawyer, and that's frankly the problem. Great lawyers think they can win every time. That's why they're so good.

"This, however, isn't a personal injury case. This isn't something where you can pick the jury, examine and then cross-examine some witnesses, and then settle, spinning the case that you won and maximized the gain or minimized the loss for your client.

"A murder case goes to conclusion. After the jury is picked, the openings have concluded, and the witnesses have started to testify, you're in the case to its conclusion unless your defendant folds. Melanie Stafford isn't some kid from the ghetto, nor is she some white-collar criminal who suddenly understands that she will be doomed by her turncoat partners, unless she cops a plea before the jury renders its verdict. Melanie, I fear, will be controlled by her father, and no child of his will surrender without a fight.

"Burnside will not accept the stigma of guilt being attached to the family name. Burnside never retreated in a battle or in business. I cannot imagine he will allow his daughter to do so. I apologize for being so frank, but I want both of you to understand what I feel. I may be wrong, but I doubt it."

Johnnie decided to jump in, "Erika, I've understood this dilemma from the start, and I've discussed it with Dad. Believe me, if you can discover a conflict or even create one, we all would welcome it. Until then, we've got to probe Melanie. If she killed her husband, there has to be a third party involved, boyfriend or girlfriend. The police have seized their cell phones and computers. At this point, we need Melanie to request all cell phone and landline records for the last twelve months. If she balks at that, your intuition might be correct.

"I'll call Burnside to see if Melanie is up to meeting with us at his house. After we discuss the search warrant's contents with her, I want to separate her from Burnside and take her to the crime scene.

"While I'm calling Burnside, prepare a letter for AT&T Mobility and Comcast to request the Staffords' cell phone and landline records. Also prepare affidavits for Melanie to sign wherein she requests print-outs of all calls made and received for the last twelve months from both carriers. If Melanie is willing, we'll leave within the next hour."

As Erika hurried out, Johnnie called Burnside, arranged for the meeting, and then let his father speak to him. Johnnie knew his father's reassuring demeanor would disarm Burnside and help him be more compliant when Johnnie explained to him why he couldn't accompany them to the crime scene.

13.

Burnside opened the door and led Johnnie and Erika into the cavernous cherry-paneled study, where Melanie was seated on the Chesterfield sofa. Burnside directed Johnnie and Erika to the two leather tufted chairs facing Burnside's carved desk. Burnside walked around his desk and sat in the burgundy tufted high-back leather chair. Johnnie introduced Erika to Melanie.

Johnnie noted the change in Melanie's appearance. She had combed her hair and had applied lipstick and makeup. She was wearing a gray tailored pantsuit. Pearls adorned her white silk blouse. She looked ready for court. She greeted them in a soft-spoken voice. Her green eyes momentarily sized up Erika before turning toward Johnnie. Erika was surprised by Melanie's poise and beauty. She had expected someone more plain looking.

Burnside inquired whether they would like tea or coffee. They both declined. Johnnie opened his briefcase and withdrew the search warrant.

Looking directly at Melanie's unbandaged wounds, he asked, "Are your injuries causing you any pain?"

"Other than their appearance, no. My pain is psychological, not physical. I have lost my husband. Now the prosecutor probably wants to take my life. He already has tarnished my name with these baseless allegations. What do I have left? Mr. Fitzhugh, I didn't kill my husband. As I said before, my husband uncovered irregularities at work. He was ready to expose Wellington Pharmaceuticals. They silenced him before he could do it. I didn't own the gun and never saw it before I awakened on the floor. That gun was left to frame me. I have evidence that will prove my innocence."

"Mrs. Stafford."

"As I said before, please call me Melanie."

"Okay, Melanie, we will discuss all of that later. The police executed a search warrant and seized some of your property. According to this warrant, they seized last month's cellphone and landline phone bills as well as two laptops, a desk top, two cellphones, a calendar, an address book, your husband's briefcase, and his luggage. I expect the prosecutor to indict you probably within the next thirty to sixty days. Until that indictment is returned, the prosecutor doesn't have to let me see the seized items. Knowing Mr. McGuire, he won't release anything until the court rules require him to do so."

Melanie interrupted, "Can't you show him things that prove my innocence? Once he sees what I have, he won't indict me!"

"Melanie, on TV that sometimes works. In real life, it very rarely does. In this case, it won't. Mr. McGuire is bent on indicting you, and nothing will stop him. As a former assistant prosecutor, I can tell you that only an incompetent prosecutor fails to get an indictment in a murder case. Mr. McGuire, though obnoxious at times, isn't incompetent. I believe he has an agenda, and nothing I say will dissuade him. Any exculpatory evidence I provide him pre-indictment will hurt your defense. We on the defense side divulge nothing until we have to. We want the playing field to be level. The prosecution wants it tilted heavily in its favor. Once the indictment is handed down, both sides must follow discovery rules. After Mr. McGuire provides me with his discoverable evidence, I will abide and do the same. He must prove your guilt. You don't have to prove your innocence, though at trial we will provide those facts that clearly point in that direction.

"At my request, Erika has drafted letters directed to your phone providers. She also has prepared an affidavit for you to sign so we can obtain an itemization of all calls made from your phones over the last twelve months. We additionally are seeking all calls made to your phones during that same period."

"Why do you need those records? We didn't do anything wrong. My husband and I are the victims. We aren't criminals," Melanie angrily responded.

Erika glanced quickly at Johnnie who averted her look.

"Melanie, we want to be prepared. We can't see the seized records now. I know Mr. McGuire will be subpoenaing those records. I don't want to wait until he provides them. For all I know, he might not divulge them to me if he determines not to use them. While he has an ethical obligation to divulge to me any exculpatory evidence, there is nothing to stop him from not revealing any document that he doesn't intend to use at trial. If he believes the documents are not exculpatory, he need not reveal them to me. What he believes won't aid you might not be correct. I want to determine what helps you. I have no intention of letting him make that determination for me. It is imperative that we obtain those records as soon as possible. While you may know what calls you made and received, you cannot possibly know all the calls made to and from your husband. One of the calls might be the key to corroborating your defense that Richard was killed to silence his knowledge."

"Well, Mr. Fitzhugh, I know who routinely calls my husband and to whom he often speaks. There will be no big surprises in those records."

"There might not be, Melanie, but I can guarantee you that the prosecutor's investigators will determine the identity of every caller or callee and will make contact with those individuals. Your husband was away, and I assume he took other business trips during that twelve-month period. All we need is one phone call to buttress our defense position. If we are going to defend you properly, we need those records."

Burnside interjected, "Why don't we move to suppress the evidence seized under the warrant?"

"Mr. Burnside, I'll explain that to you in several minutes. For tactical reasons, I don't want to discuss this in Melanie's presence. To defend her adequately, I need her to sign these affidavits, which Erika then will notarize."

"Melanie, go ahead and sign the damn things. We will deal with any problems later," Burnside uttered.

Johnnie handed a pen to Melanie who signed the affidavits. Erika then signed, dated, and affixed her stamped seal.

Johnnie addressed Melanie. "Melanie, if you feel up to it, Erika and I would like to take you to your home. We know this could be traumatic for you, but we must have you walk us through the events as they unfolded. We have inspected the scene and obtained photos. It's imperative, however, that you re-create the scene for us before your memory dims. We need you to describe certain positioning so that we do not make any false assumptions in our analysis. Now is the time to do this. Can you do this today for us?"

"If it's really important, I guess so. I'll try my best."

"That's all we can ask. We know it won't be easy, but it is critical we do this now."

Melanie nodded her agreement. Johnnie asked that she accompany Erika outside her father's study so he could speak to Burnside alone.

"Mr. Burnside, about your suggestion that we file a motion to suppress the search warrant, it would be fruitless. The court would find no basis to suppress the warrant. Melanie's cleaning lady called the police. She had the right to allow the police to enter because Mr. Stafford had been shot and Melanie had been injured. It was a crime scene. Had she not called, Melanie would have. Remember her defense is that she was attacked and her husband murdered. How could we argue that they were both victims and then file a suppression motion? Such a filing not only would be counterproductive but also would infer that Melanie, the proposed victim, has something to hide. Moreover, even if no one had called and the police had arrived for some other reason, had they observed the broken sliding glass door, they would have had the right to conduct a warrantless search under the emergency care-taker doctrine. Our purpose is to heighten Melanie's innocence, not to create a cloud of guilt. Based on the known facts, a suppression hearing would generate a plethora of negative press coverage. As it is, there are enough negative suppositions out there."

"Okay, I see your point. How much time do you think we will spend at Melanie's home? I have an important business meeting this afternoon."

"That's another thing, Mr. Burnside. I know how much you love Melanie. Your concern for her health and welfare is obvious. You're extremely intelligent and resourceful, and what I'm going to tell you is exactly why I tried to dissuade you from engaging me as the primary defense counsel. Due to the attorney-client relationship, there are times when you have to step aside. What Erika and I discuss with Melanie is privileged conversation. Everything that Erika and I discuss with her and everything that she says to us is confidential. No one else is entitled to know the substance or content of those discussions. Were you to be present during those conversations, that privilege would be broken. The prosecutor could require you to divulge what you heard. If you refused, you would be held in contempt by the court. If you falsely represented what was said, I would have to divulge it or request being relieved as counsel. Either way, the prosecution would be given a tremendous advantage. We cannot take that risk. Erika, as my employee and investigator, is covered by the attorney-client shield. You are not. As I informed Melanie, it is imperative that she return to the crime scene and provide us with an unvarnished and unfiltered narration of the events. What she tells us is confidential. If you're present, that bond is broken, even if you don't say anything. Also, your mere presence may cause Melanie to withhold certain details, either out of embarrassment or out of fear that certain disclosures may alter your opinion of her or of her deceased husband."

"Well, she can't change my opinion of Stafford. As I alluded to you earlier, I never liked the pompous son-of-a-bitch. I urged her not to marry him. That old saying about love being blind. She was enthralled by his supposed intelligence. I saw him for what he was, a callous, shallow, weak-spined waste of a human being. As far as I'm concerned, she's better off with him dead. My wife pleaded with me not to interfere with their engagement. I relented against my better judgment. I know I can be a hard-ass, but I didn't climb the corporate ladder by looking at everything through rose-colored glasses. Like everyone, I've had regrets over the years. My biggest was condoning their marriage. She was the real breadwinner and beacon in that relationship. A far as I'm concerned, he was just the detritus."

"Mr. Burnside, how often did you see your son-in-law?"

"A lot more that I liked. Actually, Catherine had them over every Sunday for dinner. As Melanie's practice grew and Stafford started to travel on business trips, those dinners occurred less frequently. Usually, Catherine or I would talk to Melanie several times a week. Stafford I tried to avoid, but I forced myself to keep our relationship cordial for Melanie's sake.

"For all her accomplishments, Melanie doesn't seek the limelight. In public gatherings, she always allowed Stafford to be the center of attention, something he loved. He seemed to be more comfortable around women than men. At those parties we mutually attended, he seemed to pry his way into female conversations. I guess he felt more secure around them. He wasn't really into sports. He didn't play golf or tennis and would rather discuss gardening, interior design, and medical issues, especially those dealing with pharmaceuticals.

"I'm glad you pressed Melanie on those phone records. I'd be curious to see whom he called on his cell phone. I still think he was cheating on her. He was away a lot. There's a saying in the pharmaceutical industry, 'wings up, rings off.'

"As I told you earlier, I considered putting an investigator on him but deferred. If anything was uncovered, it would have devastated Melanie and upset Catherine. They would have blamed me for intermeddling and destroying a presumed blissful marriage.

"What Melanie hasn't and probably won't tell you is that Stafford had a temper. I was somewhat surprised myself. While he had a melba-toast type of personality, the guy's arrogance led him to believe that he was an authority on certain subjects. If someone questioned him on his opinion, he initially would listen politely. If the questioner continued to press the matter, his mood would change. He would become indignant and caustic.

"The guy didn't have a real sense of humor. He didn't joke or laugh often unless someone was praising him on his work. If you sought his approval, all you had to do was wheedle him. Nothing made him happier than recognition and flattery. I guess that was the reason he intermingled so often with women. They were more likely to provide the approbation he constantly chased. To me, he wasn't a 'guy's guy.' He couldn't be one of the boys. He possessed that innate insecurity that he didn't quite measure up. Melanie somehow overlooked that characteristic. Because she was around self-assured surgeons so frequently, maybe his personality was a pleasant change. Who knows? Many years ago, I gave up trying to ascertain their chemistry."

"Do you think he ever hit her?" Johnnie asked.

"I remember one time I stopped over unannounced one afternoon when Melanie wasn't working. When she opened the door, I noticed a welt on her left cheek. I definitely caught her off guard. I asked her what happened, and she stammered for a moment before replying that she had tripped and slammed into a wall corner. She said she had applied ice on it earlier and it soon would disappear. She quickly changed the subject and commenced rambling pleasantly about something I now don't recall. Richard obviously wasn't at home. I probably stayed for a couple of hours. When she wants to, Melanie can hide her feelings pretty well. If she had told me that he hit her, I would have beaten the living shit out of him, if not worse. Who knows if he hit her then or even more often? It was very rare that Catherine or I ever appeared without calling."

Burnside paused, shook his head, and then added, "I'll abide by your instructions and not accompany you to the scene. All I ask is that you let me review those phone records. The prosecutor, no doubt, will obtain them, so my knowledge of their existence won't cause any prejudice to Melanie."

"I will, Mr. Burnside. Please keep the substance of our conversation private. It would not be prudent for Melanie or Mrs. Burnside to be privy to our exchange."

"Consider my lips sealed."

Johnnie shook Burnside's hand and exited the study in search of Melanie and Erika.

14.

Melanie insisted that she accompany Johnnie and Erika in a separate car. Even though she knew her return could be unsettling, she declared that she needed some time alone at the house after completing her reenactment. Johnnie and Erika followed her on the winding township roads.

"I caught your look," Johnnie bantered.

"I knew she'd resist the phone record affidavits. I'm telling you she did it," Erika smugly replied.

"Just promise me you will hide your skepticism during her narration. I've had enough combativeness from her father. I don't need to clash with my client. By the way, Burnside actually wants the records. He's convinced Stafford was cheating on her. He considered hiring an investigator but deferred for fear of alienating both Melanie and her mother. He also recounted one unannounced visit to Melanie's. When she opened the door, he immediately noticed a welt on her left cheek. When questioned regarding the bruise, Melanie immediately stammered before quickly regaining her composure. She insisted that she had tripped and slammed into a wall corner. She quickly changed the subject and warmly interacted with Burnside. Stafford wasn't present. Burnside volunteered that had there been any further corroboration, he, at the very least, would have given Stafford a very intense thrashing. It was patently obvious that he detested his son-in-law."

"Are you going to question her about marital infidelities, fights, beatings, and the like?"

"After she reconstructs the assault and its aftermath, I'll gently probe her on those subjects. Erika, you'll have to watch her reactions and body gestures. I won't stare at her. That, in itself, would make her uncomfortable and cause her to withdraw."

"May I suggest, Johnnie, that you preface your prodding with the fact the McGuire's theory is that she killed her husband because of third-party involvement. If there were any liaisons, we need to know it now so we can minimize their impact. Similarly, if there were any assaults by him or her, it's better to disclose them rather than to be surprised at trial. Such unpleasantries, as they say, can be marginalized if divulged quickly and voluntarily. At least, that's what some of my lesbian sweethearts proclaim."

"Erika, you read my mind, except, of course, about your lesbian girlfriends."

"Johnnie, you're so square. You have to admit that most of my past flames have been real lookers."

"Yeah, and that's what's so frustrating."

"You know, Johnnie, if I come back to the other side, it will be only for you!"

"Yeah, Erika, I guess hope is eternal."

As Erika playfully jammed him in the shoulder, Johnnie turned right into Melanie's driveway.

Melanie walked hesitantly toward the front door. Johnnie produced the key and stated, "Erika and I will enter first to ascertain whether anyone has altered the inside since our last visit. Melanie, the police outlined Richard's body on the rug. There is blood spatter on the wall. I know this will be disconcerting and horrific for you. You will have to steel yourself to what you observe. Erika and I are here to help you. Let your emotions free, if need be. We understand. If you need to be alone, we will go outside until you tell us to reenter. All we ask is that you not move anything if we are not present."

Melanie looked forlornly at him and commented, "I remember every detail from that morning, the blood on the walls and rug, the overturned table and lamp. I don't think the nightmare ever will end, but my life now is at stake. The prosecutor will not defeat or conquer me. I have been distraught, almost felt disemboweled, but Mr. Fitzhugh, I am a fighter and a survivor. Since they arrested me, I knew this day would come. I have rehashed everything in my mind. Richard is gone. I can't bring him back. I have one mission: to find, kill, or convict his killer or killers. Every waking moment, and even in my somnolent state, I have thought of nothing else. I have primordial emotions like anyone else, but my medical training also has inculcated me with dispassion to combat those feelings, in situations of extreme stress or sadness. I will follow you in without trepidation, but with loathing for the beast or beasts that slaughtered Richard. I will be relentless in proving my innocence and their guilt. If I were a free woman, I would hunt them down and kill them without the slightest trace or remorse. This may shock you, but I am my father's daughter. I have feelings, but I can be just as ruthless. Let's go in."

As they entered, Johnnie asked that Melanie first inspect her jewelry and valuables to ascertain whether anything was stolen. Melanie explained that her valuables and jewelry were stored in a bank safe deposit box. Neither she nor Richard believed in keeping cash in the house, other than that in their wallets. Richard had a small rare coin collection, which he also secured at the bank. The various paintings that adorned the walls were only of sentimental value. None were museum pieces. The silverware had not been disturbed. She canvassed the house. While it was evident that the police had searched thoroughly, nothing was missing other than the seized items.

Johnnie inquired as to their cellphones and computers. Melanie replied that the police confiscated her only laptop and their joint desktop. She and Richard each had cellphones, which had been seized. She was uncertain whether he had a cellphone for work. She assumed that Richard had an office desktop but had no direct knowledge. Richard routinely used his personal laptop for business and pleasure.

They had a joint checking account. She had a separate business account from which she would transfer funds to her pension account as well as to their joint account. Richard had a pension account through Wellington. He also had a separate bank account, which contained funds he inherited from his parents. She likewise had a separate account, which Burnside had established for her. Periodically, he would deposit funds into that account in allowance with the Federal Gift Tax regulations. Both she and Richard treated the accounts containing funds from their parents as their own to be used as each saw fit.

Melanie mentioned that both were self-sufficient and never argued over money. Richard would deposit a portion of his salary into their joint account, as would she. Neither had exorbitant tastes or hobbies. Even if they had desired such indulgences, their work consumed most of their time, even periodically on weekends. They would spend a portion of their evenings reading or watching TV and would recharge their batteries by vacationing at the Jersey Shore or in Europe. Both loved to frequent museums, palaces, churches, historical sites, and world-renowned gardens. Typically each year, they spent a week at the shore and one to two weeks in Europe. While Melanie's practice was confined to New Jersey, Richard traveled throughout the country on business and occasionally journeyed to Africa, Europe, and Latin America regarding drugs being tested by his company.

Johnnie realized that Melanie had been able to harness her emotions. She related their finances and lifestyles concisely and logically. This was accomplished devoid of any emotion or hesitancy. Melanie glanced at the crime scene without emotional withdrawal. Her demeanor didn't change from the undisturbed rooms to the crime scene.

"Melanie, earlier you mentioned that you weren't working that day. Was that always your day off?"

"No, it depended on my surgical schedule, which was set by the various hospitals."

"What did you do that day?"

"Relaxed in the morning, probably paid some bills. Went to the gym in the afternoon. Took a spinning class and worked out with some light weights. Also used some of the Cybex machines. Came home, showered, and grilled some chicken and cooked some green beans and pasta. That's why I had unlocked the sliding glass door earlier, so I could use the outdoor grill. After dinner, I watched some news shows on CNN and Fox and then did some light reading on the couch. Richard was supposed to be home by 11:00 p.m. I was lying on the couch reading. I don't know when, but at some point, I fell asleep. I didn't awaken before he kissed me on the forehead. Without opening my eyes, I asked him how his flight was. He said something about a long delay in Dallas. I mumbled something about being glad he was okay and then fell back to sleep.

"I have replayed that scene over and over. Had I just left the couch and gone to the bedroom, maybe something would have been different. Possibly, one or both of us would have heard the intruder or intruders before they entered the bedroom. Had I not screamed, Richard wouldn't have exited the bedroom. Had we both been in the bedroom, they wouldn't have known where we were. They might have gone to the right, not to the left. At that point, they could have stumbled over something, and we might have awakened. We then could have had some time to try something. Then I think of the alternative. We might both have been murdered in our bed. You know I have that survivor's guilt. I screamed and lived. He ran out and died."

"Melanie, you shouldn't feel that way. They drugged you. They had no intention of harming you. Otherwise, they would have killed you immediately. They either thought you were away or had planned to frame you. If they had surveilled the home that day, they would have known of your presence. Obviously, they had some prior knowledge of your home's layout. They entered at the most vulnerable location. Why didn't you have an alarm system?"

"We didn't live our life that way. I guess we were too naïve and trusting. We didn't store any valuables at home. Even if someone broke in, what would they get? A TV? Our laptops were usually with us as were our cell phones. I had nothing critical in my computer that would benefit someone else. The contained medical articles and notes would be too technical and boring for some marginally educated thief. I don't know about Richard's computer, but I assume it would be the same. We did not bank online. We had friends who had been victims of identity fraud. We tried to minimize that risk. Our bankers and brokers urged us to streamline our finances, but we refused. So we really didn't think we needed an alarm."

"Melanie, do you have any idea when you awakened to go to the bathroom?"

"No, I know it was still dark out, though."

"Had you been asleep on your back, side, or stomach?"

"On my back."

"Was the book on your chest or stomach when you awakened?"

"I don't remember. Maybe Richard took it when I said I was remaining on the couch."

"Why didn't you get up and join Richard in your bedroom?"

"As I said earlier, he awoke me from a deep sleep. I didn't feel like undressing. I know if I did I wouldn't fall back asleep quickly. The spinning class, combined with the weightlifting, really did me in. Usually, I do one or the other. For some reason, I wanted to push myself that day. In retrospect, it was a bad mistake."

"When you started toward the bathroom, had you intended to return to the couch, or would you then have stayed in your bedroom?"

"That's a good question. In my slumbered state, I probably wasn't thinking about that. I just knew I had to go to the bathroom. I hadn't intended to fall asleep on the couch. I don't know how long I was asleep, and I don't know what time Richard arrived home. As it was, I only took several steps before I was grabbed from behind."

"Do you know how many steps you took before you were attacked?"

"No. All I know is that I was grabbed from behind. There are end tables and lamps at each end of the couch. He must have walked around the back of the couch and then grabbed me from behind as I was walking. The first thing I felt was this vise-like arm crushing my breasts. Then the cloth was over my face. I twisted and bucked but couldn't get free. I grabbed his gloved hand and tried to tear off the cloth, but he kept pressing it harder against my nose and lips. I kicked backward with my right leg. I think I hit his right shin. I seem to remember falling forward. He never said a thing. Next thing I recall is being groggy and hearing Inez scream. I was on the floor. I looked over and saw Richard on his back on the floor. Blood was all around. The gun was next to me. The cloth was nearby. The table and lamp were overturned. I was bleeding from my forehead and the bridge of my nose."

"Melanie, at the jail, you told me that your assailant's fingers were thick. You didn't mention any gloves."

"I didn't? Well, he had on a glove. His fingers felt thick through the glove. I could feel the glove as I tried to pull away the cloth."

"Was he wearing a hood or mask?"

"I don't know. All I could grab was his gloved hand. His other arm constricted my chest. I thought he was going to crush me."

"Did you try to hit his face by head-butting him?"

"As I said, I tried to twist and push back, but he was too strong. When my head went back, it didn't strike anything. This all occurred so quickly. I was able to scream, as I was twisting, but that was it. I got out 'Richard!' and then lost consciousness. I didn't even hear the lamp or table crash to the floor. From my cuts, I must have fallen on them before I landed on the floor."

"Melanie, did you hear or feel the presence of anyone else in the living room?"

"Everything was so sudden. I don't think I would have had any time to process that. Initially, my focus was on getting to the bathroom.

Then, I felt the cold air. I had closed the drapes after cooking on the grill and closing the sliding door. I thought I had locked it, but then I felt the cold air. I didn't know whether Richard had gone outside after I fell back to sleep and had forgotten to lock the door upon returning, or whether I inadvertently had forgotten to lock it. All I knew was that cold air was coming inside. I started to move in the direction of the sliding door and then — boom! — I was attacked. It was pitch black inside. I was grabbed from behind, while still half somnolent. It felt like everything happened within several seconds. I reacted instinctively the moment I was pinned from behind. You're asking me all these questions, as if I have a stop-action and instant replay in my head! You've got to understand. One moment I'm hazy, and then I'm assailed. All this occurs not in daylight, not in twilight, but in utter darkness. I'm pounced upon when the only thing in my mind is a full bladder."

"We understand, Melanie. Erika and I realize this is disturbing and difficult. We're not trying to harass or besiege you with details. Our purpose is to peel back as much of your memory as we can. Better now than later when your recollection dims. You can expect that McGuire will be just as thorough. Believe me: His questioning won't be as supportive and conciliatory."

"Don't worry. I'll be ready for them, Mr. Fitzhugh. He will meet his match. When that time comes, we will have already seen his evidence. The advantage will be ours."

"Melanie, don't be lulled by that assumption. A trial isn't like a tennis match where one player serves and the other returns. In the courtroom, the server's purpose is to serve two or more balls at once to defect the possibility of any return. That's the way McGuire plays. Don't expect anything less. Erika and I need your best recollection, warts and all. That's why we probe before your memory recedes."

"I understand, Mr. Fitzhugh. I am so accustomed to being in control. As an anesthesiologist, I literally hold the patient's life in my hands. One mistake and that patient doesn't wake up or awakens in a damaged or vegetative state. I hate to admit it, but it's almost akin to playing God but in a perverse way. I fear killing them. You may have dreams about losing a case. I have recurring nightmares about killing a patient. You see, we both have our demons. You, however, have an appellate process to cure your, or the court's, mistakes. I have none, just my conscience and my guilt. If there is a heaven, do I get to enter if my negligence kills someone else's patient? If I and the surgeon are sued by the deceased's heirs, do you think the surgeon sides with me? Not a chance! He throws me to the wolves to save his ass and a rising malpractice premium. So I understand pressure. It keeps me up at night. That's why when I'm lucky enough to fall into a deep sleep, I don't arise from a couch when my husband strolls in late. I try to remain in my often-sought but rarely achieved blissful state. That's when I'm really at peace."

Taken aback by Melanie's retort, Johnnie changed his line of questioning.

"Melanie, when Mrs. Garcia's scream caused you to regain some of your senses, what, if anything, did you do when you saw Mr. Stafford and the blood on the floor?"

"I remember screaming and telling Inez to call 911. I rushed to Richard. There was blood all over the rug. He was on his back. I immediately started chest compressions and also gave mouth-to-mouth. It was to no avail. He was gone. I tried to grab him and hold him, even though I knew then he was dead. I had his blood on my face and hands. I started yelling, 'They killed him!' I was crying. At some point, the EMTs and the police arrived. I think the EMTs arrived first. They went to Richard, tried CPR, and recognized it was useless. Obviously, I was very emotional. I was crying. I also told them someone killed my husband. I said the same thing I yelled to Inez, that 'they killed him.' The EMTs checked me over, strapped me to a gurney, and took me to the hospital, where my forehead was stitched, and the bridge of my nose was bandaged. I'm pretty sure at the scene I also said to the police, 'they killed him.' Of course, the cops took me from the hospital to the stationhouse. I was arrested there, and you know the rest."

"Melanie, did you wash the blood from your hands and face before the police arrived?"

"No."

"How about at the hospital?"

"They washed my face because they had to inspect my head wound. The big cop who came with me in the ambulance told the emergency nurse not to wash my hands. Earlier, the cop had asked me if I had any hand injuries. I said no. The emergency nurse asked me the same question after the cop told her not to clean my hands. When I replied negatively, she didn't touch them. Another officer arrived at the ER and opened a kit. He dabbed the palms and backs of both of my hands. He told me he was looking for fingerprints from the man who grabbed me."

"Melanie, he lied to you. He was checking for gunshot residue. He was using stubs to attempt to collect particle blowback. If you fired that gun, there might have been some burnt, unburnt, or semi-burnt particles on your hands. If so, it will buttress McGuire's argument that you were the killer."

"Well, I didn't shoot him! I don't give a damn what he says!" she shouted.

"Melanie, calm down. First of all, we don't have the test results. Secondly, a positive test isn't foolproof. There are several exceptions to a positive test. Once we get the lab report, we can address it, if we have to. If the test is positive, McGuire will gloat. He won't be able to contain himself. He'll probably call me."

"Well, how long does it take to get the result?"

"It depends. Turnaround could be ten to fifteen days, I think. A rush job maybe would be three to five days. Whatever the result, we'll just have to deal with it, like we would do in any other case. Very rarely is any case perfect. There is positive and negative evidence in every trial. Lay witnesses will say anything, even if it defies logic or scientific reliability. Expert witnesses often can be retained to rebut even the most unassailable position. We trial lawyers deal with these conundrums on a daily basis. Frankly, a lot of times it comes down to form over substance. Which expert does the jury like or admire? Believe me, it's not always the most qualified expert. Any lawyer who tells you his expert will convince the jury is a fool. During any trial, the only certainty is that there will be uncertainty when you least expect it. Each case has its ebb and flow. No one really knows until the jury announces its verdict. A trial attorney who boasts he's never lost a case either hasn't tried many or is being untruthful."

"You don't exude much confidence, Mr. Fitzhugh."

"Confidence has nothing to do with it. Your father would be the first one to tell you that I don't lose cases. He wouldn't have retained me if he believed I wasn't the best attorney to represent you. Due to our relationship, I tried to steer him to other defense counsel. He refused. If you think otherwise, you should share your feelings with him. I would welcome that conversation and gladly would step aside. As an attorney, I have an obligation to explain the trial process to you. Every case contains possible pitfalls and traps. We trial attorneys comprehend those scenarios, just as you grasp the snares that manifest themselves in your field. The fact that I mention these concepts to you does not diminish my belief in your innocence or my confidence in defending you. Part of my obligation is to instill in you the fundamental workings of any jury trial. You must be composed and prepared for sudden shifts that periodically occur during evidentiary presentation. You must mask your emotions when unfavorable testimony is elicited. The jurors will be watching you closely throughout the entire trial, even during the jury selection process. How we interact will be critical. I would be derelict in my obligation to you if I failed to expound on the intricacies of the trial process."

"Mr. Fitzhugh, my father only hires the best. He chose you, so I know I'm in good hands. This process is so deflating. I scream my innocence, and no one hears or believes except you. Do you know how that makes me feel? Throughout my life, I basically have experienced nothing but adulation. Always at or near the top of my class, lead actress in school plays, student body representative, alumni coordinator, and so on. Like any girl or woman, I've experienced romantic rejections in my earlier years, but who hasn't? That's part of growing up and maturing. At least, that's what the self-help gurus profess. Now, I'm confronted with negative publicity, an overbearing prosecutor, and a justice system where I may be a pawn, subject to the whims and caprices of someone else's testimony and opinion. For a control freak, that's not very comforting or reassuring, is it?"

"From your vantage point, it's not. Erika and I have seen it in many others. I have counseled and represented many doctors, lawyers, and corporative executives. None of them reached the pinnacle of success without some tribulation, and, believe me, each of them harbored deep-down insecurities and inadequacies, often more imagined than real. I would venture to say most of us do, but we find a way to cope and plod forward, at times three steps forward, and then two back. We persevere, not succumb.

"You will endure what is thrust at you, and you will survive. Erika and I will be by your side to parry what McGuire and his minions hurl your way. That is our responsibility. We do not take it lightly."

"Thank you. I guess I needed some reassurance. To me, the pressure has seemed so unrelenting. I'm accustomed to rapid solutions to even confounding problems. It's the waiting and the unknown that is so overwhelming."

"Melanie, that is a typical sentiment. Its urgency is heightened in a serious criminal case. You are not the first to experience it and won't be the last to suffer that insecurity and apprehension. When the indictment occurs, time will accelerate as discovery is released. We will discover the holes in McGuire's case and will plot our defense. Until then, we will secure the ancillary testimony that we later will use to augment your defense. Erika and I will speak to first responders regarding what they recall regarding your appearance, your comments, and their observations of the scene and their interaction with the police. We also will question the hospital staff that examined and treated your wounds. Hopefully, they will enhance your future testimony. Do you have any more questions for us?"

"I guess not. I'm sure I'll think of something later after you've left. I need to spend some time here. Right now, I have so many emotions swirling in my head. I need to grieve here alone. I know it won't be easy, but I have to for my own sanity. Don't worry. I won't stay here tonight."

"Before we leave, there are a couple of delicate matters we should discuss. McGuire's case hinges upon the means, the motive, and the opportunity that led to Richard's killing. The means and opportunity he already has. The motive he seeks. With an alleged domestic killing, there is a triad that all prosecutors analyze: money, abuse, and infidelity. From your comments, money never was an issue for either of you."

"No. We both made good money. Mine was higher, but Richard did well. Richard also had his inheritance, and my father routinely funneled funds to me despite my protestations. No, money definitely wasn't an issue."

"Did your husband ever hit you?"

"Never."

"Has anyone ever witnessed you two have a violent argument?"

"No, that's not the way we were. Obviously, all couples have disagreements and will argue. I don't think we were different from anyone else. Frankly, we spent a lot of our waking time apart except on weekends. On the days I was at the hospital, my days were early and long. Typically, I would be on duty for multiple surgeries. Even after my day ended, I might be on emergency call if multiple casualties occurred. Richard would leave later than me in the morning, but he still left early and would return after six. Typically, we would be together Saturdays. On some Sundays, he would leave midmorning or early afternoon on out-of-state business trips. He would be gone overnight or for several days. If the meeting was abroad, he would be gone seven to ten days."

"Melanie, on those extended trips, would you talk during his absence?"

"If he was in the U.S., we would speak daily or every other day. If he was abroad, we would communicate via email."

"To your knowledge, did your husband ever cheat on you?"

Melanie momentarily regarded Johnnie quizzically before intoning, "No."

"So you found no unexplained correspondence, cryptic notes in your husband's luggage, files, or books?"

"I didn't uncover anything because I never looked. A marriage is supposed to be about trust. I didn't poke into his professional life, and I assume he didn't intrude into mine. Could he have had an affair at a conference or while abroad? Sure, he could have, if that was his inclination. How would I know? He's intelligent enough not to reappear, luggage in hand with some exotic perfume emanating from his clothes. Had he cheated on me, there would be no notes or billets-doux to peruse. I know my father never approved of our marriage, but even he would acknowledge his son-in-law wouldn't be that stupid. No, Mr. Fitzhugh, I didn't attempt to ferret out any possible dalliances. My husband was a big boy. If he was going to cheat, he had ample opportunity. Maybe I'm too guileless. I trusted him, and that's that."

"Melanie, did your father ever tell you that he disapproved of your marriage?"

"He didn't have to. My father is a blunt man, not just by his words but also in his emotions. There was no effusive praise of Richard. Probably silenced tolerance would be a more apt description. You have to understand my father had my best interests at heart. Of that, I have no doubt. For me, only the best, brightest, and most athletic would have sufficed. Richard was none of those in my father's eyes, but he was my choice. My father knew I would be steadfast in that decision. He grasped this was one battle he would not win, without losing the closeness and love of his daughter. Mom would have been overjoyed with whomever I adored. She would not have countenanced any outright resistance from my father, and he knew it. So rather than tear asunder our familiar bonds, my father did something alien to his personality. He retreated. He relented from his ironclad belief. Did he mask his feelings? No, they often simmered just beneath the surface. In public gatherings, he was the genial father-in-law. In private familiar settings, he was cordial to Richard, but that's all. There were no intimate father and son-in-law outings. No ballgames attended. No friendly games of golf or tennis played. Granted, Richard wasn't gifted athletically, but he probably would have tried, especially if urged by me. But there was no point. I sensed my father's subsurface disdain. Maybe that word is too harsh. Let's say disapproval instead. After several attempts at congeniality, Richard perceived my father's subtle rebukes would not dissipate. Like my father, he settled into a state of mutual tolerance. Neither invaded the other's space. There was no outward caustic inter-play. Turned shoulders, evasive glances, nonexistent humor suffused their interplay. I guess that answers your question. I'm feeling really drained. If you need any other information, could it wait for another day? I don't mean to be rude. I guess I overestimated my mental and physical strength."

"Of course, Melanie. The tragedy you've endured and its concomi-tant emotions would overwhelm even the most strong-willed. Please promise us you will not remain here tonight."

"I'll leave within the next hour. If you think of anything that needs an urgent response, you can reach me at my father's. Thank you for your understanding. Tomorrow should be a better day."

Johnnie handed Melanie the key and exited with Erika. After closing the front door, Erika blurted out, "Johnnie, we forgot to ask her what lights she had on that evening before Richard returned."

"We'll speak to her tomorrow, get the key, and return at night to photograph the various lighting conditions. She's starting to unravel. Let's give her some peace and space."

As Johnnie was driving away from the house, Erika blurted, "You know, Johnnie, there's still something about her that doesn't ring true. First, she tells you how the guy's fingers were thick. Today, she gives a different version. Now, the assailant was wearing gloves. What gives? How come the change? Did she do it and then wipe the gun clean, realize she erred earlier, and now conveniently remembers the intruder wore gloves?"

"Maybe, Erika, she was so distraught when I first met her at the corrections facility that she didn't think to differentiate between the gloved hand and the fingers. After all, if you're fighting for your life and grabbing at someone's fingers, you still could feel the thickness of the fingers through the gloves. When I mentioned the discrepancy, she responded quickly. You might be reading too much into it. If she gave McGuire the same ungloved version, he will grill her during cross. She'll have to deal with it then. She said McGuire will have met his match. We'll see if she was correct. There's nothing we can do to alter the discrepancy. She'll have to deal with it."

"That's not all, Johnnie. What woman who'd been assaulted, awakens, and discovers her husband dead tells her lawyer that, after being kissed on the forehead by her returning husband, decides to remain on the couch rather than accompany him to the marital bedroom, because he 'just strolled in' and wakened her from a 'rarely achieved blissful state'? Give me a fucking break!"

"Erika, neither you nor I have ever been married, nor have we held the lives of surgical patients in our very hands. You're delving into areas we've never experienced. I think you're being overly critical. Don't you think she has a right to being pissed and angered if unjustly accused of murder, especially when accused and arrested after awakening from being assaulted and drugged?"

"Johnnie, that's utter bullshit, and you know it. Don't play the devil's advocate with me. We have too much of a history. Yeah, we're defending her, and we, or I mean you, will do your best in that regard. But we have to view this defense from McGuire's vantage point. If she uses 'stroll in' with McGuire, he will crucify her on cross. Also, let's not forget her other gratuitous comment that McGuire will 'meet his match.' Watching CSI doesn't provide the acumen to withstand a blistering cross-examination. Even a blowhard like McGuire wouldn't think he could play anesthesiologist. What makes her think she can outwit him, just because she believes she will have seen all the evidence before she testifies? Does she really think that her acting skills will carry the day? You better pray she doesn't volunteer on the stand that she was an actress. Of course, she wasn't just an actress. She was always the lead actress. What does that tell you? She thinks she can manipulate anyone and any situation. Is she playing you, Johnnie? Is that her ultimate goal to ensure her innocence? The young but experienced good-looking lawyer swept into her web? God forbid she mentions her acting skills on the stand. If she does, she's dead in the water. Not even you and your scintillating summations can save her then. In your trial prep, underline in red that you warned her never to mention the word acting on direct or cross, unless McGuire somehow uncovers it. Better he unveil it than her. Let him insinuate she's a liar, because she's acted on a stage. A jury will see he's overreaching in an effort to save his case. Let him argue to the jurors that she knows how to craft her lines, alter her personalities, and filter her emotions."

"Erika, actors and actresses often have screwed-up personal lives. They are harmonious on the stage while their own interpersonal relationships are in disarray. Very rarely do they kill their spouses. They cheat on them, embarrass them, maybe, but they don't slaughter them."

"That's my point, Johnnie. The tabloids expose the alleged sordid lives of the rich and famous on a weekly basis. Sometimes, they strike it rich. Most often, their claims are baseless. In either event, the public's prurient interest thrives on the misfortunes or peccadilloes of the so-called upper strata. Let McGuire enter the gutter first. The jury will sense his deceit and will punish him for it. Now all you have to do is convince your actress to heed your advice."

Erika paused for a moment. Then before Johnnie could proclaim Melanie's fragile state, Erika added, "Why didn't you ask her if she ever cheated on her husband?"

"Because, Erika, why would she kill him if she were unfaithful?"

"How about, Johnnie, if Richard discovered her infidelity and exclaimed he would file for divorce? She made more than he did. He could argue he was entitled to live in the same lifestyle he was accustomed to before her adultery. Sure, they both had ample funds, but Burnside provided a frequent stipend, and I feel Melanie probably indulged her husband with some of the money."

"Erika, I think you're stretching it a bit. Also, I didn't want to know. If she admitted to it and then testified on cross to the contrary, I didn't want that playing in the recesses of my mind while I was putting her through redirect after McGuire was finished with her."

"You mean, Johnnie, you didn't want two or more tennis balls flying toward you simultaneously. Great analogy, by the way. You know I had a similar experience. Several years ago, one of my tennis friends convinced one of the top-ranked men to play a set with me. After his first serve, I thought I had diplopia. The ball's abrupt change in elevation and direction as a result of its reverse spin threw my spatial orientation completely off balance. I really thought I was seeing two balls. Moments earlier, I had bantered with him. Told him 'hit me with your best.' When he hesitated, I told him I was serious. He smiled, shook his head, and exploded one by me. My racket didn't come close to it. He was a lefty. After that, he laughed, apologized, and actually let me win two games. He claimed he was really trying hard, but that I was too resilient. What a gentleman. That guy did, and still does, carry himself with real class."

Johnnie looked toward her, gave her a wide smile, and replied, "I'm starved. Let's get something to eat."

15.

August 1974
Munich, Germany

The meeting had gone much better than envisioned. Before Hitler's rise to power, the gentleman had been a member of the Arts Faculty at Munich's Ludwig Maximilians University. While he had lectured on the Renaissance, he specialized in classical art and architecture.

When Hitler invaded France, he, his wife, and infant son fled to Switzerland, where they remained until returning to Munich in 1954.

The man had been appalled that Hitler had looted priceless art and antiquities from France, Belgium, and Holland. Like other historians, he yearned for the discovery and return of the hidden works.

Presently, he taught part time at the university and also served on the board of one of the city's museums. West Germany was prospering, as was Munich. The museum, like others, had its share of benefactors. What was needed, however, was the return of stolen treasures. For a fact, he knew that museums, even surreptitiously, would pay for the reacquired works. Some items, of course, were pilfered from private collections. Were their owners still alive? Even if so, could they be located? If not, the museums also would purchase those treasures. What mattered most was that those masterpieces again be on public display. Art was timeless. It depicted history and culture. It fostered knowledge, imagination, and creativity.

The American sensed an opening and pounced. As an exporter, he had learned from clients that some of the stolen treasures had been shipped to South America. He also was an art lover and believed that the sculptures and paintings should be returned to the museums and individual owners. But who best could determine ownership of each item? Who would have the knowledge and resources? The museums, of course. Their curators would be the most knowledgeable and scrupulous.

As an exporter, he could not deal directly with the museums. He lacked the pedigree.

Would the German act as the intermediary should the American be able to arrange for the transfer of the art to Munich? Of course, the present holders and the museum would have to negotiate the price. It would be no easy task, yet the transfers would be advantageous to all participants. The sellers would avoid detection and prosecution by relieving themselves of the stolen items, and the museums would see the return of the magnificent works of art. Of course, both he and the German would be paid handsomely for their expertise in facilitating the transfers.

Would the German be interested in participating in such a noble cause?

The man smiled and responded, "Of course! It is my duty to help the world again see such invaluable riches."

The American extended his hand, which the German quickly grasped.

The German said that he would confer with the museum's curator. He was certain the museum would authorize his journey to New Jersey where more detailed discussions could occur.

16.

Princeton, New Jersey

Shortly after nine o'clock the next morning, Catherine Burnside heard the front door's chime, crossed the spacious marble foyer, and opened the heavy front door. Standing at the entrance was a solidly built, baby-faced man. From the right pocket of his black overcoat, he retrieved a black leather billfold. Bringing it to chest level, he opened the small case and displayed a gold shield.

"Good morning, ma'am. My name is Detective Daniel Stenkowicz. I'm with the Mercer County Prosecutor's Office. Is Mr. Burnside home? I'd like to speak to him for a couple of minutes."

She hesitated for a moment before replying, "He's doing his daily workout in the gym. Let me see if I can disturb him." With that, she closed the door and quickly walked to the carpeted gym.

Within minutes, Burnside opened the door forcibly. Wearing a gray sweatsuit and perspiring heavily, he glowered from the door's threshold.

"Mr. Burnside, Homicide Detective Dan Stenkowicz. Can I come in? I'd like to ask you a few questions about your late son-in-law."

Burnside snorted.

"You must be kidding, Detective. An intruder or intruders invade my daughter's home, drug her, kill my son-in-law, and your office immediately arrests her without even a cursory investigation, opposes her bail, and now you want my cooperation?"

"Sir, I'm trying to complete the investigation. Perhaps you have some information that might cause us to look in a different direction."

"It's a little late for that isn't it, Detective? Before your office rushed to judgment, it should have considered that possibility. Prosecutor McGuire, at the bail hearing, didn't seem like he needed any additional evidence. He bellowed to the court and press the certainty of my daughter's guilt. Now he wants my cooperation. You can take McGuire's gold badge and stick it up his ass. From his added girth, it should glide up easily."

"Sir, Prosecutor McGuire, in deference to your position in the community, asked me to make this informal overture. He didn't want to have to subpoena you before the grand jury."

"Detective, how long have you been with the prosecutor's office?"

"I've been there now twelve years. Before that I was with the Trenton PD for thirteen years."

"How many times have you been shot at, Detective?"

"Fortunately, never."

"Well, I've been shot at more times than I can count. I've been wounded several times and have been awarded numerous medals for my battle service. I find it laughable that your prosecutor would infer that the threat of a grand jury subpoena would cause me to tremble and cower. If he subpoenas me, I'll invoke my Fifth Amendment right against self-incrimination. What will that subpoena accomplish?"

"Sir, he could request that the court compel you to testify."

"Not without immunity he couldn't."

"Sir, your response seems to imply that you somehow were complicit in Mr. Stafford's murder."

"Well, Detective, I guess you'll never know without my immunity protection. It's amazing what surprises may unfold before a grand jury when one is insulated from prosecution. I wonder if Mr. McGuire desires to risk that potential embarrassment. Is he an aficionado of those Medieval Knights Fairs? Does he joust well? Rumor has it that the prosecutor is seeking a judgeship, and that First Assistant Terry avidly hopes to slide into that vacant position. He's very fortunate that the governor and I are playing a friendly game of tennis this weekend. When he's available, we usually play every other weekend. Please tell Terry for me that I'll put a good word in for him and his boss with the governor. I'll make certain His Honor easily defeats me, so he'll be more amenable to my entreaties on behalf of dear Terry and his boss. Have a pleasant day, Detective."

Burnside gave his Cheshire cat smile, abruptly turned his back on the officer, and slammed the door in his face. As he crossed the foyer, he mused to himself. What if they provided the immunity and I then testified I killed that shithead? What would the grand jurors do then? I know my prints aren't at the scene, at least not on the gun. Catherine couldn't testify against me because of the spousal privilege. He laughed to himself. Let the games begin.

It was noon, and Johnnie, per usual, was starved. With no scheduled court appearance, he had worked out early and had his coffee and fruit before scurrying to his office. His morning was filled with incessant calls from and to carrier claim reps regarding interrogatory answers, deposition scheduling, discovery deadlines, arbitration hearing dates, and trial scheduling and postponements. Eleanor Dodson buzzed to alert him that Terry McGuire was holding. Johnnie frowned, sighed, and picked up the phone.

"To what do I owe the pleasure, Terry?"

"Pleasure? What the fuck are you advising Burnside?"

"What do you mean?"

"I sent Stenkowicz to interview Burnside regarding the late Richard Stafford. All he gets is an earful of shit and veiled threats. He refuses to divulge anything, claims that he'll take the Fifth if subpoenaed to the grand jury, and implies that he'll fuck up the works if granted immunity. He then tells Stenkowicz that he understands the boss wants a judgeship and that I'm itching to fill the supposed vacant prosecutorial slot. Says he plays tennis frequently with the governor, will see him this weekend, and will put a good word in for boss man and me. Also tells Stenkowicz I should take my prosecutor's badge and shove it up my fat ass. What a cocksucker! Thanks, Johnnie, for hypothesizing with him regarding the ambitions of your former friends and associates. Not all of us are blessed with a paternal safety net to guarantee our livelihood, brighten our future, and eradicate our worries and insecurities."

"Terry, you're way off base. First of all, I don't represent Burnside. He's not charged with murder. Melanie is."

"You might not represent him, but I seem to recall that he was at the bail hearing and posted the security. He also is one of your prized clients. There's no doubt in my mind that if I haul his ass before the grand jury, he will assert the Fifth and direct me to Fitzhugh and Fitzhugh. You're his puppet. He knows it. You know it, and we here know it, so cut out the sanctimony. He orders, and you march. The master has his puppy dog on a very short leash. For your pride's sake, Johnnie, don't grovel for the bastard. I'd hate to see him telling you when, and if, you could piss."

"Thanks for your advice. It warms my heart, Terry. You know there is a fine line that we all walk as advocates. You call the man's daughter a murderer. You defame her in a public courtroom, knowing full well you have absolute immunity in that arena. You don't have the courtesy to advise me that you would like to speak to the accused's father so that under the guise of a benevolent detective you can elicit information to bury his daughter. Your ruse borders on the diabolical."

"All we wanted, Johnnie, was a little cooperation. Your client claims Stafford's employer had him killed. Well, maybe the father can shed some light on the subject. Now that you're on board, we can't question her. The employer will stonewall us."

"Well, Terry, maybe if she hadn't been arrested immediately, you would have learned from her what you needed. As it was, she spoke openly to the officers, despite being drugged and injured. Her statement was recorded. You ask for her cooperation, for her father's cooperation, even obliquely for my tolerance, but what do we get in return? Nothing. It's been days since that statement was recorded. Have you divulged it? No. Where is the typed police report? That was prepared quickly. Have you forwarded it to us? No. Trust is a two-way street. Duplicity will get you nowhere."

"Johnnie, you know the rules don't require me to release anything now. I also get my orders from others."

"Then let he who issues the orders have the balls to try this case, Terry. If Burnside has the power he infers, boss man isn't getting a judgeship from this administration. Give him my regards. Let him know I'm waiting for the report and Melanie's statement. I've got an important call on the other line. That person pays the bills. Boss man doesn't. Have a good lunch, and tell Stenkowicz no hard feelings. He's got more class than to pull that stunt without someone ordering him there. Terry, if you reach for the sun with the help of the devil, you'll burn with the devil. In my heart, I know you have a decent core. Don't let outside influences and pressures rot it. Life's too short, and memories can be cruel."

Johnnie pondered whether he should call Burnside immediately and decided to mull over his thoughts while at lunch. Erika was out on another assignment, so he casually walked to his favorite luncheon haven, the Tap Room in the basement of The Nassau Inn.

Favored by underclassmen and alumni for its charm, winter coziness, and stock of good beer and spirits, the Tap Room always caused Johnnie to reminisce about his college days. Then, his life was carefree. Fall Saturdays filled with cheers and male bonding rapidly overshadowed the aches and pains from multiple blocks and tackles. Winter brought indoor track meets at Jadwin Gym and other Ivy locales, followed by the outdoor track season and house parties. Sandwiched among the frolic were the junior papers and the anxiety-fraught senior thesis that every senior dreaded but came to appreciate post-graduation. For many, the time spent researching and then laboring over the mandated research project represented a culmination of four years of initial apprehension followed by social growth and intellectual enlightenment.

Only when he entered the practice of law did Johnnie comprehend it also represented a false sense of security and self-importance, bordering on hubris. Suddenly, one's alleged pedigree meant nothing. It had opened doors, which quickly closed, once he ventured into the courtroom. Background meant nothing. You succeeded or failed on your wits and your preparation. Where you went to college, what educational or athletic renown you achieved there were meaningless before that jury comprised of your client's alleged "peers."

Even the word peers was a mirage. More than likely, most of those confined to the uncomfortable chairs didn't want to be there and couldn't care less about the lawyers or their clients. Many had educational backgrounds dissimilar from those arguing before them. In today's age, few read newspapers. Knowledge of current events, if at all, was gleaned from the televised talking heads, the Internet, and the self-invented bloggers.

Justice often was an ephemeral concept often exploited by those well versed in chicanery and obfuscation. If well staged, form could vanquish substance. Two wrongs didn't make a right. Rather, two wrongs might nurture a cash windfall. Mendacity often bested logic and truth.

The battle-tested litigator, in the end, often settled his cases. Otherwise, the pitfalls and minefields were too many. Judicial administrators harped on judges to move cases, not try them. Reduce the backlog. Cases were not to be tried to prove a point. That was frowned upon by all but the most misguided and quixotic. Of course, there were certain cases that had to be tried, but, as years flew by, they became fewer and fewer on the civil side with the advent of court-compelled arbitrations and mediations. Judicial pressure could come in a plethora of ways, none of them pleasant.

Johnnie was jarred back to reality with the gentle push on his shoulder.

"How come your picture's not there?"

Johnnie laughed and quipped, "They didn't set the bar that low."

Across from his table was a wall lined with black-and-white photographs of famous Princeton graduates.

"What brings you to this Ivy-laden town, Douggie boy?"

"I was hoping by osmosis I could experience how the upper class lived," responded Crawford.

"Bullshit. If this is upper crust, I'd hate to dwell in the bowels of society."

"Why don't you leave this lifestyle and return to us? You can then grovel with society's filth."

"I don't think that welcome mat will be extended anytime soon, if ever. Seriously, where you been?"

"Boss man sent me to our local Princeton constabulary to see what dirt exists on Burnside. Boss man and McGuire are really pissed with you. Do you know why?"

"Yeah, Stenkowicz tried to interview Burnside today and was given some very unpleasant news to deliver to boss man and McGuire. If his predictions are correct, those two will be your bosses for some time. I bet you relish that thought. I guess you'll have to toil in the bowels of Trenton's nether world without my company. How did you find me?"

"Your office said you went out to lunch, which they said meant here."

"Pull up a seat and join me for old times' sake."

"Johnnie, I can't. If someone sees me here yucking it up with you, I'll be on weekend call for months. That's how pleased they are with you."

"Doug, they are only reaping what they sowed. They have been busting me from this case's beginning. McGuire mistakenly saw this homicide as a career game changer. Fortuitously, it may be, but not in the manner he sought. If Burnside holds true to his word, McGuire, and maybe boss man, is fucked. Win or lose, he'll become a lifer in your office."

"That pleasant thought will prompt me to an earlier retirement than planned, Johnnie."

"Doug, when I was there, you were the best investigator and trial team liaison by far. You saved my ass any number of times. If you ever want to jump ship, call me. I'll hook you up with a plaintiff's firm that will double your present salary. How are Lois and the kids?"

"Lois is fine. Jimmy is a freshman at William and Mary. He got a partial scholarship. Leslie is two years behind. That means we'll be looking at colleges all over again this summer. She's playing field hockey and lacrosse. Made second team all county in field hockey. Lacrosse is actually her better sport, so we're hoping some college will offer her at least a partial scholarship. Like her brother, her grades are real good. She's a real plugger. I guess we did something right."

"Doug, you did a helluva lot more than something right. Thanks for the heads-up. Like McGuire, even a favorable outcome in this case doesn't preclude failure. Whoever wins may also lose. Notoriety comes with consequences, often those unwanted. Take care."

After finishing his lunch, Johnnie returned to his office, gathered his thoughts, and called Burnside.

"Johnnie, you read my mind. I was going to call you. A prosecutor's detective visited me this morning. Wanted to talk to me about Stafford. I told him to tell McGuire to stick his badge where the proverbial sun don't shine. The utter balls of that bastard. He wants to destroy my daughter's life with my assistance. The detective told me McGuire could subpoena me before the grand jury and informed me that McGuire could grant me immunity, if I invoked the Fifth. I dared him to do it. Let him know I'd turn his case upside down with my testimony. Implied I might testify I was the killer. Wouldn't that confuse the grand jury? Here McGuire presents to them all this circumstantial evidence of my daughter's guilt, and I confess to the killing. He would look like a fool or an incompetent."

"McGuire called me in a huff. He claimed that I advised you how to react, as if I knew Detective Stenkowicz would appear at your doorstep. It's a shame Stenkowicz bore the brunt of your feelings. He's really a good guy. McGuire knew he couldn't send anyone to see you. He assumed Stenkowicz's good nature would garner your cooperation."

"Well, as usual, Johnnie, he assumed wrong. How did that guy ever become first assistant? Does he grate on everyone, or is it just on me, as a result of my meekness and timidity?"

"When he joined the office, I was assigned as his mentor. From the outset, I detected his ambition. In our office, new hires were eased in gently. The initial assignment often was to juvenile court, where you couldn't screw up. The judge controlled everything. You learned how to ask questions of police officers and witnesses. On occasion, you were afforded the opportunity to cross-examine the juvenile and his parents. Then, you would be off to the grand jury. You would prepare cases and would present them. You also would assist other prosecutors on their files.

"Then the big day arrives, your first trial. With labored breathing and sweaty palms, you pick your first jury and present your case. Little do you know that it's a case no one else wanted to try. It is of little significance and, most likely, is an absolute loser. You, of course, assume an indicted individual must be guilty and that the jury readily will agree. When word of a quick verdict is reached, you confidently report back to the courtroom for the good news only to be head-slapped by the 'not guilty' result. Crestfallen, you slink back to the office with hope everyone has left for the day. Rather, all are there. The other prosecutors barely acknowledge your presence as they speed by, more concerned with their own problems. If you're really snake-bitten, someone else also takes a verdict that afternoon. He or she enters beaming from that sudden success. Without any malevolence, your partner inquires how your trial is proceeding. With a lump in your throat, you lower your chin and mumble 'lost.' You receive that quick condolence, 'you'll win the next one,' as your compatriot merrily proceeds onward to celebrate with others.

"Days pass before you again enter that foreboding arena. This time you're filled with self-doubt and even more fear of additional humiliation. You assume another pounding will occur. This time, however, the case really is a better one, and you have the same trial judge, who now guides you through the trial. Subtlety through his demeanor, he makes the jury aware of his own feelings that the defendant is guilty. You win. Your skills continue to improve, and you slowly gain confidence that with arduous preparation coupled with excellent trial investigators you can win many more than you can lose. Defense attorneys, who usually are public defenders, begin to respect your ability and sometimes actually fear your competence. More guilty pleas begin to occur, even without the entry of plea bargains. If you're really fortunate to become very accomplished, you eventually try only the most difficult cases. You no longer fear defeat, because all know you try only those important cases that most prosecutors are afraid to prosecute. The stigma of losing no longer intimidates you. All the while, you seek justice. That is more important than a win. Better a guilty man go free than an innocent one be incarcerated.

"McGuire, he seemed cut from a different mold. He was on the fast track to the top. He thought he knew better than most. He took advice but often didn't follow it. He charted his own course, even to the disadvantage of others. Numerous detectives and investigators grew to dislike him after I left the office. He worked them like dogs, always asked for more, often more than he needed, and gave them very little credit for their efforts and his concurrent success. A prosecutor is only as good as his investigators and detectives. McGuire apparently very rarely acknowledged their efforts and contributions."

"Johnnie, how then did he ever become first assistant?"

"He became the prosecutor's attack dog and his overzealous fall guy. McGuire readily accepted his role. If things went south, McGuire would step forth and take the blame. He was the good soldier, willing to fall on his sword for his boss. Deep down, he's not a bad person.

He's just consumed with personal advancement. He hasn't comprehended that his thirst for success will drown him in the end."

"Well, Johnnie, I guess I added more water to his glass. Told the detective to inform McGuire I was playing tennis this weekend with my good friend, the governor. Told him I'd put in a good word for him and his boss. Heard they sought higher positions. Said I would see how I could help!"

"Yeah, McGuire got the message. No doubt that prompted his call. Any chance of him not indicting Melanie just evaporated."

"Look, the bastard was never going to let my daughter walk free. If he had any doubts, he wouldn't have so viciously opposed you at the bail hearing. You read him right. He thought this case was his ticket to fame and fortune. If I have anything to do with it, and I will, he'll see neither."

"Mr. Burnside, I'm afraid you've pushed him too far. He'll probably call you and Mrs. Burnside before the grand jury."

"No, he won't call me. There was a method to my alleged madness. If he didn't know before, he knows now that I'm a loose cannon. He can't risk giving me immunity for fear of what I might say. Hypothetically, if I were to tell the jurors I was the killer, what would he do? Indict me? On what evidence? My prints aren't on the gun. I can assure you. Who broke into the house? Would I have assaulted and drugged my own daughter and then set her up for murder, just to then get her off? That's preposterous! Don't you see, he can't call me before the grand jury or during the trial? He knows I'll screw it up. He thinks if anyone calls me, it will be you to demonstrate what a loving and caring person my daughter is. We both know I won't be a witness, for fear my real feelings toward Stafford will surface.

"As to Catherine, she would make a sympathetic witness. Much to my surprise, she liked Stafford. She didn't recognize him for what he was. The jury would be enamored by her grace and dignity. They would conclude that she couldn't produce a monster. Johnnie, I've saved you from him or you calling me. A tour de force, you might say!"

"I hope you're correct. As to Mrs. Burnside, I don't believe I'll call her as a witness."

"Why not?"

"For several reasons. First of all, if I call her, how can I not call you? The mother testifies, but the renowned father doesn't. What signal does that send? You're right. I can't call you. Even if McGuire doesn't try to antagonize you, he will bring out our business relationship. All you need is one juror to believe I was forced to defend Melanie, and that juror could poison the others. Secondly, Mrs. Burnside might do very well on direct examination, but she could wilt on cross. The net effect would be that McGuire, at worst, would neutralize her. A best, he would elicit some testimony that inadvertently could damage or diminish our defense. She isn't court-wise and, frankly, is too much a lady. Unintentionally, she would want to please the prosecutor as much as she would desire to please me. The net effect is a wash. Circumstances might alter my thinking. For now, however, I'm inclined not to use her.

"I forgot to mention that McGuire sent an investigator to the Princeton chief to uncover any sordid events in your past."

"Johnnie, you don't have to worry. That inquiry will go nowhere. The police chief and his fellow officers have been recipients of my largesse. I contribute to their charities and provide donations when municipal officials fail to meet the chief's budgetary requests. Need I say, I have excellent police protection?

"As to skeletons in my closet, I have none. Quasi-skeletons perhaps, but those missions are buried so deep in the bowels of the Pentagon that no Congressional subpoena or presidential inquiry ever would uncover them. As a soldier, I followed the orders of my generals. I did my duty in honor of my country and bear no shame for doing so. I will go to my grave without fear of meeting my Maker.

"With your permission, I'd like to sanitize Melanie's home. I have contacted the appropriate people to remove her living room rug, clean and paint the walls, and repair the sliding door. I'd like to start tonight. Everything will be completed by tomorrow afternoon."

"That's fine. Erika and I wanted Melanie to return with us to the home early tomorrow evening. We need her to show us exactly what the interior lighting was from initial darkness until her husband return home."

"I guess that's okay, as long as you drive her there and return her here. When she returned last night, it was quite evident that leaving her there alone for several hours was our mutual mistake. Everything still is too fresh. She still is reliving it."

"We'll arrive before sundown tomorrow. In the interim, please don't call the chief. I'd like to keep that information confidential. Any disclosure would have severe repercussions for my confidential source. That person is a good friend. I have no doubt that source will provide other salient information if it has a critical bearing on our defense."

"Mum's the word. Melanie will be awaiting your arrival. See you then."

17.

The following morning, Johnnie attended a case management conference at the Mercer County Civil Courts building. The matter was a complex civil case that required periodic monitoring to address discovery problems. Both sides were objecting to certain written questions that had been served by opposing counsel. Judicial intervention was required to determine which of the contested interrogatories had to be answered. Dates also had to be entered for the inspection and production of requested documents. The plaintiff's counsel had delayed in producing his expert reports, and both counsel accused the other of stalling in scheduling the depositions of various witnesses.

For Johnnie, the morning meeting in the products liability case was no different from scores of others he had handled on behalf of defendants. The plaintiff's counsel complained that the manufacturer was stonewalling his document request, while Johnnie proclaimed that the request was overly broad and requested the disclosure of trade secrets or confidential information. The plaintiff's attorney harped on the continuing severe physical and emotional suffering of his incapacitated client. Johnnie countered by sympathizing with the plaintiff's plight but stressing it was precipitated by the plaintiff's negligent conduct. In the end, the court ordered for an in camera inspection of specific documents, at which time the court would opine which documents had to be produced, what parts had to be redacted, and what sanctions would be meted out, if plaintiff's office, his client, or his experts revealed the contents to the press or public.

When the conference concluded, Johnnie ascended one flight of stairs and participated in a non-binding arbitration proceeding that centered on which driver had the green light and whether the plaintiff's detailed injuries were substantial enough to overcome the State's limitation barring recovery for non-permanent injuries. In this instance, Johnnie knew the proceeding was meaningless. Whoever lost, that party would pay the statutory appeal fee to vacate the award and would proceed eventually to trial, unless the trial judge, in response to Johnnie's future summary judgment motion, ruled that the plaintiff's injuries failed to meet the statutory threshold.

After the hearing concluded, the plaintiff's counsel informed him that he would file the trial de novo form. Johnnie joked, "Better you than me, Art. You're the one with all the money."

"Spoken like a true defense counsel, crying poverty like his parsimonious insurance carrier. See, I'm creating more billable hours for you, Johnnie. Just do me one favor. Don't file your summary judgment motion for twenty days. I have a two-week trial starting next Monday."

"You got it, Art. Is Watson's firm on the other side?"

"Yeah."

"Well, I hope you clobber him. His firm tried to steal one of my carriers by offering a lower hourly rate and a flat daily fee for trial days. Carrier nixed his overture. Recognized his offer for what it was. Cheap rates for cheap service. Good luck with him."

Later that afternoon, Johnnie and Erika were met at the door by Catherine Burnside, who escorted them to an elegantly furnished living room, resplendent with antiques and formal paintings. As they were being seated, Burnside approached from the hallway and mentioned, "Melanie just got out of the shower. Would you like C.C. to bring you tea or coffee?"

"No thanks. We're fine," replied Johnnie. As Catherine Burnside excused herself, Erika inquired, "C.C. – is that Mrs. Burnside's nickname?"

"I guess you could say so. I started calling her that after our first date. It's short for Catherine Clarendon. Her father was a very distinguished professor at Princeton, a brilliant scholar, and a real gentleman. One of the finest men I've ever met. Johnnie, were you in any of his classes?"

"Unfortunately, no. I knew he was a world-renowned antiquities expert and classical scholar. Also knew he was one of the Monuments Men during World War II. I majored in English and dabbled in psychology courses. In retrospect, I probably should have majored in history."

"Melanie was very close to her grandfather. Actually, she accompanied him on several trips to Europe and South America during the summers of her college years. She took his death extremely hard. Up to the end, he still was pursuing those who trafficked in stolen antiquities. A week before he died, he confided in me that he feared he might have uncovered a conduit in stolen antiquities here in Princeton. He inferred that it would shake the local legal community to its core if his intuition was correct. The suspect apparently took occasional trips to Munich and surrounding areas. He related that he still had to tie up some loose ends with the U.S. Attorney's office. Next thing I knew, he was dead. A passerby found him lying face down on McCosh Walk. He had bruises to his face and the right side of his neck. Glasses were broken. Wallet and watch still were on him.

"The police believed his heart gave way. For years, he had been experiencing cardiac problems. Due to our earlier conversation, I immediately thought he had been murdered, but the autopsy was inconclusive. What a shame. He was eighty-five. His mind still was very acute and insightful. He had a great sense of humor. Always had a kind and encouraging word. His heart literally may have been weak but figuratively it was strong, so strong. Johnnie, you really would have enjoyed his company. He probably watched and cheered for you. Loved football. Was an ardent Princeton rooter."

Burnside's words froze Johnnie. Munich trips, stolen antiquities, and possible links to the Princeton legal community seared his brain.

It couldn't be true. He knew only one Princeton lawyer who made such excursions. They shared the same DNA. The thought was impossible, so far-fetched and alien to his own moral fabric that he couldn't countenance or comprehend it. His father a thief and maybe a killer? Unthinkable, inconceivable, unimaginable. The man who instilled in him honor, respect, rectitude, responsibility, duty, courage, and, most of all, morality would not debase himself that way. Their bond and their beliefs were so intertwined. His father had been a church elder and had served on the Mercer County Bar's ethics committee. There had to be some mistake, some lacuna in the professor's hypothesis. Wouldn't an antiquities thief leave some obvious trail?

He had grown up with his father and mother. Never once did he see a Greek or Roman bust, relief, or any other telltale sign that his father was an art thief. Even now, he visited the family home weekly and had free roam of the house. His father didn't have expensive tastes or habits. He was down to earth and blended so well with others. Never showy or hedonistic, friend to all, that was Jack Fitzhugh. The professor was eighty-five with a failing heart. Were his powers of rationalization also failing? Had his synapses widened, causing improper transmittals that impaired his ratiocination?

Melanie's voice shocked him back from his nightmare. She appeared in the living room wearing a black velour jogging suit and gray sneakers. Gone was her disconsolate countenance replaced with a radiance Johnnie hadn't witnessed.

As if she read his thoughts, Melanie advised, "Robert Sutcliff called. All the area hospital administrators want me back. They are confident of my innocence. He assured me that the staff would be supportive, that there would be no hostility or avoidance. He has scheduled me for surgeries starting Monday. I feel like my life is being given back to me, at least for the moment. I need that routine, that stabilization, the concreteness and certainty that I belong to something. Without it, I feel aimless and devoid of any purpose. Dad said I need to return to our house for more pictures. I'm ready and anxious to get those visions behind me. There, we can talk about something that will prove my innocence to you. Then, maybe the prosecutor will realize I'm not the heartless woman he has depicted for the media and public."

Erika studied Melanie's tone and mannerisms. The change was dramatic, but that was fitting for a former actress. She still had reservations. Melanie declaimed her innocence, but she had witnessed many others do the same, only to be entwined in their pathological lies. Johnnie was much more trusting than she. Firsthand, she had experienced the deceit, dishonor, and disloyalty by advisors, agents, and sponsors on the tennis circuit. Of course, most were honest and admirable. Those who were not, however, appeared just as honorable and trustworthy as the others. Only through the nuances had Erica, upon reflection, stripped away the façade that separated the two. To her, Melanie appeared both naïve and calculating. Which was the real Melanie? One was innocent, the other a murderer. Erika knew she had to befriend Melanie to discern the truth. Johnnie was perceptive, but beauty could blind his senses. Melanie could be striking. Johnnie was no match. He would wilt like the others. She had to take the lead, be more interactive, and engaging. She was the investigator. That provided plausible deniability. She would trumpet Melanie's innocence before her. If Melanie was untruthful, Erika's enthusiastic support would lure and then ensnare her. Now was the time to play Melanie's strings.

"Melanie, McGuire is smart and persistent, but he also is a petty blowhard. Clearly, Mr. Sutcliff recognized you for what you are, a wronged spouse unfortunately pursued by a deluded and misinformed prosecutor. Your friends and associates will fill that emptiness until Johnnie and I can prove your innocence."

Johnnie, somewhat surprised by Erika's overt involvement, stated, "It's about to get dark. Let's go now. I want to take pictures during different times of the evening under lighting circumstances similar to that night. We'll all go together so we can discuss our staging issues. We'll stop at a deli on the way."

As Melanie opened her front door, the new paint smell wafted out. The white rug had been replaced by a beige one that blended harmoniously with the furnishings. Melanie described the lighting that illuminated the house through various states of the evening and then handed him a folder.

"This will prove my innocence." Johnnie started to open the folder but stopped as Melanie stated, "Several days before he left for Hawaii, Richard became even more agitated about his discovery. He really feared for his life yet refused to tell my father or the authorities. He had divulged his findings to John Furber, Wellington's Executive Vice President for Pharmaceutical Research and Development. Furber said he would investigate and get back to him. Weeks went by without a response. Richard sought him out. Furber seemed cold, almost distant. He asked Richard if he understood the magnitude of his allegation. The company had spent millions on the drug's research and development. The drug, Youtheria, was a blockbuster. There were no competitors. The baby boomers were euphoric. They believed they had found the fountain of youth for facial aging. While the rest of their bodies might be aging, the drug was erasing crow's feet, boosting collagen, and minimizing or eliminating brown spots when used in conjunction with the company's facial cream. Furber admonished him that nothing good could come from his contention. Reputations would be tarnished, jobs lost, and finances devastated. The drug had been approved by the FDA. Wasn't that enough? To assert such a baseless charge would shake, possibly destroy, the company's foundation. Wellington's parent Swiss company would be damaged severely. Furber cautioned that Richard was charting a very dangerous course. Neither he nor the company could protect him from those who suffered harm from his revelations. One never knew what people would do when livelihoods were threatened, careers destroyed, or families torn apart."

Melanie looked down and paused for a moment before adding, "Richard was shaken. He knew Furber was right. How could he convince the U.S. Attorney's office of the truth of his findings? The might of Wellington and the FDA would crush him. On the other hand, his conscience ate at him. Richard lived for his work. He believed he, in some small way, was helping the world. As a biochemist, he sought answers to life's scourges and maladies. It gave him a purpose, a way to do good in a world so populated with chaos, war, and political dysfunction. If he divulged his findings, that purpose would be obliterated. If he didn't, he would bear witness to the company's deceit. Millions would take a drug that for most was just a placebo. Some might see transitory facial improvement. The drug was not toxic. The Phase One Trial had proved that. Originally, Wellington had created the drug with the belief that it would cure melanoma and squamous cell carcinoma. The Phase Two study, however, failed to substantiate its efficacy. Like many drug companies, Wellington engaged an independent company to conduct the drug testing abroad. It was during those tests that the anti-aging properties were supposedly uncovered. Consequently, when the melanoma prevention and retardation claims were unsubstantiated, Wellington resubmitted the drug as a facial skin anti-ager."

Johnnie interrupted, "Why was the drug tested abroad?"

Melanie snickered, "Because tests can be falsified. The FDA allows pharmaceuticals to outsource their testing to clinical research organizations. Those concerns decide where the clinical trials will be conducted and who will be enrolled in the testing. If the tested drug is for both genders, the patient population should approximate 50 percent male and female and should be consistent with the age group for which the drug will be marketed. Some drug companies that shift their trials abroad also farm out all phases of the projected drug's development and testing. For-profit companies, not researchers associated with colleges, universities, and teaching hospitals, coordinate the testing. As a result, several problems can arise."

Johnnie interjected, "Like what problems?"

Melanie accelerated her pace. "Drug companies use foreign areas because labor is cheaper. Test enrollees can be paid a lot less. Doctors engaged in backward or impoverished countries are more likely to be tempted to shade the test results when tendered sums far in excess of their monthly wages. Fear of litigation is much lower, if existent. Regulations often are less or more pliable. Depending on the chosen country, diseases in a particular area can skewer results. Also, people in poverty-stricken regions might metabolize a drug differently than a well-nourished American. The poor and uneducated are easier to recruit. They may believe they are being treated for a particular disease when, in reality, they are being given a placebo rather than an actual drug. Those given the placebo can also be utilized to distort the results. The FDA doesn't have any authority in those foreign regions where an American drug company is performing the testing. Companies aren't required to report all studies managed overseas.

"The for-profit independent contractors, who oversee and implement the testing, solicit the enrollees, determine the rules for the clinical trials, conduct the trials, determine the results, prepare the report, ghostwrite the technical articles for the medical publications, and initiate the promotional campaigns. The FDA receives the information on these foreign trials from these independent contractors. Although the FDA has the authority to visit the foreign sites, it rarely occurs. It doesn't have sufficient manpower to visit all the sites. Moreover, the companies can withhold the foreign test data until the applications are submitted to the FDA for approval. At that point, it is too late for the FDA to inspect how the foreign trial was regulated, determine whether acceptable standards were followed, and ascertain whether data was altered. The FDA tries its best, but the task is overwhelming. There just are too many drugs tested overseas. The job is daunting enough when examining drugs tested here."

Johnnie asked, "Where are drugs tested overseas?"

"You name it: Africa, India, the former Eastern-Bloc countries, just to name a few. Don't get me wrong. Not all drugs tested overseas are manipulated. A pharmaceutical company takes a huge financial risk if it discovers an irregularity and fails to disclose it. Greed, however, has no limitation.

"Richard was certain he was correct. As a senior medical statistician, he was required to travel to sites in the U.S. and abroad to verify testing protocols and results. Youtheria was being tested in Bulgaria, Romania, and the Ukraine. Because of pigmented differences, it was decided not to perform testing in Africa. If the drug proved efficacious for Caucasians, then further research and testing would be implemented for African Americans, Asians, and so on.

"What he discovered was mindboggling. The testing was rigged. The participants were to be at least forty-five years old and were to have shown obvious signs of aging before being placed in the clinical trials. Richard determined physicians and clinicians also were accepting subjects in their early thirties. Facial photos were taken of all participants before testing was commenced. One group for six months was given Youtheria, while the other group was administered a placebo. The results weren't as promising as anticipated. Only about 30 percent of those ingesting the pill showed any facial improvement, and that alteration was no better than that produced by over-the-counter facial creams. Based on those results, Wellington knew that the FDA never would approve the drug's marketing. Wellington had spent years and millions attempting to create a drug that would impede and retard facial aging. The financial upside from such a drug would be staggering.

"Someone high in the corporate hierarchy deemed the results unacceptable and plotted another course. The testing protocol was altered. Wellington manufactured an over-the-counter facial cream similar to others already on the market. The cream was added to the testing procedure. Participants were required to utilize the cream daily with the drug. The facial improvements were marginal at best and short-lived. Pictures were taken of those facial improvements before they receded. Those photos then were contrasted to the pre-testing shots and were used to tout the drug's alleged effectuality."

Erika interrupted, "Why didn't Wellington just market the cream? I know for a fact those creams are money makers. Even with the number of brands, there's still a lot of money to be had."

Melanie replied, "Because they aren't the 'magic bullet.' At best, those creams last for only a short duration. They sell so well for that reason. Women don't want to lose the benefit those creams temporarily provide, so they buy and buy.

"Collagen is the support structure that provides our skin with that firm, young look. As we age, we lose collagen, and wrinkles, fine lines, and other skin blemishes start to appear.

"Facial skin creams contain ingredients that tighten the skin and, thereby, reduce the appearance of lines and wrinkles. Many of the utilized ingredients interact to restore the collagen that raises the sagging skin and restores its firmness. This skin reversal, however, is of short duration. To maintain the desired effect, the cream has to be applied often. Remember, these creams are marketed as cosmetics, not as drugs. They don't need the years of extensive testing and approval of the FDA.

"Moisturizers will temporarily plump the skin by infusing it with moisture, but these creams don't work like Botox. Botox is injected. It breaks the connections between nerves and muscles, thereby relaxing and paralyzing the muscle, preventing the formation of a wrinkle. Botox injections are expensive and must be repeated. Wrinkle-filling injections also are expensive and also must be repeated. Not many women can afford those continuing processes.

"Other expensive alternatives exist. Laser skin resurfacing creates microscopic tears deep in the skin. These tears cause the stimulation of collagen production. Chemical peels remove damaged skin levels, creating a more youthful appearance. Again, these procedures are expensive and sometimes painful. They are performed by superbly trained physicians.

"I'm not saying the anti-aging creams are useless. They have utility. They moisten and exfoliate the skin. They provide short-term skin enhancement. To provide longer effectiveness without reapplication, I believe ingredients would have to be injected under the skin. That requires a physician's assistance.

"In the future, will the cosmetic industry develop some more lasting product? Who knows? I'm not a dermatologist or a plastic surgeon. All I know is that today there is no drug that definitely retards or reverses facial aging. For that, you need the services of a plastic surgeon or the assistance of an expert makeup artist."

Erika asked, "How did your husband uncover this fraud?"

"Frankly, he was very lucky. Wellington paid the foreign doctors very well for their involvement in the testing process. Sums much more than they could ever earn by practicing medicine in their countries. At the outset, most, if not all, assumed the testing would be legitimate. Once it became apparent that the drug was ineffective, the money's lure overcame their conscience. Fortunately, the drug had no toxicity. It was more like the placebo. The test subjects weren't hurt by the drug. They just weren't helped. It didn't matter to them. They were poor people getting paid well for ingesting a pill they thought would protect their skin from melanomas and sarcomas. There were no side effects. It was a financial windfall for them. The doctors could sway their consciences, as long as the subjects weren't hurt. No one in their country's medical community would know, so there would be no repercussions. Even if they discovered the truth, how would it have mattered? The rich would undergo plastic surgery, so who really cared what happened to the drug. Of course, doctors not in the testing loop would envy those who were, but their time might come, if more drug companies used their country for testing. Surely, the politicians would promote it, and, no doubt, some were already on the take through Wellington and its contracting agency.

"As with any conspiracy, all you need is one disgruntled or disillusioned conspirator. Fortunately, or in retrospect unfortunately, one doctor had a conscience. That physician later surreptitiously approached Richard at a foreign conference and divulged the truth. He went so far as to relate how Wellington's subcontractor sought out identical twins as test subjects. Identical twins only represent about one-third of all twins. Medically, they are referred to as monozygotic twins. When a single egg is fertilized by a single sperm, and when that egg divides into two separate embryos, the twins have the identical DNA. They also are of the same sex. They may look very similar. It may be difficult to tell them apart. Yet, they may age a little differently.

What a boon for fraudulent testing. Take a picture of both twins at the commencement of the testing, but enter only one of the twin's names in the record. At the conclusion of the testing, use both pictures to show the supposed dramatic facial improvement. What could be better? No one would know that the younger-looking twin's photo was substituted for the older ones. That's why fraternal twins weren't sought. They don't have to be of the same gender, and they do not possess the identical DNA found in identical twins."

Erika broke in, "Will the doctor testify for us?"

"Not a chance. He wouldn't even provide Richard with a written statement. Richard had promised him anonymity. The man had a conscience, but he also valued his life and livelihood. Richard never told me his name, so there's no way we could locate him, much less convince him to come here."

Melanie withdrew a piece of paper from her pocket and handed it to Erika. "This proves the tests were manipulated."

Erika looked at the paper. It contained three colored photos. The top depicted the exterior of the Romanian test facility. The middle revealed the interior of a closet filled with vials of various substances. The bottom picture was a close-up of an aged laboratory table. On it were three bottles of a named substance Erika didn't recognize, four vials of Botox, several hypodermic needles, and towels spotted with a blue substance.

Erika looked up from the photos. Before she could speak, Melanie uttered, "The middle photo shows a typical storage closet where Wellington's testing contractor stored the various agents employed to manipulate the test results. Besides the obvious in the bottom photo are bottles of hyaluronic acid fillers utilized to treat deep smile lines, forehead wrinkles, and crow's feet. The fillers would be injected to present a more youthful visage. The blue spots on the towels are evidence that chemical peels were applied to some of the subjects to exfoliate the aged surface skin. You don't need a Romanian doctor to testify to the picture's content. Any dermatologist or plastic surgeon would suffice. If the testing was legal, none of these items would have been present. Richard gave a copy of these photos to John Furber. It represented indisputable proof that the earlier testing had been fallacious. Wellington knew its marketed drug was, to some degree, premised upon inappropriate testing. It could have stopped production or even done additional testing quietly. Instead, it silenced Richard.

"The one thing Wellington didn't consider was that I urged Richard to back up the photographic evidence. With my assistance and in my presence, Richard typed an 'In the event of my death' memo on our home computer. That memo is stored in our safety-deposit box with the original Romanian photos."

Melanie took back the paper and read the memo addressed to the authorities in which Richard outlined his position and duties with Wellington, the information divulged by the Romanian doctor, together with the doctor's photos, his conversation with Furber, and Furber's veiled threats.

She then handed the file back to Johnnie and exclaimed, "Give that to McGuire and see what he thinks of his case now!"

Johnnie, somewhat taken aback, replied, "He has the computer. At some point, his technicians will discover it. I'll be curious to see if he contacts me about it. If you're indicted, which we all expect, it means he has dismissed its evidentiary value and probity or hasn't uncovered it. Post-indictment, he has to reveal it through the discovery exchange. If not, we will and then cross-examine his lead detective and technician why it wasn't disclosed to us as an exhibit during discovery. The prosecutor must reveal any possible exculpatory evidence. He can't assume I already know it. Melanie, does anyone else know about the photos or Richard's statement?"

"No. I didn't tell my father. I thought I'd leave that to you, if you so choose. I was fearful he might inform the press or the prosecutor. He's smart, savvy, and very outspoken, but he's not a trial lawyer, although he frequently believes he knows more what to do at trial than the attorneys he employs."

Before Johnnie could misspeak, Erika answered, "Melanie, you're correct. Let Johnnie handle it. He knows how to deal with McGuire from past experience. Your father doesn't."

As the evening progressed, Erika took the requisite exterior pictures from the appropriate sides of the house as lights were turned off and on to match the illumination present on the night of the murder. Johnnie noted that Melanie's mood altered as the evening progressed. Her outward persona dimmed. She became more reticent and detached. By the time only the table lamp and the front exterior lights remained lit, she had become silent. Her earlier banter and interaction had receded. Clearly, she was reliving the night of the killing. Johnnie suggested they leave, and Melanie slowly nodded her agreement.

As they drove away, Johnnie tried to posture that evening. Because there was no plausible reason to assume Melanie was the intended target, the killer or killers had to know Stafford was returning home that evening, unless that night was an accidental choice.

Wellington would have known his travel plans because he was attending its conference. More than likely, the company booked the flights.

In either event, due to the length of the driveway and the surrounding forest, there were ample areas to hide and watch the evening unfold. Once all interior lights were extinguished, those lurking outside only had to wait a sufficient time to allow the Staffords to drift off into a deep sleep. How long would that take? An hour? Two? The murder occurred closer to darkness than daylight. That was obvious from Melanie's own recollection.

The photographs evidenced the coverup. The memo corroborated the photos and gave credence to Stafford's conversation with Furber.

Johnnie could depose Furber, but what would that gain? Furber would deny that Stafford provided the photos. If shown the photos, he would act shocked and express disbelief that the independent contractor had phonied the testing and that Stafford knew before the FDA gave its approval and only typed the memo to provide an alibi should the scheme be uncovered. After all, Stafford was a senior medical technician. He was to validate the protocols. He possessed the expertise. How could he not have uncovered the irregularities before the FDA gave its approval?

No, Johnnie wouldn't depose him. He would subpoena him to trial and would subpoena the testing results. How many times had Furber been on the witness stand? Probably none or very little. How many times had he appeared as a hostile witness in a criminal trial? Never, for sure. A different arena, a far different atmosphere for a novice. Let McGuire object to Johnnie's questions. Let the jury ponder why the State's representative was objecting to questions concerning a possible monumental fraud on the public. If Johnnie could get the photos and Stafford's memo before the jury, then Wellington would be on trial with Melanie. Then where would the jury's sympathy lie? With Melanie? With Wellington? Johnnie liked the odds, provided nothing else surfaced to upset them.

Little was said on the drive back. Johnnie found a classical music station to break the awkward quietude. Erika pretended to doze. In the rear, Melanie maintained her silence.

Upon their arrival, Johnnie walked Melanie to the door and cautioned her not to disclose the photos or memo to anyone. He said he would be in touch when something developed and asked her to call the office if she thought of anything important.

He urged her to be polite, friendly, and circumspect when interacting with associates and the public when she returned to work Monday. She should act professional and dignified under all circumstances. As a grieving widow and criminal victim, she should not be exuberant, even if others tried to lessen her pain. Most of all, she should not talk to or lash out at the press. Any inquiries should be directed to him upon advice of her counsel.

Johnnie warned that she might be met with stares or downward glances. She might overhear impolite or infuriating comments. Under no circumstances was she to reply. The ever-present cellphone would record her reaction, which then would find itself on the evening news. She was to maintain her work schedule but, otherwise, avoid public places and public functions. She was to let her parents do the food shopping and errands for the time being. With luck, some other tragedy would develop to distract the public's short-lived interest.

Melanie looked Johnnie directly in his eyes, placed her right hand on his upturned collar, and thanked him for his advice. She then opened the door and gracefully entered.

Closing the car door, Johnnie stated, "What a night."

"Especially the end," Erika retorted. "I loved how she touched your collar. I was waiting for a peck on the cheek."

"Erika, do I sense pangs of jealousy?"

"No, I sense an accomplished actress. You're so frozen by her looks that you miss the obvious. How about the drama? She takes a paper from her right pocket and then later pulls one from her left. I was waiting for a rabbit to jump from her coat. Why not produce both of the damn papers at once from one pocket?"

"How about she didn't want to wrinkle the photos?" Johnnie answered.

"Give me a fucking break, Johnnie! The photos were copies. She has the originals in the safety box. Are you so blind that you can't ascertain what's in a wrinkled photo? I remind you that the piece of paper was folded in half when she produced it. I grant you this helps her defense, but you'll have to tone down her staged responses. Otherwise, the only stage she'll be playing will be the one in a cell."

Johnnie drove Erika to her car. Erika started to exit the car and then suddenly turned back and kissed him on the cheek.

"You look so miserable. That's for the kiss you didn't get from her. See you tomorrow. Sweet dreams."

Johnnie smiled at her. She read his inner feelings. When Melanie touched his collar, he actually feared she was going to kiss him. Yes, he now felt miserable but not from an unwanted kiss. The evening's end brought him back to his own fears. Burnside's comments seared his insides. Could it be? Was his father really involved in stolen antiquities? Was Melanie's grandfather murdered? Did his father kill the grandfather of a woman he was defending for allegedly killing her husband? The proposition was insane, although circuitous. It was eating at his soul. He had predicted nothing good would come from his involvement in Melanie's defense. He had hoped to somehow extricate himself from Melanie's defense, but this was not the route. No, Burnside's idle chatter was just that. There was no way his father was involved in something so base. Tomorrow, he would talk to him and extirpate such nonsensical thoughts. Now all he had to do was get some sleep. He feared that might be impossible.

18.

Johnnie awakened from a fitful sleep feeling more somnolent than rested. Despite how much he dreaded this morning, he knew he couldn't avoid the subject. To ask his father if he was involved in the antiquities trade would border on the obscene. He could not stomach such an inquiry. The man was his father, a man he loved deeply. A false inquiry would sever their bond irreparably. He would rather die than make that egregious blunder. He didn't believe it anyway, so why even bother. Why? Deep down, he knew why. Erika heard Burnside's remarks. She knew his father had made several trips to Germany. Would she also have considered the same erroneous link? Not much eluded her. She would not verbalize her concern, but it would be there. That he would not tolerate. He would not let his father be besmirched by false innuendo. He deftly would approach the subject with his father, receive a logical response, and banish forever this nonsense.

He showered and skipped breakfast, knowing he'd have trouble keeping anything down. His father was an early riser and would be at the office. It provided an avenue to escape the morning solitude precipitated by his wife's passing.

Johnnie pulled into the office lot, saw the familiar vehicle, and caught his breath. The dreaded moment had arrived. He prayed his initial misgivings had been unfounded.

"Good morning, boss."

"Boss? Since when have I been your boss?" smiled his father. "Any new developments in the case?"

"What case?" Johnnie replied.

"Son, it's the only case that has you scared shitless," laughed his father. "Sit down and take the world's weight off your shoulders. As I told you before, this case will pass as they always do. We may get bludgeoned and bloodied, but we will survive with or without Burnside's work. I'm having lunch with Judge Ellison. His son-in-law has been hired as general counsel for our state's next casino. I pushed hard for Jeff's elevation to the bench. He had faced fierce opposition from a particular state senator. The governor pulled the senator aside and promised him something in return for his cooperation. Jeff got his judgeship and said he never would forget my good words. I believe we may have a new client in the foreseeable future.

"Hear anything from McGuire?" his father returned to case.

"No. Erika and I took Melanie back again to the scene so she could recreate the interior lighting conditions that were present the night of the murder."

"Was Burnside present giving his advice?"

"No. So far, he's been the good soldier and followed my gently referenced requests. He told me yesterday that Melanie's grandfather was Professor Clarendon. Did you have any of his courses at Princeton?"

"No, I now wish I had. He once spoke at the Princeton Bar Association meeting. I had an opportunity to speak to him. For all his renown, he was a down-to-earth gentleman."

"What did he speak about?"

"His specialty, classical art and the wartime plunder of antiquities. He showed us pictures of works he and others had retrieved. Of course, he was dismayed that much still had not been located. What a tragedy! Such priceless beauty and history irretrievably lost."

"Did he mention what cities and regions he worked in as a Monuments Man?"

"Basically, all through France, Germany, Austria, and parts of Italy."

"All that intrigues me. Maybe I'll tag along with you on your next Germany visit. I'd love to roam the streets of Berlin, Munich, and Nuremberg."

"That trip you'll probably have to plan yourself. I think I've seen it all. Next is Greece, maybe Italy and Switzerland. Maybe go three to four weeks next time. You're welcome anytime. Would love to have you. Would be fun, so long as you left thoughts of work at home. Maybe once this case is behind you?"

"I wish that were yesterday. Once the indictment comes, the frenzy will commence. I might need you to placate Burnside if he becomes too intrusive. As it is, I'll be bouncing some ideas off you once discovery commences. Just promise me you won't wander back to Europe before this thing is over."

"How about Latin America? Buenos Aires or Rio, do they count?"

"Yeah, Dad, everyplace counts. Enjoy your lunch with Ellison. Butter him up well. I fear we might need all the work we can get."

Johnnie left relieved. His father had been forthright. There was no evasion or misdirection. He was the same old dad. He had met Clarendon and spoke glowingly of him and his work. He welcomed him on his next European foray. Two or three weeks? Johnnie knew with his schedule, that would never happen. A week? Ten days? That was doable. He could hold the judicial dogs at bay for that duration, if not the constant client emails. Erika could fend off those annoyances. She could melt even the most abrasive client. Johnnie felt buoyed by his father's directness and humor. Sure, he might have to hold his father to his promise. But Buenos Aires? Rio? He knew there was no real interest there. What could be of interest in Buenos Aires? Germany, yes, but Buenos Aires, no way.

Johnnie turned the hallway's corner and almost ran into Erika.

"I've been looking for you," she stated. "I've been mulling over the case. We still don't know when Stafford arrived home. We know the flight took off late, he arrived home after she fell asleep on the couch, but we don't know when that flight arrived in Newark. We need to know. We then can guesstimate his arrival home. Melanie said he drove his own car to the airport, so all he had to do was get his luggage, if it wasn't a carry-on, take the bus to the lot, and drive the 90 to 120 minutes home."

"Does it really matter?"

"Sure does. What if he got home really late? Add an hour for him to fall asleep, and there wouldn't be much of a window before daylight. If so, this would aid Melanie's defense. Remember, the maid always arrived early. When she appeared that morning, Melanie was still on the floor and awakened only when she heard the maid's shriek. The narrower the window, the more favorable for us."

"Good point. Check with Melanie. I think she said it was an American flight. Ascertain the departure time from Honolulu, the arrival and departure times at Dallas, and the arrival time in Newark. I have a one o'clock deposition in Flemington in the Stroper case. I'll call you later on your cell."

The deposition took longer than anticipated as a result of the contentious personality of the plaintiff's counsel. Fortunately, Johnnie was able to contact the case managing judge who ordered that plaintiff's counsel allow his corporate client to answer the questions.

As he left Flemington, Johnnie called Erika.

"Any progress on the flight information?"

"Yeah. I spoke to Melanie. Stafford flew direct to Honolulu on a Sunday. The conference was to commence Monday and end Thursday. Stafford told her he wanted to visit the volcano on the Big Island on Friday so he would be checking out of The Royal Hawaiian on Thursday. He planned to fly Saturday to LA and then from L.A. to Newark through Dallas on Sunday. The expected Newark arrival time was 7:55 p.m. Are you going to be home tonight?"

"Unless you have a hot date for me, I will."

"That means I'll call you tonight, once I've gotten the flight's actual arrival time. Oh, I forgot to mention that Melanie said she last spoke to Richard that Wednesday. Due to the time difference and her busy surgical schedules on Thursday and Friday, she didn't have the opportunity. That Saturday, she was on emergency call and actually had to work. Sunday, she had free, as she earlier told us. Richard called her from Dallas that Sunday and related that his connecting Dallas to Newark flight was delayed. I'll call you later."

That evening after dictating for his client a summary of that afternoon's deposition, Johnnie turned on ESPN. Duke was playing UNC. The score was tied with two minutes to play in the half. Duke called a timeout. A commercial broke in, and Johnnie headed for the refrigerator. The doorbell rang.

"Who is it?" he yelled.

"It's me, stupid. Open the door."

Johnnie opened the door, and Erika quickly rushed by him.

"How many beers have you had?"

"None. Why? Do I look inebriated?"

"No, but you'll wish you were. We have a problem, a big fucking problem!"

"What now?"

"That Dallas flight wasn't delayed. It took off on time and arrived in Newark on time."

"So? Stafford still would have to get his luggage, his car.... Maybe there was some delay?"

"Johnnie, you don't get it! He wasn't on the fucking plane to Newark!"

Mouth agape, Johnnie looked like he had been smacked in the face.

"Once I learned the flight was on time, I called back American and impersonated Melanie Stafford. I said my husband was on a time-and-expense account and, in his haste, had forgotten to save his tickets to and from Hawaii. I informed her that my husband needed a copy of both tickets so he could receive reimbursement from Wellington. I gave her Melanie's address and requested she send the tickets to Melanie's home address. I asked her to pull Richard's flight records just to make sure everything was correct. The lady put me on hold while she searched the computer. Guess what? Stafford didn't leave Honolulu on Saturday. He took a red-eye Wednesday night! He arrived in Dallas Thursday and immediately flew to Regional Southwest Airport, which is in Fort Myers, Florida. On Sunday, he flew via American to Newark, arriving at 10:15 p.m. That's why he was late. Mark my words, the bastard was cheating on her."

Johnnie just stared at her.

"Do you know what this means, Johnnie? If McGuire does what I did, we're in big trouble."

"Hold on, hold on! Let's think this through," he replied.

"Johnnie, don't you see? She killed him. She must have known he was cheating on her. Maybe this wasn't the first time. Maybe this was just the last straw. She's got the perfect alibi, Wellington!"

"Wait a minute. You're jumping to a rash conclusion. Let's look at this from the Wellington angle. If Wellington had engaged someone to kill him, would they have followed him to Hawaii? If so, then the killer would have planned to kill him there or staged an accident leading to his death. If not, the plan hadn't been set in motion before Stafford left Honolulu. Did the killer follow him to Florida and not have the opportunity there? Then, he would have had to follow him to Newark. How would he have known which flight he would be taking back to Newark? Without that information, the killer couldn't have purchased a ticket and passed through the security point. I guess he could have checked the departure board and purchased a ticket for one or more flights to Newark. He would have known the flight was to Newark because Wellington's corporate office probably booked the original flights for him. Let's say he was able to secure a ticket. Why didn't he kill him in the Newark parking lot or run him off the road on one of those winding Hopewell Township roads? Why make it a break-in? On the other hand, if Wellington wanted to frame Melanie, the only way to accomplish that was to stage a home invasion and a killing."

"Wait a minute, Johnnie. That now makes no sense. Why would Wellington, knowing that Stafford had uncovered testing falsification, stage a break-in by breaking the sliding door? Shouldn't the killer have murdered them both, ransacked the house, stolen TVs, jewelry, silverware, and such?"

"No, Erika, because there wasn't time. His flight was too late."

"Not really."

"Erika, how about the possibility that no one followed him to Hawaii? The killer could have known his return time from the scheduled ticket. All he had to do was case the place that evening and wait."

"Possibilities. There are a lot of possibilities, Johnnie. All I can say is there is one certainty. We need Stafford's cellphone records sooner rather than later. He had to make calls to someone in Florida, and that person probably called him."

"Erika, maybe that person had information on Wellington, and Stafford had gone there for that reason."

"Maybe. Whichever way, Johnnie, one of us will be heading to south Florida once those records arrive. Let's hope McGuire's boys are so confident that they don't contact American."

"Erika, let's keep this from Melanie. Either way, it's going to be upsetting. We don't need that now. As to Florida, you're going. Your wiles are captivating. Mine are nonexistent. Tomorrow, call the phone carriers and prod them for the records. If they are resisting the subpoena, let me know. I'll then call their corporate counsel."

"Are you going to discuss this development with your father?"

"In time. I want those phone records first. I fear the person on the other line of those calls might determine Melanie's fate. Get some sleep. Let me do the tossing and turning. Unfortunately, it's getting to be a bad habit."

"Johnnie, we can only follow the evidence. We didn't create this scenario. In the end, we'll walk away from this mess. We will have done the best that we could do. That's all Burnside requested, and that's what he'll get. Losing sleep isn't going to alter the outcome. Our sanity and health are more important than the whys and wherefores. I don't want to see bloodshot eyes tomorrow."

Erika blew him a kiss before closing the door.

Johnnie turned off the incessant sports babble and walked again to the refrigerator. This time he would get a beer to dull his thoughts and anxieties. Was he defending a killer or a wronged spouse? Did it really matter? Either way, his and Melanie's lives now were interwoven. Not lovers, not really friends, rather two people brought together under the worst of circumstances. He feared neither would walk away unscathed when the story line was completed. Had their lives intersected for a purpose? Was it preordained, or was it just a cruel and random twist of fate? He would never know the answer. He just knew he would have to endure what was forthcoming.

19.

No matter what he tried, Johnnie couldn't fall asleep. What would those phone records reveal? Suddenly, it dawned on him. In one sense, it didn't matter. Lover or not, Wellington still was a major player in Melanie's defense. Stafford's email was embedded in the seized computer. McGuire's technical staff would unearth it. McGuire might not accept its relevance or authenticity, but it was still there. In one way or another, McGuire would have to deal with it. He had no doubt McGuire would dismiss it. He had no other viable alternative. He coveted the prosecutor's job. In fact, he lusted so much for that position that his desideration blinded his reasoning.

The initial arrest had been sudden but explainable. A murder had occurred, and the weapon was found next to Melanie. The local police had arrested her. Given the scene, that made sense. Had the arrest not occurred, the locals would have been chastised. Without really delving into the details, McGuire pushed forward with celerity and with venom. At the bail hearing, he shouted for justice. The woman was evil. The evidence was overwhelming. She would flee if allowed bail. With those public comments, how could he now investigate Wellington? He would look like a fool, a hotspur, a person whose reckless judgment debarred any realistic consideration for the prosecutor's position.

No, if he read McGuire correctly, Johnnie recognized that there would be no investigation of Wellington. Johnnie was almost certain of that. So what could he do to force the issue? It came upon him like a lightning bolt. He would send a letter to McGuire and would enclose a copy of Stafford's email together with a copy of the three photographs. He would request McGuire obtain the names of all test subjects as well as all test results. He also would require that McGuire subpoena Furber for trial, a trial he knew was forthcoming. The likelihood of McGuire's cooperation was almost nonexistent. McGuire's recalcitrance then would provide the impetus for his own motion before the court to issue an order requiring that Wellington produce the testing information for discovery and that Furber be compelled to appear for trial. To be sure, Wellington's own counsel would oppose the motion vigorously. His motion might be a long shot, but he had nothing to lose. It would be an appealable issue if the jury's verdict was unfavorable.

Johnnie had no viable alternative. He couldn't institute upon Melanie's behalf a wrongful death suit against Wellington. That wouldn't accomplish anything. Due to the criminal case, all civil discovery would be held in abeyance until the criminal trial had been concluded. Wellington, of course, would resist discovery until the trial's conclusion. He would have to concur, because he could not submit Melanie to answering lengthy interrogatories, nor could he submit her to days of deposition testimony by skilled defense counsel whose courtroom experience and trial savvy would far outweigh McGuire's.

No, the letter would be his modus operandi. He would send his request by mail and by fax to McGuire and, more importantly, to Detective Stenkowicz. He knew Dan would go immediately to McGuire and offer to lead the Wellington investigation. He was even more certain that McGuire would emphatically shut him down. There would be no investigation. McGuire's response wouldn't be an enraged phone call or sarcastic, bombastic letter. No, the indictment would be fast and furious. Dan Stenkowicz would be his witness, even if McGuire never called him. Johnnie immediately dictated the letter. It would be faxed within minutes after Fitzhugh and Fitzhugh opened that morning for business.

Stenkowicz saw the fax, read it and the attachment, and then mused to himself and hurried to McGuire's office.

"Have you seen this?"

"Yeah. So what?"

"Terry, do you want me to contact Wellington?"

"No! Fitzhugh will get my response shortly after the next grand jury session," he angrily responded. He then added, "The GSR test came back. She's got residue on her. She fired the fucking gun. Fuck her! Fuck him! Fitzhugh can obfuscate all he wants. Stafford's all mine. Let Johnnie come groveling to me for the plea bargain. He's a little too late!"

Stenkowicz nodded and left McGuire to his gloating. He inwardly laughed. Johnnie was Stradivari, and McGuire was his violin. He had no doubt Johnnie would call him as a witness. He could see the courtroom scene unfolding with such clarity. McGuire would take the bait. He wouldn't be able to resist. He would strut about and pose one question on cross: "Did Burnside cooperate with him?" Then, Johnnie would lower the boom. He could hear his own response resonating, and the jury's cascading laughter. No, Johnnie hadn't lost his touch, and yes, he might be asking him for a job reference.

20.

Two Weeks Later

Dan Stenkowicz entered McGuire's office and immediately sensed the prosecutor was even more tetchy than usual. The information he had to relay only would amplify his boss's foul mood.

"The Glock info finally arrived from Austria. It's not helpful. The Glock 17 was purchased in 1988 in Munich by one Seigfried Hauer. He died in 1992. There was no subsequent gun registration there or in the U.S. Neither Melanie Stafford nor her husband ever purchased a gun where a registration was filed. Neither attempted to obtain a permit to carry, or State records would have indicated that the appropriate motion was filed and denied. We already know there were no prints on the gun or on the shell casings."

McGuire interrupted and responded, "So what? Maybe she wore gloves when she loaded and fired the weapon. All I know is that the GSR test revealed powder residue on her left palm. She fired the weapon, and that's all we need. She probably wiped the gun and the three shells clean after she killed him."

"Terry, if she did that, then why didn't she clean her hands? She had plenty of time to do that."

McGuire surprisingly smiled before stating, "Because she probably had no inkling that a scientific test could uncover microscopic evidence of blowback powder when she pulled the trigger. Hell, she spends most of her waking hours putting people to sleep, not killing them. I don't care how smart she is or how long she planned this murder. She had to be rattled after she pulled the trigger, not once but three times. The sound had to be deafening to her. Her first instinct would be to assume someone else may have heard it. It wasn't raining or thundering. While the neighbors weren't close, the night was still. There would have been minimal, if any, vehicular traffic that early. When did she kill him: one, two, three o'clock in the morning, or somewhere around then? If later, she knew the cleaning lady would arrive early.

"She staged this damn killing. She probably knocked over the lamp and table after the fact and purposely fell on them. The cuts were to the bridge of her nose and forehead. There were no hematomas to the occipital, basilar, or temporal areas. There was no bruising on her neck. You mean to tell me that her alleged assailant wouldn't have applied pressure to her neck as he was allegedly drugging her? His arm would have been pressed tightly against her neck as he was pressing the cloth against her nose and mouth. There should have been welts or surface bruising to her neck, and there was none. No, she panicked. When you panic, your thought processes accelerate to the detriment of your reasoning. She thought she had planned for everything, but she couldn't plan for the rush and horror that suddenly engulfed her.

"We know she's an accomplished and well-respected physician. I don't doubt for a moment that she has empathy for those she sees on the operating table. That empathy ironically is what will convict her. Once she pulled the trigger, she realized the enormity of her act. This was not a sixty-minute tele-drama interspersed with multiple commercials. Her husband's blood didn't appear in just a little puddle. It continued to flow over her white rug. Brain matter flew out of the back of his head and mixed with the blood as it sprayed on the back wall. Even if this was a passion killing, she had to have some residual feeling for him, especially once she saw all the gore. Her subsequent actions went into overdrive, but her reasoning slowed. That she hadn't prepared for, and that is what will be her downfall.

"In three days, I'm taking this case to the grand jury. Don't worry: I'm not calling you as a witness. All I need is one of the Hopewell Township cops and the GSR test. I don't care how she got the gun.

She fired it, and that's all I need. Let Fitzhugh be surprised when he learns the existence of the third party to this unseemly triangle."

21.

Three Days Later

A little more than two weeks had elapsed since her call to American Airlines. In the interim, Erika had spoken to the EMTs who had responded to the crime scene, examined and treated Melanie, and thereafter transported her to the hospital. All described that Melanie had been extremely distraught. She had appeared as very agitated and frantic. She had repeatedly stated, "They killed him." None of the EMTs had pressed her as to the identity of "they." That was left for the police to investigate.

The EMTs were more concerned with Melanie's well-being than with her guilt or innocence. When the police arrived, they described her earlier mental and physical state while also mentioning the comments she had voiced to them. If questioned on the witness stand regarding any assumptions they had formed, all replied that they were trained emergency personnel and lacked the expertise to posit any opinion on her guilt or innocence. Most importantly, they all concurred that Melanie's emotions were real, not feigned. Her external injuries were self-evident and easily could have occurred during a struggle. Either she could have fallen on the overturned objects, or they could have landed on her. While the surface cuts were obvious, Melanie seemed more emotionally frazzled than in acute physical pain.

From her interview, Erika concluded that all three technicians would corroborate Inez Garcia's testimony regarding Melanie's appearance and her comments on the assault.

Erika also had reached out to Melanie, who indicated that she had been working without any adverse incidents. She had not been confronted by anyone and had not experienced any overt hostility. Heeding Johnnie's instructions, Erika avoided divulging to Melanie the stratagems he intended to employ during his interactions with McGuire. When questioned about what was transpiring with her case, Erika only responded that Johnnie was continuing his investigation and was awaiting information from the prosecutor's office. Erika added the information actually didn't have to be released unless and until an indictment was handed down. From prior conversations, Melanie understood that indictment was almost a certainty.

After spending all morning and a good part of the afternoon interviewing witnesses to a construction accident, Erika exited the general contractor's office and realized she was famished. After starting her car, she turned on a local sports station. Nothing like sports drivel to void one's mind of tension and anxiety, she thought. Almost instantaneously, she knew she was wrong. A bulletin crossed the air waves. It came from a news reporter standing outside the Mercer County Courthouse. "Breaking news," he uttered in an excited voice. "Well-known physician Melanie Stafford was just indicted for the brutal murder of her husband."

"So much for lunch," Erika muttered to herself. She activated the car phone and headed directly for the office. Now the hand-holding and encouragement would be required. Melanie would need to be consoled and bolstered. Burnside would have to be constrained and placated. The legal game would commence in earnest. Everything would accelerate to be followed by obfuscation, posturing, and delay. Then the anticipated day would dawn, the players would take their positions, the judge would mount the referee's chair, and the players would start pounding each other into submission.

The spectators, in this case, the jury, would root for one player or the other – or maybe neither. Their alertness would fluctuate with lassitude and boredom. Regardless, the players would pound their points at them, hoping that some would be heard, grasped, and accepted as actual truths. The player with the most supposed truths might, if lucky, actually win the match. All would be in the hands of the spectators who didn't pay to enter the stadium, didn't want to be there, and couldn't wait to leave to return to the banality of their daily regimen.

22.

November 1986
Northern New Jersey

It had been twelve years since their initial meeting. The German had been true to his word. He had made the requisite contacts. He had wired funds to numerous offshore accounts held by the American and had forwarded shipments from Buenos Aires.

At first, purchases were initiated covertly by various European museums, large and small. Recently, however, a new dynamic had arisen. The individual market had blossomed. Wealthy Europeans, with money to burn and status to be elevated, had entered the market. Some purchased for individual pleasure. Others viewed the works as investments to be held short term then resold for substantial gain.

The German suggested expanding the market to the States. Surely, American museums and tycoons would salivate at the opportunity. The American quickly dispelled the overture. Now was not the time. The risk was too great. Certain Americans, who served in the war, specialized in searching for the stolen art and antiquities. Those men wanted the thieves prosecuted and the booty returned.

The Europeans were willing to overlook past transgressions and not ask questions. All they sought was the retrieval of the lost treasures.

Everything had been running smoothly. Did not the German agree that his profits had been far more than anticipated? The German inwardly knew others would conclude their profits were obscene.

The American handed him a photograph. Depicted was a bronze sculpture of a scantily clad youth with a baton in his outstretched hand.

"A runner at Olympus?"

The American uttered, "Probably from 150 BC. Turn over the picture."

The German complied and regarded the seven-figure sum.

The American added, "We won't take a dollar less. Let's get an early dinner. Your flight leaves in five hours."

The German nodded and smiled. Yes, the American was cautious and rightly so. There was no reason to overreach. There were more than enough European clients. Leave America alone.

23.

Princeton, New Jersey

Ensconced in the firm's library and mired in dictating a brief in opposition to the plaintiff's appeal in a Dram Shop case, Johnnie was startled when his cell phone rang. After telling his secretary to hold all calls, he inadvertently had forgotten to silence his phone. As he reached to turn off the device, he noticed it was Erika. At the expense of losing his train of thought, he answered.

"Hi, what's up?"

"What's up? Where are you? In a cave?"

"I might as well be. I'm toiling away on our opposition brief in the Maranz case."

"Well, I'm here to rescue you from your labors. Breaking news! Melanie has been indicted!"

Even though he knew it was inevitable, the sudden news rattled him.

"How did you learn of the indictment?"

"Just heard it on the car radio, which means McGuire, or his boss, has held a news conference or will be doing so soon."

"Knowing McGuire, that's his way of responding to my email and letter with the Wellington test photos. I guess it was too fanciful to think he would pause in his rush to judgment to explore Wellington's possible involvement. I hope you don't have any plans for tonight. I want you to accompany me. We're going to see Melanie and Burnside.

I want to quell his explosions before they reach the press. She's going to need some reassurance and hand-holding. Hopefully, she's already home. Where are you now?"

"Until I heard the news flash, I was on my way to a very late lunch. I'll hit a deli and head back. Should be there in twenty to thirty minutes."

"I'll call Burnside. If there's a change in plans, I'll get back to you. Pick up an extra sandwich. Just another dinner on the run."

Johnnie clicked off and called Burnside's cell. Clearly, Burnside had not heard the news, or he would have called the office. Now Johnnie would bear Burnside's fulminations directed at McGuire and his office. Aspersions were one thing. Threats were another. These had to be silenced before they were uttered. What Burnside did behind the scenes could not be averted. That was his domain.

What concerned Johnnie were Burnside's overt actions. Burnside was a doer. Action was his realm. Others might internalize their aggression and hatred, never letting it boil to fruition. That was not Burnside. He would strike quickly. Maybe by stealth, but the onslaught would be sudden and overwhelming. The recipient would be shocked and routed. What might work on the battlefield or in the boardroom would be ineffectual in the court of public opinion. Johnnie knew he had to silence Burnside before he misspoke and unintentionally damaged Melanie's defense.

Johnnie had no doubt that McGuire and his boss were in Burnside's crosshairs. What he did to them covertly was not his concern. That was a foregone conclusion, once Melanie had been arrested. The public arena, however, was Johnnie's. What was said was his province. He knew not to provoke or alienate. His voice would be one of reason and civility buttressed by logic and vindication.

"Hello, Johnnie, only have a couple of minutes. I'm rushing to a board meeting. What can I do for you?"

"Mr. Burnside, did Melanie work today?"

"She had several morning surgeries, but she should be home now or at least heading there."

"Good. Would you call Mrs. Burnside and tell her Erika and I will be there soon?"

"Sure. Is there anything I need to know or can help you with?"

"I want to be with Melanie. I just heard she was indicted."

"Those fucking bastards! They will rue the day they did this! McGuire can forget about being Mr. Prosecutor, and his boss's desire for a judgeship is gone! Oh so gone!"

"Mr. Burnside, I'm sure it is. You have to promise me you will not voice those opinions to the press. In fact, you have to promise me you won't talk to the press. Believe me: Nothing good can come of it. We can't have any distractions. You know the press. They feed off distress, misfortune, and misery. It's their staple. Killing sells their papers and pays their salaries. You and Melanie are just their fodder. They care no more for you or Melanie than you do for McGuire. Sensationalism sells. Happiness and harmony don't. I beg of you, for Melanie's sake, please do not speak to the press or call the prosecutor's office.

"What you do secretly to derail the aspirations of McGuire and his boss is not of my concern. Even if it were, I know I have no power to dissuade you. But for Melanie's sake, I beg of you to remain silent, no matter how prodded you are by the press. If approached in person, your only response should be that you fervently stand behind your daughter and her innocence. Any other inquiries should be directed to me upon my advice. This is critical! I don't want to be hounded by the press for any responses made my Melanie or her family.

"A case such as Melanie's is won in the courtroom, not in the papers. A misspoken word or statement could unfavorably predispose our jury pool. At the outset, the deck is always stacked in favor of the prosecutor in any murder case. Our job is to chip away at that advantage, and chip away we certainly will. What we want to avoid are outside pretrial distractions that unintentionally might ease the prosecutor's burden. Promise me you won't be one of those distractions.

"I know you have close ties to the governor. What you want is his sympathy, not his ire. He is a politician and a good one. For any politician there is one golden rule, self-preservation at any cost. Politicians thrive on adulation and power. Their thirst is insatiable. Whatever you do, don't let the governor quench his thirst by gulping away at Melanie's freedom."

"As I told you earlier, I get it. Against my better nature, I'll rein in my natural impulses. Melanie's life is in your hands, Johnnie. To use an apt analogy, I'm your owner. There's one play left in the game, the biggest game of your life. The game-ending pass is coming to you. I know it. The coach knows it. The quarterback knows it, as do the defensive backs. Don't drop it. If you do, you and I both know there will be no tomorrow. You will be cut and cut summarily. After all, we all know it's just a business. Life goes on. A new receiver is signed, and you look for employment elsewhere. Dejected and disillusioned no doubt, but you will survive, maybe even catch on with another team and revive your career. But you never will forget that dropped pass, nor will your teammates, your fans, or even your family. If the dropped ball had feelings, I wonder how it would have felt. Well, we will never know.

"What I do know is how I will feel, how Catherine will feel, and most importantly, how Melanie will feel. Her life, as she knew it, will be over, as will ours. You, Johnnie, who knows? You may get to chart a new course. Melanie, however, will languish in a cell, a hellhole, surrounded by society's human vermin. She will be preyed upon by the skulls and jackals that floated through their lives until deservedly caught in the prosecutorial net. The flotsam and jetsam of society. The human waste discarded to our society's architectural bowel, the impregnable prison. Don't let that happen, Johnnie. I pray to God for Melanie's sake and our sake it doesn't happen. And, Johnnie, I also pray for your sake it doesn't happen. Hell hath no fury like a woman scorned or a father betrayed.

"I'll be home as soon as I can conclude the director's meeting. Call me if any further crises occur. Until then, I know you will comfort Melanie and counsel her wisely. And, yes, I will be the good foot soldier and obey your requests. For both of us, let's hope your intuition and counsel was the wiser option."

Johnnie heard the phone click and sat back in stunned silence. The bastard had made his thoughts crystal clear. Win or get set to be destroyed. Burnside would pull his files and badmouth him and the firm to any other claims manager, corporate executive, and politician who crossed his path. Burnside would upend his life as punishment for his daughter's conviction. If this were a television drama, Burnside's threat would have been visible. But there was no tape. Burnside was dead serious. He would pummel Johnnie with as much force as possible, if Melanie's life was altered.

What out did Johnnie have? If he resigned as counsel, Burnside still would unleash his fury. It would appear to the public that Melanie was guilty. Johnnie knew he was viewed as an ethical and accomplished trial lawyer by the legal community and the public. His withdrawal would be tantamount to signaling Melanie's guilt. He couldn't cite health as a reason. He had no infirmities. To claim to the contrary would be detrimental to the firm's business.

No, he was stuck. Burnside had forced his hand. Burnside wanted to control this passion play but knew he couldn't. Well, Burnside would get his wish in a way he hadn't anticipated. Originally, Johnnie had decided to keep Burnside out of the loop. That, in retrospect, was a mistake. No, now Burnside would be in, way more in than he could have hoped for.

If Melanie was convicted, Burnside would play a prominent part. Burnside would get to see all the prosecutor's evidence obtained through discovery, especially the unfavorable part. Let him see his daughter's warts, if they existed.

Johnnie had no doubt that McGuire harbored some bombshell that reverberated Melanie's guilt. McGuire was cocky, but he wasn't a fool.

Something in that prosecutorial file pointed directly to Melanie's guilt. Something that easily could sway a jury toward conviction. Burnside would see it and see everything else that pointed toward guilt.

Melanie was docile in front of her father. If he asked to see the evidence, she wouldn't balk at his inclusion. Let the bastard in. If Johnnie was going down, so was Burnside. He would share the blame, share the guilt, share the angst, and share in the second-guessing.

Burnside was dead on when he averred that he and Catherine's lives would be upheaved by a conviction. What he didn't presage was that he would be instrumental in precipitating that eruption.

Burnside had insinuated Johnnie's reaction. He hadn't considered how his own hubris might precipitate his daughter's demise despite Johnnie's valiant efforts to the contrary. Burnside's grandiosity and impetuosity was his Achilles' heel. It would be he, not Johnnie, who would sever the Burnside familial bond.

The evidence would speak for itself. Burnside would have the opportunity to interpret it, as would Johnnie and Melanie. If guilt were evident from the prosecutor's pretrial discovery, Burnside would see it. Let him evaluate his daughter's chance of victory or defeat. Let him discuss with his daughter the wisdom or rashness of a plea bargain. While the decision would be Melanie's alone, let him try to intercede or, at the very least, voice his opinion, however misguided it might be.

In the end, Johnnie would counsel Melanie that it was her decision alone, not his, not Catherine's, and definitely not Burnside's. But Burnside would know the die was cast and that he somehow had played a part in it.

Johnnie left the library and returned to his office. On the corner of his desk was that day's mail. He was in no mood to wade through the inevitable discovery requests, interrogatory responses and demands, and opponent's deposition notices that were buried in the plethora of stacked envelopes and packets. Burnside's tone and threats had addled him more than he wanted to admit. Now was not the time to direct his attention to other cases, which contained their own vexing conundrums.

From a glance at the return addresses, he usually could foretell which missive contained a problem he didn't want to address but knew couldn't be avoided. He did not need those distractions now. He had to focus on his meeting with Melanie and the probable appearance of her father. He had to calm her, reassure her, and conceal his distaste for her father.

Johnnie ejected the cassette from his tape recorder and attached it to the appellate file. As he opened his desk drawer to retrieve another cassette for his meeting with Melanie, he noticed a solitary envelope near the desk's edge. It was from the Mercer County District Ethics Committee.

Recently, Sam Pollack, its chairman, had asked him to fill the seat of one of the attorneys who had resigned from the voluntary unpaid position.

Johnnie opened the letter and gasped. Dr. Lewis had filed an ethics complaint against him. Lewis had charged him with a dereliction of the attorney-client relationship. Lewis alleged that Johnnie conspired with Supreme Insurance Company to sabotage Lewis's legitimate defense, that the carrier and Johnnie settled without his consent, and that Johnnie and the plaintiff's counsel plotted against him to his detriment and standing in the medical community. Lewis had warned Johnnie that he had not heard the last from him, and Lewis was correct. The charge was baseless. Johnnie knew it, as did Judge Fleming and the plaintiff's counsel.

Burnside normally would be the wild card in the equation, but here he had ordered Johnnie to settle the case – not, of course, out of concern for Lewis's interest but rather to expedite Johnnie's involvement in Melanie's defense. Lewis's claim was an entanglement Johnnie didn't need, given the demands on his time and conscience. A response would be required, but first he and Erika had to calm Melanie and control Burnside.

As he had anticipated, Melanie's nerves were frayed. Uncharacteristically, she gestured and fidgeted with her hands. Her head darted back and forth as she turned to address them simultaneously. Burnside had not returned, and his wife quickly retreated to the kitchen after offering them tea and coffee. Johnnie immediately had attempted to quell her anxiety but with little success. Fortunately, Erika's soothing cadence initiated a calming effect. Within minutes, Melanie's rapid speech slackened, and her focus became more direct, which allowed Johnnie to explain what immediately lay ahead.

"Melanie, realistically you knew this day would arrive, maybe not in your heart, but your instincts had to forewarn you. As we explained to you earlier, an indictment is only a vehicle by which a prosecutor can bring a case before a jury for a resolution. It does not mean you are guilty. In fact, the trial judge emphatically will instruct that fact to the jurors when they are selected to sit on your case. He will tell those jurors on several occasions that you are presumed innocent and that the prosecutor must prove your guilt beyond a reasonable doubt. You don't have to prove anything. In your case, however, we are going to take that extra step. We will show the jury that there are gaps in the prosecutor's case that prevent the return of a guilty verdict.

"Up to now, McGuire has not provided us with his proofs. Now, with the return of the indictment, he must do so and must do so quickly. The criminal division case manager will be scheduling a pre-arraignment conference, at which time McGuire has to hand over his evidence. Then, we can analyze and probe the validity of that information. We can engage witnesses and experts to demonstrate the inconsistencies and improbabilities inherent in those documents, reports, tests, and statements.

"For you, it's a novel and horrifying experience. You are entering uncharted waters. It is an arena completely alien to your upbringing, a vista only viewed from afar through newspaper headlines and television sound-bites. Yet it happens to thousands of people each year. Not many have your father's resources, and only a select few have your intelligence and persona. While it may sound trite, Erika and I deal with this type of stress on a daily basis. Think of your most mundane work task. That would be analogous to our situation here. Pretrial discovery, communication with adverse counsel, and trial preparation are our daily staples. While the personalities of those counsel vary dramatically, the system and the procedures are the same. We all have to operate under the same legal guidelines. If we don't, the judge will punish us and correct any misdeeds.

"McGuire likes to grandstand and intimidate those accused of crime. He prefers to bully those who aren't on equal footing, those who are not familiar with the criminal process, those who he easily can terrify. He can't and won't do that to us. I was his mentor in the prosecutor's office. I wasn't a bully. He strayed from my admonitions. I was always looking over his shoulder. I know, and he knows that I was, and still am, his master. He can threaten, boast, and whine all he wants. It has no effect on me. The trial judge will slap him quickly should he try such histrionics in front of the jury."

"Well, can't you get this case dismissed before it goes to the jury? I'm innocent! I shouldn't have to be put through this stress and aggravation. The hospitals need me. The surgeons need me. Why doesn't he go after the real killers? It's not right. Where is the justice?"

"Melanie, if I read McGuire correctly, all he sees is your husband on the floor, you near him, and the gun near you."

"How about the cloth, cut-out glass, the overturned table and lamp? Does he really believe I cut a hole in the sliding door, shot Richard, knocked over the table and lamp, fell on it, and then drugged myself but was foolish enough not to dispose of the gun? Isn't that the theatre of the absurd?"

"Put simply, yes. He believes it, and nothing will change his mind. Had he any reservations, he would have contacted me, after I forwarded him Richard's email and the photos. I didn't hear a peep from him. The indictment was his response."

"So I have to suffer because he is such a hard-ass?"

"Unfortunately, yes."

"Can't the judge throw the case out?"

"Hypothetically, he could, but he won't because of the gun's presence. There is something else in the evidence packet that ensures that McGuire has enough proof to allow him to overcome our motion to dismiss at the end of his evidence. Otherwise, he never would have sought your indictment. Our job is to question the validity and worth of that evidence. We don't have to prove the evidence definitely wrong. All we have to do is create a legitimate doubt as to its accuracy and weight."

"So I'm in this for the long haul. The publicity, the ridicule, the scorn. Not to mention my own anxiety, mental stability, and physical well-being."

"Melanie, I won't sugarcoat it. This will be the biggest test you have ever faced. You have overcome every obstacle thrown in your way. Very few can say that. This is just another one, another hurdle. Together, we will strive not only to clear it but also to destroy the person or persons who placed it in your path."

"Are you confident we can do that?"

"As an anesthesiologist, you know you cannot guarantee that your patient won't suffer some mishap while sedated, but you do the best you can based on your training and learned skill. That is what we do. We do as thorough a job as possible. What fate has in store for us or our clients we cannot control, even if we could prognosticate that predetermined outcome. Instead, we journey forward and pray our efforts are rewarded."

"And if they aren't rewarded? I end up rotting in some hell hole for the rest of my life, surrounded by crazed, uneducated ghetto dwellers and white-trash addicts?"

"Melanie, we can concentrate only on the present. You must do the same. McGuire is using you as a stepping stone to a higher position, a brighter future, one worth more power and acclaim. He is focusing on his future. We will use that to distract him. The more he is disconcerted and angered, the less acute will be his reasoning. You will be arraigned approximately one week after the pre-arraignment conference. At that time, you will plead not guilty. The judge then will schedule periodic status conferences to make certain that both sides are providing to each other everything required by the rules. The judge, not McGuire, will control everything. The judge will be our ally, not our enemy. We will build on that. During this process, you must trust us and must not hide anything from us. Anything that might hurt your defense, we must know. We can deal with it, as long as we know it. If the prosecutor discovers it and we don't, we won't be able to defend you properly. What you tell us cannot be divulged without your permission as a result of the attorney-client privilege. Do you understand what I've said?"

"Yes. I have nothing to hide. How do you know the judge will help me?"

"No judge wants to be reversed on appeal because he hasn't provided a defendant with an obviously fair trial. McGuire will have to be on his best behavior in the courtroom, or the judge will rebuke him. We can't control McGuire's present aggressive posturing. At trial, it's a different matter. For now, you must dismiss his combative attitude and sarcastic demeanor. It is irrelevant to our defense and is meant only to intimidate you and others whom he prosecutes. It is meaningless to the facts of your case. I know it, the judge knows it, and McGuire knows it. Now, you know it. You must focus on what is important – your defense."

Melanie looked directly at him and, with tightened lips, nodded.

From the hallway, Johnnie heard another familiar voice. Within seconds, Burnside strode quickly into the room, approached his sitting daughter, and lightly grabbed her shoulders.

"We will win. Don't you worry, honey. We will crush them, and they will pay for this. Pay more than they ever could imagine."

Burnside turned to Johnnie and inquired, "What's your plan of attack now? I can't believe that bastard really went through with the indictment. I warned him. He's going to regret this to the end of his pitiful life."

"Our plan is this. I'm calling the criminal case manager to accelerate the pre-arraignment conference, at which time McGuire has to provide me with all the reports he has as well as his projected witnesses. He can add to them during the discovery process, but he has to give me what he has now. I'll call him tomorrow morning to see if he will supply it to me before the conference. The arraignment probably will take place one week after the conference. The trial judge then will hold frequent status conferences to ensure that both sides are sharing all their proposed trial documents, including updated witness lists. Once I receive McGuire's pre-arraignment discovery packet, our work accelerates."

"I want to see everything, Johnnie. I'm your client, too. After all, I'm paying you to defend Melanie."

"If Melanie has no objection, I don't."

"She doesn't. Do you, dear?"

Melanie responded softly and submissively, "No."

"Okay. That's settled, Johnnie. I want to see a copy of everything as soon as you get it."

"Mr. Burnside, when I receive it, I'll call you, and then we will meet. There is a procedure we will have to follow to make certain the prosecutor cannot call you as his witness and require that you divulge certain confidential communications."

"I'll never divulge anything, not even if the court orders me to."

"Well, we don't even want that scenario to arise, so you and I will plan accordingly for your daughter's sake. I've also told Melanie that she has to ignore McGuire's future actions and comments. He thinks he can intimidate and discourage his defendants through supposed damning evidence leaked to the press. His use of gratuitous bombastic comments is part of his strategy. Anything to prey upon a defendant's psyche. I have warned Melanie not to succumb to his nonsense. McGuire likes to bully those unfamiliar with the criminal law. Any experienced trial lawyer recognizes it for what it is, just a deep-rooted insecurity of future success. One fears the quiet assassin, not the vainglorious boor."

"Point well taken. That's one of the reasons you're Melanie's lawyer."

Johnnie wanted to inquire the other reason but knew the main one: control.

"Is there anything else we have to discuss?"

"Mr. Burnside, there is another matter you and I have to consider. It has nothing to do with Melanie, but it is important."

"Let's go into my study. Melanie and Erika can keep Catherine company in the interim."

Johnnie followed Burnside into the study. As Burnside closed the door, he asked, "What's so important it couldn't wait?"

Johnnie pulled the ethics complaint from the back of his legal pad and handed it to him.

"This asshole has a lot of gall! When you told me he didn't fare well before the jury, I thought you were getting gun-shy. Now, I see why. I sure as hell wouldn't want him operating on me with that kind of thought process. What do you want me to do? I'll do anything you suggest. I want your attention directed to Melanie, not to this delusional fool."

"I'm preparing my responsive affidavit and am submitting copies of all of the plaintiff's expert reports. I'm calling Judge Fleming and am asking him to supply a supporting affidavit. Normally, judges avoid interjecting themselves into disputes between attorneys and litigants. These charges, however, go right to the heart of the judicial process. Fleming knows me well and respects me. He knows there was no conspiracy, especially with Silverman. He also realizes he put considerable pressure on me to settle the case, because the exposure was enormous, the plaintiff was a wonderful guy, and Lewis came across as an arrogant prick. Fleming won't desert me. He and my father have a mutual respect. I'll call Silverman who would love to nail Lewis. The only problem with Silverman is that he has such a high opinion of himself that he inadvertently may say something stupid. I will warn him but not seek an affidavit from him.

"I need you to write a letter stating that your company did not betray the doctor and did not conspire against him. Rather, the actual trial evidence was so compelling against him, and his projection on the witness stand was so detrimental that you determined it was in the doctor's own best interest that you save him from himself. You had an ethical duty to protect him from the distinct probability that he would receive a verdict far in excess of his policy limits.

"Send me your letter. I'll put it in affidavit form. You then can sign it and have your company's notary affix the appropriate seal. I'd like it as soon as possible."

"I'll dictate it tonight and fax it tomorrow. Now what's your concern with me seeing the evidence?"

"Technically, you're not my client. Melanie is. Of course, you're supplying the payment, but that's it. I can't hire you as an investigator when you are the president of your own company. Because of your position and because you are Melanie's father, I have to be careful how we discuss the evidence. You can share your thoughts with me, but I don't want to discuss my strategy with you. Any concerns you have, you should voice directly to Melanie. If she passes them on to me, that's fine due to the attorney-client privilege. I don't think McGuire will call you as a hostile witness, but he might if he's desperate. I want you to be able to testify that you looked at the evidence per Melanie's request but saw no reason to interfere with the defense. You're not a lawyer, and Melanie has a good, honorable, and honest one.

"You'll see the prosecutor's discovery and our own documents that we provide him. You, however, will not see any of our strategy notes. Therefore, you will be protected, as will we.

"I wholeheartedly believe in Melanie's innocence. If, by some chance, I receive from the prosecutor evidence that is damning against Melanie, you will see it. Then you and she, but really she, will have to decide whether to accept a plea bargain or go to trial. Hopefully, we never reach that point, but you have to be prepared for that occurrence. It's what you encounter on a daily basis in your malpractice cases, except for one actual difference. This is your daughter, and it is her life. The stakes never will be higher. I can appreciate your fervid desire to be involved. I would feel the same way. I just want you to be prepared. In the end, Melanie has the final say. I hope we never face that prospect. If we do, you and I will have to accept her decision. All three of us will have to live with the result."

Burnside, for the first time Johnnie could recall, looked troubled. Behind that mask of omniscience and omnipotence, there seemed to creep a sliver of self-doubt and fear. It was only fleeting, but it was there. The façade hadn't shattered, but there was a hairline crack. Johnnie's admonition had awakened that primordial fear, deeply suppressed but still ever present — a fear that while dormant was embedded in one's conscious state, a fear of the unknown, a fear of some supernatural evil that lurked in the shadows and that could be unleashed at any time. Good people — innocent, caring, God-fearing people — died in earthquakes, floods, mudslides, and other calamities through no fault of their own. And, yes, upstanding, innocent people got wrongly convicted and discarded to oblivion. Was that through fate or through evil? Did it really matter? The result was the same, and nothing would reverse it.

Johnnie arose from his chair.

"It's been a long and stressful day for all of us. Tomorrow, we go on the offense. The moment I receive the prosecutor's file, you will receive a copy. Just remember no comments to the press. Everything goes through me. You are the grieving and concerned father, certain of her innocence and reliant upon her attorneys."

Still pondering Johnnie's comments, Burnside raised his hand in acknowledgment.

24.

Early the following morning, Johnnie reached Judge Fleming before he resumed his trial. Fleming immediately voiced his scorn and distaste for Lewis. He readily agreed to advise the Ethics Committee that Johnnie had acted ethically, that the plaintiff's case far exceeded Lewis's policy, that Lewis had not done well on the stand, that there had been no conspiracy between counsel, and that Fleming repeatedly had urged the carrier to settle for it was in the best interest of all the parties. Fleming added that as a jurist, he felt obliged to save Lewis from himself in order to minimize any long-lasting damage to Lewis's professional reputation and practice.

Later in the morning, Johnnie made contact with Silverman, who had to be restrained from calling Lewis. Silverman was outraged that Lewis would impugn his integrity, much less Johnnie's. He threatened to contact the New Jersey Medical Society regarding Lewis's surgical conduct and post-trial spurious allegations. Eventually, Johnnie was able to dissuade Silverman who promised he would prepare a reply affidavit and allow Johnnie to edit and revise it before Silverman signed and forwarded the document to the committee. Silverman ended the conversation by complimenting Johnnie on his trial skills and by stating that he would pay a very reasonable referral fee should Johnnie steer any plaintiff's cases his way. Johnnie replied that he would keep him in mind, knowing full well that Silverman would be the last attorney with whom he would dare associate. The guy was a rogue who would stretch the ethical line to its furthest boundary and then some.

Johnnie then phoned the criminal case manager, advised him that McGuire had failed to provide any pre-indictment discovery, and requested an expedited conference. After some wheedling and prodding, he secured a late appointment for the next day and was told to advise the prosecutor's office.

"Don't tell me you're already calling for a plea deal."

"You're overoptimistic Terry. Why would I do that when you haven't even provided me with any pre-indictment discovery as required under Rule 3.13-3(a)?"

"Johnnie-boy, you've been away from the criminal practice too long. Check the rule. Only when the prosecutor has made a pre-indictment plea offer need I do that, and then only when I have determined the discovery wouldn't hinder or jeopardize the prosecution or investigation. Lest you forget, I never made a concrete offer. Ergo, no discovery until you have obtained a date for the pre-arraignment conference."

"The delay's over, Terry. It's tomorrow at 3:30 p.m. Make certain you bring the discovery with you to the conference. As to the items seized under the search warrant, I want them released to my client. You've had ample opportunity to inspect the computers and cellphones. My client also needs her address book and calendar. By now, you've reviewed them and made the appropriate copies. If the originals are needed for trial, I'll provide them voluntarily, assuming the warrant's issuance was proper."

"As a former fellow prosecutor, Johnnie, I'll accede to most of your requests. I don't think boss man, as you call him, will object. You might want to keep that appellation between us. Peters wouldn't take kindly to it. Unlike our old boss Sapienza, Bob doesn't have a great sense of humor. By nature, he's mordant, especially when dealing with the opposition. He views defense counsel and the accused as cut from the same cloth."

"That's very interesting, Terry. One would expect a man with such a myopic view not to shy away from personally handling this case. Is he fearful it could damage his chance for a judicial appointment? Isn't it a little selfish to seek the reward without taking the risk? I guess you don't mind being the fall guy, should everything turn sour. Well, let us not digress into such philosophical issues. It is what it is. You and I are just players, those who Shakespeare would describe as being poor players that strut and fret about on the stage. Will one, or both, of us be heard of no more? That remains to be seen.

"Rumor has it the governor takes a keen interest in judicial appointments. Merit actually is considered, along with common sense and fair play. Does Peters possess those qualities? If not, I would watch your back. You know your boss, not me. One who falls on his sword is remembered that way, but he's still dead. I'll see you tomorrow at 3:30. Tell boss man I want the discovery then, or I'm going right to Scholman. Enough with the head games. Watch your back. Don't let this be your professional eulogy. Think hard about who placed you in this position. You might have sought it. If there wasn't any resistance to you being the lead on this case, you might want to ask yourself, why not?"

25.

Shortly before 3:30 p.m. the following day, Johnnie entered the Criminal Division Manager's Office. McGuire arose from a waiting chair, approached him, and handed over a thick folder as he led him to a vacant side room.

"Delivered as requested. Where's my reciprocal discovery?"

"Had you provided me with the police reports, tox reports, crime scene photos, and so on, maybe I'd have something for you. I sent you Stafford's lengthy email and the Wellington photos, hoping that would stir your office to investigate. Apparently, it didn't."

"Why bother, Johnnie? You and I both know that's a red herring meant to confuse and misdirect our focus. Why should we bother? Once you review what's in this packet, you'll see there's no need to look elsewhere. I grant you she's attractive and smart, probably too smart for her own good. She tried to stage it well. I give her that, but here she's out of her element. She did it! It happens time after time, the eternal love triangle – shock, sadness, humiliation, jealousy, and then uncontrollable rage. Killers come in all sizes, shapes, colors, and professions. The names on the blotter change, but the result is the same.

"In a way, I feel sorry for you, Johnnie. When you left this office, I knew you'd be a success. You joined your father's thriving practice, mingled with well-heeled clients, and, no doubt, prospered financially. Think of all the respect and admiration you have earned, and deservedly so. This case will tarnish that. How much, who knows? You talk about me being the fall guy. But what about you, Johnnie? Will you emerge unscathed? Has it already scarred you emotionally? If not, I fear it will. You mentored me well. I absorbed your suggestions, mulled them over, and then discarded a few. That's my personality and my uniqueness. You glide through interpersonal relationships. I tend to agitate them. That's me, and I'll never change. But one thing we both know is I go for the jugular. Melanie Stafford is in my path. She will regret it."

"I take it there is no plea offer to be conveyed."

"Nothing has changed my mind, Johnnie. That's your task, and the time is short. Use it wisely."

"I want returned the items seized by the search warrant. Do I need to make a motion?"

"If you will sign a stipulation that you will produce them at trial if requested, I will release everything but Stafford's luggage and its contents."

"Have you made a record of everything stored on the computers and cell phones?"

"No. Frankly, we didn't find anything probative."

"Terry, are you telling me at trial, no one will testify that they contain damning evidence to my client's detriment?"

"I'm telling you we found nothing. Obviously, should you produce independent evidence that alters our position, I will advise you and provide you with time to attempt to rebut it. If nothing else, I think we both can agree we don't want to try this case twice. I don't want her conviction overturned on some tenuous technicality."

"Have you supplied me with all your discovery?"

"You have everything I have. I intend to engage one or more experts beside the medical examiner, whose report is enclosed. I anticipate receiving their reports within the next sixty days."

"I'll need their CVs with those reports and then I'll obviously need time to engage my experts."

"We should have plenty of time. We have accrued a one-year backlog. It all depends on which trial judge gets this case and what he plans to do with it. I'm assuming Scholman won't keep it. Frankly, I found it odd he handled the bail hearing."

"You didn't suggest he handle it or ask for an in-person bail hearing for the publicity? Come on, Terry!"

"I didn't. Frankly, I thought you did."

"How could I do that? You're the one who sees him often. The only time I run into him is at an infrequent bar function, and then the discussion usually is perfunctory."

"Well, Johnnie, as much as we may plot, both our assumptions, I guess, were wrong."

"There's one other thing we have to address. I trust you won't object too strenuously if I attempt to schedule the arraignment in conjunction with my client's surgical schedule. She runs from one hospital to another. I either need to schedule it on a day off or late in the afternoon, provided the trial judge concurs."

"Johnnie, as long as I'm not in trial, I don't care. Just let me know the proposed date and time before you clear it with whoever is assigned to her arraignment."

"Fair enough. I'll discuss it with the case manager before I leave and then check with my client."

"Johnnie, don't read me wrong by my acquiescence. I expect you to provide me with discovery when you receive it, or I'll move to strike it."

"Terry, it's a two-way street. I shouldn't have had to wait so long. I'll give you a pass. Let's both cooperate. I agree that neither wants a replay of this trial. Let's keep our errors to those unintended and unappealable."

As McGuire quickly left the office, Johnnie spoke with the case manager regarding the possibility of coordinating Melanie's arraignment. Johnnie left a message on Melanie's cell and requested that she quickly send him her seven-day schedule. He then headed to the office. How would McGuire's packet alter his strategy? Was the alleged evidence as damning as McGuire contended? As to McGuire not wanting a retrial, Johnnie didn't believe that for a moment. If McGuire thought the jury doubted his theory of the case, he would do his best to mistry it and take his chances with another jury. McGuire had hitched his advancement to Melanie's hide. Absent an acceptable face-saving guilty plea, the race was on.

26.

After dinner, Johnnie settled into a living room chair and opened McGuire's discovery packet. On top was an enumerated summary of the enclosures. As expected, there were the EMT records, emergency room documents, Hopewell Township police reports, crime scene photos, autopsy report, and typed rendition of Melanie's recorded statement. What caught his attention, however, was the listing of a recorded statement from a Sally Huffmire. So she was the apex point of the triangle. Johnnie scanned the remaining items on the list. He had expected forensic documents regarding fingerprints and gunshot residue as well as detailed cellphone and landline records. What he hadn't anticipated were documents relating to a second cellphone for Richard Stafford.

Johnnie immediately pulled Huffmire's statement and commenced reading the four-page transcript. He pulled a notepad from an adjacent desk and wrote down her address, landline, and cell phone numbers. She was a childless forty-two-year-old divorcee. She was self-employed as a travel photographer and writer. She maintained a small apartment in Red Bank, New Jersey, and owned a condo on Sanibel Island, which she used as her travel base from October through July. Three years earlier, she had been seated next to Stafford on a Philadelphia flight to Venice. She was on assignment for a well-known travel magazine while he was spending two days in Venice before flying to Romania on behalf of Wellington. During the flight, they realized they shared a mutual interest in Italian art and architecture as well as opera. Upon arrival in Venice, they agreed to have dinner that evening. The next day, they toured several museums and galleries where she photographed paintings and sculptures in conjunction with the article she was preparing on the city. Before parting, they exchanged cellphone numbers and entertained the possibility of meeting sometime after they returned to the States. She assumed Stafford was single.

A couple of months later, Stafford contacted her. He was concluding a pharmaceutical conference in Manhattan. He asked if she would be interested in accompanying him to the opera the following evening. She readily agreed. They enjoyed each other's company, and she stayed the night. He confessed that he was mired in an unhappy marriage. His wife was a workaholic, consumed by her profession. His father-in-law was a haughty son-of-a-bitch who derived satisfaction from seeing others genuflect in obeisance to his whims and commands. He dominated those around him and exercised considerable control over his wife and daughter, whom he loved deeply. At their rehearsal dinner, he had been pulled aside and warned, "Do not hurt or betray my daughter. If you do, you will rue the day that you did."

Melanie also had her own faults. Though attractive and intelligent, she was emotionally insecure, probably due to her father's overbearing presence. Not able to bear children and usually unable to accompany him on his frequent business trips, she often berated him for being lax in calling while abroad. Was he too busy sleeping with some pharmaceutical rep? That was a frequent refrain. Once when he returned from Geneva, she had been particularly angered. She immediately accosted him and slapped him on the face. As he backed away, she continued to hit him. Tired and irritated, he shoved her violently. She fell sideways, hitting the corner of the kitchen island before falling on her face. Her irritation was not quelled when her face quickly bruised. Melanie's moods could vary quickly. She could be sweet and caring and then somber and irritable. What was so vexatious was the suddenness of the change without any precipitating provocation.

Johnnie stopped reading the statement. The mention of facial bruising shook him. He remembered Burnside commenting that he had appeared once without notice at Melanie's house. When she answered the door, he instantaneously observed her facial discoloration. Melanie offered that she had "tripped and slammed into a wall corner." Were the described incidents one and the same? For certain, Burnside now couldn't testify. Any mention of his observation could minimize the Wellington defenses. Was Melanie really the woman depicted in Huffmire's statement, or was that narration the concoction of a conniving, manipulative, and vengeful paramour distraught by her lover's murder?

Johnnie returned to the statement. The trysts became more frequent as the months flew by. At times, Stafford would meet her at her Red Bank apartment or in Manhattan. Because he traveled by himself to Romania and Bulgaria, she met him on two occasions there, never returning with him on the same flights. Both were very discreet. All telephonic communications were from and to his office cell phone. Although she had heard much about Melanie, she had never met her. Being an adventurer, she valued their noncommittal relationship. She could go as she pleased without fear of any real emotional entanglement. She had undergone an acrimonious divorce and had no pressing desire to bind herself to another mate. She liked her freedom, and Stafford accepted her lifestyle.

While her Sanibel condo could be his safe haven, she never provided him with a key. Ten days before his death, they had planned a short rendezvous at her condo as he returned from Hawaii. When he left Sanibel, he was in good spirits and promised to call several days later so they could plan their next liaison. When she did not hear from him, she left several messages on his work cell. After a couple of days, she called his office and learned of his murder. She knew he lived in Hopewell Township, so she called the police there. A Township detective took her name, address, and number. Within minutes, the Mercer prosecutor's office called and obtained a telephonic statement.

Johnnie put down the statement. No doubt, it was damning. On the other hand, about what could she testify? Their lustful relationship? Of course. She admitted she never spoke to or met Melanie. All she could recount was her version of what Stafford allegedly confided in her. McGuire could press fervidly for its admission, but would the judge allow it? It all depended on how it was offered, and that hinged on a number of factors. For the moment, Johnnie would assume the worst, that it would be admissible. Somehow, he would have to deflate its deleterious effect. He would have to know more about this woman, and he knew just the right person to shadow her.

He picked up his cell and punched in the number. She answered quickly.

"Where are you, lover boy? Obviously not with someone of my gender?"

"Get a good night's rest, and bring your suitcase with you. Fill it with shorts, tops, a bathing suit, sandals, and maybe a light sweater."

"Wow, where are you taking me?"

"I'm not. You're flying solo and hopefully tomorrow."

"To where, for how long, and why?"

"To Sanibel Island, Florida, for an unknown duration, and to spy on Richard Stafford's lover."

"I warned you, Johnnie. Like I said, it's a woman's intuition."

"Yeah. Your intuition has been borne out by a written statement. I have McGuire's discovery. I'll have a copy for you tomorrow. I'll try to get you a flight for tomorrow afternoon or night. If I can't, I'll get the quickest one I can. See you at 9:00 a.m. Get your beauty rest."

Despite his efforts, he could not secure a flight until the following day. He informed Erika, and they still agreed to meet at 9:00.

Johnnie grabbed a beer from the fridge and returned to McGuire's file. The crime scene photos were just as he expected. Shot from every angle, they depicted the blood spatter and blood-mottled rug. Most of the colored photos were taken before the print dusting. There were four pictures of the deceased taken from different vantage points and distances. Close-up images revealed the gun, white cloth, overturned table, and lamp. The briefcase and luggage were depicted open and closed. Several shots illustrated the sliding glass door. Viewed externally and interiorly with the drapes open and closed, the circular cut-out was revealed.

Exterior shots of the residence were taken from all directions and revealed the driveway and woodlands. Interior pictures were taken of every room and were accompanied by a sketch enumerating the dimensions.

In a separate envelope were the autopsy photos. Stafford was naked on a slab. The entry wounds were identifiable. More visceral photos illustrated the Y-shaped incision and specific body parts.

Johnnie put the gruesome images back in the envelope. Burnside would view the same with dispassion. Melanie would not. He would warn her of their stomach-turning effect. At trial, McGuire would exploit them for dramatic effect. Johnnie wanted Melanie to be as horrified as the jury. They would be watching her reaction. He did not want her prepared for what she would witness.

Johnnie culled Melanie's and Inez Garcia's statements from the discovery pile. What Melanie related to the police was basically what she told him with one exception. She failed to mention to the police that the assailant's thick fingers were covered with gloves. On the other hand, the police overlooked asking her. Therefore, this was explainable, especially under the extreme circumstances that surrounded the inquiry.

Inez Garcia's statement was surprisingly consistent with what she told him. He was certain the police had not given her a copy of the document. They probably viewed her as an adverse witness. Even without a copy of the statement, she described the facts accurately when she spoke to him and Burnside.

Johnnie then pulled the fingerprint reports. There were no identifiable prints on the Glock or on the fired shells. There also were no prints on the unfired rounds. Whoever loaded and fired the weapon probably used gloves.

Melanie's prints were on the table and lamp, which was understandable because she would have turned on the lamp and probably would have touched the table that evening or earlier.

There were no identifiable prints adjacent to the glass cut-out. Melanie's were on the inside latch, which would have been expected because she locked the door that evening. Her prints also were inside at other locations consistent with her opening the door.

The GSR test revealed trace powder on Melanie's left palm but none on her right palm. There also was no trace evidence on the outside of either hand. Melanie was right-handed. Had she fired the gun, presumably there should have been some blowback residue on her right hand. There was none. Johnnie knew Melanie did chest compressions on Stafford. Had Inez described which was the top hand? He would have to check with her. The police hadn't inquired when they got her statement.

He then reviewed the reports of the responding Hopewell officers. The narratives focused on the crime scene site, the presence of the EMTs, and Melanie's physical and mental states. While mention was made of the maid, there was no detailed inquiry at the scene. Most importantly, one of the officers specifically mentioned that Melanie repeated several times that "they killed him" without stating whom.

The EMT records recorded Melanie's physical status. Mention was made that she was hysterical. Again, there was a notation that she said "they killed him."

The hospital reports described in more detail than the EMT report the nature of Melanie's injuries and the treatment rendered. The GSR test was noted as requested and taken by the police. No significant concussion tests were administered. The police were advised that if she exhibited thought inconsistencies, visual difficulties, or other aberrations, she should be returned immediately for a follow-up. Her forehead was sutured, and her nasal abrasion cleaned and bandaged. Her emotion was described as labile. She was prescribed pain medication and given Tylenol. Mention was made of her agitation and distraught condition, precipitated by the assault and her husband's murder. Again, there was a notation that she said repeatedly, "they killed him."

Stafford's work cellphone records covering a twelve-month period were replete with calls made to and from Sally Huffmire's cellphone. Johnnie checked the landline records as well as the personal cell records for Melanie and Stafford. Huffmire's number was absent. He made a note to ask Melanie to review all the other numbers contained in the family's records. Any unfamiliar numbers would have to be verified.

Tomorrow would be an interesting day. Now it was time to sleep.

27.

Erika finished reading the statement's final sentence and looked seriously at Johnnie. Gone was her early morning frivolity.

"My guess is she found out, plotted her moves, and expertly orchestrated the scene. Do you finally agree?"

"My conclusion, if any, is irrelevant. Only the jury's judgment is pertinent, and that is beyond our control, regardless of what evidence McGuire and we produce. Huffmire's statement is damning, especially as to Melanie's inferred alternating personality."

"Johnnie, what she says regarding Stafford's account is pure hearsay and, thus, inadmissible."

"Maybe, maybe not. It depends on how the statement is used, when it is offered, and for what purpose. Depending on the foundation for which it is offered, it could get in. If not during the prosecutor's case, then what happens if I put Melanie on the stand? Without referring to the statement, McGuire will probe Melanie's relationship with her husband. He will refute her denials by calling Huffmire as a rebuttal witness. If the hearsay is admitted, she'll be much closer to a conviction."

"Will the judge have to admit the hearsay?"

"It depends on the judge and how he perceives the hearsay. More importantly, it depends on what he thinks of the prosecutor's evidence and how he views Melanie. Judges always tell jurors that they have no opinion of the evidence and that the jurors should not consider their rulings as indicative of their opinions. While that instruction is correct, you better believe they have opinions, just like everyone else. Most take copious notes during the testimony so they can buttress their subsequent rulings. Like any good attorney, they want to cover their asses. They have an adversarial relationship with the appellate courts. They view every appeal as a possible rebuke or embarrassment. That's why they are hyper-vigilant when providing their rulings. Judges try to mask their opinions during a trial, but sometimes you get that glimmer of what they really think. We don't know yet who will be trying this case. Once we do, we might have some insight before or, at least, during the trial. Let's hope so. It could alter our chances of an acquittal, mistrial, or conviction."

"Do you really believe that?"

"Here, yes. This is an explosive case. It's not a rear-end accident. A very prominent and well-respected woman is on trial for her life. The stakes couldn't be any higher. Even if Huffmire's hearsay is admitted, what do we have? A cheating husband and a complicit woman who cares not one iota for the philanderer's spouse. Huffmire comes across as self-absorbed and noncommittal. She globetrots and has her flings without concern for their ramifications. What is the outgrowth of her entanglements? She couldn't care less. By her own account, Stafford doesn't come across much better. He's an unfaithful wimp. He knows his wife's insecurities and does nothing to mitigate them. She implores him to call more frequently, and he shrugs her off. You can sense his disdain through his actions. The guy's a weasel, and it will be apparent to the jury if Huffmire verbalizes the hearsay."

"What about all those vacations Melanie remarked about?"

"I'm sure they took them. If Huffmire is to be believed, I'm not so certain how much time they spent in each other's company. It's easy to get immersed in your own interest when travelling to some foreign location. On the other hand, maybe that was the one time when they really connected."

"Okay, so I'm going to Florida. Do you want me to interview her or just surveil her?"

"If she knows you represent Melanie, she'll either clam up or provide a more negative picture of her. Then on cross-examination, she'll rehash your meeting in an unfavorable way to our defense. Just tail her. See how she spends her day. With luck, maybe she's on to another man. If so, that would diminish her likability and credibility."

"Why don't I befriend her? If I can gain her confidence, she might really open up. We might find out Stafford was more despicable toward his wife than we thought."

"Only problem with that is it cuts both ways. It provides more of an impetus for Stafford's killing. Also, what reason would you have to approach her that would lead to a lengthy conversation?"

"She's a professional photographer. If she's by herself on the beach or by the pool, I casually approach her with my camera and ask her where's the best place to photograph gators or something. Believe me: I'll have no problem extending the conversation in a congenial way. I'll be wearing a wire. With luck, maybe she'll divulge something that you can use on her cross. She'll deny it. You'll call me after McGuire has rested his case. I'll play that part of the recording. Huffmire will be long gone. She'll never know she was recorded, unless McGuire later tells her. If she reveals nothing, during our conversations, she won't link me to you. I won't be in the courtroom when she's on the stand. By the way, where's her picture?"

"Google her. Let me think about your suggestion. Here's the rest of McGuire's discovery. Look it over. I got the feeling last night that something was missing, but in my tired state, I couldn't place it. This is your copy, just don't take any of it to Florida, not even Huffmire's statement. See me after you've read everything. I have to call Burnside. He wanted to be kept in the loop. After he sees this discovery, he'll be second-guessing himself."

Johnnie walked down the hallway to his father's office. As he entered, he saw his father looking at a framed picture of his mother.

"Dad, you got a second?"

"I have as many seconds as you need. I still really miss her."

"So do I. We all had such great times."

"You'll appreciate it even more when you find that perfect one."

Johnnie laughed, "What makes you think she'll find me?"

"Maybe she has, and neither of you know it."

"I know what you're thinking. Don't even go there."

"What do you need?"

"I just received McGuire's discovery. I made a copy for you. I'd like you to review it. I'm arranging a meeting with Burnside. I'd hope you'd be present as a calming presence. The meeting will be here. Are you available tonight or tomorrow night?"

"Either one is fine. What's with him?"

"He basically commanded me to allow him to be involved in his daughter's defense. At first, I rebelled at his suggestion. The more I considered it, though, I realized that if her defense goes south, I want him to shoulder some of the blame. Let him enjoy the angst and regret. Why should I or the firm bear that solitary burden? We will do our best, but we cannot control the outcome. Burnside thinks he can manipulate everything and everyone. He says he and Melanie are my mutual client. He's fronting the defense, not her. In his mind, they're one client."

"Do you think she killed him?"

"I don't know and, at this point, probably don't want to know. She could have done it by herself or with someone's assistance. On the other hand, maybe Wellington sanctioned it. Maybe even he did it. He despised Stafford. There's a statement in the discovery from a Sally Huffmire. Erika was right. There's a love triangle. At this point, it's uncertain whether Melanie knew. Huffmire asserts Stafford feared both his wife and her father. He believed either or both would kill him if his dalliances were discovered.

"McGuire hasn't targeted Burnside. There's no direct evidence pointing to him. Melanie's a much more convenient suspect. She's there and has GSR on the palm of her left hand. She's right-handed. There was no blowback on that hand or the backs of either hand. There's enough to convict her from the scene and from Huffmire's statement, if the hearsay is ruled admissible. Burnside will need to be counseled and constrained. He'll try to lord over me. Hopefully, in your presence, he'll be more circumspect and malleable. He has to recognize the inherent risks of proceeding blindly through a full-blown trial. We'll be gearing up for it, but he has to be prepared if things change dramatically."

"I'll do my best to placate him. I'll read the discovery. Let me know which night."

"Thanks, I'll try to reach him now."

Johnnie returned to his office, called Burnside's cell, and left a message. An hour later, his call was returned.

"What's so important?"

"I've received the prosecutor's discovery file. There are things you and I have to discuss. In private and soon. Can you meet me at my office tonight?"

"I'll be there at seven."

"Please, no mention to Melanie or Mrs. Burnside."

Burnside agreed and quickly terminated the conversation.

Johnnie returned to the prosecutor's file. With a clearer head, he wanted to read it again. He knew something was missing. What was it and why?

Deep in thought, he didn't hear Erika enter. She handed him a photo. An average-looking brown-eyed woman stared back at him. She had thin lips, an upturned nose, and straight auburn hair.

Compared to Melanie, she was plain and almost nondescript. Johnnie was stunned. Stafford would betray his wife for this woman? It made no sense, but his litigation experience reminded him that often there was an absence of logic in matters of the heart and bank account.

"You look perplexed?"

"I expected someone with sultry thick lips and deep-set eyes framed with a radiant smile."

"No wonder you overlooked what was missing from McGuire's file. There's no record of the Glock's ownership. There were no prints on the gun or on the shells. As prosecutor, what would you have done?"

"Had my investigators contact Glock to ascertain the initial purchaser and then attempt to follow the chain. The gun was manufactured abroad. Europe's gun laws are a lot stricter. McGuire had to have pursued that course. What he learned couldn't have pleased him."

"That's why it was missing. There's no direct nexus to Melanie or Stafford. McGuire knows the identity of the initial purchaser and doesn't want it disclosed."

"He has to provide me with any exculpatory evidence. In his twisted mind, what's not inculpatory can't possibly be exculpatory. I'm preparing a motion for other discovery, so this will join the demand list.

"Erika, don't engage Huffmire. Just track her for now. Later, I might change my thinking. McGuire had to caution her that we would approach. Let's back off and just watch. Maybe we'll get lucky. For now, enjoy the sun and sea, compliments of Glen Burnside."

"When are you going to show the discovery to Melanie? I wanted to gauge her reaction when she reads Huffmire's statement and observes her photo."

"I'm meeting with Burnside first. That shock will be enough. I'll meet with her later. At this point, it's more important that you watch Huffmire than Melanie. You already think she did it. Her reaction, or lack thereof, likely won't alter that opinion."

"But you need a woman's intuition."

"I need that intuition focused on Huffmire. She's the one we have to break. McGuire already is focusing intently on Melanie. She's his ticket to fame if not fortune. Remember, daily reports and lots of sunscreen."

Erika sashayed from his desk, turned, and blew a kiss as she exited his office.

Why hadn't he thought of the gun? Wellington was a Swiss subsidiary. The gun was manufactured in Austria. Melanie's defense was premised on Wellington's involvement. If the weapon wasn't shipped for sale in the U.S., then that lessened the likelihood that Melanie or Stafford had acquired it. McGuire must have ascertained it was sold in Europe. That explained the report's absence. More than likely, Dan Stenkowicz knew the answer. Stenkowicz couldn't divulge it voluntarily, but he also wouldn't sign a false affidavit as to the record's nonexistence. A discovery motion would compel McGuire to release it. If he didn't, he knew Stenkowicz wouldn't be a party to such deception.

28.

Early January 2000
Northern New Jersey

The American couldn't believe what he read. The newspaper article recounted the Princeton professor's sudden passing from an apparent heart attack.

In late December, the professor had written to him. In that correspondence, he had described his background as a former Monuments, Fine Arts, and Archives Officer who had continued his pursuit of stolen antiquities while teaching and lecturing at Princeton University.

In conjunction with his ongoing investigations, he had corresponded to other export-import companies to ascertain whether those concerns had imported to the States any antiquities or European paintings. The professor also had inquired whether any employees had booked business trips to Germany within the prior ten years.

The professor's inquiry had alarmed the American. Had the scholar uncovered his real business? Several years earlier, the American had divulged to his son the hidden and lucrative aspect of his company.

The son was an accomplished attorney with a Princeton law office. While very bright, his son apparently had inherited certain less-desirable characteristics from his father. He was very self-absorbed. He thirsted for advancement and monetary enrichment. Corners would be cut, and ethics skirted, if personal advantage, prestige, and wealth could be attained.

As the American had predicted, his son quickly grasped the opportunity being afforded. Due to his father's advancing age, he readily agreed to travel to Germany to meet with the Munich contact. Often, he took his wife to mask the trip's real intent. Very few flights were booked directly to German cities. Most purposely landed in and departed from other European venues. The ordinary investigator would assume the couple were tourists interested in immersing themselves in European history and culture.

The American had shown the professor's letter to his son, who advised there was no concern. Nothing would be uncovered, and no prosecution would occur.

Now within days of that conversation, the scholar was dead. How likely was that? Was it really a mere coincidence, or was it something more? Did that something more involve his son?

The American knew one thing for certain. If his son thought there was a threat to his own career and wealth, nothing would stop him from eradicating that impediment.

29.

Princeton, New Jersey

Glen Burnside arrived sharply at 7:00 p.m. His face revealed his marked concern. Gone was his authoritarian persona. Johnnie escorted him to the firm's spacious library.

"Jack, I didn't expect to see you."

"Johnnie asked me to join the discussion. I've read the discovery, and he wanted my input in case you had any questions."

Johnnie had prepared a copy of the discovery. He handed the top document to Burnside, who gazed intently at the photo.

"Who is she?"

"She's our problem, a big problem."

Johnnie then handed him Huffmire's statement. Burnside was on the second page when Johnnie noticed the man's tension rise. Burnside bit his lower lip. His right hand tightened on the typed document. He flipped each page more forcefully. When he had finished, he flipped it to the table.

"That self-righteous bastard! He railed at Wellington's deception and falsehoods. Yet he thinks nothing of betraying my daughter. The perfidious prick got what he deserved! To think he would desert her for this tramp. Look at her. If you passed her on the street, you wouldn't even notice her. Well, he was right about one thing. He's lucky I hadn't found out earlier. The bullets saved him from the agony I would have inflicted. Is this woman still in Florida?"

"Glen, Johnnie and I both agree you have to stay away from her. You can't contact her. It will blow up in our faces and really hurt Melanie's defense. Promise us you won't."

"Okay, I won't contact her. Am I a target? Her statement implies if Melanie didn't do it, then I did."

"Mr. Burnside, McGuire may be many things, but he's not a fool. You're too difficult a target. Nothing links you to the scene, except for your comment to Stenkowicz about what you might say or do if called to the stand."

Burnside turned away from Johnnie and looked directly at his father.

"Jack, as of now, I view myself as a suspect. I've just hired you as my lawyer. Prepare the retainer agreement. Anything we discuss from now on is privileged, correct?"

Johnnie's father smiled and nodded.

Johnnie then handed him the next document and stated, "She's not our only problem."

Burnside slowly read the gunshot residue findings and then asked, "How bad is this?"

"Not good, but it could have been much worse. She's right-handed. There's no blowback there. McGuire will want the jury to accept that she staged the killing and then washed her right hand. How do you scrub your right hand without using your left? Why not scrub both hands? If she staged everything, did she just panic? There also are other plausible reasons to explain the powder residue. We will be hiring an expert to elucidate them before the jury. That is, if you still want me to defend her. Earlier, I told you there might come a time when this would prove to be too awkward for all of us. Maybe now is that time?"

"I told you I wanted you. Now I also have your father. As long as your experts are top-notch, I'll be satisfied. I want to see their reports and know their credentials. How long before the trial?"

"McGuire guesstimates a year due to the current lengthy backlog."

"A year! That's too long. Melanie can't endure this uncertainty that long. She will crack under that long of a disruption in her regimented life."

"After all the expert reports are in, depending on the trial judge, maybe we can accelerate it. I don't think McGuire will oppose it. This is his baby. When he's ready, he'll be chaffing at the bit to start. The sooner he sends me his expert reports, the quicker I can employ our experts. Until then, you have to remain in the background and direct all your efforts to comforting and bolstering Melanie's spirits and optimism."

"What about the woman? What are you going to do with her? I can put a tail on her."

"Mr. Burnside, let us deal with her. You can't be associated with her in any way. Dad agrees it only could hurt our defense. Let us deal with her. If you can't agree with our request, then I strongly would have you reconsider whether you want us trying this case. We will keep you apprised of our findings, but we need you to be separate from our investigation. I hope this doesn't sound rude, but for your sake and Melanie's, you have to keep your distance. If something arises where we need your direct assistance, we will reach out immediately."

"If they are the rules, I can abide by them. I won't have any of my company's excellent investigators interfere. Case closed."

"I intend to meet with Melanie in the next day or so. Please do not reveal our meeting or the discovery. Her arraignment will be within the next week. At that time, she will appear with me. She obviously will plead not guilty. I will learn the name of the trial judge and will ask for an immediate discovery conference. I will keep you informed of all developments. In the interim, if you have any concerns, contact me or Dad."

"Don't worry, I will, and, of course, I won't share the discovery with Catherine. She's upset enough. This only would dismay her further."

Johnnie and his father walked their joint client to the door and thanked him for his patience and understanding. Both wondered whether he really could be controlled. Neither thought for long.

30.

As he walked to his car, Burnside reflected on their admonitions and rapidly disregarded them. He was their client. What they didn't grasp was that he was their conductor. He was paying their fee. He was their boss. He would do as he always had done. He would lead the charge. They might fall by the wayside as unexpected but accepted casualties. He would prevail. This was just another battle. The strategy initially might be theirs, but the tactics would be his. Different situations necessitated alternative methods. He lacked a law degree but possessed a keen sense of survival. Lawyers were bound by their rules and ethics. He was unshackled, left to implement the schemes that guaranteed the mission's success.

He drove his black Mercedes to the Palmer Square parking garage, obtained the ticket, and proceeded to the second level. He turned off the engine and pulled the untraceable phone from his coat pocket. He dialed the number. The voice brought back memories of missions past.

"Can you talk?"

"Yes."

"I need you."

"Is it urgent?"

"Urgent, urgent. Can you be in Princeton tomorrow?"

"By late afternoon."

"Book a room at the Hyatt on Route 1."

"For how long?"

"Just one night. Clean up, and wear a suit and tie. I'll meet you at six thirty at your room."

"Got it, boss. Glad to hear your voice. It's been some time."

"Nothing's changed. I'm the same old guy. 'Til then."

31.

Johnnie awakened and checked his messages. Melanie had texted him at 6:00 a.m. She was en route to Capitol Health for an early morning surgery. She was off in three days and would appear for her arraignment that Friday. If he needed to see her before then, she would meet him any day after 5:00 p.m. On surgical days, she often went to bed by 9:30 p.m. Johnnie suggested that they meet the following day at 5:00 p.m. He then called the criminal case manager and requested a Friday afternoon arraignment, the later the better. Within minutes, he was advised that Judge Scholman would handle the proceeding at 3:30 p.m. The judge had requested no word to the press, and McGuire had been cautioned. No one needed a circus atmosphere at the end of a long week. Johnnie assured that he would be mum and hoped McGuire would obey. He then texted Melanie regarding the arraignment's scheduling.

Erika was on her way to Florida and probably wouldn't call him until the following day. She would need to familiarize herself with Sanibel before spying on Huffmire. Now was a good time to consider what experts to employ. That meant phoning numerous criminal defense counsel for their recommendations. The experts would have to be vetted. He wanted to avoid those who frequently traipsed the courtroom corridors. He would focus on those with sterling credentials and impeccable reputations. Would he need a separate ballistics expert, or would a chief medical examiner suffice? Money was not an object. Burnside would pay quickly and often. He needed experts who could teach the jurors as well as mesmerize them. The conversationalist, the person who spoke to them, not at them, the person with whom they could relate and see as a friend, not as a high-priced advocate — that's whom he sought. All he had to do was find the one he desperately craved.

32.

Having read the prosecutor's material that morning, Burnside had a handle on the case. The solution was simple. He would effectuate it. He knocked lightly at Room 304. The door opened slowly without revealing its occupant. Burnside entered and walked toward the center of the room as the door closed behind him.

"Just like old times," said the voice behind him.

Burnside turned and smiled as he quickly approached the grinning man. They shook hands and firmly touched each other's right shoulders.

"Short hair, clean-shaven, bespoke suit, regimental tie, you still know how to follow instructions."

"When my old boss calls, I recall how to follow orders."

"Five years, and you still look the same."

"Yup. In my business, appearance counts as does a certain aptitude, as they say."

"Are you now solo or attached?"

"I'm still affiliated with the company on an as-needed basis. I'm also associated with a security firm. Go with them to the hot spots for the government or for the agency. The firm gives me leeway to contract out for solo jobs. I guess you could say I'm a world traveler, usually to areas others fear to tread. I still maintain that same apartment in Arlington. All I have to do to hone my skills is walk the streets east of the Capitol. It heightens my awareness. It lacks mountains and sand, but it's still a battle zone. You'd think the seat of our democracy would have been cleaned up by now. The politicians have gotten worse, so I guess we shouldn't expect any improvement elsewhere. My grand-daddy used to say 'politicians are like apples in July. Some are firm, most are tainted with brown spots, and the rest are rotten to the core.' I think they all are gravitating to the latter."

"Spoken like a true soldier."

Burnside walked to the desk and sat in the adjacent chair. His fashionable soldier sat on the bed's corner.

"What's the mission?"

Burnside pulled a colored photo from his suit pocket and handed it to him. The man gazed at the photo and then looked up.

"She's a professional photographer and journalist. Apparently, she travels the country and abroad, usually on assignment for travel publications. She's an immediate threat to my daughter's well-being. My daughter has been indicted for a murder she didn't commit. Her husband was killed by his employer when he was set to reveal a global scandal. His company would have lost millions by the revelation. Unbeknownst to my daughter, this woman had been engaged in a long-standing affair with her husband.

"The woman falsely claims that my daughter shot him, even though my daughter was drugged and knocked unconscious by the assailant who then shot her husband. This woman is out for vengeance without any regard for the truth. My daughter is a prominent anesthesiologist. She is very respected and much loved by her peers. As a result of this woman's lies, the prosecutor indicted my daughter. He sees his advancement tied to her conviction. This woman was the impetus for the indictment.

"Terminate her. Her name and address are on the back."

"What's the time period?"

"My daughter's attorney says that the trial won't occur probably for one year. I'm not that patient. My daughter's emotional suffering must end. I think her attorney is putting a tail on this woman. I do not want her disposed of in Florida, nor in New Jersey. Abroad would be ideal. Can you handle it?"

"You saved my life. I told you then I was yours. I don't renege on my promises and especially not to you."

Burnside pulled a thick envelope from his suit coat's interior pocket and handed it to him.

"This should cover your expenses. If not, reach me only through the untraceable. If I can't pick up, leave the appropriate number. Once done, you will be paid handsomely. It goes without saying, use alternative identification in her presence and when on the mission. Sanitize everything. Her demise should appear accidental or drug-induced. Needle to the arm, prescription overdose, car accident, or any other means that points to a guilt-ridden woman who ends her own life. Any problem?"

"No."

"Any questions?"

"No."

"Then let's go downstairs, have some dinner, and catch up on non-sensitive subjects."

33.

Sanibel Island, Florida

The flight was uneventful and arrived in Fort Myers at 1:20 p.m. Earlier, Erika had booked a room at a cottage located near Huffmire's condo at the island's eastern end. Being it was mid-April, the spring breakers had returned to their nests, and the snowbirds were contemplating heading north. Rooms were available, and rates would be dropping in May, even on Sanibel.

Erika exited the car rental lot, followed the signs, and made a left onto Daniels Parkway. At the junction with Six Mile Cypress, she made another left, passed the Minnesota Twins spring training complex, and continued to follow the rental agent's instructions. Within thirty minutes, she arrived at Punta Rassa, paid the toll, and started her journey across the three-mile causeway. She ascended a high span. At its summit, she had a 180-degree view of aquamarine San Carlos Bay. To her left and right were boaters and sailors heading toward, or coming from, the emerald Gulf of Mexico, which adjoined the island's eastern end at which was stationed a brown-colored lighthouse.

As she continued across the causeway, Erika traversed spits of land interconnected by low-lying bridges. The islets reminded her of Key Biscayne. Palms lined both sides, as did picnickers, swimmers, fishermen, and windsurfers. She glimpsed a trio of dolphins as she crossed the first low bridge. Off to her left, brown pelicans were rising and suddenly diving toward their prey swimming under the water's surface.

She had been told that there were no traffic lights or high rises on the island. She left the last bridge and joined a line of slowly moving cars. As she approached the first intersection, she observed an officer directing the four-way traffic. His hand movements mimicked an exuberant maestro. She turned left onto Periwinkle Way. A paved bikeway to her right was populated with bikers, joggers, and walkers. Lushly landscaped homes fronted both sides of the roadway. Palms of all sorts and sizes were everywhere. Some lawns also were graced by Banyan trees and Gumbo Limbos. Hedges of varied heights separated numerous residences from the roadway.

Erika arrived at her destination, quickly checked in, and changed into beach attire. Huffmire was on the island. Of that, she was almost certain. The prior evening, she had used a phone card and posed as a pollster. A female had answered and politely declined participation. Her voice was not youthful nor elderly. It had to be her. Johnnie had urged her not to make direct contact. For now, she would heed his instructions. The condo was nearby. She decided to approach from the bike path, not the beach. She looked like any other tourist sporting sunglasses, casual top, shorts, and sandals. She purposely left her camera in the room. If needed, she would use her Smartphone.

Except for a small cluster of shops, the area definitely was residential. The further she walked, the more secluded the surroundings. Side streets changed from macadam to crushed shell and sand which led to San Carlos Bay or to the Gulf.

Within several minutes, Erika reached the condo complex. Seagrape hedges, native vegetation, and palms were parted by a crushed stone driveway that led to a series of two-storied buildings set back at different angles. Their beige color blended seamlessly with the native vegetation and assorted palms that encircled each structure. Each building was numbered with parking underneath.

Erika could hear the ping from tennis racquets on the courts hidden behind twenty-foot hedges that adjoined the bike path. She passed several buildings before reaching an enclosed hexagonal pool, hot tub, and bathhouse. Huffmire's building was adjacent to the pool and was closest to the beach. A winding gray-planked walkway bisected over a hundred yards of sea grass, seagrape, and sable palms that separated the complex from the shell-speckled beach. All the parking spaces were occupied at Huffmire's condo. She was not at the pool.

Erika headed down the walkway and passed a child washing her shells at a shower spigot overhanging the walkway. She reached the hard-packed sand and gazed at the Gulf. Unlike the bay, it was calm. The tide was low, and avid shell pickers were forty yards offshore. They bent, plunged their hands in the ankle to knee-deep water, and scooped up sand and shells. At the shoreline, others rummaged through small shell mounds. The shell pickers and walkers easily outnumbered the loungers at that hour.

Huffmire was a part-time resident. Her quest for shells probably had been satiated. More than likely, she'd be lounging nearby or walking, if not occupied in her condo. It was maybe a quarter of a mile to the lighthouse. Erika proceeded in that direction, rounded the island's curve, and walked to a public fishing pier. She reversed her direction and returned to the pool. No Huffmire. Tomorrow was another day. She'd be up early and would scour the complex. The woman would surface. She couldn't be that reclusive.

Erika followed the pebbled pathways toward the entrance. As she neared, she heard that familiar sound. It stirred her competitive juices. She walked toward the courts, and there she was. Solo. Dressed all in white. Slightly tanned and very thin. In the near court, with her back to her, the woman was fixated on mastering her serve. Ball after ball hit the net or landed out of bounds. Clearly a novice yet persistent in her efforts to improve. She wasn't throwing the ball high enough or straight enough. A simple instruction would improve her chance of success.

Erika was so tempted. What an opening, casual and believable. Huffmire would welcome her advice and would loosen her guard. A friendship would develop, and she would open up. She never would suspect. Johnnie's admonition returned. He wouldn't forgive her if her actions led to Melanie's conviction. Erika turned away and exited the complex. She would report to Johnnie. It was his call. It was his to win or lose. She couldn't interfere. Huffmire was here. That's all that mattered. She would watch from afar and follow all orders. Johnnie was not rigid. He would alter the surveillance if necessity mandated it.

34.

The night had been a restless one. Sleep had eluded her. All she could dwell on was the missed opportunity to connect with Huffmire. It was 7:30 a.m. Johnnie was in transit or already at the office. He answered immediately.

"How burned are you?"

"Plenty, but not in the way you expect. She's here, and I blew it. I scouted her complex and beach to no avail. As I was leaving, I spotted her trying to improve her horrendous serve. No one else was there. It was the perfect opportunity to assist her without suspicion, and I failed because of you. I obeyed your warning and kept walking. That's what still is burning me, not the sun."

"No, you played it right. Just tail her for the next several days. Let's see how she interacts with others. Does she seem despondent over her lover's death, or is she carefree and engaging?

"Does she differ much from her photo?"

"I had no trouble recognizing her. She was dressed in tennis whites. She's real thin and about five foot four, nothing eye-catching about her. I couldn't tell if she was graceful because all she did was serve the ball into the net or out of bounds. My guess is she's had a few lessons but needs a lot more. Tennis is a good way to meet people, especially those of the opposite sex. Maybe she's on the hunt for another companion. Wouldn't that be a bonus for us?"

"That's one of the reasons I want you to give her some space. Burnside is paying the tab, and we surely have the time. Her arraignment is Friday. I spoke to McGuire. He's releasing the computers and the personal cells but is keeping possession of Stafford's work phone. I'm meeting with Melanie at five o'clock tonight. Don't worry, I'll make note of any mood swings, body signals, and all that. What do you think of the island?"

"If the rest of this place is like the east end, I can understand its allure. Real tropical. Being athletic, you'd love it. No high-rises, no billboards, no traffic lights, no honking taxis, what's there not to like? I had a great blackened grouper dinner at this small shopping area a stone's throw away from my cottage. I spotted a long line at an ice-cream place called Pinocchio's. I figured it must be good. The Sanibel Crunch was to die for. I topped it with a scoop of the Mocha Java, which had a real kick to it. Met the owner, real nice lady. Former corporate executive who traveled often to Europe for her employer. She also owns Geppetto's, a cute little bakery. She flies her dough in from France. Makes her own French baguettes, croissants, and pastries as well as takeout lunches. As soon as I hang up, I'm off to Geppetto's. Do I save my receipts for Burnside?"

"Of course. If your mission is a success, he'll pay for anything. Huffmire's statement set him off and confirmed his suspicions of Stafford. Before, he strongly disapproved of him; now, he loathes him. Stafford was lucky his demise was sudden. Burnside inferred had he known of the affair, Stafford would have incurred more pain. Burnside promised me he wouldn't contact Huffmire. The way he thinks, that was a personal agreement. He probably feels it doesn't apply to someone else he employs. While you're tailing Huffmire, someone could be watching you both. If you sense it, back off and observe whether the tail makes a direct contact with Huffmire. The tail could be under the control of Burnside or McGuire."

"Got it. Any other instructions?"

"No. I think we've covered everything. I'm in the process of contacting possible forensic experts. Until I have McGuire's experts' reports, they can't help me too much. I anticipate a long evening with Melanie. She's coming to the office. I don't want Burnside's interference. Call me only if something urgent develops. Otherwise, follow Huffmire and report back in two or three days. Watch out for any frisky seniors on the prowl!"

"Yea, that's just what I need to add to my already conflicted personality. Watch out for your client. Patients fall for their analysts as do divorcees for their attorneys."

Erika clicked off. She would be missing his 'long evening with Melanie.' That both annoyed and troubled her. She read women much better than he did. He was handsome, athletic, and intelligent, a woman's trifecta. Yet he had more.

She had dated her share of men and only had become disillusioned. They could be disgusting, self-absorbed, and condescending. If they had feelings, they remained latent, unless prompted by an ulterior motive. She found it easier to bond with women. They shared their feelings and admitted to their fears and insecurities, at least the ones who maintained her interest.

Beneath the surface, Johnnie was much more sensitive and tender than he even wanted to admit. That's what conflicted her. He was so different from the others. He projected strength and confidence. Beneath that mask, there was emotional lability, a tenderness and feeling that she realized was drawing her to him as a moth to a night light. The more they collaborated, the stronger the magnetic pull became. Her resistance was receding, even if he was blind to its movement.

Melanie Stafford was pulling them closer, but he didn't even sense it. How could he plunge into the depths of Melanie's psyche if he couldn't comprehend his own? Johnnie assured her that he could assay the real Melanie Stafford. In that, he was delusional. The woman had been an actress in her younger years. Age only burnished that craft.

Under Melanie's spell, he would be a rudderless sailor on the open sea. More to the point, a thirst-starved mariner who hadn't even realized that the rudder had separated from the bobbing craft. Johnnie needed her insight now more than ever.

For several days, she would bide her time. If it proved uneventful, she would leave the sunshine and, figuratively, return to the darkness. Burnside readily dwelled in the shadows and mists. Had his daughter inherited that gene, or was she the innocent victim of a sinister conspiracy? Johnnie's duty was to her regardless of the DNA. Erika's onus was to shield Johnnie from the fallout. She questioned herself. Was she up to it?

Erika left her room and headed to Geppetto's. Its owner had touted her signature confection the Sanibel Blossom.

35.

Princeton New Jersey

She arrived on time. From her appearance, he wouldn't have surmised that she'd spent eight hours monitoring intubated patients as surgeons practiced their art. She was well- groomed, alert, and ready to proceed. She grabbed a bottle of water from the credenza and replied that the deli food could wait.

"I've received materials from the prosecutor. I want you to review them. If anything differs from your recollection, note the document, the page, and the inconsistency on this yellow pad. In the packet, there are also phone records that itemize calls received and made within the last twelve months. Pay particular attention to the numbers. If you don't recognize any, note the date and the number. When you've finished or need anything, hit number 15, and I'll be in. The bathroom is two doors to your right. Take your time, and don't be shocked by the police reports. I've seen thousands like them. I've removed the crime scene photos. You don't need to relive them now."

Melanie thanked him as he retreated from the library. He had withheld from her the damning documents. He wanted her clearheaded as she perused the reports from the EMTs, Hopewell cops, and hospital personnel. He also included the statements she and Inez provided to the authorities. After she had digested and analyzed those evidentiary items, he would confront her with the GSR report, Huffmire's photo and statement, and her husband's office phone log. That's when things really would get interesting.

Two hours elapsed before she buzzed him. As he entered, he glanced at the yellow legal pad he had provided her. There were very few notations.

"Let's start with the phone records. Were there any unfamiliar numbers on the landline records?"

"Not really, most were Jersey numbers. Based on the time of year, I could figure out the unfamiliar ones. Calls to my places of employment, physicians, pharmacies, and the like were obvious, as were calls to Wellington."

"How about your cell?"

"None at all."

"And your husband's cell?"

"I didn't see anything that would have raised a red flag."

"Are you sure? Even it if is detrimental to our defense, I have to know. It's the only way I can defend you properly. I can deal with bad news as I prepare for the trial. Once it commences, it's too late."

"As I said, so far, there's nothing that has set off my antennae. If anything does, I will alert you."

"Anything in the EMTs' reports?

"In my state at the time, I obviously can't verify or dispute anything they recorded. I was emotionally overwhelmed to say the least. I probably was irrational. Reading Inez's statement, clearly I had lost it. If her recollection is correct, when her screams awakened me and I went to Richard, I didn't even assess his condition. I just started CPR without looking at the wounds and their location. I can't believe I didn't notice the head wound immediately. Even the chest wound, I didn't recognize what effect my pumping would cause. He probably was dead, and I didn't see it or didn't want to accept it. My focus was on the blood and him on the ground. Defensively, I must have had tunnel vision on his body. As an anesthesiologist, I'm accustomed to standing over and behind a gowned body encircled by known and competent specialists. In most cases, everything has been planned and needs only to be executed. It's rare I see trauma patients in the ER. Usually, they are prepped and brought to one of the surgical suites after they have been stabilized to a degree.

"On that day at that hour, what I did and why, who knows? All I was trying to do was revive my husband. Nothing else mattered. Everything else was foreign to my thought processes."

"How about the reports of the arriving officers?"

"Not really. I must have had some clarity at that point."

Melanie looked toward the yellow pad.

"I told them, 'They've killed him.' Inez mentioned she heard it as did the EMTs and hospital personnel. Once I knew Richard was dead, I focused on his killers. I wanted them caught and punished, probably even killed. I had been attacked, but he had been murdered, snuffed out like a squashed bug."

Johnnie found her analogy odd. Did she view him as a bug? He knew what Erika would have concluded.

"Anything else about the police reports?"

"Again, I can't question their recollections. I don't even remember much of my own actions. I'd be foolish to quarrel with their opinions. Even I know it wouldn't help me before a jury. They'd believe them over me."

Johnnie considered her response. Was it one from a patient woman or a calculating one? Whichever, she was still his client. His opinion didn't matter. He wouldn't be pronouncing judgment.

"And the hospital reports?"

"They are trained professionals. They evaluated as best as they could. I noted they were unsure as to whether I had suffered a concussion. All I know is that I had a splitting headache and felt outerworldly. Whether that was due to the head trauma or to the shock of the assault and murder, I can't say. The headache lasted several days, but that was the least of my concerns. My husband was dead, and I was incarcerated. Viewed as a murderer, I wasn't a sympathetic figure to my jailers. Could I have complained of my headache? Of course. What would they have done about it? You and I both know: nothing."

"Ready to take a break to eat?"

"After reading this, definitely."

At first, they were quiet while eating. Johnnie felt somewhat uncomfortable with the stillness, which didn't seem to bother her. He figured she was deep in thought and probably reliving that night. To distract her, he broke the quietude. Had she had any unusual surgeries? She replied that nothing much anymore was unusual to her. What was troubling, however, was that they were cutting back her hours. They had obtained additional help. She wondered whether this was the beginning of the end. Was the public pressure too much to bear? Were they getting ready to let her go or, at least, suspend her so that hospital life could return to normal? No one wanted a putative killer among the staff and patients. She shuddered at the thought but seemed resigned to the probability. He tried to bulwark her spirits but was met by no positive response. When they were finished eating, he asked if she was too drained to continue. She though it better to see everything now. The damage to her composure already had been done. Why repeat it later?

Johnnie excused himself. Little did she know what came next never would leave her, especially if she really was unaware of Huffmire's existence.

When he returned, he mentioned, "There were no fingerprints on the gun or on the shells. There also were no fingerprints adjoining the glass cut-out on the sliding door. Your prints were on the door's inner side adjacent to the lock. That would be expected since you locked the slider."

He then handed her the GSR report.

"What is this?"

"It's called a gunshot residue report. Read it slowly. Then we'll discuss it."

Johnnie watched her concentrate on the report. She looked troubled. Maybe confused, but definitely concerned.

"I don't understand. If my prints weren't on the gun, how could I have powder on my palm? And why my left hand? I'm right-handed."

"Have you ever fired a gun?"

"No. When I was a kid, I fired a rifle at camp, but that's it."

"When you fired the rifle, was your right finger on the trigger or the left?""

"The right, of course."

"Are you sure you remember that?"

"Yes. Not a doubt."

"One explanation for the powder on only your left palm would be if you compressed your husband's chest with your left palm on his chest. The bullet pierced his heart. The compressions would have been near it. There would have been powder near the entrance wound. The gun was fired from short range, leaving powder burns. My guess would be the powder was transferred from his shirt to your left palm."

"Then I guess that's it. That's how it happened. "

"Melanie, this is not a guessing game. Do you know what McGuire will do with a guess on cross. He will tear you apart."

"Well, it had to be that way. My right hand is stronger than my left. I would have used it to apply the force to my left hand. It wouldn't make sense any other way. That's it. I know it."

"Let's hope so. It's a logical explanation. Mrs. Garcia saw you do the compressions. As long as she corroborates you, it becomes an issue of fact. The prosecutor's detective never thought to ask you, probably because the test hadn't been analyzed yet."

He then handed her the photo. She studied the woman longer than Johnnie had anticipated.

"Who is she?"

Johnnie stared at her. "She's your husband's lover."

"What?! On my God! Oh my God! No! No! No! It can't be. Why would he do it? We had everything! Money, respect. How could he throw it all away? For what? For her? Look at her! She's a plain Jane!"

"What could he see in her? What does she have that I don't? Looks? Not a chance! Education? Not to my level! Acclaim? Was that it? Was she renowned? Was she?"

"Not that I know of. She's a photographer. Apparently, she takes photos and writes articles for travel magazines."

"She's a fucking freelancer! That's what she is! How could he throw me away for her?"

Johnnie was rattled by her fury. She continued, "What did she do? Stroke his ego? Inflate his self-worth? Make him feel like the man my father said he wasn't? Is that how she ensnared him? How could he stoop so low?"

She buried her head in her hands. "What about me? What about my feelings, my hopes, my dreams? Didn't he even care? Was that how little I meant to him?"

She started to sob and then convulse. Johnnie didn't know what to do. Should he touch her and console her? How would she react? Would she lash out and strike him? Would she blame him for revealing the ugly truth? He just froze and watched her shake and weep. He couldn't even hand her tissues from the credenza. Her head was buried too deeply in her palms.

Finally, it occurred to him. "I'm so sorry, Melanie. I dreaded this revelation, but there was no other way. There was no escaping this moment. As horrible and gut-wrenching as it is, now was the time, not in McGuire's opening statement to the jury. That would have been calamitous. You would have been overwhelmed and collapsed. The jury would have believed you staged your response. Everyone would have believed you already knew it. McGuire would have crucified you on cross. Not one person would have believed you saw everything else but not this particular discovery. Not the jurors, not the judge, not the bailiff, and definitely not the press in the gallery. You would have been doomed for sure. I'm your lawyer, not your witness. I can't say I never showed you. If I did in open court, the judge would extirpate me. My credibility before the jury would be lost, and the verdict would be swift."

Melanie, without looking up, blubbered, "I don't blame you. You're the messenger, not the actor. The actor's dead, and I'm left all alone to wallow in my sorrow and my hate. Yes, my hate. I can't believe he violated my trust. But her? She had to know he was married, or was this a short romance?"

"From her statement, no. Was it love? I seriously doubt it. At least, from her vantage point, it doesn't seem so. She was once divorced and appears to have valued her freedom. But it really doesn't matter. I'm convinced her statement guaranteed your indictment. Up to then, McGuire had you near the weapon and had the GSR results. Her statement was the hammer he needed. He's convinced you killed him."

"Let me see the statement. Does my father know? He will explode."

"Yes. He commanded that I share everything with him. Your prognostication was correct. He wanted to be here when I revealed it to you. I strongly counseled him otherwise. He finally relented. He's hired my father as his counsel. He believes he could be a target based on the paramour's supposed parroting of your husband's thoughts. He's wrong. McGuire doesn't have him in his prosecutorial sights. It only would weaken his case against you. I've ordered him not to contact the woman, and I also order you. Not a call. Not a letter. Nothing. Any contact by you, and you can kiss your defense goodbye. Our focus is, and must be, on Wellington. McGuire refuses to investigate that angle or any other. Your husband feared Wellington and for good reason. Now we want the jury to realize he was right."

"Please let me read the statement. I have to see it with my own eyes. I don't want to, but I have to."

Johnnie, with some regret, handed it to her.

As she read the statement, she looked defeated. She sighed several times and just shook her head. There was no escaping the truth. Was the statement accurate, or was it embellished by a vengeful woman who had lost her admirer? Who knew? What was undeniable was that Stafford had cheated and had cheated often, obviously without shame or remorse. Did he deserve to die? For that, no. But he wasn't the first casualty of unrequited love and wouldn't be the last.

She slid the document back to him. "How many others did he sleep with? Did they accompany him, or were they locals, impressed by an American on a company expense account? And I felt sorry for him, for those elongated flights, many to impoverished lands. How could I have been so obtuse? When I was a teenager, my father warned me that trust was a one-way street and told me that I should always listen but verify. I heard him but discounted the aphorism as uttered by an overprotective father."

"Melanie, we learn from our experiences. Unfortunately, often it's too late. You gave him your trust. There was nothing else you could do. His weakness nourished his deceit. Those three bullets have victimized you twice."

"What will happen to her?"

"Nothing. Maybe her former husband also was duplicitous and destroyed her marriage, leaving her initially desolate then hardened and narcissistic. Frankly, it doesn't matter."

"She should be punished for what she did."

"In other ways, she may be, but not by you. I repeat you must not contact her in any form. If you do, you will have destroyed all the efforts we will be undertaking to defend you."

"So she just gets to go on with her life as if nothing happened? I may spend the rest of my life in a ten-by-six-foot cell, and she can merrily continue with her flings?"

"Who knows what life has in store for any of us? None of us realize, but we all live in the moment. That's our only guarantee. It might be fleeting or of longer duration but never everlasting, at least not here.

"Despite the double shock to your psyche, you must focus on one thing, your defense. At this point, nothing else matters, not even your job. It won't be easy, but that is what you must do."

"Will she testify?"

"Absolutely, and there will be no outbursts by you. The jury will expect you to stare at her, but that's all. If you scream, curse, rant, or rave, the jury will interpret those actions as corroborative of the probable fact that you killed your husband to punish him and destroy her. The link will have been made, and we won't be able to shear it. Heed this and heed it well. If McGuire promotes an outburst, he has probably won. Through witnesses and your cross-examination, that will be his purpose. To you, he will be antagonistic, sarcastic, over-bearing, and intemperate, all to provoke your anger. You must be the thoughtful and intelligent spouse, one unknowingly betrayed by her adulterous husband yet convinced that he was murdered by his employer. When asked how you would have reacted had you known, you will reveal your sadness but also will demonstrate your humanity. You would have asked him why, suggested counseling, and if not suc-cessful, would have parted. Sorry, of course, but able to move forward with your profession. You both had your own funds, so each could live without any real financial concerns. Am I right so far?"

"Yes. What else have you held back from me?"

"The crime scene and autopsy photos."

"Give them to me. Better now than be surprised before the jury."

"Are you sure? We have plenty of time."

"Now! I remember the scene. The photos won't change it, unless the pictures were staged for maximum effect. If so, I'll know. As to Richard, I guess I'm a little more dispassionate having read that woman's statement."

He returned with the envelope-enclosed photos. "When you've finished and feel ready, call me. They're not pleasant. Do the best you can, especially with the scene photos."

Forty minutes elapsed before she summoned him. She looked exhausted. He chided himself for pressing on with the photos. They could have waited. Maybe, however, she was right. Get it all out, and then try to repair the damage. A task they both knew would be difficult, if not impossible.

"I wonder which shot was first?" she pondered. "How much did he suffer? Was he still moving forward after the first one? Is that why there were more, or did they just want to make certain he was silenced?"

"I can't answer that. Maybe the forensics will."

"What will the prosecutor argue?"

"That it had to be you. No professional would have needed three shots."

"How about if it was completely dark?"

Her response blindsided him. None of the statements covered that issue. Neither she nor Inez ever mentioned whether the master bedroom was illuminated when Inez arrived. If it wasn't, then there would have been total darkness. Unless the killer was wearing night vision goggles, he would have been unfamiliar with the layout. His eyes probably wouldn't have adjusted. He easily could have missed the kill shot with the first bullet, maybe even the second if he still was struggling with Melanie.

"Before the police arrived, did you enter your bedroom?"

"No. I never entered it before they took me away."

"How about Inez?"

"I don't know."

"Call her now, but don't ask her. Just tell her I have to speak to her. Then leave the library. Whatever her response, you can't hear it. I'll explain why later."

Melanie placed the call, briefly chatted, and handed him the cell.

"Mrs. Garcia, when you arrived that morning, was there daylight?"

"Yes, it light enough. I see colors but no real sunny yet."

"Were there any lights on when you entered the house?"

"No. I going to put on inside light but instead saw Mr. Stafford on floor then Mrs. Stafford on floor."

"Were there any lights on in the master bedroom?"

"No."

"Did you put any lights on before the EMTs arrived?"

"Only light near front door. I too shook up. Melanie, she screaming and running to Mr. Stafford and blood on rug and wall. I call 911."

"So the only light you turned on was the one just inside the front door?"

"Yes. Only one."

"Did the EMTs turn on any lights?"

"I don't know. I too shook up."

"How about the police?"

"I don't know. I still too shook up then."

He thanked her and went for Melanie.

"What did she say?"

"It was light enough outside that she could see colors. There were not lights on inside. Sometime after seeing you and Richard on the floor, she put on the inside lights adjacent to the front door."

"So that helps me?"

"It helps you, as much as it helps McGuire. I can live with that. Did you notice anything unusual or interesting from the crime scene photos?"

"They depicted what I recalled. Unsettling but accurate. What else have you not disclosed?"

"Nothing. As my client, you're entitled to see everything, and you will. Nothing will be hidden from you, and nothing should be concealed from me. I mean nothing."

"You told me earlier. I haven't forgotten. What's next on the agenda?"

"For you, Friday. Be at the office by 2:00 p.m. My dad will accompany you to the courthouse. I'll be there before you arrive. I'll probably stay after you leave. If possible, I want to see the judge with McGuire. You are not to comment to anyone who asks you anything about the case. Nothing. Be pleasant, courteous, and smile if appropriate, but that's it. My dad will take care of the rest. I will tell the judge that we waive reading of the indictment. He will ask you if you understand it, and you will say 'yes, Your Honor.' He will ask you how you plead to the indictment, and you obviously will say, 'not guilty, Your Honor.' He will inquire if you had an opportunity to review what the prosecutor has given your attorney, and you will state you have. Anything else he asks, you respond directly to him unless I answer for you or tell you not to respond. Do not say anything in response to questions or comments made by McGuire. Nothing. I'll address those issues. Understand?"

"Yes."

"Do you have any questions?"

"I understand. Nothing to anyone, not even the press."

Johnnie walked her to her car. As she drove away, he still couldn't comprehend why Stafford would have cheated on her. She seemed to have it all. What was it about attractive women being drawn to nondescript men? Did it embolden them to cheat? He guessed a psychoanalyst might have at least a plausible theory.

36.

That Friday, Johnnie and Melanie met in a conference room between the courtroom and the public hallway. She was dressed in a black suit. Her nerves were apparent. He assured her the procedure would be perfunctory. He reviewed her role in the proceeding, and then he and his father escorted her to the empty courtroom. Within minutes, McGuire entered, and both counsel advised the attending sheriff's officer that they were ready for her arraignment. Shortly thereafter, Judge Scholman entered, greeted them, and commenced the proceeding. Johnnie waived the indictment's reading. Melanie pled not guilty and advised the court that she had read the discovery provided by the prosecutor's office. Both counsel informed the court there had been no plea negotiations. Johnnie then requested an immediate conference with the judge regarding discovery issues. The judge mentioned that he had a short conference call he had to take and then would see them in chambers. As the judge was leaving the bench, Johnnie briefly conferred with Melanie who then exited the courtroom with his father.

McGuire approached him. "What are the discovery issues? I've given you what I've got."

"It's not so much what you haven't provided me, but more about what you're not going to do."

"Like what?"

"Like investigate Wellington and its testing lab."

"Why should I? It's a smoke screen, and you know it."

"That's where you and I differ, Terry. By the way, who owned the gun?"

"She used it, so either she or her husband obviously did."

"When and where did they purchase it?"

"How would I know?"

"You can't tell me Stankowicz or some other detective or investigator didn't run a check on the gun. It was manufactured in Austria. Glock would know where it was shipped. Terry, if I have to file a motion on this issue, I'll be asking for counsel fees if it turns out you have the information. When we see Scholman, I'm going to bring it up. You might want to check now before we see him."

"Yeah, I'll check to see." McGuire exited the courtroom.

Ten minutes later, he returned. "I apologize. A check was run. I'm having a stipulation typed for you now."

"And what will that stipulation generally say, Terry?"

"The Glock was sold to a German who died many years ago. There is no record how it ended up in Melanie Stafford's possession."

"That won't cut it, Terry. There's no proof it was her gun. It's a contested issue of fact as to whether she owned it or even shot it. I want a revised stipulation. I want the date of sale, where it was sold, to whom it was sold, and what the last registered owner did with the gun. Also, include the date of death for the original purchaser. I expect that document on my desk by Tuesday."

McGuire did not respond. He just walked back to his counsel table and made like he was inspecting his file, which Johnnie knew he already had memorized.

Several minutes later, the courtroom's side door opened, and the judge's law clerk summoned them to a long brown-carpeted hallway that separated the chambers of the various criminal judges from their courtrooms. They then entered an outer office manned by the judge's secretary and continued to the actual chamber. Scholman had disrobed and was seated at a u-shaped desk. Behind him was a large fan-shaped window. To his right were two elongated windows. To his left was a large built-in bookcase containing the green bound decisions of the lower and appellate courts and the off-white volumes of the state's Supreme Court. Scholman motioned for the attorneys to sit in the two chairs that faced him and directed his law clerk to the chair next to the elongated windows.

"Johnnie, I don't think you've met my law clerk, Grace O'Neill. I've decided to keep this case. I expect you and Terry to try to iron out any discovery problems before calling me. If you can't resolve your differences, call Grace. She'll schedule a telephonic conference for me. With the publicity surrounding this case, I want to minimize your court appearances. I don't want this case tried in the press. As of now, I'm entering a gag order. This will spare both of you from having to grandstand before them. I expect you and your offices to honor it, as well as Dr. Stafford, although I'm sure you already have instructed her on that issue. When you both leave, provide Grace with your cell and home numbers. Now what are the discovery problems?"

Johnnie pulled a copy of Stafford's email and the related photos from a folder and handed them to the judge.

"Your Honor, from the beginning, it has been our position that Mr. Stafford was murdered to silence him. He possessed explosive information that financially would have caused severe economic damage to his employer, Wellington Pharmaceuticals."

Johnnie briefly described the damaging information, the reason for the email, and the relevancy of the photographs.

"I've asked Terry and his office to investigate our allegations. They have declined. They've concluded Dr. Stafford murdered her husband. We vehemently disagree. Our only recourse is to file specific motions directed to Wellington and the testing lab utilized to implement and analyze the drug trials. I will be directing the motion not only to Terry's office but also to Wellington and the testing lab. I will file the notice of motion directly with the court clerk but the actual affidavits and supporting documents under seal directly with Your Honor. That way, Wellington and its lab will be protected at this stage of the litigation. I have no other alternative. My client must be protected. We need the requested information. Without it, we can't defend her properly. I'm certain Wellington will claim its documents are confidential and privileged. I will be asking Your Honor for an order requiring copies of the requested documents be shipped directly to you for an in camera inspection so a determination may be made as to which documents can be divulged to us within the parameters of a specific court order."

Johnnie then handed the judge copies of the EMT, police, and hospital reports.

"Your Honor will see that Dr. Stafford repeatedly told the responding emergency personnel, the cops, and the emergency room staff that she had been assaulted and drugged by an unknown assailant or assailants, and that 'they killed him.' This is not some bogus assertion mentioned weeks after the crime. She uttered it immediately at the scene and for hours thereafter. She readily provided a statement the day after she was arrested. While it's not our burden to prove her innocence, we will. The prosecutor won't, so it's left to us."

"Who owns the gun?"

"Your Honor, that's what I want to know. Neither Dr. Stafford nor her husband owned a gun. I asked Terry today if his office ran a search on the Glock. He said they did. The gun was manufactured in Austria and sold to a German who died years ago. I told him I wanted by Tuesday a stipulation as to all the known facts on the gun."

Scholman looked at McGuire. "Get it to him by Tuesday. Did the Staffords own it?"

"She used it, Your Honor."

"Did you find her prints on the weapon?"

"No. The gun was wiped clean."

"So you don't know who owned it. I want that stipulation to leave out any gratuitous assumption that she owned it and fired it. Those are issues of fact that you must prove and she doesn't have to disprove. Got it?"

"Yes, Your Honor."

"Also, once the stipulation is signed by both of you, keep copies for yourselves and send me the original. "How about expert reports, Terry?"

"Judge, we're in the process of getting our reports."

"How much time do you need?"

"We hope to have them in forty-five days."

"And you, Johnnie?"

"Judge, we can't do anything until we see his reports."

"That makes sense. Terry, send me your reports when you send them to him. Johnnie, I'll give you sixty days from your receipt of the reports. If either of you need more time, arrange a conference call with me through Grace. I expect both of you to cooperate. You're both very experienced. I'm not going to tolerate any game playing, so be forewarned. Everything that's discoverable should be exchanged sooner than later. Understand?"

Both attorneys nodded and stated affirmatively.

"Okay. Back to the courtroom. The gag order is being placed on the record. That way there will be no misunderstanding by either of you. Let's go. You, too, Grace."

After Scholman had placed his comments on the record and left the bench, Johnnie approached the young lawyer. Her short strawberry-blond hair blended with her slightly pimpled pale complexion. Wire-rim glasses shielded her gray-blue eyes. She blushed as he approached. He sensed that behind her studious and serious semblance was a substratum of shyness and quietude.

"So how do you like the clerkship?"

"Judge Scholman is very demanding, but he is also helpful. At first, I was really intimidated but relaxed a bit when he kept praising my thoroughness. I had been warned he was a taskmaster, but I've adjusted to his demands. The hours are long, but I expected that."

"Trust me, they're no longer than private practice, but there the pay's better. What do you want to do when your clerkship ends in August?"

"I'm not sure. The judge told me he'd help me hook up with a good firm, but I still don't know what type of law I want to practice. I can't see matrimonial. There's too much acrimony and sorrow. Maybe corporate or educational law. I don't think I'm cut out to be a trial lawyer. I'm definitely not suited for criminal work, not on either side. My dad would like me to focus on banking or corporate. I don't know how you guys can think so fast on your feet. I'm too deliberative for that. I'm also too set in my concepts of right and wrong, whether it be in civil or criminal matters. Sometimes, I question whether I should have gone to law school in the first place."

"Well, if right and wrong bother you, how about that gray area in between? That's often where we lawyers troll. You're gonna discover that's where lawyers earn their keep or lose their clients. We can mold our facts to the black or the white to some degree. It's the gray where both sides really become creative."

"Well, who determines right or wrong in the gray?"

"The Judge Scholmans of the world and their overseers. Why do you think so many civil cases settle? It's because of the gray. Most cases contain some gray, and usually each side equally partakes. Most cases have some right and wrong on each side. I'm not talking here about criminal law. There, the person either committed the crime or didn't. On occasion, there may be some extenuating circumstances, but that is the exception, not the norm. The civil side, for the most part, is very different."

"But how about the black letter law?"

"You remember your torts class? The accidents, the product defects…. What did you need to know for your exam and also for the bar exam?"

"The exceptions. For every concept, there were numerous exceptions."

"Exactly. And that's what leads to the gray area. For example, you might have a great case on the issue of fault but weaknesses in your damages. That's where you enter the gray area. That's where the really good lawyers earn their reputations and reap their rewards. Don't limit yourself. A reputable attorney has to be honest with himself or herself. Be true to your sense of self-worth and honor, but also recognize no one has a monopoly on the gray world. As long as you play by the ethics, you can enter it. In fact, you will have to enter it if you want to survive. Here are my phone numbers. Anytime you want to talk about honor, ethics, and the gray zone, call me. I guess you, me, and Terry will become companions over the next several months. Nice meeting you."

As Johnnie turned to leave the courtroom, she pondered what he had related. He projected such a strong presence, yet he spoke with such calmness and sincerity. The contrast was so alluring.

37.

Sanibel Island, Florida

"Throw the ball higher!" The prior evening, he had spotted her walking on the beach. The following morning, he had parked himself at the pool from where he surveilled her condo. At 8:30 a.m., she had exited and walked to the courts. He observed her from a distance. She was alone and practicing her serve. She turned toward him when she heard his instruction. He was extremely well built. She guessed he was around six foot two and 215 pounds.

"If you're going to beat anyone, you have to get the serve over the net." He smiled and said, "Sorry. Don't mean to be rude, but you looked like you were really struggling."

"Struggling isn't the word for it. I think my shoulder will give out before I master this."

"Throw the ball higher and arch your back a little more. The ball should be above you and not so far forward. You're losing distance and power. Do you want me to show you?"

"Please do. My instructor will be impressed if suddenly the ball gets in the proper court with some regularity."

He picked up two balls near the fence and went to the serving line. The first one he served with little effort and speed.

"You're not hitting it much faster than I did, but at least it's in."

He took the other ball and rocketed it over the net. "Does that satisfy your need for speed?"

"I'm impressed."

"Don't be. You'll learn it's not just the speed that's important. Any decent pro could have returned that ball and placed it where he wanted it. It's the kick, spin, and placement that make the difference. Are you a baseball fan?"

"Rabid Yankees fan."

"Then you probably know any hitter in the American League can smash a fastball. A fastball pitcher has to change the location, speed, and movement on the ball. Otherwise, he's toast. Why do you think starters have more than one pitch? They need deception. Angles, speed, location, and movement fool hitters. It's the same in tennis. Watch Nadal, Federer, Djokovic. You'll see how they're different, yet they all vary their shots and speed."

"Are you renting a condo here?"

"No. I had gone for a run on the beach and suddenly realized I had overextended myself. I saw the condos. Figured there would be a pool, a water fountain, and some unoccupied chaise lounges. Thought I'd take a breather and then head back on the bike path. Closed my eyes and probably dozed off for ten minutes. Awakened, started toward the road, and saw you whacking away. Do you live here?"

"Usually October through July except for business trips."

"Now that's the way to live. What type of business?

"I'm a professional photographer and freelance travel journalist. How about you?"

"Now a self-employed idler and traveler."

"If you're self-employed, how can you be idle?"

"Got very lucky when I was younger. Got hooked up with some techies, did very well when they sold their companies, and invested very wisely. Now I advise a limited number of clients. Actually, I agree to handle only a portion of their portfolios. I want the bulk of their assets with the private wealth managers at the big institutions. I dabble with their play money in various ventures in which I also invest. That way, if they lose, I do also. If I reap gains, so do they. Fortunately, the winners have outpaced the losers."

"Where do you travel?"

"Mostly Europe. Love the history, art, and architecture. I've also been to the Middle East, Israel, Saudi Arabia, and other places."

"I take it you don't live here."

"No, I was visiting a client in Naples. He had mentioned I'd probably enjoy Sanibel's quietude, so I booked a room for several days. So far, so good."

"Where do you live?"

"My home base is in Chicago."

"Do you have family there?"

"What's with all the questions? If I tell you too much, I'll have to kill you." He laughed and then continued. "I was married for a while before I realized I had made a terrible mistake. Fortunately, we hadn't had kids. Been single and carefree since. Haven't met the right person I could love and also trust."

"Have any regrets?"

"Don't we all have regrets in one way or another? We have to look forward. If you dwell too long on the past, you can't enjoy the present, and no one can predict their own future. At least I can't. Can you?"

"Not that I know of."

"Listen, if I keep philosophizing, you'll never improve your serve. I'll stop by tomorrow on my jog to see if you've improved."

"I have a lesson at the Dunes at ten o'clock. You can catch me there if you're interested in my progress. Thanks for the advice."

"I'd be curious to see if your pro corrects it. Enjoy your day in the sunshine."

As he jogged away, he had second thoughts about his mission. She seemed so friendly. But a mission was just that. Orders had to be obeyed, especially when your commander saved your life.

38.

She had tailed her to a restaurant, followed her as she took pictures in the 'Ding' Darling National Wildlife Refuge, and even watched her from afar as she took tennis lessons at the Dunes Golf and Tennis Club. All to no avail. Then one day, she witnessed a tall, good-looking guy approach her at her condo's tennis courts. Her serve still hadn't improved. He showed her how to serve properly. They talked for several minutes. Then, he jogged away. The following day, she watched her lesson at the Dunes. The man reappeared. He borrowed a racquet and hit with her for an hour after the lesson. That evening, he took her to dinner at a local restaurant. As they exited the restaurant, she was laughing and playfully hitting his arm. He grabbed her around the waist, raised her right arm, and pushed it forward as if she were serving. They appeared to be bonding. He dropped her off at the condo and returned to his hotel. The following day, they played tennis for two hours at the condo and then lounged around the pool. That evening, they dined out, and he spent the night at her condo. When they emerged the following day, they were holding hands. She kissed him on the tennis court following their playful tennis practice. They returned to her condo, and they emerged for dinner that night. Again, he stayed overnight.

Erika had videos and pictures to substantiate their budding romance. Not two months had elapsed, and the paramour was grieving no more, if she ever had. Erika had the date-stamped evidence to prove it. Sunburned and tired, she phoned Johnnie.

"I thought you forgot about me. Did the sun rot your brain?"

"I think we hit pay dirt."

Erika explained what had transpired and what she had recorded. He told her to back off and return before her cover was exposed. He also lauded her for her thoroughness. McGuire's office had researched the Glock. It was manufactured in Austria and purchased in Munich in 1988 by a Seigfried Hauer who died in 1992. The chain ended there. How it got to the States was anyone's guess. There was no direct proof that the Staffords owned or even possessed the gun other than by its presence at the crime scene and possibly by the GSR test. McGuire had tried to conceal the truth, but Erika's quick thinking had led to its revelation.

She called the airline and luckily was able to secure a seat on the early afternoon flight. She packed, checked out, and headed to her car. Then she saw him. He was jogging on the bike path adjacent to her cottage. They would cross paths. There was no way to avoid him without arousing suspicion. As he neared, he glanced at her suitcase, smiled, and asked, "What, leaving paradise?" Then he was gone. Had she been exposed, or was he just an outgoing guy? He definitely was a charmer.

39.

November 2008
Princeton, New Jersey

His father had died at eighty-seven in 2004, necessitating the sale of the legitimate side of the export-import company. In a sense, it was a relief. To remain associated with the law while simultaneously operating a northern New Jersey company was impossible.

While the company had generated a decent profit, that sum paled when compared to the money engendered from the illicit trade of antiquities and art. Within months of the German's passing in 2002, his son had made contact and expressed an interest in continuing the relationship.

Thereafter, the son visited him in Princeton. He reciprocated on several occasions. The trips now were different. He flew solo. His wife had died recently.

Transactions were facilitated through agreed-upon codes with funds still wired to offshore accounts. Changes however, had occurred. The Russians had entered the bidding. The German had been reluctant to accept the new clientele but eventually relented upon realizing their voracious appetite for the looted items.

Prior to his passing, the American's father had disclosed the European locations where buried treasures still remained. Armed with that knowledge, the American understood that unconscionable profits could be realized for a long time provided only he knew the locations.

40.

Princeton, New Jersey

After Erika's call, Johnnie placed Silverman's and Burnside's supporting affidavits in the large envelop along with his exhaustive affidavit and relevant expert reports. Judge Fleming already had transmitted his report to the Ethics Committee. That body would have to decide whether oral testimony was necessary. He didn't relish seeing Dr. Lewis again. Lewis had consumed enough of his time and had no appreciation for the effort he had expended on his behalf.

Inez Garcia had agreed to meet him at the office at 5:30 p.m. He needed to probe her further without Melanie being present. McGuire's office had promised that the agreed-upon seized evidence would be returned to his office that afternoon.

Johnnie then turned to his most daunting task, completing his motion to compel discovery from Wellington and the independent testing lab. He had prepared the notice of motion directed to the prosecutor's office, Wellington, and the lab. From the prosecutor's discovery, legitimate inferences and deductions could point to her guilt or innocence. Richard Stafford's lengthy 'To Whom It May Concern' email embedded in his computer provided the nexus to Wellington's involvement. At least, that's the way he viewed it. Would Judge Scholman concur?

While McGuire would oppose, the heavyweight resistance would flow from Wellington. He would be assaulted with the defenses of trade secrecy and privacy. He had to craft his affidavit to convince

Scholman that Melanie's right to a fair trial outweighed both concerns and that they could implement steps to preclude harm emanating from the utilization of the requested documents.

His affidavit and supporting documentation, as agreed, would be forwarded directly to the judge. He would file only the notice of the motion with the clerk's office. He would not prepare a proposed order but would request leave to submit one after the court had determined what would be allowed.

In his affidavit, he would describe Furber's involvement, as detailed in the email, and would voice his concern that Wellington would not produce him voluntarily for trial. To prevent Wellington from hiding him abroad, he would request that an order be entered requiring him to appear for the trial. Furber was a critical hostile witness. Melanie's defense would be compromised severely without his appearance. A pre-trial de bene esse deposition would be ineffectual, because preceding trial evidence probably would alter the line of questioning. If the judge ruled against him, Melanie, more than likely, would be convicted.

Inez Garcia arrived promptly. She was short and stout. She wore her hair in a bun. What was most pronounced was her radiant smile and gentle nature. Johnnie knew she would be liked instantly by the jury. McGuire would offend the jury if he tried to bully her. He had feared her docile nature might allow a cross-examiner to alter her memory of the incident. He was surprised when she resisted his efforts to confuse her recollection. She was adamant as to her perception that early morning. He had her demonstrate how Melanie reacted when she arrived. She did so with conviction and emotion. When asked how Melanie applied the CPR, she went to her knees, bent over, placed her right palm over her left hand, and pushed down rapidly. She was certain that was the way.

That was what he needed but feared he wouldn't see.

After she left, he recorded all he saw. Before he put her on the stand, he would rehearse those movements so that they would be ingrained in her. All he could hope was that McGuire's chicanery wouldn't alter her certainty.

41.

Two Months Later Mercer County Courthouse
Trenton, New Jersey

Johnnie had argued cogently in support of the motion. To solidify his position, earlier he had provided the judge and all opposing counsel with Malcolm Gideon's expert report that detailed the inner workings of the FDA and its relationship with the pharmaceutical industry. Gideon had an undergraduate degree in chemistry and a doctor's degree in pharmacy. Actually, he had worked as a pharmacist before being lured to a well-known drug company. There, he participated in the research and testing of numerous drugs that were submitted for FDA approval. Some were successful; others were shelved. Eventually, he became disillusioned with the industry and obtained employment with the FDA, where he used his knowledge to attempt to police the industry. He had testified before Congress for the agency. Despite his exhortations for more funding and more employees to oversee the industry, his pleas typically fell on deaf ears. Now retired, he consulted and wrote on pharmaceutical issues.

McGuire had started to argue in opposition, but Scholman cut him off. McGuire had a duty to provide possible exculpatory evidence to the defense. Johnnie had argued the same point. The requested evidence wasn't under McGuire's control. Scholman said he had no real standing to oppose the motion. Scholman then turned to separate counsel representing Wellington and Sterling Labs.

"Gentlemen, I've read your opposing briefs. Your points are well articulated. Is there anything else you want to add that's distinct from the briefs?" Wellington's counsel arose.

"Your Honor, the FDA approved the drug. There have been no recalls. There is nothing to support the defendant's motion, other than an email from the deceased. Who knows his motivations? How truthful are his allegations? No one else has come forth to support these claims. My client views them as scandalous and defamatory. The company's good name will be tarnished, and for what?"

Judge Scholman interrupted. "For what? How about the defense of one accused of murder? If Wellington is blameless, it has nothing to fear. Mr. Petito, the defense is asking only for the testing records of the Romanian participants and the documents forwarded to the FDA exclusive of the drug's formula."

"Your Honor, Wellington is obligated to protect the identity and privacy of the subjects."

"And how do you think, Mr. Petito, the world will learn of their participation? It won't in this courtroom. The jurors will see their names and faces. No one else will, except for me and counsel. Do you really think an American juror is going to trumpet to the world the names of these people? How do you suppose that is going to occur? Jurors can't take their notes with them. As to the documents sent to the FDA, I will review them."

"Well, Your Honor, leaks do occur."

"Not in my courtroom. If they do, the person who ventured to disobey my instructions will get to taste the culinary delights of the Corrections Center. Let's move on to the defense's motion regarding Wellington's Mr. Furber."

"Your Honor, the request is baseless. No one other than the deceased has accused Mr. Furber of any possible wrongdoing. Unfortunately, Mr. Stafford can't be cross-examined."

"Then what does Mr. Furber have to fear, Mr. Petito? Like any other witness, he can assume the stand and tell the truth. He has nothing to lose except for some time for which I'm sure his employer will pay him. If not, I'll order the compensation."

"But, Your Honor, what if Mr. Furber has to be out of the country on business?"

"That's simple, Mr. Petito. It's mid-June. I'm scheduling this trial for the first Monday in October. From what I understand, Mr. Furber can fly back to one of four airports. I doubt Mr. McGuire will call him as his witness. If so, I'm sure he will cooperate. If Mr. Fitzhugh wishes to call him as a hostile witness, then he will notify me at the end of Mr. McGuire's case. Understood, Mr. Fitzhugh?"

"Yes, Your Honor."

"Gentlemen, I want to compliment all of you on your briefs. The arguments were well researched and well presented. This is a murder case. I'm obligated to consider the rights of the accused. If I err, I have to err on the side of caution in favor of her rights. I want all the testing records and photographs for the Romanian subjects on my desk within twenty days. Everything should be sent under seal to me. I will review them and decide what must be disclosed to the prosecutor and the defense. Whatever is released will be only to opposing counsel and is not to be disclosed to anyone other than any retained experts who must provide an affidavit to the court that they will not divulge the documents to anyone and will return copies to counsel for their destruction. I will prepare the order. It will apply to Sterling as well as Wellington. Mr. Petito, you will advise Mr. Furber and his superiors of the order and that same must be complied with."

"Yes, Your Honor."

"All right, gentlemen, that's it. Have a good day."

Johnnie couldn't believe he had won on all fronts. What was even more surprising was Scholman's tone and decisiveness. Before he could leave, the judge's clerk, Grace O'Neill, approached him.

"Hi, Mr. Fitzhugh. I've given a lot of thought to your gray-zone concept. I finally see where you're coming from. Thanks for the advice. I'm not as conflicted now with my choice of a profession."

"Listen, most of us have self-doubts. If we didn't, we'd all be foolhardy and egocentric. What a gaggle of attorneys that would make."

Johnnie said goodbye and left the courtroom. Yes, he still had self-doubt. Would he be able to use Furber to Melanie's advantage? One thing he knew for certain – Judge Scholman had no doubt as to whom was controlling the case. McGuire and he were participants, but Scholman was director. Hopefully, there would be more rulings in his favor. But then, that self-doubt raised its ugly head.

42.

March 2015
Munich, Germany

The lanky art purveyor walked through the Propyläen. Modeled some-what on the ancient Propylea situated on the Athenian Acropolis, the structure featured Doric porticos and served as a large neoclassical city gate to the Konigsplatz, one of the city's largest squares. In an effort to aggrandize his power and to intimidate the masses, Hitler used the square to parade his troops.

To his right sat the Staatliche Antikensammlungen, which housed one of the world's finest collections of ancient vases from the sixth and fifth centuries BC, together with treasured samples of Etruscan, Greek, and Roman ornamental art and jewelry. To his left stood the enormous Glypotothek with its central eight-columned portico. Niches containing sculptures embellished three sides of the edifice. King Ludwig I erected the building to house his collection of Greek and Roman sculptures.

As a young man, he had marveled at the grace of the Apollo of Terentia. Sculpted in 560 BC, the figure portrayed a perfectly propor-tioned unclothed male, his long tightly sculpted locks flowing behind his shoulders. Even with part of the figure's right arm and forearm absent, the mesmerizing effect was undiminished. He walked toward the classic Greek temple-like museum, mounted its steps, and entered. He wandered through the Roman Hall and viewed the busts and statues of famous philosophers and emperors. He continued to stroll through the museum. He passed a sculpture of a fallen soldier on his left side, bracing himself with his circular shield. He then encountered a stone carving of a seated and drunken elderly woman arching her neck backward while fervently cradling a cherished urn.

His father, an art historian and professor, had survived the war and eventually had profited, despite Munich's ruin and devastation. Over a six-year period, some seventy Allied air raids had blasted the city. The Feldherrnhalle, with its wide arches open to the street, somehow had avoided destruction. Constructed to mirror Florence's Loggia dei Lanzi, it had been the scene of the Fuhrer's Beer Hall Putsch, his November 1923 attempt to overthrow the Weimar Republic. To some, it still remained a stain on the city's history, as did the 1972 Olympic venue.

Like his father, he had been drawn to the ancient classical culture of Greece and Rome. From the ashes of war-torn Germany, Munich has reclaimed its splendor as the "Athens on the Isar." Known for centuries for its love of the arts, the capital of Bavaria had become a cosmopolitan metropolis. Its shops rivaled those found in Paris, Milan, and Zurich. Recognized for its high tech and media industries, the city, as its politicians boasted, had become Europe's largest publisher.

It was fitting that his own art gallery was located here in the Maxvorstadt. This upscale academic and art district rivaled the city's historic center. Despite his wealth, he liked to keep a low profile. The varied paintings and bronzes that populated his shop acted as a veneer for the historic and priceless works that remained unseen to the general public. Those iconic items crossed continents to the wealthy and privileged. They remained hidden from public view. Transported by private jets and yachts, they brought awe and wonderment to their patrons. Sums were wired through banks, large and small, in safe financial havens throughout the globe. The accumulation of such art became a sport and a badge of prestige. For decades, the mavens of the art world had lusted for the recovery of the looted items. Despite all the forensic advances, few had been uncovered, so concealed were the transfers. His father had schooled him in the clandestine trafficking of such priceless artifacts.

His contact had moved decades before from Buenos Aires to America. Coded messages were sent detailing provenance, location, and price. Photos, when sent, were placed in innocuous pamphlets. Yearly, he would travel to America to meet with his contact, discuss purchases and resales, and alter codes and wired accounts. On occasion, his American friend would journey to Munich under the guise of a scenic tour or a work-related conference. The world-wide recession was finally easing. While the very wealthy were recession-proof, monetary activity was less likely to rise regulatory suspicion when profits were abounding across all aspects of the world economy.

As he exited the Glyptothek, a middle-aged woman approached. Bundled in a fur coat and hat, she grasped a stylish Louis Vuitton bag with her right hand. With a smile, she uttered, "It's been a month since my patron wired the funds to your Cayman bank. Immediate delivery was required and guaranteed. The terra cotta statuette of the Greek tragic actor has not arrived. You have exactly seven days. We wouldn't want your gallery to suffer an electrical fire, would we?"

With that, she mounted the museum's steps and disappeared inside.

Shaken, he accelerated his stride and hurried toward his gallery. In his business, trust and dependability were paramount. The very wealthy didn't pose idle threats. Promises were kept, or consequences quickly followed. He had seen others suffer hideous consequences when bonds were broken. The dark side wasn't very far from the surface. His American contact needed to fear the same.

43.

Still rattled from the woman's admonition, he entered his closed art gallery and rushed to his back office. As it was Sunday, he assumed the American would be at home. With the six- hour time difference, he could have been at church, but he seriously doubted his contact had the time or the inclination to partake of that ritual. On his visits to the States to discuss their mutual business, he never felt comfortable around the American. While he found him to be cordial, he disliked the man's imperial attitude. His demeanor reminded him of those German businessmen who deluded themselves into believing that Germany was still the axis upon which the rest of the world revolved.

On occasion, he and the American had been in the company of others. When it suited him, the American could be charming, especially to women, but, more often than not, he was a bit standoffish as if he was superior to the others. While his business partner masked his temper in public, he had been the victim of the American's outbursts, especially when funds had not been relayed to accounts with celerity. Pure and simple, the American was punctilious. His demands were exacting. He had suffered the man's vexatious nature because the remuneration was excessive. The woman's warning, however, was not an idle threat.

This particular buyer had amassed his fortune through his ruthless power grab of his county's mineral and petroleum deposits when the wall was finally torn down. The populace's freedom was illusory for those who remained. A plutocratic class had ascended. Most of the masses remained impoverished. Some of the intellectuals, professionals, and small businessmen who lacked the proper connections fled with their families to Europe or America. They were followed by a criminal element sent forth by the power-grabbers to infiltrate various sectors of the economy, both legitimate and illicit. This Russian titan was not to be angered.

The art dealer picked up his scramble phone and dialed the American.

"Horst, what is it? I'm very busy," the American abruptly answered.

"We have a serious problem. The Russian has not received his purchase. The funds were wired to the bank account one month ago. He has threatened me. The art must be in his possession within seven days, or I will suffer severe consequences. Have you already shipped it?"

"No. I've had more pressing matters. He may think the world revolves around him, but it doesn't. Tell him I am a man of my word, and it will be forthcoming. I really don't have time for his threats."

The dealer frenziedly replied, "Believe me. He is not bluffing. My gallery will be gone next week. This is my livelihood. I will not see it destroyed. You also have a reputation. A very high one. In the States, you have much more to lose than me. We both understand that. One phone call and a few documents to the proper organization will do that. I beg of you not to test this man. Remember, we had deliberated whether we should approve him as a client. Against my better judgment, I acceded to your request. You argued the man's ego was such that money was no object to his desire to accumulate as many treasured items as possible, that such works would give him the prestige and worldly acceptance he so dearly craved. Do you think that desire will be thwarted by me? You will be next in his sights. As your friend and associate, please email him from your business that shipment has been made."

The American huffed and muttered that he would. After the conversation ended, the dealer could only hope that the man valued his life as much as his word.

44.

Princeton, New Jersey

Burnside knew the motion was critical to Melanie's defense. It was late afternoon. Surely, the arguments would have concluded by now. Had the judge ruled or reserved decision? He dialed Fitzhugh's cell.

"What happened in the motion?"

"I planned to call you and Melanie tonight. The judge agreed with our position. The identity of the Romanian test subjects and their pictures, the testing data, and the documentation forwarded to the FDA has to be forwarded to the court for an in camera review. The judge then will decide which documents will be released to all counsel. Furber must be presented at the trial. Once I receive the judge's order, I will have it and the subpoena served on Wellington and also on Furber. The trial has been set for the first Monday in October. Let Melanie know so she can alert her employers."

"What's the next step?"

"Until I receive McGuire's expert reports, not much can be done except review any Wellington documents that the judge releases. I'll call Melanie tonight and explain everything to her."

"What can I do?"

"See her often and reassure her. The more she interacts with you and Mrs. Burnside, the better. I don't want her to think that she's all alone in the world. As the trial date approaches, she'll become more agitated and alarmed. There's only so much I can do to lessen her fear.

You will have to do the rest. I want her new life to appear as routine and well structured for as long as possible."

"Remember, I want to see everything when you receive it."

"You will, probably even before I review it with Melanie. Just remember our agreement. No action. No interference. Leave that to me, Erika, and my father."

"Understood."

After the call ended, Burnside called the number.

"How are we progressing?"

"Better than expected. I'm meeting our prospective client in Vienna in late August."

"I expect you to seal the deal then. The launch date is September 1st."

"Don't worry. With my powers of persuasion, it will be completed there."

"I expect to hear immediately."

"You will. Once the deal has been finalized, do I get a bonus?"

"Of course. A real good one for such excellent work."

"Wow! That's great! I'll be in touch."

Burnside returned the phone to his suit pocket. His protégé was referred to as "the cleaner." Stealthy, quick, and efficient, he employed an arsenal of tools and tricks. Some jobs required a violent statement as a warning to those who lived by aggression and terror. Others necessitated quietude and normalcy. People died in many ways. Some made the front page, some the agate, but most just the normal obit section. Would she be agate or obit? He really didn't care, just as long as she was dead and soon.

45.

Late August 2015
Vienna, Austria

They had seen each other a couple of times after he left Sanibel. She had mentioned that she'd be on assignment in Vienna in late August. He had lied and told her that he'd be in Zurich on business. Would she like him to drop by when he was finished? Of course, she welcomed the input from a seasoned traveler who could highlight the city's oddities that might interest the magazine's male readers.

He flew to Zurich under his assumed identity, stayed a day, and then took a train to Vienna. They met at her mid-priced hotel just off the Ringstrasse. She had to photograph the Stephansdom Cathedral, which dominated the city center. The edifice was a Gothic church in a city whose architecture accentuated the Baroque. From the Sexton's Lodge, they climbed the stairs to the viewing platform situated in the 450-foot Gothic spire. The sight was impressive.

After getting the needed photos, they descended, and she photographed the Baroque High Altar below the cathedral's vaulted ceiling. She promised she needed to make only one more stop. Off they went to the Staatsoper, the city's Neo-Renaissance State Opera House. They entered through the five-arched loggia containing bronze statues of heroism, drama, fantasy, humor, and love. They ascended the exquisite marble staircase enriched by statues of the seven liberal arts of architecture, art, dance, drama, music, poetry, and sculpture. She photographed everything from different angles and heights. Finally, after inspecting the auditorium with its three box circles and two open circles, they left.

"I feel like eating in tonight," he announced.

"On your first night here? I wonder why," she replied as she tightly grabbed him around the waist.

They stopped at a local supermarket. She selected the salads and sandwiches. He grabbed a St. Laurent, a soft red wine. Then he remembered he needed wine glasses. He spotted them on the adjacent shelving. How convenient, they were tinted dark blue. The thought momentarily turned his stomach. He quickly dismissed it. He owed his life to the man. The debt had to be repaid. His word was his bond. She would not suffer. He owed her that.

He found her in the pastry section. They jointly agreed upon the desserts, including a mouth-watering Sachertorte.

By the time they reached her hotel, darkness had descended. She was in an amorous state. She ripped at his belt. He convinced her a condom was necessary, as a result of a recent cystoscopy. He grabbed her tightly and slowed down her movements. For the first time in his life, he felt like a mechanic. He tried to choreograph every move, which proved arduous due to her feverish passion. He knew he had to be gone before midnight. He had to get the wine in her soon. Although she seemed spent, she did not want to release him from her grasp. He kissed her softly and then traced his finger around her lips, as he slid to his right. She wanted more and tried to pull him back. He asked her if she had ever made love after drinking Viennese wine.

"What? You've got to be kidding. It's an aphrodisiac?"

"I guarantee you it will be like nothing you have ever experienced." He walked to the bathroom. The opened wine bottle and two glasses were next to the sink. He poured the wine. Quietly, he slid open the drawer containing his toiletry bag. He removed two pills and dropped them in her glass. He then removed another condom from his bag just in case her ardor hadn't subsided.

"Now the secret is to drink this quickly." He handed the glass to her. "Cheers!" He drank his rapidly and urged her to do the same. He refilled his glass and hers.

"What's the first sign it's working?" she asked.

"You'll begin to feel a little mellow, maybe even a little sleepy." He drank his second glass. She did also. He took her glass and placed it with his on the night table. He then put on the condom and turned toward her. She pulled him to her. He kissed her breasts and then her navel. He explored her body while monitoring her responses. The drug was working. Her movements were slowing. He synched his body with hers. Each touch was lighter and softer. Her eyelids started to close, and her arms became flaccid. He moved away from her and checked her pulse. He pinched her nipple and got no response. He grabbed her ear. Again no voluntary response. He gently exited the bed and went to his suitcase. He removed the hypodermic needle. He waited ten more minutes and again checked her. The pills had worked. He lifted her left arm. He inserted the potassium chloride into the vein. The dosage was more than sufficient. When they found her, there would be no evidence. The drug absorbed quickly and left no trace. He had promised himself she would die peacefully. Those who really deserved to die weren't so fortunate. For them, succinylcholine was the drug of choice. They got to watch him as the drug paralyzed their breathing. In essence, they got to view and feel their impending demise.

He flushed the condom down the toilet. He removed gloves, a cloth, a hairdryer, and a plastic garbage bag from his small suitcase. The hairdryer really was a minute vacuum cleaner. He put on gloves and turned on the TV and shower before activating the cleaner. He vacuumed the bedspread, sheets, and pillow for stray hairs. He then washed down and wiped every object he might have touched. He wiped her glass and the wine bottle. Then he placed her right hand on the cleaned glass as well as on the wine bottle. He removed from the garbage cans anything he might have placed there and put those objects in the plastic bag. He hung up her clothing. He placed both salads and one sandwich in the plastic bag, leaving the other one on a paper plate next to the television. He placed the Sachertorte in the room's mini refrigerator and dumped the other desserts in the plastic bag.

He then turned off the shower and the TV. He pulled up the sheets to her chest and turned the thermostat to a much colder temperature. He placed the plastic bag in his garment bag, took one last look at her, turned off the lights, and placed a Do Not Disturb sign on the door handle. He descended the stairway and exited through a side door. Mission accomplished. It left a bitter taste in his mouth. Why hadn't there been some other way? He had repaid his debt. He feared this one would haunt him. Burnside would dismiss her death as collateral damage. In the fog of war unintended things occurred. This wasn't war. For Burnside, the reward always outweighed the risks. Well, he had his reward. Now they were even.

He found a taxi and returned to the hotel he had booked in the Belvedere Quarter. It was 5:00 p.m. in New Jersey. He placed the call.

"The deal has been finalized. I'll be at my hotel in three days."

"I'll meet you at six o'clock at the hotel. You had a tough client. I'll be interested to learn how you closed the deal."

"I believe I've earned that bonus and then some."

"I don't renege on my promises. See you then."

46.

The pretrial discovery was complete. All that remained was today's court appearance with Melanie and McGuire to finalize the judge's pretrial memorandum. Scholman quickly released all the Romanian documents and photos. Despite the number of participants, there were only six before-and-after photographs. Why didn't each testee have such a comparison? Did this validate Stafford's claim that identical twins were photographed with only one twin listed as a test subject?

Johnnie forwarded the documentation to Malcolm Gideon, who filed an amended report commenting on the test documents as well as on the data he had received from the FDA. At Johnnie's request, Dr. Robert Stanton, a plastic surgeon, rendered a report that identified the objects depicted in Stafford's photos and explained the current nonsurgical alternatives utilized to retard facial skin aging.

To negate the medical examiner's report, Johnnie engaged Dr. Eric Honig as his forensic expert. Despite those additional reports, McGuire had not sought the services of any other experts. His forensic evidence would rise or fall on the testimony of the county's chief medical examiner, Dr. Mahesh Kapoor.

Johnnie had explained to Melanie the purpose of today's conference. It had been agreed that motions regarding the various statements would await the trial for disposition.

The bailiff announced the judge was entering. Both attorneys and Melanie arose.

"Gentlemen, everything okay with the pretrial order?"

"Yes, Your Honor."

"Then sign it."

"Mr. McGuire, have you offered any plea to Dr. Stafford?"

"No, Your Honor."

"Then, gentlemen, I'll see you on the first Monday in October. Have a good day."

Melanie appeared shocked by the suddenness of the event. It appeared over before it had commenced. The judge abruptly left the bench. No detailed discussion. Nothing.

Johnnie recognized her consternation. The dreaded date now was seared into her consciousness. Its permanency was apparent. Barring some calamitous event, the trial would proceed as scheduled. She would know her fate sooner than she had hoped. She looked toward him for reassurance. He touched her lightly on the shoulder and stated, "We, and I mean we, will get through this. Inform the hospital administrator that you will be on leave from the second week in September until the trial is over." He led her from the courtroom. Except for his forced conversation, the ride to his office was a quiet one.

47.

September 2015
Munich, Germany

It had rained steadily since noon and poured since three o'clock. No one had visited his gallery since noon, so he decided to close for the day. He turned off the lights in the adjunct gallery and started toward the front door when it opened suddenly. In she walked. His stomach tightened, and his pulse rose. Behind her was a bearded brute whose width seemed to match his height. With a half smile, she remarked, "Relax, I have come to inspect those paintings featured in your recent online brochure. My patron was intrigued and somewhat surprised. A German with your background, touting impressionism and modernism? Quite intriguing and surprising, I would say."

She walked passed him and stopped in front of an ornate gilded frame encasing an impressionistic seascape. She then moved slightly to her right for a head-on view of a similarly framed impressionistic pastoral setting.

"Your brochure does not do these paintings justice. My patron's assumption was correct. These are fitting for his expanding taste." She barked, "Sergei, take these."

The hulking presence moved forward and lifted the seascape from its attachment. He then removed the other painting.

She turned back to face him and indicated, "I trust you can pack these quickly for us. My patron will be so pleased with his new acquisitions."

He replied, "You can't just take these. Your patron first has to wire the funds to my account. No credit card company will approve this monetary transaction."

"My friend, you don't understand. We are taking, not buying, these. For the second time, your source has failed to deliver his order within a reasonable time. He followed your instructions. He wired 20 percent to your bank account and the remaining to the American's bank in Buenos Aires. The Greek amphora, the one depicting the warriors, has not arrived. You must remember our prior meeting. Well, my patron had a change of heart. Why burn paintings? Why destroy such creativity? Isn't it always better to preserve, not destroy, beauty? So, you see, that is may patron's wish. He will preserve these. He will even send you a picture of their placement in his personal gallery. You will be able to gaze upon how they have embellished his collection. I can assure you their placement will befit their exquisiteness. Now, please prepare them quickly. We are in a hurry."

"You can't just take these. You're stealing them. I won't allow this."

"Let's just say they're on loan, as a guarantee that future deliveries will be timely. Now hurry. Otherwise, Sergei will provide you with a very unwelcome present. Sergei, please show him the present. We didn't have time to wrap it as part of our exchange."

Sergei unzipped his coat and pulled a short black baton from his waist.

The dealer recoiled.

"Time is fleeting, my friend, and Sergei is hungry. It's best not to keep him waiting. He's not as patient as my patron."

After they left, he frantically hurried home. This was intolerable. He could be ruined. His nurtured reputation in art circles destroyed. His dealings with the American were only a small part of his business. The return for the effort expended was immense, yet that business was concealed from the public. Disclosure would lead to ruin and prosecution. He had evaluated the risks and allowed cupidity to overcome caution. Wasn't that human nature? Success and greed interfaced. Each fed off the other. Ethical boundaries disappeared with morality being a waste product. Maybe now was the time to cut the cord. His father had exposed him to the profession's seaminess.

He had always loved art; he had majored in it at the university. He'd tried to paint himself but wasn't pleased with the results. His father provided the seed money for his gallery and paved his way. He introduced him to established artists and their benefactors, helped open up social circles, and attended art soirees. Then his father took ill. Before his passing, he revealed his past, the old Germany that was crushed by the Allies, and his indirect complicity in the Nazi art pilferage. Others had fled to South America. He had chosen to stay, his past deeds not akin to those who had escaped for their lives. He urged him to contact an exporting firm based in northern New Jersey. Its founder had access to stolen antiquities. Beseeched, he tried to seek clients who would purchase and then eventually sell or donate to museums. It was a way of making right, of coming full circle.

After his father's death in 2002, he contacted the firm's founder. He began the process. Transactions took place, and museums covertly acquired long-sought antiquities. He acted as a middleman and refused compensation. Then the old man died in 2004, and his son took over. After that, procedures changed. The son required that he hold 20 percent of the fee as a presumed down payment from the purchaser. The son led him to believe that the remaining amount was paid after the museum inspected the antiquity and verified its authenticity.

After several transactions had been completed, the American visited him and said how pleased he was with his professionalism. Then, he dropped the bombshell. The money in the account was his. He initially refused. The American replied that there was no other option. The museums required that he, as an art dealer, receive compensation. They valued his services as a guardian to the operation's legitimacy. Priceless works now would be shown to the world. Long lost artifacts again revealed. The American persisted. Their relationship worked so well. Could he trust another dealer to be so proficient? Hardly, he must continue. The museums needed him. The art world was benefitting through his aid. His father would have been proud. That's what the American exhorted. He was a part of history. Darkness was receding, and light again was surfacing. He told the American he needed time to reflect. The American encouraged him to ponder. He would return before leaving for the States.

On that revisit, he brought a museum curator who pressed him not to impede the progress that had been made. The museum directors trusted and needed him. What was long hidden now was being revealed. Eventually, he relented. He could see the good. The American was correct. His father would have been proud. But now? No! Now the American was selling to the highest bidder. The Russian pigs, with their stolen wealth, were the acquisitors! Who's next? The Chinese?

He looked at his watch. With the time difference, it was too early to call. The American would be involved in legal matters and definitely wouldn't take his call. He would have to wait until the American arrived home. Then he would set everything straight. Those paintings had to be paid for or returned. The fools probably tried to penetrate his wired account before coming to his gallery. He hoped they had. To their surprise, they would have found nothing. What entered immediately exited. He knew better than to trust others. He also would close that account.

At 9:00 p.m. he placed the call to the American.

"Hello?"

"The Russian stole two of my paintings. His goons came and just took them because you never shipped the amphora. Why didn't you send it to him? I need those paintings returned immediately or their value. What happens if the artist walks in and sees them gone? He'll want his money. I can't pay it. Even if I could, I wouldn't. You need to call that vermin now and get them or the money. This is inexcusable. Why wasn't it shipped?"

"I've been distracted here with some delicate matters."

"You might be distracted, but I had my life threatened. I had a choice of surrendering the paintings or being beaten to a pulp. That was my so-called distraction. Those paintings are worth €600,000 combined."

"Well, then I suggest you file a theft claim with your insurance carrier."

"How do I explain to the carrier that those two specific paintings were stolen? There were other impressionists worth more than the stolen ones."

"Well, tell the carrier the thieves need an Art 101 class."

"This isn't some joke. My business and reputation are at stake."

"Let's not go overboard, my friend. Business maybe, but reputation? You entered this relationship freely. You knew there were risks as well as rewards."

The dealer seethed to himself.

"Rewards? Where's my reward? I'm now responsible for paintings worth €600,000. How do I call the police? The building was broken into. Do I just say two people entered during business hours, held a gun to my head, and walked off with the two paintings? No one will believe that."

"Of course not, leave the front door unlocked, set the alarm, and then break the front window. There's just enough room for someone your size to climb through, take the paintings, and exit the front door. By the time the police arrive, the would-be burglars probably would be gone anyway."

"So you're telling me now several hours before daybreak to return to my store, disarm the system, break the window, then rearm the system, run out the unlocked front door, drive home, and hope neither the police nor anyone else observes what I have done?"

"Yeah, I'd say that's your best bet."

"No, my best bet is for you to send me a check for €600,000. You then can return the Russian his money or ship him the amphora. Are you going to do that?"

"I'm not sure I can do that at this time. I suggest you follow my suggestion while I work on yours, unless you want to gamble the artist won't pay your gallery a visit. I have an urgent call on hold. She's in a more life-and-death situation than you."

The line went dead. He stared at the phone. He had no alternative. He had to follow the American's scheme, even with its inherent risks. The American, more or less, told him there wouldn't be a quick resolution. He would wear gloves, enter the gallery, ransack his desk, take some other paintings off the walls, and leave them scattered on the floor. He then would break the alarmed window, run out of the front door and pray he wouldn't be caught. He'd drive halfway home, turn around, call the police on his cell, and return to the scene of the crime.

But things would change and change dramatically. The American said he knew the risks. That was tantamount to saying he never would see the €600,000 or the paintings. If his deduction was correct, then the American soon would understand those risks were mutually shared. He was done with their relationship, done with the antiquity trade. What the American didn't grasp was that he also was nearing the end, just not in the manner he intended. The American would pay dearly. He would become a pariah in the eyes of his profession. He would earn the world's scorn. The only antiquities he would behold would be those gleaned from a dog-eared magazine. In the end, justice would be served. He would see to that, if it was the last thing he ever accomplished.

PART THREE

PART THREE

48.

October 2015 Mercer County Criminal Courthouse
Trenton, New Jersey

Seventy-five pairs of feet shuffled into the back of the courtroom. For most, it was an unwanted experience. A few were captivated by the allure of a murder trial, but for others it was an unwelcomed intrusion into their programmed routine.

It was always like this, but now the stakes were higher. All the preparation and the strategizing would be for naught if these people weren't entertained. They had been conditioned to focus for ten-minute intervals interspersed with one to two minutes of blaring, mindless commercials.

KISS was the first rule for trial advocacy: Keep It Simple Stupid. The idea was to use monosyllabic words when possible. Vary your tone and sometimes your cadence to awaken the daydreamers and disinterested. Employ hand gestures and body movement to create at least some eye movement. Use visual props when appropriate and allow the individual jurors to handle the photographs and documents. Keep them involved.

Talk to them, not at them. Let them feel like they're making all the decisions, even when hopefully you have preconditioned them through your own actions. Be likeable but also steadfast in the conviction of your position. Stress logic and common sense, the utilization of inferences and deductions based on life experiences and innate reasoning. To be sure, the witness being examined or cross-examined would necessitate variations as would the type of case being tried.

In this instance, Johnnie had to be likeable but also outraged. His client had been wrongfully charged, and the prosecutor had refused to conduct a thorough investigation of the most likely suspect.

As her counsel, he would look each juror in the eyes, speak to each as if he or she were a friend, and make each feel important and involved. Each had to feel Melanie's pain and horror. Each subconsciously had to slide into Melanie's position as a victim battered by an overzealous and misguided prosecutor.

He had prepped Melanie and would prep her again just before she took the stand. Unless something unforeseen occurred, she probably would have to take the stand. He, of course, would not mention that in his opening statement, but the pretrial discovery almost mandated that she testify. He also knew that Burnside would compel her to take the stand. More importantly, he evaluated her demeanor and responses during their prep session.

Melanie was forceful, assured, and almost combative. Gone was the meekness and timidity. Her controlling personality surfaced. It almost seemed like she was leading him, not he advising her. He counseled her that she must be the sympathetic aggrieved widow.

She replied that she knew that. She told him she would not be sarcastic but rather firm on cross-examination and she would answer all McGuire's questions professionally. She would look McGuire in the eyes and would look to the jury with her responses when prompted by him on her direct examination. She would answer only what was asked and wouldn't volunteer information. No matter how offensive McGuire's question might be, she would answer it. If the question contained facts or hypotheticals she knew not to be true, she would state so and then provide the proper response. She would not accept anything as true unless she knew it to be. She never would guess. Rather, she would say she did not know. If she didn't understand a question, she would say so and ask that it be rephrased.

She would avoid unfavorable facial and body gestures and, of course, there would be no outbursts. If caught in an inconsistency, she would admit it and then explain why her earlier or present statement was more accurate. She would not quibble with McGuire. She would remain the lady and would be logical in her responses.

Whatever the judge inquired of her, she would respond and also would heed his instructions. She would be self-deprecating, not arrogant or condescending. She would study any exhibit before providing an answer regarding its content. She never would guess unless the judge ordered her, to provide a guesstimate. She knew the jury had to like her, had to empathize with her, and ultimately had to believe her. She told him she knew that, and by the time she walked off the stand, each juror would believe she was a good person and a doctor in whose hands each would entrust his or her life.

Johnnie remembered Erika's admonition that once an actress always an actress. Maybe she was correct.

He heard the familiar words, "All rise," and responded reflexively as did his client. Conservatively dressed in a navy suit and white blouse, she was wearing a cross. On all the occasions he had been in her presence, he never had observed it. Was it just a prop for its effect?

Scholman ascended the bench quickly, introduced himself to the jury, described the case, and explained that he was looking for impartial jurors who would view the evidence with an open mind until a verdict was reached. He stressed that those chosen through the voir dire process would be the judges of the facts while he would be the judge of the law, and they had to accept that, whether they liked it or not. He forcefully informed the prospective jury panel that the indictment was not evidence of Melanie's guilt but was merely a vehicle utilized to bring the case before them for their determination on the issue of guilt or innocence. The defendant was presumed to be innocent and would remain so unless each and every element of the charged offense was proved beyond a reasonable doubt. The defendant need not prove anything. It was not her duty or obligation to prove her innocence, testify, or offer any evidence on her behalf. The burden rested solely with the prosecution, and that burden was much higher than satisfying the mere preponderance of the evidence standard used in civil cases. Here, the State had to prove the defendant's guilt beyond a reasonable doubt. The burden never shifted to the defendant. Each and every element of the offense had to be proved beyond a reasonable doubt. Otherwise, a verdict of not guilty had to be returned.

Scholman estimated the case would take two to three weeks to try. He introduced all counsel and Melanie. He then directed the panel to the provided standard criminal jury voir dire questions. Any juror who could not sit for the three weeks due to medical, personal, financial, or vacation issues was asked to rise. Each then was brought to sidebar where Scholman quietly questioned him or her in the presence of both counsel. Those with legitimate excuses were dismissed and told to return downstairs to the jury assembly room. The unhappy others were told to return to their seats without realizing that counsel might dismiss them anyway during the selection process.

Unbeknownst to the prospective jurors, the judge had before him the entire list of seventy-five jurors, of which fourteen had been selected randomly by a computer. Two extra had been added as a precaution so that a mistrial would not occur should one or two of the normal twelve be dismissed for any number of reasons. The judge called the fourteen jurors individually to sidebar and questioned them in the presence of counsel regarding that individual's responses to the standard voir dire questions.

Scholman also asked additional questions that each attorney had submitted. After each of the fourteen was questioned, the judge, out of the presence of the juror, heard challenges for cause by the attorneys and then decided whether that person would be seated or sent back to the jury assembly room. As was expected, many were excused. Eventually, fourteen filled the jury box. The judge then asked those fourteen jurors to describe their educational history, work experience, military service, marital status, work experience of their children, television shows they watched, papers and magazines they read, bumper stickers if any, and leisure activities they enjoyed.

As defense counsel, Johnnie had twenty peremptory challenges. McGuire had only twelve, giving Johnnie a tactical advantage. Each could excuse any juror for any reason without disclosing to the court or the juror the thought process involved. Whenever one was removed, a new juror would be selected by lot, and the sidebar process would be initiated again with the prospective new juror.

Johnnie assumed that McGuire wanted conservative individuals, divorced men, unattractive, and uneducated women who might resent Melanie's looks, education, and earning power. Administrators and those holding positions of authority also would be considered as more favorable for the prosecution.

On behalf of Melanie, Johnnie desired divorcees, teachers, sociologists, psychologists, artists, nurses, and health field technicians. Professionals whose jobs required logic and precision, such as engineers, architects, and mathematicians also were favored because they would be less likely to convict where the defense was able to provide logical responses to the prosecutorial evidence. If gaps existed in the State's presentation, those individuals would be more likely to acquit. Pharmaceutical employees, of course, would have to be avoided as a result of Wellington's asserted involvement.

It took almost two days and 225 jurors before fourteen were sworn to adjudge Melanie's fate. As in almost all cases, neither attorney got his perfect jury. Each had managed to seat a few that might be predisposed to his side, but, in reality, the whole process was a guesstimate. Johnnie knew that firsthand. He had won many cases when he had been displeased with the makeup of the selected jurors. His most disheartened loss had been announced by his supposed perfect jury. A jury trial was a crapshoot. That's why experienced civil trial practitioners settled 90 percent of their cases.

Murder cases were a different beast. Johnnie would be looking into fourteen pairs of eyes. What those eyes were seeing, and what those brains were thinking, no one knew. Did those fourteen people even care? Would their interest wane? Would employment and family issues utterly distract them from their required focus? Would they hear and then grasp what was said as well as what important information was absent? Sure, trial lawyers lost sleep over courtroom testimony. What was left unsaid was how much time they squandered wondering what was heard, grasped, and believed by those blank faces in the jury box.

After the jury was selected, Judge Scholman dismissed the jury for the day and told them not to discuss the case in any way with anyone.

Johnnie was talking to Melanie as he was gathering his files when he noticed the courtroom door open abruptly. Domenic Carlucci, McGuire's lead detective, rapidly approached his boss and gestured forcefully. McGuire listened, threw up his hands, and stormed toward Johnnie.

His face florid, McGuire exploded. "She's dead! He killed her!"

Johnnie looked at him dumbfounded. "Who's dead?"

"Huffmire! I'll get him!"

"Get whom?"

"Burnside! I know he did it or had someone do it for him! I want to see the judge now!"

Without waiting for a response, McGuire rushed toward the side door that led to the judicial corridor. After telling Melanie to sit at counsel table and speak to no one, Johnnie followed. By the time he had entered the outer office, McGuire already was gesturing wildly before Scholman who waved Johnnie to enter his chambers.

"Sit down and calm down," Scholman ordered McGuire. "Don't say another thing. Count to twenty to yourself. Then compose yourself, and tell me in a calm voice what Carlucci told you."

"Our office last spoke to her immediately after Your Honor advised us of the October trial date. That was in late August. She told us she was leaving for Europe the next day and would be back by mid-September. She said to send the trial subpoena to Florida. All her mail was being held there. Within the last couple of weeks, Domenic tried to reach her by phone to no avail. I sent him to Sanibel, which was her official residence. The condo's office manager hadn't seen her since late August.

"Huffmire was one of the few owners who remained in the condo during most of the summer. Usually, the other condos were rented out to vacationing Europeans. The post office indicated that she had not retrieved her mail. We knew she kept a small apartment in Red Bank. Domenic met with her landlord. She paid him quarterly and had paid through September. He hadn't seen her in months, which wasn't unusual because she spent most of the year in Florida and used the apartment infrequently due to her job demands. She apparently was a very private person and didn't associate with the three other tenants.

"Domenic assumed she actually had traveled to Europe. He contacted Customs. He just got word that she had died in Vienna in late August, actually died two or three days after her arrival."

"How'd she die?"

"Customs said she was found in her bed. The hotel notified police. She was taken to a morgue and then embalmed. Nothing had been disturbed in the room. Customs said there was no evidence of any violence. Police notified our embassy. Embassy had no list of kin and called the Lee County Sheriff's Office. Apparently, the condo super was notified after Domenic had left Sanibel and had assumed we already knew. Judge, we believe she was murdered."

"How so?"

"We don't believe it was a coincidence that this woman died within days of our late August pretrial conference when you assigned the trial date. We believe a hit was put on her."

"By whom?"

"Either the defendant or her father."

"What proof do you have?"

"No actual proof to date."

"Well, considering there was no violence, and considering she already has been embalmed, you're not going anywhere, Terry."

"Judge, we want the trial delayed."

"For what reason? We know Dr. Stafford turned in her passport when she made bail. Did you check to see whether her father left the country?"

"He didn't, Your Honor."

"So you're telling me that there was no overt evidence of foul play, that the defendant and her father didn't leave the country, yet one or both plotted Huffmire's demise."

"Yes, Your Honor."

"Where's the proof?"

"We need time to prove it."

"Well, you can try to prove it after this case is tried. You're not going to be allowed to mention any of this to our jury. This case is going forward. If you want to put your objection on the record, we will do it. I am not having this case tainted by your office's assumptions. Do I make myself clear, Terry?"

"Yes, Your Honor."

"I'm instructing you to tell your boss what I have conveyed to you. If I read in the press anything about Ms. Huffmire's death and your assumptions, you will pay dearly for your transgressions."

Scholman buzzed his secretary and told her to clear everyone from the courtroom except Melanie and then lock the courtroom's door.

McGuire then put his request on the record. Scholman repeated his reasoning and warning. Johnnie and Melanie left the courtroom in shock.

Johnnie wondered, Could Burnside have ordered a hit? What would be the evidentiary effect of Huffmire's death on the trial evidence?

Could McGuire introduce her statement? If so, how much could he keep out?

Melanie had asked him what all of this meant. Would the prosecutor now have to dismiss her case? No, he wouldn't, he had replied. There still was the blowback evidence. The residue's presence probably would allow the prosecution to survive a dismissal motion. He also explained to her the significance of Huffmire's statement. All, or part of it, would be read to the jury. What effect it would have on the jury was anyone's guess.

Johnnie drove her home and then headed for the office. He and "Pops" would have to hit the books.

Melanie drove away troubled. Had McGuire been correct in his assumption? Yes, he probably had been. She knew her father better than anyone, even better than her mother. She wouldn't ask him because he only would deny it angrily. Did he have the boots on the ground to accomplish it? Without question. No one was more resourceful. Had he made the right decision? Had he grossly miscalculated? Who knew? But there was no question in her mind that he had issued the order. He wouldn't pay any price, but would she? The clock was ticking, and twelve people soon would provide the answer.

49.

It was a crisp October morning. A soft northeasterly breeze added a pleasant coolness to their walk from the parking lot to the courthouse. Johnnie knew the judge would instruct the jurors that the opening statements were not evidence, yet they were critical. Studies supposedly had demonstrated that 80 percent of the time cases were won in opening statements in civil jury trials. Frankly, he didn't believe it because he had won many "losers," even when his openings weren't as strong as his adversary's. But this wasn't a civil trial. No matter what the jurors had told the judge, they had a preconceived opinion. Melanie was guilty.

He had to sow the seeds of reasonable doubt immediately while holding back some critical information. With Huffmire's death, McGuire had lost the one witness who could have described the depth and emotion of Stafford's entanglement. This had not been a mere dalliance. It had continued over a three-year period, a sufficient time to have been discovered. Yet Huffmire had inferred that Melanie had been clueless. McGuire had no proof that she knew.

Lurking underneath the surface was another potential problem for the prosecutor. Johnnie, through Melanie, would be making Wellington the critical player. To shred that defense, McGuire would have to undermine Richard Stafford's character. Inferentially, he would have to paint Stafford as a misguided, overzealous malcontent. He could not give credence to Stafford's allegations against Wellington. Otherwise, he would be bolstering Melanie's defense. The mere fact that he hadn't investigated those claims demonstrated that he gave no credit to Stafford's accusations. Had McGuire been so consumed with his own potential advancement that he had been blinded by this obvious inconsistency? In prosecuting Melanie, McGuire could not avoid disparaging the slain victim.

McGuire didn't turn as they entered the courtroom. He didn't acknowledge Johnnie's greeting. So that was how it would be.

Promptly at nine o'clock, the jury entered the courtroom followed by the judge. Scholman instructed them on the purpose of opening statements and cautioned them that his rulings on objections and motions would be based on the law and not on his feelings as to the guilt or innocence of the defendant. He had no predisposition, and they should not view his rulings as evidence as to how they should decide the issue of guilt or innocence. He defined direct and circumstantial evidence and explained how they should assess the credibility of witnesses. He again instructed them that the indictment was not evidence, that the defendant was presumed innocent, and that the prosecution had the sole burden of proving guilt beyond a reasonable doubt.

McGuire opened as Johnnie had anticipated. Melanie was the scorned wife. She had been successful at every level. She would not accept rejection. Her husband's infidelity branded her as a failure in the eyes of her peers and community. She eradicated this stain as a surgeon would a tumor. She staged the break-in, killed her husband, and then caused her own injuries. To cover her culpability, she cleverly fictionalized Wellington's involvement. As an anesthesiologist, she knew how to drug herself after the killing. Despite her brilliance, she was no match for well-tested and well-proven forensic science. Standard scientific tests demonstrated that she had handled the gun. She had wiped the gun free of her prints but had failed to remove the trace gun powder from her hand. Her blind rage was no match for scientific proof. She was guilty beyond a reasonable doubt.

Johnnie approached the jury box but stayed several feet away. He did not want to encroach upon the jurors' space. He started with a soft tone and explained that Melanie had suffered an unbearable tragedy.

Within the space of several hours she had become a victim, a widow, and a defamed citizen. With his voice rising, he explained how she had waived her constitutional rights and given a voluntary statement, even though she had been bruised, battered, and emotionally distraught. Suffering from probable post-concussive symptoms, she had given an oral statement because her mental faculties precluded her from providing a written one. The facts contained in that statement have been corroborated by the emergency personnel, the hospital staff, and Inez Garcia, her maid.

Despite her urging, the prosecutor had refused to investigate the case fully. He had rushed to judgment even after being provided with documented emails from the deceased as well as corroborating photographic evidence. While Melanie had no obligation to prove her innocence, he would produce lay testimony and expert opinion that the prosecution was flawed from the beginning and that an innocent woman, loved by her peers and community for her medical expertise and charitable works, had suffered a grievous injustice together with unconscionable and unwarranted humiliation. Even though the evidence would fail to show her guilt, she would be emotionally tarnished forever. The killer or killers had their freedom, yet she would have her pain and sorrow forever.

When Johnnie concluded, the judge ordered a twenty-minute recess for the jurors. Johnnie walked Melanie to the ladies' room. The real drama would commence shortly. He viewed the courtroom as a cocoon. There was a prevailing stillness. Absent testimony, all that was heard was the intermittent hum of the court clerk's computer and the ticking of the wall clock. Quickly both blended into the silence. The anticipated opening of a rear courtroom door always jarred the eerie spell.

When a witness was sworn in, the clerk's words punctured the silence and heightened his senses akin to a sprinter awaiting the crack of a starter's gun. He viewed direct examination as a Ping-Pong match. The lawyer posed his question, and his witness uttered the rehearsed response. Only on cross-examination did the tension appear. Trial lawyers earned their living on cross-examination. A simple question could impale a witness, eviscerate the opposition, and shatter financial dreams, or lead to guilt or innocence. On cross-examination, the witness had to be led, contained, and forced to provide yes or no answers. Usually, the witness would not be allowed to explain his reasoning or ramble.

Police officers were trained to testify forcefully and professionally with an air that evoked certitude. McGuire's first witness was Hopewell Township police sergeant David Plesser. He had been on routine patrol with a rookie officer when he received the police dispatch. He arrived at the crime scene within minutes of the dispatch. He was greeted at the door by a visibly upset domestic, Inez Garcia.

The EMTs were tending to the defendant, so he immediately went to the deceased, who had been shot in the head, chest, and lower abdomen area near the groin. There was blood splatter on the wall adjoining the bedroom as well as a copious amount of blood on the white rug. A Glock 17 was on the floor as was a white cloth. Both were bagged only after he had photographed the crime scene and had outlined the victim's body. He called the Mercer County Prosecutor's Office and followed the EMTs to the hospital only after securing the crime scene with backup officers. At the hospital, at the direction of the prosecutor's office, he swabbed the defendant's hands with the appropriate gunshot residue test stubs and delivered the samples to Detective Carlucci.

He described the home's layout and surroundings providing distances of the home from the roadway, the woods, and the closest neighbors. He ended his direct testimony without describing Melanie's physical or mental state.

Johnnie immediately pounced.

"Officer, you had the GSR test kit at the scene, did you not?"

"Yes, sir."

"You could have done the test at the scene, correct?"

"Yes, sir, but the defendant was being treated by the EMTs."

"What was she being treated for?"

"She was bleeding from the forehead, and there was blood on the bridge of her nose."

"Was she bleeding heavily from her forehead?"

"Yes, sir."

"Was she very distraught?"

"Yes, sir. She was hysterical."

"Did you hear anything she said?"

"Yes, sir."

"What did you hear?"

"Several times she said, 'They killed him.'"

"Did you ask her who 'they' were?"

"No."

"In your report, did you say she was bleeding, that she was hysterical, and that she stated several times that 'they killed him'?"

"Yes, sir."

"Dr. Stafford was cooperative with you at the scene and at the hospital, wasn't she?"

"Yes, sir."

"Was she still distraught and upset at the hospital?"

"Yes, sir."

"She had blood on her hands at the scene and at the hospital?"

"Yes, sir."

"Was anything in the living room disturbed?"

"Yes, sir."

"What?"

"The end table next to the sofa had been overturned as had been the table lamp."

"Was there any blood on either item?"

"Yes, there was blood on each."

"Was a piece of glass cut out of the sliding door?"

"Yes sir."

"Officer, how much time were you in the presence of Dr. Stafford at the scene?"

"I would guess fifteen to twenty minutes."

"How about at the hospital?"

"Probably sixty to ninety minutes."

"You stated on direct exam that Detective Carlucci met you at the hospital. Did he question Dr. Stafford there?"

"I know he spoke to her, but I didn't hear the conversation. He told me to arrest her and take her to Hopewell. He said he was taking over the investigation and would question her there."

"Did you participate in that questioning?"

"No, sir."

"Did you hear it?"

"No, sir. Detective Carlucci was given a room and said he would take it from there."

"After you gave the GSR stubs to Detective Carlucci, did you ever see them again before today?"

"No, sir."

"Detective Carlucci told you to charge Dr. Stafford that early morning with murder?"

"Yes, sir."

"Who took her to the Mercer County Corrections Center?"

"I did at Detective Carlucci's request, sir."

"Sergeant, when you arrived at the crime scene, were any lights on in the master bedroom?"

"No, sir."

"Were any lights on in the house?"

"Only the hall light that is just inside the front door."

"When you arrived, was it light enough outside that you could see colors inside the house without illumination?"

"Yes, sir."

"No further questions, Your Honor."

McGuire arose quickly and asked, "Did you believe the defendant when she said, 'They killed him'?"

"Objection, Your Honor."

"Sustained," Scholman replied and called both counsel to sidebar.

"Mr. McGuire you know better than that. Don't repeat your mistake. Do you understand me?"

"But, Your Honor…"

"What don't you understand, Mr. McGuire? Do you have any more questions of this witness?"

"No."

Scholman immediately turned to the jury and sternly said, "Ladies and gentlemen, I want you to disregard that question. Remove it from your thought processes completely."

Johnnie was stunned by Scholman's dramatic response but excitedly pleased. McGuire had been slapped by the judge. The response was quick and authoritarian. McGuire had made a tactical mistake and had been rebuked harshly. An impression had been made. Hopefully, it would be indelible. Scholman was in complete control. Both counsel had been warned. Tow the evidential line, or suffer the humiliating consequences.

Detective Domenic Carlucci strode confidently to the stand. In a booming voice that harmonized with his barreled chest and massive shoulders, he recited his experience and explained his involvement in the homicide's investigation. He reviewed the crime scene photographs taken by Sergeant Plesser and earlier shown to the jury. He narrated the details depicted in the photos taken at his direction after the prosecutor's lab technicians had examined the crime scene. He obtained the GSR samples from Sergeant Plesser and delivered them to the crime lab, which concluded that there was gunshot residue on the defendant's left palm. He described his interaction with the defendant and the taking of a voluntary statement, which he then read to the jury.

Carlucci produced the blood-stained pajamas of the victim and revealed the bullet holes. The Glock and the three spent shells were also marked into evidence after he described the gun, the number of chambered rounds, and the weapon's operation.

He briefly mentioned that he took a statement from Inez Garcia. McGuire did not move it into evidence.

At his request, a search warrant had been obtained. He specified the seized items.

Carlucci produced a printout of all calls made and received by the deceased on his company-issued cell phone. He highlighted one number, which was identified as belonging to Sally Huffmire of Sanibel Island, Florida. He related that he called Huffmire.

Johnnie quickly asked for a sidebar conference, which Scholman granted.

"Your Honor, I anticipate that Mr. McGuire intends to use Detective Carlucci to introduce Ms. Huffmire's statement. Most, if not all, of that statement is inadmissible as hearsay. I'd like to be heard on the statement and would request that Mr. McGuire give you a copy."

"Okay, I'll give the jury an early lunch break."

Scholman then excused the jury, took the statement, and returned to chambers.

Within fifteen minutes, Scholman returned and asked Johnnie to explain his position.

"Your Honor, the applicable rule permits the admissibility of hearsay statements when the declarant is deceased provided those statements don't contain inadmissible hearsay statements supposedly made by others. Here, Ms. Huffmire describes not only their interaction but also describes the supposed words and feelings of Mr. Stafford. None of these alleged words or feelings of the deceased are admissible because they weren't made under the belief of imminent death, weren't made as excited utterances, weren't present sense impressions, and weren't statements of existing mental, emotional, or physical conditions. Moreover, references to my client weren't to her feelings but rather to Mr. Stafford's belief. Ms. Huffmire's statement alludes to what the deceased believed his wife or his father-in-law would do if they discovered his infidelity. The statement doesn't mention what his wife said she would do. Ms. Huffmire admits she never spoke to my client. She also admits Mr. Stafford believed his wife knew nothing about their affair."

"What parts of the statement are you asserting should be stricken?"

"Your Honor, first of all, nothing should be mentioned about Mr. Burnside. He is not on trial."

"I agree with you there. What else?"

"Mr. Stafford allegedly said he was mired in an unhappy marriage. His wife was a workaholic, consumed by her profession. She was emotionally insecure. She often berated him for being lax in calling when he was on business trips because he was too busy sleeping with pharmaceutical reps. She allegedly slapped him when he returned from Geneva. Her moods varied. None of that is admissible under any hearsay rule in this particular instance."

"What say you, Mr. McGuire?"

"It all comes in. Mr. Stafford is deceased."

"Well, that's not how I read the rule and, more importantly, Rule 805 when read in conjunction with Rule 802. I agree with the defense. I already have stricken those sections in addition to some others. Detective Carlucci, I am handing you a copy. You can read anything that hasn't been stricken. Please review it now. Tell me if you are uncertain about any of my markings."

Carlucci studied the document intently and then replied that he had no questions. Scholman told them the trial would reconvene at 1:30 p.m.

Before Carlucci resumed the stand, Scholman advised the jury that Huffmire recently had died in Europe while on a work assignment, and that Carlucci would be allowed to read a portion of her statement based on the evidence rules.

Carlucci ended his direct examination by reading to the jury Huffmire's background and residence, how she met Stafford, how often they saw each other, what they did, that she called him only on his work-issued cell phone, that they were very discreet, that Stafford forbade her from taking his picture, that she liked her freedom and didn't want any long-term commitment, that she never met Melanie, and that she last saw Stafford in Florida several hours before his death.

Johnnie knew Carlucci was very court-wise and always looked for an opportunity to offer a gratuitous damaging response. Most of his questions would be phrased to elicit a yes or no response.

"Detective, were there any fingerprints on the gun, the fired shells, or the unfired bullets?"

"No."

"Were any other guns or rifles found on the premises?"

"No."

"Was there any record with the State of New Jersey or any other state that showed either of the Staffords had purchased a gun of any type?"

"No."

"Where was the Glock 17 manufactured?"

"Austria."

"When, where, and to whom was it sold?"

"In 1988 in Munich, Germany, to Seigfried Hauer."

"How did you obtain that information?"

"Austria and Germany have gun registration laws."

"Is Mr. Hauer alive or deceased?"

"He died in 1992."

"Do you know how this gun got to the United States?"

"No."

"Do you have any information to indicate Mr. Hauer was a relative, friend, or business associate of the Staffords?"

"No."

"A piece of glass was cut out of the sliding door near the interior latch, is that correct?"

"Yes."

"Were there any prints around the perimeter of that opening?"

"No, but there were the defendant's prints on the internal lock mechanism."

"In her statement, she told you she locked it earlier that evening, didn't she?"

"Yes."

"Well, to lock it she had to touch it, correct?"

"Obviously, Counselor," said Carlucci with a smirk.

"When the gunshot residue test was administered, both the front and back of both hands were swabbed, correct?"

"Yes."

"And the only trace evidence found was on Dr. Stafford's left palm, correct?"

"Yes."

"You even asked her before the test results if she was right-handed, and she answered that she was, correct?"

"Yes."

"You first saw Dr. Stafford at the hospital?"

"Yes."

"Where did she have blood on her body?"

"Her forehead already had been bandaged. There was a cut on the bridge of her nose. She had blood on her hands and on her clothes."

"Was the blood on her hands just hers?"

"No. Testing showed also Mr. Stafford's blood."

"Didn't both Dr. Stafford and Inez Garcia tell you that Dr. Stafford tried to revive Mr. Stafford by applying chest compressions?"

"Yes."

"Did you ask either of them to show you how the compressions were done?"

"No."

"When you saw Dr. Stafford, was she distraught?"

"She looked distraught. Whether she really was or not, I don't know."

"You knew from the forehead bandage that she had suffered a head injury?"

"I didn't see the injury."

"Well, you talked to Sergeant Plesser. Didn't he tell you that the EMTs took her to the hospital because of her emotional and physical condition?"

"I didn't go into any details with him. I just went to the hospital."

"Well, didn't you inquire of the ER staff what they were doing to her?"

"When I arrived, she was being treated. When I first saw her, she had on the bandage."

"You required the Hopewell Police to take her back to their police station, correct?"

"Yes."

"You wanted to question her there?"

"Yes."

"Did you advise her of her constitutional rights that she didn't have to speak to you, that anything she said to you could be used against her, and that she had the right to seek advice of counsel?"

"At first, I didn't because the nurses, the EMTs, and the Hopewell officers all said the defendant repeatedly said, 'They killed him.' I just asked her to tell me what happened."

"Did you ask her to write it down?"

"Yes."

"Did she agree?"

"No."

"She told you her head really hurt, and she had trouble focusing, didn't' she?"

"Yes."

"Didn't she voluntarily agree to a recorded statement?"

"Yes."

"And you took that statement even before you advised her of her rights, even though you knew a gun had been found near her at the scene?"

"Yes."

"Did you ever ask Dr. Stafford who 'they' were?"

"All she said was that she couldn't see her assailant or assailants."

"So you assumed the 'they' were the intruders?"

"Counselor, you're assuming there were intruders."

"You're the lead detective on this case?"

"Yes."

"I provided your boss with Mr. Stafford's lengthy email that he wrote about Wellington several days before his death. Did you ever read it?"

"Yes."

"You never were requested by your boss or Prosecutor McGuire to contact Wellington, were you?"

"I didn't think it was necessary."

"Your Honor, I ask that response be stricken."

"Ladies and gentlemen, disregard that answer. Respond appropriately, Detective," Scholman strongly ordered.

"No, I wasn't told to contact Wellington."

"Detective, were any unknown fibers found on Dr. Stafford's clothes?

"Yes."

"Could you match them up with any other source?"

"No. By the time I saw her, she had been in contact with the inside of the ambulance, the hospital personnel, and the hospital equipment. There would be no way to ascertain whether the fibers came from in the house or from somewhere else."

"How about footprints at or outside the house?"

"The ground conditions weren't conducive for leaving solid prints. Inside there were no prints near Mr. Stafford, other than the defendant's."

"Those prints were from her bare feet that had walked in the blood at the scene, correct?"

"Yes."

"Based upon the content of her statement, you assumed that she had taken her shoes off before going to sleep on the couch?"

"I guess so, but obviously I don't know."

"Your office did find indention marks in the rug?"

"Yes, but we couldn't ascertain whether they pre-existed that night or not."

"Detective, you checked the landline and personal cellphone records for Dr. Stafford and Mr. Stafford, didn't you?"

"Yes."

"Did any of those records indicate calls to or from Ms. Huffmire?"

"No. Only Mr. Stafford's office-issued cellphone showed the connection between the deceased and Ms. Huffmire."

"Officer, you told this jury that you also took a statement from Mrs. Garcia who performed household cleaning for the Staffords. Did you direct that she be taken to the police station?"

"Yes."

"You interviewed her there about six hours after Dr. Stafford was taken to the hospital?"

"Yes."

"Was she cooperative?"

"Yes."

"Did you ask her to write out what she witnessed?"

"She said she couldn't write well in English, so we recorded her."

"Did you believe she was trying to deceive you?"

"How would I know, Counselor?"

"I noted that Mr. McGuire didn't ask you any questions about what Mrs. Garcia said in her statement. Would you please read the statement to the jury?"

Carlucci looked to McGuire for assistance. McGuire knew he was boxed. If he objected, he would be viewed as hiding something from the jury. He also assumed Johnnie would call Garcia as a witness. Therefore, he remained mute. Scholman looked over at McGuire and waited for a hearsay objection. When none came, he told the detective to read.

Johnnie then ended his cross. McGuire asked some unimportant follow-up questions. Scholman then dismissed the jury.

The day had gone better than expected. Scholman had given him everything he wanted regarding Huffmire's statement. He actually was surprised how quickly the ruling was rendered in his favor. McGuire could try to file an interlocutory appeal, but he would get nowhere, especially when the ruling was made by the county's criminal assignment judge.

Tomorrow was another day. The county's chief medical examiner would be expected to provide the gory details to inflame the jury. What he said, and how he said it, could impact the case significantly. With Huffmire's death, McGuire had lost the emotional and personal impact. The medical examiner would have to bring Richard Stafford to life and then depict his slaughter. Without Huffmire's presence, he probably would be the last prosecution witness.

50.

As the county's chief medical examiner was being sworn in, Johnnie's thoughts quickly returned to the prior evening. Burnside had called at six o'clock. He was annoyed that Johnnie hadn't called immediately after court had recessed. Johnnie somewhat placated him by explaining that he had been involved in critical research as a result of the day's testimony. Melanie then appeared at his office to discuss the medical examiner's projected testimony. She casually knew him from prior county medical society meetings. Johnnie knew him well. During his prosecutorial days, the man had been his crucial witness in the numerous homicide cases he had tried. Never had he lost. They had developed a good relationship.

The examiner was a quiet, methodical individual who recoiled from bombast and egoism. Johnnie always tailored his direct examination to coincide with the doctor's strengths, but he also counseled him as to the necessity to raise his voice and project emotion when delivering his medical opinion on the most important facets of the case. They had bonded well. While Johnnie never had witnessed McGuire's trial interaction with the examiner, he couldn't conceive that the doctor would have viewed him positively. On the other hand, the man was honest and took his job seriously. How did he view Melanie? Did he have genuine distaste for McGuire? Would such issues color his testimony? The next two hours would supply the answers.

There was one other issue of concern. Melanie's own actions. Throughout the trial, she had been poised, attentive, and professional in her appearance and actions. Nothing negative had been projected before the jury. Last night, however, had been troubling. He had been preoccupied and really hadn't grasped it. But Erika was there, and nothing got past her roving eyes. Because she was to be a witness, Erika had been prevented from sitting with him at the counsel table. But she obviously could participate in office strategy sessions.

She was there that evening as the three of them plotted the medical examiner's cross-examination. Twice, Erika observed Melanie place her left hand on Johnnie's upper thigh as she leaned over to inspect the examiner's expert report. Johnnie was so engrossed in his trial planning that he didn't recall it happening. Once Melanie left for home, Erika's wrath exploded. He recalled her angrily exclaiming, "I'm telling you this woman isn't angelic. Somehow she's involved. If she pulls that shit in the courtroom, she's toast. You can kiss Supreme's business goodbye."

Erika's comments had led to a restless sleep. On the way to the courthouse, he had tried subtly to explain again to Melanie how they should interact when they were looking at exhibits in front of the jury. Subtlety wasn't one of his fine points. Melanie just smiled at him and then remarked that she understood.

Dr. Mahesh Kapoor ascended to the witness box in his typical stooped posture. He was of average height and was rail thin. In response to McGuire's questioning, he related that he had obtained his undergraduate and medical degrees in India. He and his family had immigrated to the United States twenty-eight years ago. Upon arrival, he entered a residency training program in forensic pathology. He then passed the test administered by the American Board of Pathology and received his certification as a forensic pathologist. He worked in that capacity for several years before being appointed as the chief medical examiner for Mercer County. For the last seventeen years, he had testified in almost every murder case tried in Mercer County.

McGuire then directed him to Stafford's autopsy. Kapoor unemotionally described the procedure as if he was filleting a fish. He had made a y-shaped incision from the shoulders to midchest and down to the pubic region. He made a second incision across the rear of the head, joining the bony prominences just below and behind the ears. He carried incisions down to the skull, rib cage, breastbone, and cavity containing the abdominal organs. He retracted back the scalp and soft tissues in front of the chest. Without nauseating the jury with the more distasteful details, the examiner stated that he examined Stafford's brain and heart.

He opined that the shot to the chest had severed the main cardiac artery and quickly would have caused Stafford's death. He assumed that the shot to the lower abdomen had been the first shot and that the head shot had been the last. The shooter used hollow point bullets. They had mushroomed upon impact and had not exited the body. Consequently, they had created massive wounds as they ricocheted within the body.

The EMT reports indicated that Stafford had been dead at the scene. The emergency report revealed Stafford's body temperature. That reading probably indicated that he had died one to two hours before that examination.

McGuire then turned to the crux of the case, the blowback. Kapoor, without any emotion, explained the concept in very simplistic terms. Was he doing it to aid Melanie or as a result of his probable distaste for McGuire? In either event, the description was flat but accurate. A good witness would have embellished it with animation. He would have looked directly at the jurors as he explained its importance. Kapoor did neither. McGuire tried to coax him to open up, but it clearly wasn't working. The presentation was too stilted. Finally, McGuire gave up and asked the ultimate question.

"What is the significance of the presence of gun residue on Melanie's left hand?"

Kapoor softly replied, "It shows that she had handled the gun and fired it."

McGuire then turned to Johnnie and said, "Your witness, Mr. Fitzhugh."

Although Kapoor's testimony had hurt, it hadn't been dramatic. Johnnie knew he had to skirt the issues with Kapoor. He would let his experts rebut the examiner's conclusion.

"Good morning, Doctor."

"Good morning, Mr. Fitzhugh," Kapoor replied with a slight smile. Was that a sign? Would Kapoor follow his lead?

"Doctor, you've reviewed the EMT and hospital reports, have you not?"

"Yes, sir."

"Did you accept as true what was in those reports?"

"Yes."

"Doctor, did you ever go to the crime scene?"

"No."

"Do you know what the weather conditions were like on the night of the murder?"

"No."

"So you wouldn't know whether there was cloud cover that night, whether it was raining, or how cold it was?"

"No, I don't have that information."

"Did you read the statements provided by Dr. Stafford and Mrs. Garcia to the police?"

"I don't know who Mrs. Garcia is. I didn't read anything by her."

"Did you read Dr. Stafford's voluntary statement given to Detective Carlucci immediately after she was released from the hospital?"

"Yes. Mr. McGuire showed it to me."

"You don't have any proof one way or the other as to whether intruders broke into the house that night, do you?"

"No, I don't."

"Have you ever owned a gun?"

"No."

"Have you ever fired a gun?"

"No, sir."

Johnnie thanked the doctor and resumed his seat.

McGuire asked one question on redirect.

"Doctor, did you need to go to the scene to reach your opinion regarding Dr. Stafford's handling and firing of the gun?"

"No."

McGuire stated that the State had rested with the exception of moving the various exhibits into evidence. Judge Scholman turned to the jury and informed them they were done for the morning and for the day. They were to report tomorrow morning at the usual time.

After the jurors had left the courtroom, Scholman directed his words to Johnnie.

"Mr. Fitzhugh, I'll hear your motion to dismiss at 1:30."

Johnnie walked Melanie to her car. He told her the purpose of the motion and that he would lose, which was normal at this stage in a criminal case. He told her to review her statement that night. She replied that she was ready to testify. She and her father had decided that she had to testify, and she would when the time came.

Johnnie then called Erika. He instructed her to have Administrator Sutcliff and Mr. Lethridge at the court house by 8:30 a.m. The three EMTs should be there by 10:00 and the treating nurse by 11:00.

Johnnie had advised Wellington's personal counsel one week before the trial started that it was commencing as scheduled. Furber had been scheduled tentatively for tomorrow anyway. Johnnie personally called Wellington's attorney. Tomorrow afternoon and probably all the following day, he would be on the stand. Furber was required to bring the requested documents with him.

Johnnie decided to skip lunch. He called Burnside and filled him in. Burnside repeated what Melanie had proclaimed. She was testifying, regardless of any objection from Johnnie. If she was going to be convicted, it would be on her own terms, not as a result of some misguided suppositions, inferences, or deductions.

Johnnie returned to a counsel room adjacent to the courtroom's entrance. McGuire had made a tactical decision. He had relied solely on the county's medical examiner as he had done on numerous occasions. The real issue had been the gun residue. McGuire, rightly or wrongly, had decided against retaining an additional expert on that issue. McGuire probably feared that the use of an outside expert would undermine the jury's confidence in Kapoor's opinion. If Kapoor was so qualified, why was another forensic pathologist required? The defense, of course, would have to hire an expert. But why would the State need two on the same issue? Only the jury would determine whether McGuire had guessed wrong. In either event, Johnnie knew Dr. Honig, almost as much as Melanie, had to carry the day.

At the appointed time, Johnnie argued his motion to dismiss, even though he knew the eventual ruling. To protect Melanie's appeal rights, he had to place his argument on the record. He knew all possible logical inferences had to be given to the prosecution at this stage in the proceeding. The gun residue results were sufficient to overcome his motion. Even the bailiff knew that. McGuire supplied the appropriate buzzwords, and Scholman swiftly denied the motion.

Tomorrow, Johnnie went on the offensive. Would his firepower be enough?

51.

The morning started with fireworks. Before the jury was led into the courtroom, McGuire moved to bar the testimony of Johnnie's first witness, Robert Sutcliff.

"Your Honor, this man's purported testimony will add nothing to the issue of guilt or innocence. He's a hospital administrator who knows and works with the defendant. He wasn't present at the scene, and no report has been provided to us that would indicate he possessed any forensic evidence. We would ask that you prohibit his testimony."

Johnnie immediately went on the offensive. "Your Honor, the jury is entitled to know something about my client. She has a constitutional right not to testify. Nothing in the evidence rules prevents the defense from showing her background, her personality, or her life through other witnesses. While Mr. McGuire wants to paint her as a cardboard figure bolted to a chair next to me, he cannot preclude me from evidencing her personality. She is entitled to present a legitimate defense, despite McGuire's wishes to the contrary."

The judge turned to McGuire. "Mr. McGuire, you have tried many cases in this courthouse. You know the evidence rules as well as anyone. You've made your motion for the record. It's denied." Scholman turned to the bailiff, "Bring in the jury."

Johnnie led Sutcliff through his background, employment, and working relationship with Melanie. He explained in depth Melanie's responsibilities and interactions with the various hospitals. He described her expertise and acclaim. She was recognized as one of the top anesthesiologists in the state and served on hospital advisory boards. She also volunteered her time to assist in hospital-related charity functions and even had traveled abroad to third-world countries to provide free services as an anesthesiologist.

McGuire knew what he had to do. "Sir, you would agree with me that good people can do bad deeds?"

"Of course."

"You don't know the defendant's relationship with her husband, do you?"

"Well, whenever I've been in their presence, they have seemed like a well-grounded, harmonious couple."

"You don't know what happened behind their closed doors, do you?"

"Of course not, but she's a wonderful and caring person."

"You have no personal knowledge of any concrete evidence that could prove her guilt or innocence, do you?"

"Only my opinion based on knowing her well. You don't want that, or you would have asked. The answer is no. I wasn't there."

McGuire had gotten the responses he needed, but Sutcliff had smacked him. The jury knew McGuire didn't want Sutcliff to give his opinion. Would they be clairvoyant enough to jump to the conclusion that McGuire feared the response from the pleasant gentleman?

Alan Lethridge, wearing a blue blazer, white shirt, and gray pants, comfortably settled into the witness chair. In a folksy, grandfatherly tone, he explained that he lived next to the Staffords, that they were a pleasant couple, and that Melanie had been a Godsend to him after his wife passed away. He described the area. Gunshots were routine in the area due to hunters. He had not heard any that evening. He had gone to bed early. Even if he had heard any, it wouldn't have concerned him due to their frequency.

This time, McGuire decided to leave good enough alone. He asked no questions. Fitzhugh had asked Lethridge to paint a favorable portrait of his client. McGuire would confront that depiction in his summation. Good people commit crimes, even murder.

Ronald Townsend was the senior medic that arrived at the crime scene. He vividly narrated what he observed on arrival: a hysterical domestic, an injured and distraught wife, and an obviously dead husband. Melanie had said, "They killed him. They finally did." He didn't bother to ask whom. That was the police's job. His task was to assess her vitals, initially treat her, and swiftly transport her to the closest hospital. She had blood on her face, hands, and clothing. A table and lamp had been overturned. When he arrived, the only indoor illumination came from a wall light adjacent to the front door. The Hopewell Township Police arrived several minutes later. After briefly speaking to the officers, he and his two assistants strapped Melanie to a stretcher, applied an IV, and rushed her to the hospital. Townsend added that he had tried CPR on Stafford but knew it was useless.

McGuire had nothing to gain, so he declined cross-examination.

Now it was payback time for McGuire's earlier cheap shot before the jury. Johnnie arose and addressed the judge. "Your Honor, I have two other EMTs in the hallway. They are ready to testify. I believe they will be cumulative, and I don't want to waste the court's time unless Mr. McGuire wants me to produce them so he can ask them questions."

Scholman turned to McGuire. "What's your pleasure, Mr. McGuire?"

"That's fine, Your Honor. I don't want to waste the jury's time."

They now were even. McGuire had no choice. He knew he couldn't allow the other two witnesses to repeat Townsend's testimony. The jury would hate him for causing the delay. Fitzhugh had made his point. Three EMTs all said the same thing. They helped paint the scene in Melanie's favor. But then wouldn't EMTs favor a doctor? Also, weren't they more concerned with treatment and not investigation? That's why there were detectives and forensic pathologists. He would make certain the jury knew the difference.

She had been primed for this. Melanie might be an actress, but Erika was no wallflower. Her black suit and white blouse accentuated her Nordic beauty. The plainness of her attire contrasted with her stunning face and flowing blond hair. Her voice had a tone that immediately drew the listener to her.

Erika described her educational and employment background. She then produced the pictures that she had taken of the interior of the Stafford home. She produced fourteen copies of the pictures and of the diagram she had drawn of the home's interior. The diagram contained numbers that matched the numbers assigned to the photographs. The copies, with the court's permission, were distributed to each juror. The judge was provided a copy. McGuire already had been given his through the earlier discovery process. Erika walked the jury through each room. She highlighted the dimensions of the living room and the cut-out in the sliding door.

She then handed out copies of photos taken of the home's exterior surroundings together with a diagram that depicted measurements taken from the roadway to the home and from the home to the adjacent woods. A mileage chart illustrated the distance of the closest homes to the Stafford property. Erika somberly mentioned that the prosecutor's office had not provided any nighttime photos of the premises' exterior. Consequently, she contacted the National Weather Service and obtained a weather report for the night in question. With the judge's permission, a copy of the document was handed to each juror. Erika then interpreted the document's written data.

Erika advised that she tried to replicate that evening's conditions. She waited until the weather and cloud cover were similar. On that evening, she took the exterior photos. The diagram illustrated where each photo was taken. She took all photos with and without a flash and marked them accordingly. She stated that she took the exterior photos after taking the interior photos.

Johnnie viewed the jurors during her testimony. They were rapt with attention. They looked at her and then at each photo. The men seemed to look a little longer at her. Johnnie was not surprised. Their reaction was instinctual.

On cross, McGuire asked whether Johnnie was present during the photos. In her best professional tone, she replied, "Of course, as Melanie's counsel, he should have been there, just as a prosecutor would want to visit the scene and have photos taken to duplicate the night's appearance as closely as possible."

McGuire silently chastised himself. He never should have asked the question. She had embarrassed him badly. He had allowed attention to be brought to his office's own failure. They hadn't taken night pictures, because they had given no credence to the Wellington conspiracy. Erika had made him pay dearly for the oversight. McGuire made a note to explain in summation that night shots weren't needed, because the killer resided in the home.

After the luncheon recess, John Furber still had not appeared. Johnnie immediately informed the judge who instructed his secretary to call Wellington's counsel. Furber was to be produced at 8:30 the next morning, or he and Wellington would be held in contempt. McGuire remained unusually quiet during the discussion.

Rebecca Potter was forty-four years old and had been an emergency nurse for eighteen years. She examined Melanie upon her arrival. She obviously was distraught and dazed. She required stitches to her forehead as a result of a deep gash. The cut to the bridge of her nose was superficial and was bandaged. She had facial bruising apparently caused by her fall. Melanie briefly described her assault and several times mentioned, "They killed him," referring to her deceased husband. Melanie did not resist the officer when he told her he would be swabbing her hands.

Potter was concerned that Melanie may have suffered a concussion. She was unsteady on her feet and seemed to have gaps in her responses. She advised the officers that Melanie should remain at the hospital for several more hours. A prosecutor's detective said he was taking her back to Hopewell Township. There had been a murder, and they needed information quickly. She advised him that wasn't medically prudent. It did not sway him. She provided him with a sheet describing concussion symptoms and warned him that Melanie should be returned if her symptoms persisted or got worse.

Potter's narration was straightforward and professional. She delivered it in a methodical and serious manner. The woman was all business. McGuire realized nothing would be gained by examining her. She left the witness box unscathed.

Inez Garcia was nervous. This was her first time in a courtroom. She had dressed conservatively. Her tan slacks and brown silk blouse blended with her dark hair that was pulled back in a ponytail. Johnnie had told her to answer the questions as best she could and to face the jury with her responses. That she did.

She had worked for the Staffords for many years. Melanie was her favorite employer. She was so kind and nice. Never once did Melanie scold her or utter a harsh word. She gave her extra money for Christmas and always bought her a birthday present. Mr. Stafford was pleasant but much more reserved. Melanie treated her as an equal, unlike the other women whose houses she cleaned. She knew Melanie was right-handed because she signed her checks. She cleaned the entire house and never saw a gun.

On that morning, she arrived early. While it isn't bright out, she could make out objects. She opened the door and noticed that no lights were on. She flicked on the hall light next to the front door, saw Mr. Stafford on the floor, and screamed. Mr. Stafford was on his back. He had blood all around him. He was motionless.

She then saw Melanie to her left. She was on the floor and trying to get up. Melanie screamed. She had blood on her face. The table and lamp next to the couch were on the floor. The lamp's light was shattered. There was a gun on the floor near Melanie. There also was a white cloth. Melanie screamed for her to call 911 and then ran to her husband. She put her hands on her husband's chest and pushed forcefully and repeatedly.

Melanie had blood on her hands. Melanie tried to blow into Mr. Stafford's lips. She got blood on her face. Then she stopped and fell on her husband's chest. She screamed, "No! No! No! They killed him!" She said it numerous times. She was crying and appeared hysterical. The ambulance arrived and then the police. One of the medics pushed on Mr. Stafford's chest a short time and then stopped. Melanie kept crying and screaming, "They did it!" The ambulance people treated Melanie. The police talked to Melanie. She was still crying and shaking. Melanie was unsteady on her feet. The ambulance people placed her on a stretcher and then took her away. She heard the siren.

Inez remained at the scene. A big policeman left the house with Melanie and the EMTs. Other officers remained and were joined by more officers who took photos and applied black dust over various parts of the room. She saw the hole in the sliding glass door and felt cold air coming in from the outside.

Later, she was taken to the police station where she gave an oral statement. After it was typed, she asked the officer to read it to her. She then signed it. They didn't give her a copy, although she asked for one.

Johnnie then asked her to show the jury how Melanie gave the chest compressions. Johnnie held his breath. Would she do it correctly? She did, forceful downward pushing, right hand over left hand.

McGuire cut to the chase. "Mrs. Garcia, the defendant paid you well over the years, didn't she?"

"Yes. She a wonderful woman."

"She's still paying you, correct?"

"Yes."

"So you still see her often?"

"No. She not yet returned to house. I clean it, but she not back yet. She tell me she probably sell house. Too many bad memories."

"You would do anything for her, correct?"

"Yes, as long as I tell truth. I tell what I see. I love Melanie, but I answer to God first."

She had remembered. Johnnie had prepped her. He told her to tell the truth, but McGuire would try to show that she was lying. During their pretrial prep, he had played McGuire. He had crossed her nicely, but all with the intent of showing her bias. He had explained what McGuire would do and how he later would tell the jury that she was a liar. His thoughts had not been forgotten. She had stood her ground. McGuire had not scored any points. After several innocuous questions meant to show he wasn't a bad guy, he stopped.

The jury was excused for the day. Johnnie then made a motion to have Furber declared a hostile witness should he appear the following day.

McGuire opposed the relief. How could Furber be assumed to be hostile when he hadn't yet uttered a word? The defense should be forbidden from asking leading questions until Furber proved uncooperative.

Scholman commented that Furber had failed to appear that day despite the notification. That was sufficient to demonstrate his hostility. Moreover, Dr. Stafford's defense was premised upon the alleged misconduct of Mr. Furber's employer. Leading questions would be allowed.

McGuire then moved to prevent the use of Stafford's email and the accompanying photos. They were hearsay documents and weren't admissible. Melanie had caused her husband's death. Therefore, she could not benefit by their introduction. For all anyone knew, she may have written the email herself when her husband was in Hawaii. She had planted it in the computer to deflect suspicion from her. She had staged the whole thing, just as she had cut the glass from the sliding door while her husband was in Hawaii. She should not benefit from her own culpability.

Johnnie countered. The State had not introduced even a scintilla of evidence that the email wasn't genuine. Had Stafford survived the shooting, the email would have been admissible. Moreover, a declarant's statement was admissible when he was absent from a hearing due to death. Additionally, the email's content revealed that Stafford feared for his life. As the email specifically stated, it was to be provided to the authorities should Stafford not return from Hawaii or be killed. He had evidence harmful to his employer, had been told to suppress it, and had been warned of the consequences. The email represented his fear of imminent death and was admissible. This was a criminal proceeding. Stafford was the unavailable victim. Therefore, it was admissible.

Scholman ruled swiftly. It was admissible under both exceptions to the hearsay rule. The defense could utilize the email and the photos when examining Furber. If the defendant took the stand, she also could refer to them.

After Scholman left the bench, McGuire motioned Johnnie over. Out of Melanie's presence, he addressed Johnnie. "Did Burnside get to him also? Something stinks, Johnnie. I knew I had a worthy adversary. I didn't know I had two. Just remember who's paying you. You might win this battle thanks to Scholman, but I'd be worried about the overall war. Burnside can cast you aside, just as easily as he did Stafford and Huffmire. Physically, you'll be fine. Emotionally, I don't know. What if you discover she really did it? That we weren't wrong, just manipulated? Not just us but also you? Are you controlling this defense, or is Burnside? My guess is both she and he have told you she's going to testify despite your admonitions. Maybe I'm wrong. If I was a betting man, I'd wager I'm not."

Johnnie smiled and replied. "Our die is cast, Terry. Maybe this case is part of our fate. I didn't want it, and you thought you needed it. How it plays out and its ramifications are matters we cannot control. Maybe we are pawns. If we are, we have contributed to our own fate.

We had our choices and did not make them blindly. We have no one to blame but ourselves. Our motives may have been different, but our blame is the same."

Johnnie returned to his client.

"What was that about?" she asked.

"Just a philosophical discussion, not worth repeating. Let's get out of here."

"How'd we do today?"

"I think well, but I don't get to cast a vote. It's all up to those seats over there."

52.

The next morning, Furber arrived on time with corporate counsel. He was wearing a bespoke gray pin-striped suit, a starched white shirt, and a solid blue tie. His black wingtips were well polished. He was tall with well-groomed gray hair. All that was absent was a sign proclaiming corporate success.

He testified that he was Wellington's executive vice president for pharmaceutical research and development. He had hired Sterling Labs to conduct Youtheria's testing as an anti-aging drug. He admitted Youtheria initially had been touted as a possible cure for melanoma and squamous cell carcinoma but had failed to prove its efficacy during FDA testing. Millions had been spent without any return on that investment. By chance, however, testing indicated it might have anti-aging possibilities. As a result, foreign testing through Sterling was commenced in Romania, Bulgaria, and the Ukraine.

Richard Stafford was in charge of verifying the testing procedures and results. He was Stafford's boss. He never journeyed to the testing facilities and solely relied on Stafford's expertise. Stafford never mentioned any testing irregularities. He denied ever threatening Stafford. Not once did he ever imply that Stafford might be harmed or terminated. Had Stafford voiced his concern to him, he would have launched an investigation.

The FDA approved the drug. That stamped its legitimacy and safety. Yes, the drug had earned millions and increased the company's bottom line. As to why Stafford would compose such an untruthful email, he could surmise only that Stafford had become disgruntled because he had not received a promotion despite the drug's remarkable financial success.

No, he had not contacted Sterling or the FDA after being advised of the email's existence. As to the accompanying photos, he didn't know whether the building was the Romanian testing facility and never attempted to ascertain the picture's validity. Yes, he could have called Sterling regarding the photo but never did. When shown the photo depicting the various bottles and hypodermic needles, he had no knowledge as to the named substances, had no information regarding the use of hypodermic needles, and definitely possessed not even a guess as to the identity of the blue substance that spotted the towels. And, no, he didn't contact Sterling about that photo. For all he knew, Stafford could have taken that photo anywhere.

As far as he was concerned, the FDA had sanctioned the drug's use. That was enough for him. Yes, Stafford's position had been filled within days of his death, and Wellington still used Sterling for its overseas testing. And, yes, almost all his company's testing was performed overseas. The prior locations were still in use. The company also had opened facilities in Croatia and Albania.

To pierce Furber's testimony, Johnnie called Dr. Malcolm Gideon as his next witness. He had a doctorate in biochemistry and also a degree in pharmacy. For many years, he had worked for several pharmaceutical companies in research and testing. He then joined the FDA at the urging of the agency's director. He spent several years there monitoring testing protocols used by various drug companies and their independent testing labs. He retired last year at sixty-five. Over the years, he had published numerous articles on the pharmaceutical industry and also on the foreign outsourcing of drug testing. At the request of Mr. Fitzhugh, he had investigated the testing of Youtheria and had discovered several abnormalities. He, of course, was being paid for his services as all experts were. He charged an hourly fee for his investigation and for his testimony. The fee was commensurate with what others charged when offering opinions on pharmaceutical matters.

Gideon then walked the jury through how drugs were tested and why most testing was done overseas. There was a lack of adequate verification of overseas due to the FDA's insufficient funds and staff. He related that, without inspection, it was impossible to monitor overseas testing. There were no real safeguards to ensure proper testing protocols. Drugs had to be tested on individuals for whom they would be marketed.

Consequently, test subjects had to be consistent in age, gender, and race. For example, one wouldn't utilize young females or males as test subjects for a menopausal drug. Individuals suffering from diseases were to be excluded from testing unless the drug was being tested for that particular malady.

The reasons that drugs were usually tested overseas were the cost benefits and the absence of valid monitoring. The independent testing labs determined the rules for the clinical trials and the results. They prepared the reports, ghost wrote the supporting technical articles for medical publications, and initiated promotional campaigns.

While the FDA had authority to inspect the foreign testing, it lacked the manpower. On a percentage basis, it visited very few foreign labs. Companies could withhold foreign test data until applications were submitted for FDA approval. By then, it was obviously too late to inspect how the trial was regulated, ascertain whether acceptable standards were implemented, and investigate whether data had been compromised.

The depressed economy of the testing country provided a haven for rampant fraud. Foreign doctors could be easily swayed by financial inducements that far outweighed their normal earnings. Test subjects would be overjoyed to receive any remuneration while also being misled as to the drug's purpose. People in poverty-stricken areas might metabolize a drug differently from well-fed Americans. Placebo testing could be used to distort results.

Gideon had obtained the FDA file on Youtheria. There had been no foreign inspection by the FDA. It had relied solely on Wellington and

Sterling. He had read Stafford's email and had been intrigued by the possible use of identical twins to falsify the data. He had reviewed the names of the test subjects and the limited number of before and after facial photographs that had been submitted to the FDA as evidential proof of the drug's success.

Through governmental contacts, he had requested a listing of all identical twins born in Romania from 1940 to 1970. He received the requested documentation and compared the names to the test subjects. He found sixteen surnames that matched names of females born with an identical twin.

There were twenty photos submitted to the FDA as proof of the drug's anti-aging properties. Sixteen of those photos referred to women who had an identical twin. He found it statistically improbable that a test sampling would include that high percentage of women who had an identical twin and even more improbable that almost all the photographs were of women who had an identical twin. No identical twins should have been enrolled in the testing. Identical twins do not have to age at the same rate.

Numerous factors can accelerate or retard facial aging. That is why identical twins should have been removed from the study. Otherwise, a picture of the older-looking sister could have been inserted as a before-testing picture, and a portrait of the younger-looking sister substituted for the after-testing result, even though the younger-looking twin never had participated in the study. There was no doubt that the testing had been manipulated.

Furthermore, why did one of the photographs reveal the presence of Botox and hypodermic needles? Botox was used to mask the aging process. The presence of the needles suggested injections had been made. Neither item should have been stored at the facility. Youtheria was a pill, not a liquid.

McGuire commenced with the photos. "Sir, you don't know whether these photos were taken at the Romanian test site, do you?"

"Can I be certain? No. On the other hand, no one has provided me with any documentation to refute that the building was not the testing lab or that the photos of the Botox and needles were not at that facility. Mr. Stafford's email refers to an identical twin presence, and the photos bear that out, as I have already explained. The likelihood of almost all the pictured women being an identical twin is astronomical."

"Sir, I will represent to you that Mr. Stafford's boss testified immediately before you. Under oath, he adamantly reported that Mr. Stafford never complained to him of testing falsification. Are you saying that Mr. Furber lied?"

"That's for the jury, sir. I can only state what my investigation uncovered. I wrote Wellington of my findings and never received a response. I'll leave it at that."

"Sir, are you saying that Wellington ordered the killing of Mr. Stafford?"

"I have no knowledge as to who killed Mr. Stafford. All I know is that the testing of a very profitable drug was tainted. Profits would have been lost and careers ruined if the procedures were revealed."

"Sir, how much were you paid for this report and your courtroom testing?"

Gideon differentiated between the research and the testimony. McGuire then ended his cross.

Johnnie then went on redirect. "Sir, when I requested you to conduct an investigation, what were you led to believe was asked of you?"

"Look into the testing procedures, and provide an honest report without any biases. Just provide an accurate assessment without regard to the consequences for either the defense or the prosecution. That's what I did to the best of my ability."

"Had you ever met me or anyone in my firm before I called you to ask if you would do this investigation for me?"

"No, sir. I knew nothing of you or your firm. I'm not even from this area."

After Johnnie concluded, Scholman addressed the jury. "Ladies and gentlemen, I should have addressed you before Mr. Gideon testified. Experts are used routinely in civil and criminal cases. Unless they are employed by the Federal Government, a state, a county, or a municipality, they are entitled to charge a reasonable sum for their services, and they all do. They are considered experts because they possess detailed knowledge on matters not normally known by the average juror or even by the sitting judge. The fact that experts often are paid considerable sums of money should not be of concern to you. They work for it and should be paid what others in their field of expertise receive. The fact that Mr. Gideon received the stated sum does not mean he tailored his testimony to favor the side for which he testified. Sometimes, experts are employed and then never called as witnesses for any number of reasons. They still must be paid. When considering Mr. Gideon's testimony and that of other experts, you should consider what they said or didn't say. The fact that they were paid is immaterial. You might be surprised by the sums, but believe me this is routine. I, as a judge, and both counsel see this daily as we practice our trades."

Scholman had done him a favor. Actually, he had gone further than Johnnie ever would have expected. Implicitly, McGuire had been chastised. The jurors saw that he had tried to obtain an underhanded advantage over the witness. The judge then had evened the playing field.

"Your next witness, Mr. Fitzhugh."

Robert Stanton, a board-certified plastic surgeon, settled his lanky frame into the witness chair. He had obtained his undergraduate diploma from the University of Virginia and his medical degree from Penn. He was a Fellow of the American College of Surgeons and had offices in North Jersey and Manhattan. While he performed tummy tucks and breast augmentations, the majority of his practice was devoted to facial trauma, elective facial surgery, and skin rejuvenation. Through the use of exhibit boards and photographs, he explained how facial skin aged and the surgical procedures that were often undertaken to reverse or retard the process.

He then contrasted the utilization of Botox injections, laser skin resurfacing, and chemical peels with the short-term skin enhancement provided by over-the-counter skin creams. Many of his patients had tried Youtheria with minimal success. Most had supplemented the pill with skin creams but still were dissatisfied with the short-duration improvement. From what he had observed, the drug was not an elixir. Although it did not damage the skin, its effect was minimal. The application of facial creams and makeup seemed to be just as beneficial. Perhaps, the future would produce a more effective drug.

Johnnie showed him the photos in conjunction with Stafford's email. Stanton questioned why there was a need for hypodermic needles, Botox, and hyaluronic acid filters at a site devoted to drug testing. What most shocked him was the presence of the blue spotted towels. The towels clearly revealed that facial chemical peels had been performed to exfoliate aged surface skin. If the drug worked as touted, none of the aforementioned items would have been needed.

McGuire arose for his cross.

"Doctor, other than Mr. Stafford's alleged email, you don't know where these photos were taken, do you?"

"Correct."

"Are you saying that someone at Wellington or Sterling labs sanctioned a killing of Mr. Stafford?"

"No. All I'm saying is that the drug is not as effective as claimed. If those photos were taken at the testing facility, then Wellington or the lab has a real problem if any of those items were used in conjunction with the pill's administration to the test subjects."

"Doctor, isn't it a fact that if Youtheria were a miracle drug, that your business and your income would suffer dramatically?"

"Not in the least. Most of my facial patients need or want surgery due to trauma or developmental deformities or irregularities. I perform nasal reconstructions, lip modifications, eyelid and eyebrow alterations, chin enhancements or reductions, ear reshaping, and more. Those people often have real physical or psychological issues that compel the operations. I don't hold myself out as a so-called 'doctor of the stars.' For those who wish to lessen their aged appearance, I try to accommodate them. They have the right to alter their appearance. They understand there are inherent risks. I can't guarantee optimum results, only surgical skill. I have more than enough patients. Frankly, my wife and kids wished I had less."

McGuire had forced the doctor to admit that he was relying on the information contained in Stafford's email. If the photos weren't taken at the testing lab, then they were meaningless. Stanton could not refute the proposition that Melanie killed her husband. He also couldn't verify that Stafford's email was premised on legitimate facts or even written by Stafford. McGuire had received all he could have hoped for. He ended his examination, and Scholman dismissed the jury for the day.

Johnnie phoned Detective Stenkowicz. He could relax. He would not be needed. Carlucci had admitted that there had been no investigation of Wellington. Stenkowicz breathed a sigh of relief. Had he testified for Johnnie, he would have become the office pariah, banished to menial tasks and constant tedium.

Tonight, Johnnie and Melanie would meet to prep again. If Dr. Honig finished by early afternoon, he had to know if she really wanted to testify. If so, she would be the next and final witness. She advised him she would be bringing her father that evening. Her father was demanding that she testify. She agreed and would unless Johnnie could convince them that he knew that without her testimony the verdict would be not guilty. Johnnie knew already what his response would be. When you guaranteed what twelve people would decide, the only thing that you were assuring was your own destruction.

53.

Doctor Erick Honig would be the penultimate witness. The prior evening, Melanie and Burnside had made that clear. She was testifying even if Honig's testimony obliterated the opinion rendered by Dr. Kapoor.

Honig's credentials were impeccable. His undergraduate degrees in pharmacy and physiology were coupled with a Harvard medical degree. Currently, he was the director of the Northeastern Institute for Forensic Sciences and professor of pathology and forensic sciences at Yale Medical School. He was a diplomate of the American Board of Pathology in pathological anatomy, clinical pathology, and forensic pathology. He was a Fellow of the American Association for the Advancement of Science, the American College of Physicians, and the American Society of Clinical Pathologists. He was a former president of the American Academy of Forensic Sciences and had authored scores of articles in the fields of forensic pathology. He had been a chief medical examiner for several northeastern cities and a former director of a criminal investigation laboratory. He had taken various ballistic courses and was familiar with all types of firearms. He had fired many weapons when studying their effects on victims.

As a forensic pathologist, he had investigated thousands of homicides over a forty-year career and had testified for the prosecution and the defense.

He had read the prosecutor's file and had visited the crime scene. He was very familiar with the Glock 17 and explained its operation to the jury. He held one of the fired shells and explained that three substances are discharged from the gun's nozzle: the bullet, the gas, and the unburned powder grains. The burning of hot powder produces the gas that fires the bullet out of the gun. Not all of the powder grains burn. Most of the unburned grains are blown out of the gun with the same velocity as the bullet. The gas is light, so it travels only a very short distance. The unburned powder grains travel much farther.

If a gun is fired a few inches from the victim, a zone of soot will be deposited where the bullet hits the skin. If the gun is fired up to four or five feet away, a "powder tattooing" will occur. Individual unburned powder grains are blown into the skin. A small magenta-colored zone would surround each tattoo and would signify that small blood vessels had been ruptured. The shape of the individual tattoos provides a clue as to the type of powder grain used. The area covered by the powder tattoo correlates with the range of fire. Powder tattooing is typically found when a weapon is fired within five feet of the victim, although isolated powder grains could carry as far as twelve feet.

Honig had reviewed the autopsy and crime scene photos. The chest and lower abdomen entry wounds exhibited powder tattooing, meaning the gun probably was fired within five feet of the victim. The head wound evidenced soot. It was fired within a few inches and was obviously the final shot. The victim was on his back. The killer wanted to make certain he was dead.

In Dr. Stafford's statement, she said that she had screamed during the struggle. The abdomen shot was fired from an angular position. Therefore, it was fired during, or just after, the struggle. The chest shot was fired straight on. It would have been the second bullet.

Johnnie then handed him Stafford's pajamas. Honig showed the jurors where the residue was deposited on the garments.

Johnnie next mentioned that GSR testing revealed powder only on Melanie's left palm. He added that Melanie and Inez Garcia confirmed that she was right-handed. Statements and testimony disclosed that

Melanie had placed her right palm on top of her left hand when she performed the CPR.

Honig then addressed the issue of the gunpowder's presence. That residue had the consistency of flour and would remain on someone's hands for several hours. Its presence, however, would not signify that the individual fired the weapon. There were numerous alternative explanations. The person may have been in the immediate vicinity when another pulled the trigger. The residue could have been transferred from the victim's clothing if the individual had touched the victim. The facts of each case had to be considered. Different facts could lead to dissimilar conclusions.

In this instance, there were several critical factors that had to be weighed. Melanie definitely was in the vicinity of the shooter and her husband when the gun was discharged. Prior testimony had referenced that she had not washed her blood-stained hands before the test was administered. She was right-handed. Therefore, she would have fired the weapon with that hand or by holding it with both hands. Most importantly, there was no residue on the inner and outer aspects of her right hand. Had she fired the weapon, residue should have been present somewhere on the right hand. There was residue on her husband's pajamas in the chest and lower abdominal areas. Melanie applied CPR to her husband's chest. Her left palm was on the garment during those forceful compressions. He would have expected residue to be transferred to her left palm. Therefore, to a reasonable degree of forensic pathological certainty, it would be impossible to conclude that the presence of the left-hand residue proved that Melanie fired the gun.

McGuire immediately went on the offensive.

"Doctor, you're not saying that this defendant couldn't have fired the gun, are you?"

"What I'm saying is there are too many possibilities to conclude to a reasonable degree of certainty that she did. Even disregarding Dr. Stafford's statement as to the struggle, Mrs. Garcia described how she administered the CPR. That in itself definitely would have led to residue transfer to Dr. Stafford."

"But, sir, she could have already had residue on her left hand as a result of firing the weapon, correct?"

"Yes, but then there would have been residue also on the top of her left hand and also on her right hand. Neither was present."

"Well, she could have fired the weapon just with her left hand, correct?"

"Highly unlikely. People shoot with their dominant hand. If she was the killer, as you profess, she would have used her right hand. That would have been the hand she was most comfortable using when performing daily tasks."

"Sir, you said earlier that the head shot was the last shot and was to guarantee Mr. Stafford was dead. A professional wouldn't have needed three shots, correct?"

"Not correct. The prosecutor's file indicates there was no illumination in that room. There has been no proof from your file, sir, that the shooter used a flashlight. Dr. Stafford related in her statement that she tried to free herself from her assailant. She grabbed at his hand that was around her and also tried to kick back. This was a blind situation. One can assume the assailant never had been to the residence. The assailant had a struggling woman he was trying to drug, apparently was confronted with her husband rushing from the bedroom, and then had to aim in darkness. This scenario would not have been like a television show where the hero's magic bullet initially hits the moving villain."

"Sir, you're assuming that the defendant wasn't the killer, aren't you?"

"I'm not assuming anything. I'm only stating that you, sir, can assume she did it, but that the scientific evidence doesn't prove it."

"So, you disagree with Dr. Kapoor's opinion?"

"Most definitely."

"So you want this jury to accept your opinion over his?"

"Sir, I have not, nor should I tell these jurors what to do. That would be insulting to their intelligence. All I'm saying is that the facts in this case do not guarantee that she pulled the trigger. There are too many unanswered questions."

"Isn't that the case in most of the cases you get paid to provide an opinion?"

"Absolutely not, but that's not the point here. We are dealing with this case, not others. I have a professional and ethical duty to provide you with a thoughtful and well-reasoned analysis. You may not accept it. These jurors might not accept it. But I have to live with that opinion. I don't take that burden lightly. My reputation is at stake."

"Yes, but you are paid handsomely for your opinion."

"Yes. But if your reputation is tarnished, no dollar sum ever will restore it."

"Sir, you testified you went to the crime scene. Why?"

"After I read your office's file, I wanted to see for myself the house's interior, especially the area of the shooting. The autopsy and crime scene photos depicted the wounds but wouldn't really provide me with the three-dimensional information. I wanted to view the possible shot angles in relation to where the struggle took place."

"Well, you're assuming there really was a struggle between the defendant and the alleged assailant, correct?"

"Yes. I'm assuming that. If not, then I would have to assume Dr. Stafford cut out the glass, killed her husband, drugged herself, knocked over the table and lamp, injured herself, and then after all that plotting, left the gun there and failed to wash the gun residue off her hands before Mrs. Garcia and the EMTs arrived."

"Your Honor, I ask that answer be stricken as unresponsive."

"Overruled."

"Sir, are you telling the jury that couldn't have happened?"

"No. That's for them to decide."

"Sir, have you ever been wrong in your opinions?"

"Sir, anyone who tells you they have never been wrong is either a liar, an egotist, or a fool. That holds true for doctors, lawyers, and even prosecutors."

After Honig's testimony, they took a luncheon recess. Honig had elicited his points cleverly and succinctly. His credentials easily surpassed Kapoor's. Would that help sway the jurors?

Johnnie believed there was enough evidence to lead to a hung jury, if not an acquittal, without Melanie testifying. Her presentation could sway the jurors against her. Was the risk worth it? He conveyed his thought to her. She would not relent. The choice ultimately was hers. She was testifying.

After the recess, Johnnie asked the bailiff to inform the judge that he had something to put on the record before the jury reentered. When the judge was seated, Johnnie informed him that he had counseled his client and that she had decided she wanted to testify. Scholman then questioned her at length about her options and the inherent risks. She replied that she had considered all the possible consequences and desperately wanted to testify. Whatever the jury's verdict, she would know she had conveyed everything to them. She had made the decision of her own free will. She had not been influenced or coerced. She gladly would live with that decision.

McGuire smiled. Based upon Honig's testimony, he never thought she would dare to testify. Honig had done well. By testifying, she could grasp defeat from the jaws of a probable victory. McGuire always thought she was too self-assured in her own intelligence. Her ego precluded her from computing the inherent risk she was undertaking. But then if she was the killer, she assiduously and ruthlessly had plotted the murder. Everything had been orchestrated perfectly. She had created the needed implausibility that formed the groundwork for her acquittal. Why stop now? Her all-consuming vanity would not allow it. If he could pierce her façade, the game was over. Everyone would see her real persona.

Melanie arose from her chair, looked directly at the jury, and self-assuredly walked to the witness box. Now was her time. Had she lost her touch? Not in the least. She knew she still had it. No matter what the evidence purportedly demonstrated, McGuire would not defeat her. This was her stage, not his. He had no idea what it really meant to be on the stage. Well, he was about to find out. Johnnie had repeatedly coached her on how to compose herself and respond both on direct and cross. She had endured the instructions with the appropriate show of concern and consternation, masking her boredom.

In front of the jury, Johnnie told Melanie that due to the counsel table configuration, she should respond to his questions by directing her answers to the jury, that she also should do so on cross-examination unless Mr. McGuire gave her contrary instructions.

She knew the jury would be riveted to her every word and expression. Had any of them ever looked into the eyes of a killer, a tragic victim, or even a chameleon? Would they even be able to tell the difference? Was there any, or did those supposed disparities reside only in the soul? Would her words be enough? Would the mere presence of the indictment and the gun be sufficient to damn her, regardless of how she projected herself to those fourteen people? Peers? A jury of her peers? They weren't her peers and never would be. They lacked her intelligence, her education, and even her breeding. The judicial canard was that everyone was entitled to a jury of his or her peers. Well, that wasn't happening to her.

McGuire had done his best to remove as many as he could. Johnnie had saved some. Was she headed to a hung jury with a resultant retrial? Was she doomed to her fate, or could she and Johnnie mesmerize the jury? Johnnie had looks and charisma, but he was a neophyte compared to her. To save herself, this would have to be her production, not his. As long as he asked the proper questions, she could mold her answers and explain any inconsistencies. Would reason and logic convince these people, or was her cause hopeless?

Johnnie observed the jurors were rapt with attention. He started with her education and training. He asked her whether she wanted to add anything to Robert Sutcliff's narration of her charitable and civic involvement. She deftly responded that it was more than sufficient and frankly didn't really matter at this point. He then had her describe her courtship and marriage. She and Richard had many mutual interests, which she delineated. Both were passionate about their careers and worked long hours. On weekends, they would decompress and enjoy each other's company.

Johnnie next directed her to Wellington. Her husband had become very agitated. He had uncovered testing deceit and fraud. He had reported his findings to his superior, Furber. Despite his revelations, Furber had done nothing. At first, he assured Richard that he would investigate. Weeks went by without word. Richard pressed the issue. Furber warned him that further insistence could unravel his career. Furber then became blunter. While the threats were veiled, their meaning was unmistaken. Desist or suffer the consequences, which would be severe.

She had urged Richard to go to the authorities. He had insisted that he needed just a little more time to finalize everything. He was hopeful that the company's president would be at the Hawaii function. He would approach him. She had warned him that was dangerous. He could not be dissuaded. At her urging, he had typed an 'in case of my death' email memorializing his findings and referencing the photos. She had made copies and placed them in their joint bank safety deposit box. Now he was dead as a result of his valiant efforts. Wellington had killed him and widowed her.

Scholman interrupted at that point. He informed the jury that it had been a long day and they would recess until tomorrow. The jury was excused. Melanie then stepped down from the witness box. McGuire's counsel table was closest to the jury box. He was still seated. As she walked toward the defense table, her eyes never veered from him until she passed his chair. Only briefly had their eyes met before McGuire looked away. Just as she had surmised, the man was a coward. She would destroy his blind ambition on cross, or she would go to prison knowing that she, at least, had done her best.

Johnnie had been impressed by her calmness and poise. She had spoken to the jury in a soft, well-measured tone. She had looked at each of them in a respectful, dignified manner. Her tone was conversational but was touched with sadness, almost extreme sadness. She looked and acted like a victim, not a killer. At times, she would pause in her narration, and her shoulders would slump, as if she was too overwhelmed to continue. Then, her posture would stiffen, and she would resume her response. Was this all an act, or was the significance of the moment overwhelming her?

He had avoided purposely any reference to her scholastic or college extracurricular activities. He only hoped that McGuire would also. If McGuire had uncovered that she had acted, he would have all the ammunition he needed to undermine the image that she was portraying skillfully. Would she be able to suppress those flashes of anger and venom that he had witnessed? If not, even if she were innocent, the jury would not be convinced. She would be going to jail for a long, long time.

54.

The next day, wearing another conservative suit, Melanie resumed the stand. On the way to the courthouse, Johnnie had reviewed with her what he would be asking and how she should act when McGuire finally had his opportunity. Melanie told him to relax. She would handle McGuire. She had read him. He, not her, would wilt. She had played the devil's advocate. There were critical issues that McGuire had to address, and she was certain she had legitimate responses. If not, the fault would be hers, not Johnnie's. Yes, she would suppress the Burnside temper and sarcasm.

Johnnie opened the morning session with a discussion of guns. Melanie was right-handed. Everything important she did with that hand. She threw, cut, and stitched with it. She never had fired a gun. Neither she nor her husband ever purchased any guns or rifles. In fact, her husband hated them. Before awaking on the floor after he husband was shot, she never had laid her eyes on the weapon.

She had not worked the day before the murder. She had exercised vigorously at the gym, cooked outside on the grill, and awaited her husband's return from Hawaii. He had advised her that his connecting flight was delayed and that he definitely would be late. She had decided to read on the living room couch until her husband returned. At some point, she fell asleep. Her husband lightly awakened her by kissing her on the forehead. Glad he was home, she mumbled that she was too tired to move and undress. He turned off the lamp, and she rapidly returned to her slumber.

Her tone changed dramatically as she explained the assault. Her narration was word for word what she had provided to Johnnie. It was almost as if she had memorized the lines of a play. She became animated when she described her struggle and the hand that had pressed the cloth tightly against her face. The assailant's fingers were strong and thick. She could feel their width through the right glove, which was not leather. It had the consistency of latex.

Quietly, but emotionally, she slowly described what she saw and felt upon awakening to Inez's scream. She was dazed, disoriented, and in pain. She immediately observed her prone husband and the blood-stained white carpet. She rushed to him and observed the bullet holes to the chest and head. Instinctively, she applied CPR. She didn't even realize the obvious, that he was dead. She just pushed and pushed until finally her senses kicked in. There were no respirations and no pulse. The eyes were dilated and fixed.

Johnnie was transfixed by her narration. She appeared to be reliving every moment, not with shrieking or uncontrollable sobbing, but rather with tremendous sorrow and resignation. The effect was overpowering. The jurors and the judge just stared at her. The silence was deafening.

Melanie then shook her head from side to side as if shaking off a head blow.

Johnnie asked her to demonstrate how she applied the CPR, and she duplicated what Inez already had reported to the jury. Melanie added that she couldn't recall how many compressions she applied before she realized the obvious, the utter futility of her exercise.

Johnnie moved to the arrival of the EMTs and the Hopewell officers. Melanie described how she felt. She had a splitting headache. She was dazed, dizzy, and obviously emotionally shattered. Yet she also knew what had happened. Her husband had been slaughtered. She knew who had done it but never voiced the name. In her disoriented and anguished state, she blindly assumed that everyone knew who it was. Upon reflection, that obviously made no sense, not even an iota of sense. It seemed absurd now. It never occurred to her then. Her husband was murdered, and she knew who did it. The actual person or persons, no, but she knew Wellington was behind it. At stake were millions and millions of dollars in revenue and hundreds of jobs. By hundreds, she meant the corporate jobs. Those individuals with the big salaries, lucrative bonuses, and thousands of stock shares. Silence was golden. Corporate greed always outweighed public safety.

The police asked her to cooperate, and she did so quickly and voluntarily. She waived her Miranda rights and described as best she could what had happened. They had asked her to write a statement. She told them she couldn't focus well. Her head really hurt, and she felt "off." Mentally, she knew she wasn't all there, but she wanted the police to catch the killer or killers, so she asked them to let her give a recorded statement. Under the circumstances, she tried to describe everything as best as she could. Obviously, she had failed, because she never mentioned the glove or Wellington's name. On the other hand, the prosecutor's office seized the family's computer that contained Richard's email. Moreover, at her request, her attorney had sent a copy of the email and the photos to Mr. McGuire after she was released from jail.

She bowed her head momentarily and then looked up to the jury. Despite the anguish and shame she had suffered, that paled when compared to the horror and indescribable pain that Richard had suffered, as he valiantly came to her aid. All she had asked was that Mr. McGuire and his office follow the evidence. Through Detective Carlucci's testimony, she had received her answer. No contact had been made. Wellington was doing business as usual.

Johnnie ended his direct, and the judge ended the day.

Melanie walked slowly and despondently from the stand. The jurors followed her every movement and then stared at McGuire. It was a powerful moment. Had they believed her, or were they just waiting for McGuire to tear her testimony to shreds?

55.

McGuire knew he needed to make an immediate impact. He had to get the jurors thinking while they were alert. He had to surprise her, knock her off the rhythm she had gained yesterday. He needed to make her pause before responding. He needed to show the jury that she really was a calculating bitch.

He approached the witness box and handed her two crime scene photos of the living room. He asked her to study both of them and let him know when she was ready. She stared at them and then looked up.

"Where's the book?"

Johnnie gulped. She had been reading before she fell asleep. During one of their conversations, Melanie had told him that she assumed Richard had taken it into the room after he kissed her on the forehead and turned off the table light. Johnnie had forgotten to bring out that assumption on direct. Why wouldn't her husband just have left the book on the table?

When Melanie didn't respond immediately, McGuire added, "You know the book you allegedly were reading when you fell asleep?"

"Well, it's not in this picture. I'm assuming Richard must have moved it when he kissed me on the forehead and turned off the table light."

"What were you reading?"

"Actually, I was reading a medical journal. Do you have a picture of our bedroom?" She knew she always had books and journals on her nightstand.

McGuire gave her all the crime scene photos. She searched through quickly and found one that would do.

"Here, see this photo of the bedroom. My nightstand has books and magazines on it. I assume he put it there." She paused and then softly added, "Unfortunately, we'll never know."

"Now, this alleged struggle, how long did it last?"

"Sir, it wasn't an alleged struggle. I was grabbed from behind and believed I was fighting for my life. I wasn't timing how long I was fighting him. I was trying to pull the cloth off my face as he was pressing it harder against my nose and lips. To me, it seemed like an eternity, but obviously it was not."

"Well, was it a minute, two minutes, thirty seconds?"

"I don't have the faintest idea. I was focused on breaking free and calling for my husband. I yelled to him once. I remember kicking backward. I believed I hit the person's leg. Next thing I remember was Inez screaming."

"Would you please explain to this jury how you heard Mrs. Garcia screaming but never heard the three gunshots?"

"I don't know. I was obviously drugged, and in retrospect, I know I must have landed on the overturned table or lamp or both due to my injuries. I was knocked out from the drug and probably from the fall. As even the emergency room nurse testified, I had concussion symptoms when she examined me. She wanted me kept for observation, but Detective Carlucci refused her request."

"You would agree with me that the noise from those three shots would have been closer to you than the scream of Mrs. Garcia?"

"Of course, yes. All I can tell you is that I don't remember hearing the gun go off."

"Let's go back to that struggle. You testified the alleged assailant had one arm tightly across your chest while the other hand was pressing tightly against your face, that the white cloth was actually pressing against your nose and mouth. Explain to this jury, how that assailant could have shot your husband three times while holding you in the fashion that you have described?"

"Obviously, he couldn't have. I told you I didn't hear the shots. I must have been thrown or dropped to the floor before at least the last two shots were fired. Dr. Honig testified that the chest shot was direct. Therefore, the killer couldn't have been struggling with me and gotten off a straight shot. The third shot was a close-up to the head. Dr. Honig indicated that my husband was already on his back. That shot basically was a contact shot, one made to make certain Richard would be dead. Dr. Honig said the first shot was an angular one. It hit the lower abdomen near the groin. Maybe that shot was fired at the end of the struggle, and maybe the shooter was off balance due to my efforts to free myself."

"Or maybe that shot was meant for his groin as a result of his infidelity?"

"Objection, Your Honor," Johnnie clamored.

"Sustained. Ladies and gentlemen, Mr. McGuire's gratuitous comment should be discarded from your minds. Keep to legitimate questions. No more editorializing. Save your thoughts for summation, Mr. McGuire. Do I make myself clear?"

"Yes, Your Honor."

"Was the alleged assailant wearing gloves on both hands?"

"I don't know. The only hand I was able to grab was the one on my face. That was my immediate concern. I could smell a drug and knew what his intention was. I had to get the cloth off me before I was knocked out, so at the very least I could call for Richard to help me. I knew there was at least one intruder if not more. I knew why he or they were there. My husband was to be silenced. In retrospect, it was the perfect setup. Kill him, and make it appear that I was the killer."

"Well, if that was their plan, why would he, or they, be so stupid as to leave the white cloth, which would suggest you weren't the killer?"

"I think that was their mistake. In their haste and in the darkness, they forgot it. I've thought the same thing over the last several months. They had set me up perfectly, and then they leave the cloth. I even wonder whether they had planned for this break-in. I believed Richard was flying directly home from Hawaii. Wellington also would have assumed it. Wellington would have scheduled his flights. I had no idea he was flying only to Dallas and then taking a separate flight to Fort Myers. For all I know, they could have been waiting for him in Newark with the intention of killing him in the parking lot or somewhere on the way home. When he didn't arrive, maybe the killers had to change plans and do it at my house."

"You've testified that you cooked outside on the grill that evening. What time was that?"

"Between six and six thirty."

"It was dark then, and you obviously detected no one then, correct?"

"Yes. It was dark and cold. When I came in, I locked the sliding door and pulled the drapes."

"You heard no one allegedly cutting the opening in the sliding door and felt no breeze before falling asleep on the couch, correct?"

"Yes."

"So that alleged cutting had to occur while you were asleep?"

"Yes."

"Would you explain to this jury why there was no glass left on the ground?"

"Obviously, because the killer or killers didn't want the glass to fall and make a noise. Secondly, if I was to be the murderer, they couldn't leave the glass behind. They had to be wearing gloves because there were no prints on the outside of the door near the cut-out, and there were no prints on the gun according to the testimony of your investigators."

"So you're telling this jury that Wellington knew of your husband's long-standing affair with Ms. Huffmire?"

"I would have to assume so, especially when her statement mentions that she would meet him on some of his overseas work trips. Funny, isn't it, that everyone knew but me?"

"So you're telling this jury that you had no suspicion of your husband's infidelity?"

"Yes. One hundred percent yes."

"And I assume you were devastated when you learned it through Ms. Huffmire's statement to our office?"

"I was devastated from my husband's murder. I already had exhausted all my tears. All I had then were memories."

"Well, were you mad he cheated on you? That would have been a normal reaction, correct?"

"Under normal circumstances, yes. But not here. Richard was dead. His life had been sucked out of him as a result of his honesty. I don't know why he cheated, and frankly at that point and even today, I don't care."

"Let's assume for the moment that you had uncovered the affair, what would you have done?"

"I would have been upset that he violated my trust. I would have asked him why and would have asked him if he loved Ms. Huffmire. Depending on his response, I would have forgiven him and requested that we undergo marital counseling. If he had said that he loved her or if he had refused the counseling, I would have filed for divorce. I obviously would have been heartbroken, but I would have realized that was the thing to do. My profession, as does yours, exacts an emotional toll on us and our spouses. I, like you, work long hours, often with little sleep. We both are awarded professionally and economically, but there can be a price to pay. Many of my colleagues have gotten divorced, as I assume have yours. Saddened as they may be, they move on. Some remarry. Others decide it's not worth the gamble. Richard and I both were well remunerated. We had a joint bank account, but we also had additional separate accounts. He had received a substantial inheritance.

"My father, as you know, is a very successful businessman. He opened a separate account for me and deposits sums periodically. While I am appreciative of his kindness and generosity, I have told him that charities need it more than me. His response always is that he contributes to many causes, and that I'm his only daughter. My father is a strong-willed man. He does what he wants to do.

"Richard and I treated our separate accounts as our own. Neither I nor my husband ever would think otherwise. If we had divorced, we would have kept those separate accounts. We weren't into collecting priceless pieces of art or other valuable artifacts. Economically, a divorce would have been easy. We could have sold the house, or one could have bought out the other. Other than our vacation trips, we didn't live a lavish lifestyle. Our work was our passion. Even had we divorced, I believe we would have remained friends.

"Mr. McGuire, I'm a realist. I've seen so much suffering and sorrow, in the operating room and out. I've had to come out of an operating room with the surgeon and break the unpleasant news to the spouse, father, mother, or child. No matter how often you do it, it's never easy. The death of a child just tears you up; the younger, the worse it feels. When I weigh now the possibility of a divorce in comparison to what I've seen people suffer, its effect is much less. I was not fortunate enough to be able to bear children. I have missed that joy. Had there been a divorce, at least it wouldn't have affected any children. I hope I've answered your question. I've tried the best I can."

Melanie's response was dramatic. Johnnie could feel it. He was certain some, if not all, of the jurors did also. He knew McGuire had to regroup quickly, and he tried.

"You're telling this jury that you never touched the gun and that one or more assailants framed you, correct?"

"Yes."

"Would you tell this jury why the killer or killers wouldn't have placed the weapon in your hand or, at least, put your prints on it before they left?"

"For the same reason they forgot to grab the cloth. It was dark. It was obviously getting closer to daylight, and they had to get away. The gun was left at the scene. That's all they needed. They just forgot to grab the cloth. My husband got home way after his supposed arrival at 11:00 p.m. I don't know how long I was unconscious. The drug wasn't administered intravenously so it wouldn't have lasted a real long time. I couldn't have been knocked out too long, or I would have suffered severe cognitive problems. Inez typically arrived early. It was light out enough so she could see somewhat outside yet dark enough that she had to put on the hall light when she entered. You're the lawyer, not me. There had to be enough time for them to get away but not enough time for them to check on every detail. That's all I can figure out. I have replayed this horror more times than you ever could imagine. I wish I couldn't, but it won't go away, probably never."

"You would agree with me that you have achieved at each stage of your life. You went to a well-known college, graduated from medical school, became accomplished and well-respected in your profession."

"Yes, I've been very blessed. Sometimes I wonder why me? I guess that's why I'm a workaholic. I have to justify that I was lucky to have been so fortunate."

"You really haven't suffered any failure, have you?"

"No."

"You would have viewed your husband's infidelity as a failure, correct?"

"I didn't know he had been unfaithful until your office provided Mr. Fitzhugh with Ms. Huffmire's statement long after Richard had been murdered, so how could I have believed I had suffered a so-called 'failure'?"

"Well, let's assume hypothetically that you knew your husband had been cheating on you with a woman of lesser beauty and lesser accomplishment, wouldn't you have believed that you had failed?"

"Why would I have failed? Under your hypothetical, my husband would have failed to live up to his marital vows, not me. I don't get your hypothetical."

"Let me put it this way. Isn't it a fact that you found out your husband had been cheating on you, had been doing it for some time, that you were humiliated that he would stoop so low, that your reputation would be tarnished, that people would view you differently, that for the first time in your life you believed you had failed, and that everyone would feel so also, so you became enraged and plotted out this murder? Isn't that what really happened?"

Melanie looked him directly in the eyes. "No. That is 1,000 percent wrong. And your hypothesis makes no sense. How do you think I have been viewed since the day of my arrest? You have defamed me. You have irreparably ruined my reputation before those who don't know me and caused those that do to wonder and maybe believe their friend, their colleague, their daughter is a stone-cold killer. I can't go anywhere without attracting stares. Oh yes, they stare quickly and then look downward or away, thinking I won't see. Sometimes, I hear the whispering. I don't hear their words, but I know what they are thinking and saying. No matter what these good jurors decide, I have that stain. This all could have been averted had you just followed Mr. Fitzhugh's request and investigated. But, no, you just plunged ahead. I will have to live with your decision, but, Mr. McGuire, you eventually will have to live with your conscience. You will be able to wander freely. I might not have that luxury."

Then it was over. McGuire ended. Her response had left him no choice. Any follow up would have been meaningless and ineffectual.

Johnnie advised the court that Melanie was his final witness. Scholman dismissed the jury after advising them not to discuss the case with anyone, not even their spouses or relatives. Summations and his charge would be tomorrow. They would begin their deliberations early in the afternoon, if not sooner.

Scholman advised counsel that they would take a twenty-minute break. Then he would hear motions and discuss the jury charge with them.

Johnnie used the time to call Erika. She was anxiously awaiting his recital of Melanie's cross. She already had contacted the appropriate court official and ordered an updated copy of Melanie's complete testimony. She wanted to form her own opinion of Melanie's responses. She trusted her own intuition more than Johnnie's, especially with the charms of this particular client.

Johnnie instructed her to come quickly to the courtroom. He wanted her to take Melanie home. Motions needed to be heard, followed by the in camera and on-the-record jury charge conference. Melanie had been through an ordeal. There was no need to prolong her stress.

"Mr. Fitzhugh, you have a motion?"

Johnnie arose and formally placed his motion to dismiss on the record to preserve his appellate new trial rights should Melanie be convicted. McGuire then cited the appropriate case law that routinely thwarted the motion's success.

"Gentlemen, I have viewed the evidence dispassionately, and, for once, I am truly concerned. Mr. McGuire, I know at this stage I still have to draw all favorable inferences to your version of the events. I am deeply troubled by the State's evidence or lack thereof. I have decided to err on the side of caution. I am denying the defense's motion, but I have to tell you I might revisit it later after the verdict. Typically, I don't interject my thoughts into such a process, but this case really disturbs me. I make note of this so that the appellate court can consider my concern. I am a judge, not a juror. Typically, I mask my thoughts, but the Wellington issue, to my thinking, remains unresolved. There has been expert testimony. It seems to corroborate Mr. Stafford's email. The defendant has provided a logical response to Mr. McGuire's very probing and effective questioning. Before I forget, I want to commend both of you. Each of you has maximized your position based on the evidence and facts presented to you. Are there any other motions to be made before we discuss my proposed charge?"

"Your Honor, on behalf of the State, I would ask that you also charge manslaughter to the jury."

Johnnie was surprised. McGuire must have lost some of his confidence. He now was requesting a lesser included offense, thereby giving the jury an out. They could compromise. Little did they know that the penalty still was severe.

"Your Honor, there is no basis for that charge. Since Dr. Stafford's arrest, Mr. McGuire, at every stage in the process, has argued that this was a cold-blooded killing. Nowhere did he even conjecture that Dr. Stafford had shot her husband to ward off a vicious physical attack. Rather, Mr. McGuire has argued vociferously that the defendant's alleged rage and humiliation precipitated the killing. His last hypothesis before the jury was that my client's humiliation prompted her to slaughter her husband. That jealousy, not self-defense, was the motive. Not one of the State's witnesses even alluded to the scenario Mr. McGuire now is proffering. He has not introduced one piece of evidence that could warrant such an improper charge."

"Mr. McGuire, you need not respond. Mr. Fitzhugh is correct. There is no basis for the inclusion of a manslaughter charge. Your motion is denied."

Erika arrived and escorted Melanie from the courtroom as the three men discussed the appropriate instructions. With McGuire's motion denied, the rest was routine.

Exhausted, Johnnie left the courtroom. Melanie had held her own. McGuire had raised legitimate concerns, yet Melanie had provided at least adequate responses. Her conclusory remarks were probably better than he could have written. Still, there was evidence, and there were unanswered questions. The case was a toss-up. McGuire had the higher burden, yet these jurors had seen enough television. It had to be seared into their brains. When a spouse was charged with murder, the odds heavily favored the State. Melanie had not oversold herself, but those fourteen people knew she was more intelligent than they, had lived a more fascinating life, and hadn't needed to worry about finances, medical expenses, or even medical care. Would they hold that against her? Would that give McGuire the edge he needed to sway their decision making? Would Scholman somehow slant the charge's wording and delivery in Melanie's favor?

Except for denying his dismissal motions, Scholman overtly rebuked McGuire. Usually, it was the defense that received the scolding. Johnnie had been overly cautious in his demeanor. He had not given McGuire an opening that would have compelled the judge to warn him before the jury. Scholman, in his charge, again would remind the jurors not to evaluate his rulings or demeanor in an effort to determine what verdict they should return. Still, the judge had admonished only one side. How would that play before this jury?

Johnnie finally stopped pondering. He couldn't control what was to be. All he could do was prepare an effective and logical summation. His one solace was that this would be his last sleepless night for a while.

56.

Melanie's fate was in his hands. It wasn't his choice, but there had been no realistic exit strategy. Either she would walk or Burnside would exact his revenge. He would be the first victim.

After thanking the jurors for their kind attention throughout the trial, he asked that they use their common sense and good judgment that they had gleaned through their life experiences. They should look at the evidence with reason and apply the logical inferences and deductions to reach the only just verdict that could be based on the produced evidence. The State had a very high burden. It had to prove his client's guilt beyond a reasonable doubt. That did not mean tipping the scales ever so slightly in the State's favor, as would be required in a civil case. He then used the exact phraseology that Scholman would read from the standard jury charge.

He told them that their task as jurors was a very difficult one. As a result, they were entitled to the best possible evidence to make their heavy burden easier. It was the State's burden to produce all the relevant evidence. The State was required to disprove possible other explanations for Richard Stafford's murder. Dr. Stafford had no obligation to disprove anything. She had the constitutional right not to testify, yet she volunteered to explain what happened that night, just as she waived her right not to give a statement to the police. She hadn't asked for a lawyer. Rather, even though injured, dazed, distraught, and unsteady on her feet, she gave a verbal statement. Her headache and lack of mental acuity prevented her from writing it shortly after the assault, but she gave a recorded oral statement immediately after being asked.

What else did she do? She produced her husband's email and photos substantiating his claim against his employer. Not only did she produce those documents, but the prosecutor's office already had them at their disposal. They had seized the family's home computer on the day of the killing. They had searched it and knew quickly about the email and the picture attachments but did nothing. Detective Carlucci testified that they never investigated Wellington at all.

The prosecutor will claim that she never said who "they" were when she used the phrase "they killed him" before Inez, the EMTs, the hospital personnel, or in her recorded statement. So what? She was distraught, hurt, and dazed. She knew who "they" were, and it was already embedded in the seized computer. It was there for the State to see. It wasn't something that she manufactured later after she had time to reason. Her husband had predicted his demise yet had refused to allow her to go to the authorities. He wanted to bypass Furber and go to the higher-ups who would be at the conference.

What about Furber? The State never produced him as a witness. Why not? Because the prosecutor knew what type of witness he would have been. A "see no evil and hear no evil" corporate executive, more concerned about his and the company's financial well-being. He gave the typical corporate response. Stafford lied because he was disgruntled. But guess what? He hadn't been demoted or fired, just inferentially threatened to keep his silence for his and the company's well-being.

Dr. Stafford had been forced to prove her innocence, which was not what the law required. Malcolm Gideon, with years in the pharmaceutical industry and with the FDA, described the improper testing and lack of FDA inspection and oversight. The agency was underfunded and understaffed. There was a reason more drug companies were conducting their trials overseas and through independent contractors. Lack of Federal oversight and lack of accountability for the actual drug manufacturer. If anything was ever uncovered, the blame would be placed on the independent agency's so-called rogue employees.

Dr. Stanton explained that Botox, acid filters, and chemical peels shouldn't have been anywhere near the testing site. He confirmed Stafford's findings and Gideon's opinion.

What about the use of twins confirmed by Malcolm Gideon? The photos proved their presence and validated Stafford's email, yet the prosecutor just dismissed any possible connection with Stafford's slaying. As jurors, they were entitled to the best evidence and the best investigation. The prosecution had failed in its duty to them.

The only offered evidence in the case was the GSR test. Dr. Kapoor, who was employed by the same county who was prosecuting Melanie, said it proved that she fired the gun.

Dr. Honig, on the other hand, whose credentials and experience far outweighed that of the State's sole expert, explained that the mere presence of gunshot residue meant nothing by itself. In this instance, there had been a transfer. Inez Garcia independently described what later Melanie stated and also demonstrated. Her left palm was pressed down repeatedly on her husband's chest. There was no residue anywhere else on her. Honig had opined that had she fired the weapon, there would have been trace evidence on her right palm, right hand, and possibly left hand.

The State had no proof that the Staffords ever owned a gun. Inez never had observed one or been told about its presence by the Staffords. Because she cleaned the residence every week, they would have warned her about its presence and told her not to touch it. The gun was manufactured in Austria and sold in Munich to a German who had died years before the killing. The State had offered no proof how it ended up on a floor in New Jersey. Yet Wellington was a subsidiary of a Swiss Company that also had offices in Munich.

The prosecution made much out of Melanie applying CPR to her husband after he presumably was dead, yet the EMTs who arrived later reflexively did the same thing, even though they had no emotional contact to Stafford. She reflexively applied it to her husband upon awakening. Imagine the horror she faced. She had been assaulted and drugged before awakening to a prone and blood-stained husband.

The prosecution's foundation was as unsteady as the sand to which it was adhered. It assumed Melanie had cut out the glass and somehow disposed of it, killed her husband, wiped off the gun, drugged herself, knocked over the table and chair, dove on them, and faked unconsciousness until Inez arrived. If she had been that astute, she would have washed her hands.

What proof did the prosecution have that she even knew of her husband's affair? Huffmire's statement indicated everything had been kept from her. All calls had been made to and from Stafford's company cellphone. The seized phone records from the home's landline carrier, together with their individual cellphone records, substantiated that fact.

And if she had known, there was nothing to be gained by killing him, as she had explained to the jurors. It made no sense.

The prosecution had inferred that she wore gloves when she cut the glass. Where were the gloves? They searched the entire house and grounds. They found nothing.

As to the glass, the assailant or assailants would not have left it at the scene. They would have worn gloves when cutting the glass to avoid cutting themselves and leaving a blood trail. They would not have let the glass fall to the ground so as to maintain their silence. They would have taken it with them. Had they left it, then the absence of Melanie's prints would have shown that she didn't cut the glass.

If Melanie had killed her husband, why didn't she plant a knife in his hand? She still could have battered her face and then claimed that she had killed him in self-defense. He had battered her and then came at her with a knife. She killed him to save herself. There would have been no proof to the contrary. She hysterically could have called the police. That would have been an easier story to sell if she had wanted to orchestrate the whole scenario.

The assailants had made one mistake. They had left the white cloth. Why? Because nothing had gone as planned. Wellington had booked Stafford's Hawaii flights because it was a company event. Wellington had no indication Stafford was leaving early and not going directly to New Jersey. Maybe the assailant or assailants had planned to murder him in the airport parking lot where he left his car or somewhere on the way home. They would have known his arrival time as a result of the corporate booking. Maybe they originally had wanted it to appear as a motor vehicle accident.

When he didn't arrive as expected, the plan altered immediately. They had to travel to the house and wait in the darkness. They would have entered an unlit and unfamiliar home. They would have known about the sliding door because Melanie had been reading. The illumination would have been seen through the closed drapes. Once Stafford arrived, he would have turned off the table lamp before retiring. That was another reason the first shot missed its mark. The assailant had been struggling with Melanie. She had been able to scream once for her husband. At some point, he would have run or groggily walked out. Thus, the first shot was below the chest. The second was right on. The third was to leave no doubt. It was basically a contact shot. The killer or killers were way behind schedule. Soon, it would be getting light. They had to flee quickly. In their haste, they made one mistake. They left the cloth.

The house wasn't ransacked because that wasn't their intent. If they had planned to stage it as a burglary, they had run out of time due to Stafford's delay.

As to the lack of footprints, the ground was hard and dry. Had they worn flat shoes? Melanie had been out that evening. She hadn't tracked in any dirt, at least not enough to leave any definitive prints. On the other hand, there were indentations in the carpet near where the table and lamp had been. Did they signify a struggle? Who knows? The prosecution never addressed the issue.

Wasn't it interesting that the prosecution never called Inez, the three EMTs, or the hospital nurse as witnesses? Were they trying to hide how those witnesses corroborated Melanie's narration and how they confirmed her injuries and mental state? The Hopewell officers had to be called because they took the first photos. Those pictures depicted how the scene really looked. Also, why didn't the prosecution obtain night photographs that replicated how the scene would have appeared to the killer or killers lying in wait?"

Johnnie closed by saying, "Why was it that the defense, not the prosecution, brought all this information to you? The prosecution has a duty to see that justice is done. That doesn't mean to rush blindly ahead to obtain a conviction. That doesn't mean to take the easy road and make assumptions that later prove to be untenable and illogical. The duty is to examine every angle and every possibility. After that has been accomplished, it is to pursue the perpetrator or perpetrators and clear the innocent. That is all that we, as citizens, and you, as jurors, can ask and demand. Here, for whatever reason, the prosecution has failed in its obligation to you and to this upstanding and accomplished woman. She did not cheat on her husband, and he didn't improperly accuse his employer. He died for his honesty. She has suffered enough. She will live forever with the horror and grief she has experienced. Based on the evidence, or, more properly, based on the lack of the evidence, I ask that you grant her peace and some solace. Return a verdict in her favor. Thank you for your attention."

Johnnie bowed his head and walked slowly toward Melanie. He had spoken for almost two hours. It was long for him, but he had to cover everything. He had done his best. Now, he would have to sit quietly as McGuire ripped apart his argument. The prosecution had the burden of proof. For that reason, it earned the right to close last.

After a jury break, McGuire started with the obvious. Reasonable doubt did not require proof that overcame every possible doubt. Almost every case contained a little doubt. The killing wasn't televised. The State, however, had produced direct and circumstantial evidence. Even the defense did not dispute that she had gun residue on her left hand. The fact that the defendant's left palm was compressed forcefully and repeatedly against her husband's chest didn't signify that some of the residue had not blown on her hand when she fired the trigger. The blood on her hands could have covered and washed off any residue on her right hand.

Her husband had been away for several days. She could have removed the glass days earlier and then covered the hole with some object until earlier that evening.

Where were the footprints of the alleged intruder or intruders? During the supposed struggle, shouldn't dirt of some kind have been left?

She was an anesthesiologist. She would know what drug to apply and for how long. She would have wiped her prints from the gun and then laid it on the floor close to where she intended to fall. She testified the drug's effectiveness had to be short-lived, or she would have incurred a permanent cognitive injury. Clearly, from her own testimony, she had none. Who knows? Maybe she never even applied the cloth to herself. She could have placed it near the weapon, overturned the table and lamp, and then plunged on both objects. She needed an injury and knew from her medical training that she would not die from the impact. She needed facial bruising to sell her story.

If there had been intruders who were unfamiliar with the home, why weren't more items disturbed in the darkness? Without flashlights, how did the shooter hit a moving target directly in the left chest? The third shot was a kill shot. The defendant wanted to make certain her husband couldn't be revived. The contact shot provided that guarantee.

Where did the intruder or intruders come from? Certainly not through the rear woods. It was dark. The woods were dense and deep. Therefore, such imaginary killers would have approached from the driveway. Where did they park their vehicle?

If they had set her up, the very least they would have done was put the gun in her hand to ensure her prints were on it. If they had done that, they would have looked for the cloth. If she was unconscious, as she had asserted, they could have turned on a light to find the cloth. If they truly were hurried, they still could have planted the gun in her hand. They would have wanted the scene to scream out domestic abuse to the police.

Why did the defendant not hear any of the three gunshots? There were no obvious markings on the gun to indicate a silencer was applied. Even if it had been utilized, there still would be obvious noise within the house when the weapon was fired. She heard nothing, yet she claimed she was awakened by Garcia's scream. The exploding weapon would have been much closer to her than Garcia.

How many intruders were there? If there was just one, how could he have fired the gun with one hand pressing the cloth against her face while the other from behind encircled her chest? If there were two, the other could not have hit Stafford from the side. Therefore, the other had to be directly in line with the onrushing Stafford. How then did the first shot hit him in the lower abdomen near the groin? Even in the alleged darkness, the trigger was pulled from a distance no longer than five or six feet.

No. This was a rage killing. The defendant over that three-year period had learned of the affair. She knew her husband's itinerary. She knew he had a layover in Dallas. She called to check on the delay and found out there had been none. She then called American and learned he never boarded the flight and never checked in for the flight. That first shot was intended for the groin. She missed. She moved closer for the second and hit the intended area. The third silenced him forever.

McGuire's voice rose as he briefly looked at Melanie before turning back to the jury.

"Ladies and gentleman, this was a woman who had it all: beauty, intelligence, accomplishment, and wealth. But in her eyes, she had nothing because she had been scorned by her philandering husband. A man whose intellect, appearance, and charm were vastly inferior to hers. She had trusted him, maybe even forgiven him initially after she learned of the affair. No doubt, he told her it was over. He probably told her it was a stupid short-lasting dalliance. She probably learned who the other woman was and researched her. She was not in her league, not in beauty, intelligence, or in accomplishment. She had never failed in anything, always at the top of everything. This was her first failure. She couldn't handle it. Once the world discovered, she would be humiliated. With every trait she possessed, her peers and friends would conclude that she must have possessed some underlying, unattractive personality defect. A defect that she so expertly had hidden from everyone else, that is except for the one person who shared her bedroom. That one individual who had explored not only her body but, more importantly, her mind. That person had to be silenced. No divorce proceeding would ever reveal her failure.

"A murderer is not cut from a particular cloth. She or he can be rich or poor, accomplished or not, intelligent or less so. Each has a unique story, but each is driven by some internal visceral impulse that compels action. Reason, logic, and consequence are discarded. That is what happened here.

"You may view it as a tragedy, but it's still a murder, which our society doesn't countenance. If we did, there would be continuous chaos and tumult. Our way of life would fracture and collapse.

"This defendant, if she knew nothing else, knew the difference between right and wrong. In her profession, she had observed death and consoled surviving parents, spouses, and children. Maybe she became inured to death and even became devoid of feeling. Whatever the reason, a man was murdered. He didn't deserve that outcome. A divorce? Probably, but not a death. He cannot ask you for what the evidence compels you to do. For him and for this State, we speak to you. Give him what he deserves based on the evidence: a guilty verdict. Thank you for your attention."

Johnnie was impressed. McGuire had rehashed a lot of old points, but his closing words were emotional, heartfelt, and effective. They had to have resonated with the jury. Spousal killings were a common occurrence, especially on the television docudramas. This one fit perfectly. Would the jury be so easily swayed? Johnnie had his own doubts. Erika had none. Only Melanie knew the truth. For once in her life, she had no control over the outcome.

It was too late to start the jury charge. Scholman recessed for an hour lunch after instructing the jury not to discuss the case during the recess. They still had to hear his charge.

The jurors were free to roam for that hour. Johnnie wanted to avoid them. Besides, he could see that Melanie was rattled. McGuire's summation had unearthed her fear. Her hands were trembling. He escorted her to the conference room adjacent to the courtroom's entrance.

In a quivering voice, she asked him, "Will they believe him? He lied! He just plain out lied! I didn't shoot Richard, and he knows it. He just wants to destroy me to advance his own pitiful career. Why didn't you object during his summation? You could have stopped him. Why didn't you? My father never will forgive you if I'm convicted. You must know that. I don't deserve to be here! I didn't kill him! Why can't the jury see that? They were expressionless as I testified. They were expressionless during your summation. They already have me convicted! You have to do something! You have to stop this madness!"

"Melanie, calm down."

She interrupted him. "How can I calm down when all I can see is a jail cell in my future?"

"Listen, that's how jurors are. This is not television. This process is as new to them as you. They know the stakes. They want to make the right decision. They are masking their thoughts and feelings. Each probably believes the others will guide him or her during the deliberations. At this point, each is probably leaning one way or the other, yet each has some uncertainty. McGuire and I have made our points. Each juror will remember some but not all of what we've said. The judge again will tell them that our summations are not evidence. He will direct their attention to the testimony of the witnesses and the exhibits. You must remain composed during the judge's charge.

"As to your father, at the end of every courtroom day, I gave him a detailed synopsis of that day's testimony. I didn't color it one way or the other. Regardless of the verdict, I can't control his actions."

"But will they believe our witnesses? Why didn't the judge throw out the case? There was no evidence against me except for the residue."

"That was enough, Melanie, to overcome our dismissal motion."

She looked crestfallen. He placed his hand on hers. "Look, this isn't over. The judge will tell the jury that the State has to prove your guilt beyond a reasonable doubt. McGuire has the burden. You must regain your confidence. I've tried many cases where a judge has predicted I would lose. Most of those cases I have won. In each, I couldn't read the jury, so have faith. You've been strong throughout this ordeal. Now is not the time to waiver. Promise me you won't."

She stared at him for what seemed like an eternity before replying, "I promise you. I also promise McGuire that if I'm destroyed, he will be, too. My father will see to that if it's the last thing he does. That's a guarantee, not a promise."

Scholman started his charge with the defendant's presumption of innocence, the State's burden of proof, and the definition of reasonable doubt. The words were from the model jury instructions. Johnnie knew them by heart. What he hadn't expected was the tone in which the words were delivered. Was it his imagination, or was Scholman shading the charge in Melanie's favor through his word accentuation? It was obvious from Scholman's hesitancy in denying his dismissal motion that the judge questioned the validity of the State's case. Was Scholman trying to infer to the jury his own opinion? Scholman's deceased wife had worked for a pharmaceutical before dying in a traffic accident. Did he harbor any ill will toward that industry? Did he believe, or want to believe, that Wellington was probably involved in Stafford's murder?

Scholman continued reading the boilerplate instructions covering direct and circumstantial evidence, credibility, lay versus expert witnesses, and other required subjects. He told the jurors that they should weigh all the evidence. Then he reviewed some of the evidence, and Johnnie was surprised how he did it. He highlighted the gunpowder trace evidence, as the State's position for seeking a guilty verdict and then in detail enumerated many of the items mentioned in Johnnie's summation. Johnnie now had no doubts as to how Scholman felt. The judge was no fool. He read verbatim that part of the standard charge where the court had a right to comment upon the evidence and that such comment was not to be taken as how the judge viewed the case. Scholman said he had no view, and the jurors should not consider that his recitation of some of the testimony indicated a preference for either side. He had none, yet Johnnie knew by his tone that he did.

Johnnie knew McGuire also would have grasped it, but a written transcript wouldn't show it. It was a post-verdict argument McGuire couldn't win. If the State lost, there would be no retrial. McGuire never would be able to prove judicial misconduct. A written transcript would not show tone or emotion. Scholman knew Johnnie couldn't support McGuire's assertion. He would be violating his duty to his client.

Scholman ended his charge by repeating burden of proof and reasonable doubt.

As was required, Scholman called both attorneys to sidebar to inquire whether there were objections to the charge or additions that had to be made. McGuire plunged head first. He asked for a mistrial. The judge, through his tone and inflection, had favored the defense. It was too evident to overcome. The case had to be mistried. Scholman turned to Johnnie. Had Johnnie formed the same opinion? Johnnie knew the truth but replied that the judge's comments recited the evidence and were neutral in tone and inflection. Scholman then denied the motion.

Fourteen names were placed in the wooden box. It was spun, and two pieces of folded paper removed. Those two jurors were taken to a separate room from the other twelve. They would remain there until a verdict was reached, or until one, or the other, was needed for cause to replace a deliberating juror. By happenstance, neither Johnnie nor McGuire had benefitted from the draw. Each had lost a juror that each believed favored his position.

It was three o'clock. Johnnie checked his phone for messages. Erika had called and asked that he return her call.

"They just went out. He'll probably keep them to five o'clock."

"I just finished reading her direct and cross. There's no doubt she still has it. I can't believe McGuire never discovered she had acted. Regardless of the verdict, I still think she was involved. You'll never convince me otherwise. Can I now come to the courthouse? I want to be there for the verdict. Whatever the outcome, I want to see how she reacts. That will be priceless."

"No. Absolutely not. You were a witness. I don't want them thinking about you, not her. Your mere presence may cause one, or more, of them to doubt your candor or professionalism."

"I'm coming over tonight."

"Don't bother. I'll be at Burnside's doing a lot of hand-holding and encouraging. Hopefully, sometime tomorrow we'll have a verdict. You'll be the first one I call. Enjoy your evening. I guarantee it will be better than mine."

As predicted, the jury was sent home after being admonished not to discuss anything with each other, their families, or friends.

On the ride to Princeton, Johnnie tried to buoy Melanie's spirits without much success. No one was going to sleep well, if at all, tonight. First, however, he had to endure Burnside's haranguing and second-guessing.

57.

Johnnie arrived at the courtroom the next day before Melanie. He and McGuire nodded to each other but said nothing. The tension was palpable. The prior evening, Burnside had proclaimed that he and Catherine were bringing Melanie. She needed their strength and support. She would not face the verdict alone.

Burnside glowered at McGuire as he escorted his wife and daughter into the courtroom. McGuire just turned away.

On schedule, Scholman entered. Almost immediately, the bailiff led the jurors into the courtroom. Scholman greeted them, asked if they had discussed the case with anyone, and then sent them back to deliberate.

Two hours later, Scholman reentered. He unfolded a white piece of paper.

"The jury wants the complete testimony of Inez Garcia reread. I have granted their request."

The hours dragged on. Both Melanie and Burnside asked him what that meant. Johnnie had no definitive answer. He provided several alternative possibilities, some good, others not. Burnside did not mask his exasperation. Catherine remained composed and comforted Melanie. The gloom on her daughter's face was apparent.

The knock on the door came at five thirty. The jury had a verdict. The attorneys and Melanie should return to their seats. Scholman entered and instructed the bailiff to bring in the jury. Johnnie observed the jurors as they entered. Each appeared stoic. All looked down. None looked toward Melanie. That was not a good sign. He grasped Melanie's clammy hand. Her wrist was shaking. Scholman asked the forewoman to rise. The verdict sheet was shaking in her hand. She read the verdict and then almost collapsed.

The gallery erupted. Melanie turned toward Johnnie. Her mouth opened but nothing came out. She dropped into his arms and sobbed and sobbed. How could it be? She had suffered so much. She had been scorned, humiliated, disparaged, and now this. She couldn't comprehend it. She was dizzy. Her head was spinning. She felt like she was going to vomit. Her mother and father rushed to her side. The bailiff ordered the few spectators and press to quiet. The judge just looked at her as did the jurors and alternates. McGuire just stared. He was motionless as he watched the commotion. It was an almost out-of-body experience. It was over. He had asked that justice be done, and it was. Just not for him. When he looked to his right, he met those feral eyes and malevolent grin. Then he laughed. Burnside just laughed in his face.

Johnnie walked over to him and praised his effort. McGuire nodded as if he heard him, but he hadn't heard a thing. He was thinking of his future. Would he remain a career assistant prosecutor, or would he have to find another field?

As Johnnie turned to return to Melanie, Burnside bear-hugged him and exclaimed into his ear, "I told you we'd win. This is just the beginning. Now it's our turn to inflict some damage. I mean real damage."

Johnnie was numb. He was spent. He could hardly grasp what Burnside was declaring. The "we" — had Burnside really done it? Had he facilitated Huffmire's death? Had he eliminated the one witness who could have humanized Stafford from the prosecution's perspective?

Melanie saw her father pounce upon Johnnie. Her hell was finally over. She shouldn't have been in this courtroom, but she had survived. The man had made a mistake, a grievous one, but it was over. She didn't have the heart to make him pay for it. With trepidation but without a choice, she had followed her father's instructions and had prevailed. Johnnie had been her savior, a handsome and charismatic one at that. This had not been just another challenge. It had been her ultimate one. The one over which she had no, or very little, control. Johnnie had convinced twelve disparate minds to grant her freedom. Was it luck, or was it preordained?

She knew Johnnie had believed her. She could see it in his bedroom eyes. Erika had surprised her. From the moment they met, she knew the woman distrusted her, yet she had testified like a pro. Was it for her or for Johnnie? All that mattered was she had her life back. Others might believe she got away with murder, but wasn't that always the case?

Her mother still was cradling her, muttering softly that God had answered her prayers and that Melanie would soar to new heights and more joy. She would be able to return to her life's work, that of helping those who needed relief from pain and disease.

As a group, they exited the courtroom but not to calm and stillness. Burnside was not finished. It was time for him to "hold court." He motioned to the local reporters.

"I can't get back my beloved son-in-law, but I will see that the proper investigation is conducted. I will be contacting the governor, our congressmen, and senators. A thorough investigation of Wellington and Sterling labs must be conducted. As to this so-called drug, Youtheria, I call upon the FDA to reopen its file. My daughter's life was saved by the testimony of honorable men who provided the pharmaceutical and medical expertise to expose the inadequate testing and validation of this drug's effectiveness. From the testimony in this courtroom, it appears that the paying public has been duped and defrauded. Justice must be done. The sanctity of human life outweighs that of corporate greed."

Johnnie felt the bile rising in his throat. "Beloved" son-in-law. What a mockery. The man had no shame. The sooner he got out of his presence, the better.

The press turned from Burnside to him. What did he think? He exclaimed that he was overjoyed for his client. Was he going after Wellington and Sterling on behalf of Melanie and her deceased husband? No, he replied. Mr. Burnside had the power and prestige to initiate any investigations that might be warranted. He now had other clients to counsel and assist. He was grateful for the jury's decision. The case was complex, and the judge handled the proceeding superbly. He would make no more comment. His client was entitled to her life back and the peace and enjoyment that flowed from it.

Johnnie walked with his client and the Burnsides to the parking garage. He declined their celebration dinner. They needed some family time, and his father needed some help. He then called "Pops" and Erika. They were going to Philly for dinner. No one would know or bother them there. He wanted to avoid all those probing questions as to what, when, where, and why something was done.

58.

October 2015
Princeton, New Jersey

Upon his arrival in the Princeton area, he had called the American and requested he cover the difference between the insufficient insurance refund and the true value of the gallery's stolen paintings. Again, he had been rebuffed. The American scolded him for closing the conduit account. His disloyal act had precipitated difficulties and delays. Valued clients had severed alliances and sought antiquities elsewhere. Consequently, he would be compelled to travel abroad to soothe egos and repair relationships. A replacement middleman would have to be vetted. Worst of all, discounts would be necessitated to regain broken trust. No, there would be no payment. Go back to Germany. Get on with your pitiful life. Your father would have been ashamed of your avarice. You chose to cleave our relationship. Your consequences are well deserved.

Consequences? The American would see consequences. But how could he initiate them? He couldn't contact the government or the police. To do so would be to implicate himself. A quick arrest and prosecution would follow. When, if ever, would he be allowed to return to Germany? For three days, he wandered around the town without an answer. Could he go to the university and divulge what he knew? Probably not. The police would be called while he was providing the history.

He was hungry. He entered a fast-food establishment, ordered the least greasy item, and sat at a small table. Someone had left a tabloid there. The headline covered most of the front page. An accomplished physician acquitted of murder. The face of a very attractive woman looked back at him. How could a woman that stunning be accused of murder? That didn't happen in his country. He turned the page and started to read. Suddenly, he froze. The article described the trial and the woman. How could this be? He reread the paragraph three times. There was no mistake. They were one and the same. What were the odds that he would see this paper, this article? Yes, there would be consequences soon, very soon.

He had to locate her attorney. His office was in Princeton. He left his uneaten food and walked quickly to the hotel. He found and dialed the number. No, Johnnie Fitzhugh was not in. He was expected possibly late in the afternoon. His trusted assistant was present. Would he like to speak to her?

Erika couldn't believe what he was relating. Melanie's grandfather didn't die. He was murdered. This man knew the killer. He was alive. Johnnie also knew him very well but didn't know he was a murderer. The man wanted to meet but not at the office. Yes, he would call back at four. No, he would not give his name until they met. He had proof of the killing and more, much, much more.

He called precisely at four o'clock. Johnnie noted the man's foreign accent. Yes, he would meet with him. He would contact Dr. Stafford and bring her. The man refused. Only he and Johnnie would meet at a location of the man's choosing. No, Johnnie definitely could not bring his father, nor anyone else. Johnnie refused. He would bring Erika, or there would be no meeting. The man relented. The meeting would be the following afternoon at three o'clock in the university chapel.

The man asked Johnnie to describe himself and Erika. He also asked that each wear a hat and coat. The color of each was given. The man warned that Johnnie should not alert the authorities. If he noticed their presence, he would not appear. He promised to arrive with documentation to substantiate his claim. Johnnie could use that information any way he chose.

Johnnie had refused to discuss Melanie's case with the press. Was this a ruse by some overbearing reporter to gain access to him? If so, Erika would be his witness. The man would be wasting his time. He would learn nothing, and the paper's or magazine's publisher would be notified for whatever that was worth.

When would this case really be behind him? He had been the loyal servant. He wanted his freedom. Would tomorrow's encounter impede that? No. He'd listen to the man, take his information, and provide it to Burnside. Nothing more could, or should, be asked of him.

59.

Dressed as promised, they entered the chapel ten minutes early. They sat midpoint and waited and waited. After fifty minutes, they walked out, turned right, and followed the path between the university library and the chapel. As they neared the roadway, they heard, "You can stop now."

They turned. A middle-aged, white-haired man approached them slowly.

In an accented voice, he added, "I had to make certain you were alone."

He handed Johnnie a large envelope. "This will confirm what I am about to tell you. Let us take a walk through the campus."

So they walked. He started from the beginning. His father had only an incidental implication in the Nazi art and antiquity confiscation. While the major players fled to South America, his father chose to stay. He turned his efforts to assisting in the reclamation of the price-less purloined works. One of the major players had immigrated from Buenos Aires to northern New Jersey where he founded an exporting firm as a front for the sale of the stolen loot. His father had assisted the exporter in facilitating transfers of the treasured items to European museums. It was a way of righting past wrongs.

Shortly before he died, his father requested that he contact the exporter and continue the process. He became the middleman and refused compensation. He had a legitimate gallery that provided a decent living. He was satisfied that the seized items were leaving the darkness and returning to the light. The public again could enjoy their magnificence. Then the exporter died, and his American-born son acquired the business. The procedures changed. The son required that he hold a portion of each fee as a down payment. After he had amassed numerous down payments, the son arrived in Munich and explained that the down payments were his. He tried to refuse but was rebuked. The museum curators required it. It was a way of legitimizing the transactions. Without his involvement, additional lost treasures would remain hidden for years, if not decades. Eventually, he relented.

Every several years, the American visited him in Munich. He always brought his wife. Then she died. The American was a Princeton attorney. He had hidden his export business from his friends and fellow counselors.

Johnnie stopped in his tracks. He recalled what Burnside had told him months before. Melanie's grandfather believed a well-known Princeton lawyer was involved in the sale of stolen art and antiquities. The professor was in the process of finalizing his conclusion when he suddenly died while walking home from his university office. His death had been attributed to natural causes.

"Pops" was a well-known local attorney. He and his mother often traveled to Europe. They had gone to Munich numerous times. According to his father, it was one of his mother's favorite cities. It couldn't be! His father couldn't have had a side business! Wouldn't he have known of it? Was that why neither Melanie nor his father was allowed to come to this meeting?

Johnnie stopped him midsentence.

"Who is this American?"

The man persisted that he wanted to finish his narration. Shortly, all would be made clear. Erika told him to wait. He refused. Either he divulge the man's identity now, or they were leaving.

"Have you ever heard the name Benedik Schell?"

"No."

"That was the father's name before he immigrated to the States in the mid-fifties. He then changed it to Benedict Scholman."

Erika and Johnnie stared at each other in wild disbelief.

"I believe you just concluded a famous trial in front of his son, Paul. Yes, Paul Scholman killed, or had killed, your client's grandfather!"

He then continued with his narrative. Scholman had warned him that a Princeton professor, who had been a "Monuments Man," somehow had pieced together the sale of plundered works. The pipeline had to be closed temporarily. Several weeks later, Scholman had called. Everything had been resolved. It was business again as usual. There would be no further problems from the professor. Shortly thereafter, he had read Professor Clarendon's obituary in the International Herald Tribune. Scholman was ruthless. He could be charming, but that only masked his real persona.

Recently, Scholman had deviated from what his father had intended. No longer were transactions limited to legitimate art curators and museums. In his lust for money, Scholman sought the highest bidder. He made agreements with Russian oligarchs, Middle Eastern tyrants, and European nouveaux riches. None were interested in sharing such history with others. For them, it was akin to a sport. Those who could accumulate the most were attributed a preeminent place among the wealthy. The man had to be stopped.

"The envelope contains a list of all the transactions that were funneled through me over the years. Whenever possible, buyers and their purchases are depicted with approximate dates. The name, address, and phone number of the export company are included. None of the art sales will be discovered in the company's regular books. I am uncertain where all the remaining stolen items are housed in Buenos Aires. Scholman indicated that he had several safe houses and warehouses under his control.

"If you doubt my story, call the number at the top of the first page. Whenever I called from Germany, I dialed those digits. Paul Scholman always answered, as he did four days ago. The man must be stopped!

What remains hidden must be uncovered. I fear for my life. Those who sacrificed so much during the war will be looking down on you. Do them justice. See that he is prosecuted and that what still remains hidden is retrieved and displayed. That will be your legacy."

The man quickly moved away. Johnnie started to follow, but Erika stopped him.

"Let him go. The documents will substantiate or repudiate his assertions."

Johnnie's thoughts drifted to Scholman. He had theorized the judge had slanted the jury charge because he disliked pharmaceuticals. Was he misguided? If Scholman had killed the professor, had he later learned of the familiar connection? Was he atoning for his earlier sin? Having murdered the grandfather, he would save the granddaughter.

If there was any legitimacy to the enclosed documents, he had an obligation to share them with his client. Erika would corroborate the meeting.

What Melanie did with the envelope's contents was her decision. One thing was certain: He was not accusing a Superior Court Judge of killing a venerated Princeton professor. There was no proof. Not only would be he ridiculed, but he also would be shunned by his peers. He would be alone on the proverbial island, devoid of any meaningful human contact. If there was to be a crusade, Melanie or Burnside would have to lead it.

Within fifteen minutes, they had returned to the office. Johnnie dumped the envelope's contents on the conference room table. The German had not misrepresented the transactions. There were pages of them. Almost all identified the purchaser, the date of sale, and the item transferred. Most were Etruscan, Greek, or Roman antiquities. Two thousand plus years of history. The remainder were paintings by world-renowned artists. The list was mindboggling.

Included in the envelope had been the Tribune's January 2000 obituary of Clarendon. Why would the German have saved it, if there had not been a connection to Scholman?

The German had left something unsaid. It was to be Johnnie's surprise. It substantiated everything he had related. It was a photograph. There was Scholman and apparently his former wife. They were standing in front of what was probably a museum. This had to be Munich. "Pops" would know. Tomorrow he, Erika, and "Pops" would share their thoughts. If that museum was in Munich, Melanie had to know. Things were beginning to spin out of control. Where would it lead, and who would be swept into the vortex?

60.

"Pops" immediately identified the building. The Haus der Kunst was designed for Hitler by a Nazi architect. The multi-columned neoclassical edifice opened with great fanfare in 1937 with a display of "truly German" works. Ironically, after the war, it was transformed into the modern art center that Hitler would have disdained.

Scholman and his wife had been to Munich. "Pops" agreed that Melanie had to be notified.

Erika insisted she be present. The revelation would be cataclysmic. Melanie would need both guidance and hand-holding. Erika would be present to assist and to verify all that transpired. Johnnie made the call.

A light rain was falling when Melanie arrived at six o'clock. A different Melanie entered the conference room. She was cheerful and chatty. Gone was the guardedness and reticence. The sudden change was almost unsettling.

Johnnie and Erika asked of her plans. Was she taking a vacation or plunging back into her work? Was she returning to the home or looking for another? Definitely going back to work while uncertain about the home.

Johnnie then asked her about her grandfather. What did she think of the professor? How close were they? Had there ever been a question as to the cause of his death? She loved him like a second father. He took her everywhere, even several times to Europe. He opened her eyes to classical history, art, and architecture. He broadened her interest in opera and the celebrated composers. The police had ruled his death an accident. He probably had suffered a heart attack.

Johnnie placed the envelope before her. "Melanie, a German gentleman visited Erika and me yesterday. What he told us appears to be substantiated in part, or maybe completely, by the enclosed material. You must decide whether you want to pursue where the information may lead you. You will have to discuss this with your mother and father. Listen to their advice. The decision may not be yours to make. Your mother has at least an equal interest. He was her father. I wish I was not the bearer of this news. Had this gentleman not read the newspaper, we never would have met."

Then he told her. The color drained from her face. She just stared ahead. Then she exploded.

"Do you mean to tell me this man killed my grandfather and then had the gall to sit in judgment of me? That bastard! That lying, conniving son-of-a-bitch! I'll get him! If it's the last thing I do, I'll get him!"

"Melanie, we don't know if any of this is true. We know the German knew Judge Scholman. We know that they were apparently business partners. Something tore them apart. This man might be using us and you to ruin Scholman. There is no proof that Scholman had anything to do with your grandfather's death. The German may be setting you up. He doesn't care about your welfare or safety. He just desires to ruin Scholman. No one would believe you if you were blindly to accuse Scholman of murder. There were no witnesses. The police found no evidence of foul play. You will have resistance not only from Scholman but also from the police.

"What's more, a jury just acquitted you. Scholman was more than fair to you throughout the trial. To accuse him now of murder would be lunacy. People will think you're deranged. Not only won't you return to your job, you also won't return to a normal life. You will be shunned by everyone. The only avenue that you may be able to pursue is the allegation of stolen antiquity sales. Is it, however, worth the risk? If so, how do you proceed? Do you employ an intermediary to contact the authorities? Do you initially approach Holocaust organizations before the police? That would be a way to insulate yourself. Let them follow the paper trail and set forth the allegations and evidence. These are issues you must discuss with your parents. Under no circumstance should you call or approach Scholman. If you do so, you'll be back in jail. Do you understand what I'm saying?"

"Yes."

"Promise me you will not contact him. If you do, don't call me. I will not defend you under any circumstances."

She somewhat regained her composure and replied, "I will not contact him."

Erika left the room. She went to her forensic bag and removed a magnetized covert GPS tracking device. She exited the office, located Melanie's car, and affixed the device under the rear bumper. The October darkness hid her movement. The night was still young. If Melanie was going anywhere but home, she would know when and where. Things were getting interesting again. Did Johnnie really think the woman would abide his instructions?

Erika reentered the building as Johnnie was leading Melanie to the door. Erika walked with her to her car. Melanie quickly opened her door, promised she would avoid Scholman, and sped away. Erika activated the GPS, waited five minutes, and then followed. Ten minutes later, she drove by the residence and parked two blocks down and one block over. One hour and forty-five minutes later, Melanie's vehicle left the driveway. Erika noted the address and then resumed her tail. Melanie returned to Burnside's home. Who lived at that other address? Erica would know quickly.

61.

He opened the door and moved to embrace her. She forcefully pushed him backward and slammed the door closed.

"Did you do it?" she screamed.

"Do what?"

"Did you kill him?"

"You know I killed him. What the hell is wrong with you?"

"Not my fucking husband, my grandfather! Did you murder him?"

He paused and looked at her with concern. "What are you talking about, darling?"

"Don't darling me!"

"This is preposterous."

"Is it? You didn't even know me when you killed him, but you knew when we started seeing each other, because I told you about him! You could have broken off everything. I never would have known. Sure, I would have thought you were another prick like my husband, probably screwing somebody behind my back like he routinely did on his 'work-only' trips! I naively believed he had time only for work. No time? He'd jump on anything that was available!"

"Don't get sacrosanct with me! Who supplied the drug?"

"Yeah, and who fucked up by leaving the gun behind in his haste to flee! I wouldn't have been in this mess if you hadn't panicked in the darkness and fled! I saved your candy ass by wiping the gun clean! Do you think I enjoyed knocking myself out by falling several times on the table and lamp I overturned?"

"It was a mistake with the gun."

"No, it was a grievous mistake by a coward!"

"Well, you plotted this fail-proof scheme. Now you're going to blame me? And just who do you think you're going to tell? Your lawyer? McGuire? I don't think so!"

"Why not? All I have to produce are the names of your antiquities clients and the descriptions of the stolen works. A German friend of yours visited Fitzhugh. You blew him off, and he flew to Fitzhugh. How symmetric. What will you say? That I killed Richard? That I seek vengeance against you? For what reason? You ruled in my favor on every objection. McGuire and Fitzhugh both know how you stressed my innocence before those twelve cretins. No one will believe you. Did you forget, I can't be retried? Surely, you're not so foolish as to claim I perjured myself. Only an accomplice would know that. There's nothing you can do. Kill me now? You don't even own a gun. Stab me? No jury ever would believe that was necessary. Your size and strength easily would subdue me. There would be no justifiable reason to kill. Are you going to admit that you knew me, actually carnally knew me, and then presided over my trial? You'd be removed from the bench before you could blink!"

"Little lady, how are you going to trace the alleged thefts to me? You have no witnesses. Horst, he wouldn't dare remain in the States. I'll bet he never provided his first or last name to you. Do you know what would happen to him if the world ever learned of his involvement? No, you may accuse me of murder, but the lack of evidence will doom you. Who's going to give credence to your wild allegations? Most think you're a killer saved by a brilliant lawyer and an inept prosecutor. I guess we really did deserve each other! If I were you, I'd reconsider your situation. I gave you your life back. Don't squander the opportunity. Get out before I call the police!"

62.

Erika couldn't believe her eyes. The address was Scholman's! If Melanie hadn't known the judge, how could she have known that he lived there? He had an unlisted number. Her hunch was correct. They were involved. They had to be. Otherwise, Scholman would have recused himself from the case. Ethically, he could not preside over a case where he knew the accused.

Johnnie had remarked that every possible ruling went in Melanie's favor, except the motion to dismiss. Even the most inept jurist couldn't have dismissed the case with the presence of gunshot residue. Even the jury charge was delivered in a manner that strongly implied which verdict should be returned. Wellington may have produced a useless drug, but there was no direct evidence it sanctioned Stafford's murder. There was no doubt the woman had a volatile temper. Johnnie had described how she could alter her moods quickly and unexpectedly. Had she discovered her husband's infidelity? Had McGuire's summation, as Johnnie had described it, been on target?

Erika called Johnnie. He was dumbfounded. They couldn't prove she was a killer. Ethically, Johnnie couldn't disclose it even if he was certain. Yet there was something that could be done, even if its impact was minimal. It wouldn't bring closure for Richard Stafford. His killer or killers roamed free, probably forever. But inferential guilt was better than none at all. Would that surface tomorrow?

63.

The following morning, Johnnie made the early call. Donna Giordin put him through to her boss. Johnnie thanked Scholman for handling a difficult case so evenhandedly. Then he got to the point. His client wanted to thank the judge for his fairness. He advised her that was inappropriate. She should not call the judge or return to his courtroom. Had she done so? Scholman replied that she had not. Johnnie apologized for the call but wanted Scholman forewarned. His client was a wonderful woman but didn't always follow his instructions. Scholman appreciated his concern and would advise his staff.

Technically, the response was correct, yet the answer authenticated their assumption. Scholman and Melanie were not strangers. More than likely, they were lovers.

Erika then called Melanie. Could she stop by the office later that day? Johnnie needed to discuss some important post-trial matters.

She arrived midafternoon. Johnnie and Erika greeted her warmly. Had she discussed the envelope's contents with her father? Yes. He would be calling the office later that afternoon. Had she tried to contact Scholman in any way? Of course not, she had heeded his instructions. Johnnie cautioned her not to contact McGuire. He was obviously upset. Any action on her part could lead to a swift, vindictive response. Traffic violations were a simple yet effective way to harass the unwary. She also should avoid the press. She had her freedom, but danger still lurked. Silence was a tonic she should imbibe. It would not hurt her. It prevented missteps, avoided innuendos, and quelled suspicion. A neon sign was garish and not forgotten. A candle was soft and silent. She was to continue her good works but remain dignified in the background. Time was her ally. Today's story would be replaced by tomorrow's headline. People were preoccupied with their own problems. Someone else's misfortune might titillate them momentarily but quickly would be replaced by another's more noteworthy calamity. With time, her tragedy would dim. People would recall only the verdict and that the prosecution had not investigated Wellington.

Melanie nodded in agreement. She again thanked him for everything. She had her life back and would use that gift wisely.

As Melanie neared her car, she heard Erika's voice and turned.

"Melanie, I hope you heed Johnnie's admonition. Just between us girls, I have a secret to share with you. I tailed you last night. Months ago, you compared Johnnie's profession to yours. You mentioned that he always could appeal a mistake to the appellate court, but you would have to live with yours. There was no appellate relief for death or incapacity. You also questioned whether a medical mistake would bar your admittance to heaven. To me, and I'm just saying to me, not to Johnnie, you fell in love with your grandfather's killer and unwittingly conspired with him to slaughter your husband. I think you've answered you own soliloquy. Until the dawning of that day, you can dwell on your coming fate and damnation. The angels will not weep for your soul. They will close their eyes to the silence. Have a nice life."

Melanie looked her up and down. "You're so misguided. From the beginning, you've despised me. You're so transparent. Don't worry. I'm no threat to you. You can have Johnnie, but do you really think you could keep him happy? What's your pedigree, honey? More importantly, what's your real predilection, boys or girls? From what I've learned, you can't resist nipples. How's that gonna fly with your fair-haired boy? I guess we all have our demons, don't we? As you said, have a good life. Just stay out of mine."

As Erika turned, she said over her shoulder, "What's it like to fuck a murderer? I guess you and he can ask each other."

As forewarned, Burnside called, "Listen, Johnnie, I want to file a wrongful death claim on Melanie's and Catherine's behalf. Scholman has to be held accountable."

"I can't, Mr. Burnside. No one will believe us. I will be laughed out of court. Where's the proof? The German has left. We don't know his name or address. Even if we could locate him, he can't be extradited for a civil case. No one will prosecute Scholman criminally. There is no evidence. We don't even know if Scholman trafficked in stolen antiquities. Then there's the issue of the statute of limitations. While it doesn't apply to murder, it applies in civil cases. Would it be allowed in this unusual instance where the police found no crime? I don't know. The issue, however, is moot. There is nothing evidential linking Scholman to the professor's murder."

"Johnnie, we have to try."

"Then you should hire alternative counsel. I can't do it."

"Johnnie, you will do it! Do you remember what I said when you resisted defending Melanie? It still applies. You will do it, or the spigot will be turned off! Do I make myself clear?"

"Absolutely, but ethically, I can't do it. The court will not allow it. Of that, I am certain."

"How do you know? You haven't even tried."

Johnnie knew he would be shackled forever. This couldn't continue. The bond had to be severed. At this point, he no longer cared. He would not be his lapdog. He had done all that any reasonable human being could ask. The man was a bully, a tyrant, and an offish boor.

"I don't have to try. Ask your daughter. Tell her what we discussed today. I guarantee you she will agree. Tell her I informed you that ethically I couldn't continue. That's all I can say. If you wish to terminate our relationship, I can't stop you. I do thank you for your past trust and generosity. In this instance, I know I'm right. I may carry this decision to my grave, but I will do so without regret. The choice obviously is yours, Mr. Burnside. Your daughter also has a choice. Tell her for me that she should use it wisely. I think she'll understand."

Erica reentered his office.

"Where'd you go?"

"Oh, just out for a moment. You look dejected."

"Burnside called. He ordered me to file a wrongful death suit against Scholman. I told him no. He threatened me. Said he'd terminate our relationship. I told him that ethically I couldn't represent Melanie and told him to confer with Melanie. She would agree.

Also, dejected? Why would that be? I only defended a killer before a killer who also deals in stolen antiquities. McGuire had it right from the beginning. I crossed over to the other side. I, however, wasn't bringing light to the darkness. All I did was remove the stars. What do I have to show for it? I'm where I would have been had I refused to defend her. The client still leaves and now also takes my soul."

"Johnnie, you did what you thought was just. You saw goodness where there was none. You saw hope, not evil. That's one of your many admirable qualities. The fault is not yours. It's hers. You can sleep soundly. She should, and will, rot in hell. Let it be. You have much to offer. She has none."

"Thanks for the pep talk. It will get me through my meeting at five o'clock. Then, I'm going home and decompressing if that's possible."

She smiled, gave him the thumbs up, and retreated from his office.

Now what? He defended a killer before a killer. For his father, he tried to keep Supreme as a client but lost it as well as his soul. Wellington defrauded the public but did not cause Stafford's demise. Maybe Scholman would be exposed as an antiquities thief, but he never would be charged, much less convicted, of the murders of Clarendon and Stafford. Burnside would continue to deny rightful claimants of fair settlements. Melanie was free, but in whose eyes was she really innocent? In different ways, the scales of justice dispensed punishment.

64.

The meeting had lasted two hours. Exhausted, he trudged up his condo's steps and unlocked the door. He heard music from within. He looked up just as a champagne glass was thrust toward him.

"Looks like you need some loving."

She kissed him on the lips and took his other hand, pulling him toward the bedroom. He recognized the song. Sinatra's "Softly as I Leave You." He laughed. Yes, that was Erika. She knew how to break his heart.

Erika knew what he was thinking. Behind his high-octane masculinity and charm, he was so vulnerable and tender. He was not like the others. Maybe, just maybe, they really might be made for each other. At least for this night, they were.

ACKNOWLEDGMENTS:

To be successful a writer needs the encouragement and assistance of others whom he trusts. This book is no exception. My extraordinary wife, Barbara, provided advice, support, and unrivaled patience without which this novel never would have seen the light of day. Cathy Cameron of the Sanibel Public Library deciphered my yellow legal pad scribbling and somehow typed the verbiage so that it became coherent.

Bill O'Brien provided the apt title."OB" devoted twenty years of his accomplished life to Princeton University and hobnobbed with professors similar in stature to the fictitious Dr. Alexander Clarendon.

My senior law partner and superb trial lawyer, Rudy Socey, confirmed that New Jersey's medical malpractice law had not changed in those aspects relevant to Johnnie Fitzhugh's settlement of Dr. Lewis's case.

My former law partner and present Mercer County jurist, Tom Brown, and his able assistant, Donna Bartolino, provided me with a general description of the relatively new Mercer County Criminal Courthouse.

Retired Special Agent, Criminal Division, David Sergeant provided answers to numerous plot hypotheticals I posed to him.

Hugh Wachter, Princeton Class of 1968, read the manuscript and offered cogent editorial and plot suggestions.

Last but not least, two dear friends employed in the pharmaceutical industry provided background information for characters Richard Stafford and John Furber. Unlike John Furber, they have become very successful without losing their integrity.

AUTHOR'S NOTE

This book is a work of fiction. The names, characters, places, and incidents portrayed in the story are the product of this author's imagination or have been used fictitiously. Any resemblance to actual persons, living or dead, businesses, corporations, companies, events, or locales is coincidental.

There is no medical malpractice insurance carrier in New Jersey with the name Supreme Insurance. Wellington Pharmaceuticals and Sterling Labs are fictitious as is the anti-aging drug Youtheria.

While Hodge Road contains many beautiful and stately homes, Glen Burnside's residence does not exist.

I have attempted to provide a general description and history of the various locales and buildings that appear throughout this novel.

Any mistakes are mine.

In describing Munich, I have relied upon the DK Eyewitness Travel Guide and have adopted its reference of Munich as the "Athens on the Isar."

The DK Eyewitness Travel Guides on Vienna provided specific details of those edifices visited by Sally Huffmire and her assassin.

The stolen art and antiquity trade continues to this day. Additionally, many priceless works looted by the Nazis have not surfaced. For those readers fascinated by this topic, I would suggest reading The Rape of Europa by Lynn H. Nicholas and The Monuments Men by Robert M.Edsel.

Most of us unfortunately have been prescribed medicine that has effected us in unpleasant ways at one time or another. The pharmaceutical shenanigans perpetrated by the fictitious Wellington Pharmaceuticals and Sterling Labs are food for thought as evidenced by "Deadly Medicine",an article written by Donald Bartlett and James Steele and published in the January 2011 issue of Vanity Fair. It is a sobering account of the foreign outsourcing of pharmaceutical testing and the difficulty it has posed to an alleged understaffed FDA.